HIGH WHITE SUN

ALSO BY J. TODD SCOTT

The Far Empty

HIGH WHITE SUN

J. TODD SCOTT

G. P. PUTNAM'S SONS
NEW YORK

PUTNAM

G. P. PUTNAM'S SONS
Publishers Since 1838
An imprint of Penguin Random House LLC
375 Hudson Street
New York, New York 10014

The author gratefully acknowledges permission to reprint lyrics
from "Jesse James," by Ben Glover, Kyle Jacobs, and Joe Leathers,
© 2008 WB Music Corp. (ASCAP), Screaming Norman Music (ASCAP),
Curb Songs (ASCAP), Jacobsong (ASCAP), Mike Curb Music (BMI)
and Ghermkyle Music (BMI). Used with permission.

Library of Congress Cataloging-in-Publication Data

Names: Scott, J. Todd, author.
Title: High white sun / J. Todd Scott.
Description: New York : G. P. Putnam's Sons, 2018.
Identifiers: LCCN 2016051717 (print) | LCCN 2016041739 (ebook) |
ISBN 9780399176357 (print) | ISBN 9780698408289 (EPub)
Subjects: LCSH: Sheriffs—Fiction. | Motorcycle gangs—Fiction. |
GSAFD: Suspense fiction.
Classification: LCC PS3619.C66536 H54 2018 (print) |
LCC PS3619.C66536 (ebook) | DDC 813/.6—dc23
LC record available at https://lccn.loc.gov/2016051717
p.   cm.

Printed in the United States of America
1 3 5 7 9 10 8 6 4 2

BOOK DESIGN BY MEIGHAN CAVANAUGH

For my chief deputies:
Madeleine, Lily, and Lucy

Aim higher.

"There is no peace," says the LORD, "for the wicked."

—ISAIAH 48:22

Sometimes I wanna be like Jesus,
Sometimes I wanna be Jesse James . . .

—BEN GLOVER, KYLE JACOBS, AND
JOE LEATHERS, "JESSE JAMES"

BEFORE

SWEETWATER, TEXAS

1999

Goodbye stranger . . .

He had the radio up too loud, singing along with the words he knew, blasting down Texas 70, when he saw the girl standing on the side of the road waving him down. The hood of her car was up, a two-tone Ford Fiesta he remembered from a few times before parked out in the gravel at the Aces High. It was a piece of shit, more rust than car, and he wasn't surprised she was having trouble with it. He blinked his lights once to let her know he was slowing down, pulling over a few yards behind her in a cloud of quartz and dust, right where the macadam gave way to the tall, dry grass.

He fumbled getting out of his truck, feeling the heavy pull of all the Pearls he'd had at the Aces dragging him down like goddamn gravity. Truth to tell, there was a sixer he'd taken for the road still sitting in his passenger seat, and one already opened going warm in his lap. He'd planned to finish off the rest of them before pulling into his driveway; pitch the empties somewhere out in a ditch before he passed the farm-to-market road and got into town proper within sight of the familiar streetlights—now little more than gold smudges, hazy like fingerprints, stretching away into the night. But he'd also toyed with the idea of driving all the way out to Lake Sweetwater and parking out by the old Boy Scout camp and drinking 'em there, maybe even grabbing a couple of hours of shut-eye in the backseat of the cab with the windows rolled all the way down. Sometimes it was cooler out at the lake and sometimes it wasn't and he could never say why. Probably had something to do with the wind . . . that goddamn wind . . . which sand-blasted the area most of the year. It was a *living thing*, had a wicked mind of its own, leaving fine dust on everything. You could open a closed drawer and find dust on your kitchen spoons. The wind could be so loud at times you couldn't hear yourself think, couldn't hear your own car radio, which is why he kept his turned up so loud—a bad habit. Tonight wasn't like that, though. The moon was high and steady and filling everything up with its light so that the whole world glowed, and the wind was calm and relaxed, just barely moving the grass, ruffling it the same way he liked to mess up Danny's hair.

His shirt was stuck to his back, though, still so goddamn hot.

He turned down the radio some, reached for his hat and adjusted his belt . . . his holster . . . and tried to look steady as he dumped out the beer and climbed free of his truck and made his way to the girl.

SHE WAS A SMALL THING, didn't even cut a whole figure in the slip of a dress she wore—Chinese writing all over it—her tits no more than a handful, if that. She had big chunky wedges dangling from one hand, using the other to keep her hair out of her face and his headlights out of her eyes. Her makeup was a mess, and in the harsh light he couldn't tell what might be mascara and what might be bruises. He'd watched her dance before, had seen her naked, but somehow she looked even more vulnerable now, standing on the side of the road in her bare feet, holding her shoes. She was haloed in pearl light and it revealed her whole truth . . . everything. It made her look her age and that bothered him; made him feel bad for thinking he might have found a companion for the lake tonight, and for some of the other things that had crossed his mind. For the wedding band that had grown too tight on his finger.

Standing like that on her tiptoes, he imagined her on a stage somewhere else, in some high school play. Someone's daughter.

"Well, miss, what seems to be the problem?"

"My name is Sierra," she said, her accent all West Texas.

He got close, casting an eye toward the raised hood, looking for smoke or radiator fluid popping on the engine. "Well, okay then, nice to meet you, Sierra." He knew her name wasn't Sierra. Maybe it was Sara or Becky or Catherine or something else, but it sure in the hell wasn't Sierra. His sleeping wife's name was Catherine.

"She seize up on you? Run out of gas?" He gestured at the car.

"Oh, that." She followed his hands, as if seeing the Fiesta for the first time. She jitterbugged a bit, the hand not holding her shoes moving as if it had a cigarette in it, and in the light pooled at her feet he could see several spent butts, circled around her like dead moths. She'd been out here awhile. She kept on, "I seen you before, right, at the Aces? I dance there."

He nodded. "Yeah, I come in from time to time. Thought you looked familiar. I was there tonight but I don't remember you up . . . onstage." He tripped on the last couple of words and tried not to look right at her.

"Nah, not tonight. I wasn't feeling so well. I'll catch hell from Down Low, but you know, whatever."

Whatever. Down Low—Daryl Lynch—was the Aces' owner, as well as its resident bartender and bouncer and pimp. Fancied himself a biker, too. He thought he was a real badass and maybe even a bit more than that, and he kept his brand-new Softail Night Train parked right up front near the bar's door, where everyone had to pass it and it shined back twice as bright as the Christmas lights strung up year-round across the main porch. He'd known Lynch for a couple of years; knew also that he was a real shitheel and a snitch who sometimes passed him information, sometimes didn't. Lynch had paid off that nice bike with some of the money that had passed between them, but it wouldn't have been enough, not close. The Aces wasn't a gold mine, either, so ole Down Low was a real goddamn entrepreneur, a self-made man with his dirty fingers in a lot of different things. He didn't like the thought of that wannabe biker roughing up the girls, though. Maybe it was time to have another long sit-down with Lynch.

"He do that to you?" He pointed at her eye.

Her hand went up on its own, the one not holding the long-gone cigarette. "This? Nah, it was something else. You know, there's always something else."

"Yep, there always is." And goddammit, he did know it. He stared at her for long seconds, before turning his attention back to her car, trying to figure out what was wrong with it. The engine wasn't ticking and he couldn't feel any heat coming off it. It had been sitting a long time.

"You a cop, right?"

He nodded, turning enough to flash the badge at his belt. "Texas Ranger. Bob Ford."

She laughed, nervous. "I thought y'all rode horses."

He joined her. "No, not for a long time." And just like that, he was tired, so tired, already dreading the hangover he'd have to face tomorrow. *There's always something else . . . there always is.* He knew he wasn't going out to the lake anymore, either. After he got Sierra or whatever her name was up and running, or gave her a lift somewhere off this highway, he was going home. He'd slip in quiet, quiet as the grave, and look in on Danny, who should be long asleep by now, although he'd probably stayed up as late as he could reading his comics with a flashlight beneath his sheets; fighting sleep, waiting for his daddy to come home. They were supposed to go fishing on Sunday, and tomorrow they were going to get Danny a new Zebco reel at Sears they'd picked out together. Then, after checking on his son, he'd try not to wake Caty as he fell into bed next to her.

But before all of that, he'd chew a handful of aspirin he kept hidden in the downstairs bathroom and wash it all back with one last warm beer and try hard not to catch a look at himself in the mirror—at the gray feathering through his brush cut and his ever-expanding gut, pushing hard at the once bright snap buttons of his shirt.

That goddamn mirror revealing *his* whole truth. *Everything.* And Bob Ford didn't like it one bit.

"Not for a long time . . ."

HE LOOKED OVER THE COLD ENGINE, trying to make sense of it; puzzle it out, even if he wasn't much of a mechanic and never had been. Sierra was now talking a mile a minute, her words rising and falling with the breeze, lost to the radio still humming from his truck. "Goodbye Stranger." He'd always liked that song and remembered it from high school, from Midlothian. Remembered also sitting in the bed of his daddy's Chevy and sweet-talking Caty, trying to get a hand in her shirt while she pretended she didn't want him to; each of them with a Tastee-Freez cup filled with Johnnie Walker and Coke. And then, when their cups were empty and both of them were good and warm all the way through, how they'd stretch out hand in hand on his mom's old quilt, searching for fading stars and listening to crickets, counting fireflies appearing and disappearing beneath the loblollies—a magic trick that never got old. Not now, not then, but when he worked the math and realized those nights were twenty years ago, maybe more, he didn't want to think about them anymore.

"Well, goddamn if I know what's wrong here, little lady. Look, I can give you a lift back to Sweetwater. You can send someone out in the morning."

"Oh, okay," she said, not interested in talking anymore. Not interested in her car or him. Not looking at either of them but instead far out across the gently moving grass, tipped silver by moonlight.

It was north of eighty degrees, his bare arms slicked with sweat, getting in his eyes, when he realized that she'd dropped her shoes in the middle of the road, forgotten among all her burned-out cigarettes. She was shivering, watching the roadside grass.

Shivering.

Like she was freezing.

Or afraid.

SHE WAS ON SOMETHING, for damn sure—bathtub crank, pills, crack. If he looked through her car he might spy some wadded-up tinfoil or a burned-out lightbulb, some other type of homemade pipe discarded on the floorboard. If he got closer, close enough to feel the heat coming off her, he might also see the scars on her thin, bare arms. That explained it all. Down Low dealt out of the Aces, but Bob Ford had looked away on that from time to time—a necessary evil and the cost of doing hard business. The girl had been flying high all night and was finally coming down, just now staring at the earth rising up fast to meet her— *too fast.* She was going to crash and burn right in front of him.

That's why her eyes were all suddenly black and blown wide open, the irises like big windows into empty rooms. Her fluttering lids thin curtains blowing in the breeze.

She turned and did a little dancer's spin, one arm wide and the other tight around her stomach, protective. She was staring right at him and for one heartbeat he was staring right back through those windows in her eyes and all the way *through her*, into his own bedroom far away, where Caty lay asleep and lost beneath the covers. Then on into Danny's room, where his boy's walls were covered in superhero posters, and the empty fish tank he'd just gotten for his ninth birthday sat up on the bookshelf, its bottom covered with brightly colored rocks. Danny loved his damn superheroes and wanted to be one when he grew up, but he never talked about being a cop; never about being a Ranger like his old man. He never thought one could be the same as the other.

Then that heartbeat passed and he thought he heard her say *I'm sorry . . .*

"Come again, what's that?" he asked, shaking off all he'd seen, moving toward her to put an arm on her shoulder and get her steadied.

Steady himself, too.

"I'm sorry," she said again, clearer this time, and then she started to run.

THE GRASS CAUGHT FIRE, scorched by muzzle flare from the side of the road.

He turned just in time to catch that first slug under his right arm; just like getting punched damn hard, except everything important *inside* him, all the way to his heart, seemed to seize right up. His arm went numb, too, still attached but now hanging useless, so he fumbled to get at his SIG Sauer with his left hand.

Spinning—falling—to his knees.

Then he saw blood, a lot of it. More than he'd ever seen or thought was possible—a wash of it all over the road at his feet and sprayed high up on the raised hood of the Fiesta. If Sierra hadn't rabbited across the road it would have been all over her face.

The second slug got him clean in the gut and went straight through him. He heard it ricochet off the Fiesta, a metallic echo that carried off into the night. He said a crazy prayer that it didn't hit the girl, who was on her knees now, too; one hand at her mouth, the other still around her stomach, watching him die.

Pregnant. Caty had held her hands just like that, cradling and protecting Danny before he ever came into the world.

There was no way he was getting to his gun now. Not ever again. He rocked on his bloody knees, with smoke drifting above him from the two shotgun blasts.

Saw through new tears that the dry grass really *was* on fire, setting embers free to spin and dance around him before bouncing and dying on the black macadam.

Winking out like those fireflies from twenty years ago.

Two men walked out of the grass, shaking loose more embers as they moved, one holding some sort of pistol and the other a shotgun. He knew the man with the scattergun, not the other, who still had a mask on his face. It didn't matter anyway.

The wind had been calm all night, but now, suddenly, it got loud. So damn loud, a brutal rushing in his ears—a freight train right on top of him so he couldn't hear himself speak, couldn't struggle to call out the name of his killer, either, because his mouth was full of rust and sparks and blood.

But he wasn't the sort of man who was going to beg for his own damn life anyway.

Maybe his boy had it right all along. Cops weren't superheroes, after all, far from it. They were just men who got old and tired and slow and made too many damn mistakes and sometimes stopped to help pretty girls beneath starry skies.

Heroes didn't die in the middle of the goddamn road.

The barrel of the shotgun touched a spot right between his eyes.

Soft, gentle, just like Caty's fingers wrapped around his, when as teenagers—hell, as *kids*—they'd counted stars.

"Howdy, Bob," the man with the shotgun said, and then he pulled the trigger.

. . .

BOB FORD DIDN'T HEAR the greeting or his own heart beating or the radio from his truck or the blast that followed.

The wind in his face was too loud.

Almost ten years later, all along Texas 70, the first wind turbines of the Sweetwater Wind Farm came online—rows and rows of three-bladed towers stretching far into the chalky distance, standing like sentinels right over the spot where Texas Ranger Bob Ford died.

A hundred white crosses, raised up high, visible for miles and miles.

Trying to take all that goddamn wind and do something good with it.

FIFTEEN YEARS LATER

*B*reathe.
     Relax.
Aim.
Slack.
Squeeze.
That's how you stop a man's heart . . .

THIS IS NOT MY FACE.

There are parts I recognize but they're someone else's picture. A picture I might have once studied and turned over in my hands long ago.

The eyes might be mine. The color is mostly right. But there's a lot going on behind them, like too much stuff was moved in while I was away, cluttering up what used to be empty space.

Maybe nerves, maybe fear, things that have been unfamiliar to me for a long time.

Then there's the shape of the jaw and the curve of the mouth; the small scar like a star at my temple. They all make some kind of sense, even if they seem borrowed, rented by the hour.

Like all the tattoos running over my skin, inked and re-inked. They're a map to all the places I've been and all the people I used to be.

I believe all the lies I tell myself.

But most of all, the hair is wrong. There's hardly enough to run your fingers through and it still feels too long.

After I returned from across the world I let my hair grow out. A lot of us did—a bunch of damn hippies, my father might have said—but it never felt quite right to me, no matter how much I wanted it to. It was too dark, too hot and heavy, and didn't quite match the face that had been hollowed out and left empty beneath it. So I gladly cut it again when I got into the academy, and then went even shorter for my time in McKinney and left it that way for Tyler and Ballinger. Since then I've tried a second time to let it grow back, let it get thick like when I was a kid, and I try to pretend I can remember my father running his hands through it, but everything about me really has changed size and shape. My corners and edges don't quite fit together anymore and I can't arrange the pieces back again the same way. I'm missing a few. I don't know where they are.

Least of all this mirror, where all I can see is what isn't there. Every goddamn thing about me that isn't right anymore.

So I've been faking it. Smiling through my mandatory counseling sessions and the desk duty—typing everyone else's reports and helping out where I can. Smiling and joking because people feel better about everything when you smile. You only make people truly nervous when you don't. And I was taped back together, just close enough . . . almost whole.

Until today, until this morning . . . when Dyer called me in and gave me the news.

He wanted me to hear it from him first, if I heard it at all.

He knew my father all those years ago when it all happened—hell, everyone does. He knows the whole story, my story, and was part of the original investigation. He's one of those good men who is always trying hard to be an even better one, and he didn't want me getting the word from someone else. Or worse, picking it up from someone on the street, although we both know I'm not going back out on the street for a while, if at all. At least not like McKinney and Tyler. Definitely not like Ballinger.

After he gave me the news, he stared at me long and hard to see my reaction, checking my face to see if it gave anything away.

I told him I was okay.

I thanked him for telling me and for his concern. He is a good man.

I smiled when I said it.

Polite. Respectful. Calm.

I believe all the lies I tell myself.

And I was still smiling when I left.

THIS IS NOT MY FACE. *Not anymore.*

Not now.

The hair is all gone again, shaved down to stubble in some places, naked skin in others. It's the best I can do with a Gillette and a can of Barbasol.

There is blood in the sink, on my skull.

In my eyes.

I'm raw, brand-new.

My badge is on the sink, so is my gun. I'm only going to need one of them.

I point the gun at the face in the mirror and my hand shakes. I don't want to look at it anymore.

I don't want to look at what I've become. What I am.

Breathe. Relax. Aim. Slack. Squeeze.

This is how you stop a man's heart . . .

NOW,
JULY

PART ONE

THE GIRL
WITH THE GUN

1

It was damn hard to follow a blood trail at eighty miles per hour.

Not that Sheriff Chris Cherry needed to see actual *blood*; he knew it was there all the same. Thick drops of it all down U.S. 90, bleeding off the rear fender of the Nissan Maxima that was trying hard to disappear in his windshield and throwing up dust as it swerved across lanes and the shoulder.

All that blood from one of his deputies, Tommy Milford. Chris still didn't know whether he was alive or dead.

Another of his deputies, Dale Holt, was ten miles back with him. He'd been riding shotgun with Tommy when it all happened, and although he was barely one year older than the injured boy, when Chris had left them both behind, Dale had been holding Tommy's hand like a father might a son's, telling him over and over again to *hang in there, brother, hang in there* while they waited for the ambulance, because no one had been sure if it was a good idea to move Tommy or not. Honestly, it hadn't looked good either way. But Dale, even before calling it in— even before kneeling down next to his damaged friend and grabbing his shaking hand and shielding his body with his own—had gotten off a handful of rounds at the fleeing Nissan, and after this was all done they'd be out here looking for them in the desert, shining bright among the ocotillo and the cat's-claw and the creosote; prying them out of the car's metal body. At least one had definitely punched through the rear windshield, spiderwebbing the safety glass and X'ing the spot where a passenger's head might be.

Chris tried hard to focus on *that*, rather than his deputy's blood drying on the asphalt.

He prayed that Tommy was hanging on to Dale's hand right now, squeezing back just as hard with each heartbeat, letting Dale and everyone else know he was still alive.

Hanging on tight.

Please don't die. God, not today.

Not today. Not Tommy's first damn day on the job.

DEPUTY AMÉ REYNOSA blasted past Chris, shooting up the shoulder, close enough they almost traded paint. He'd already barked at her once on the radio to stay behind him but she wasn't listening and clearly wasn't going to. He caught up to her and pushed ahead. They were both pushing ninety now, heading toward a hundred, chewing up the distance on the Maxima, whose back end suddenly fishtailed, brake lights flickering on and off. The driver must have seen the red and blue strobes on Chief Deputy Ben Harper's truck up ahead, bright and clear and ominous even in broad daylight, leaving him surprised and *really* scared and unsure of what to do; maybe even bleeding out, if Dale's bullet had bent the curve and clipped the driver while passing through the car's interior. Harp had been out at Artesia most of the day but had been rolling back to Murfee when Dale fired his first shot, which put him right in the path of the fleeing car, so Chris had radioed for him to lay up at mile marker 67 and toss out the spike strip.

Chris glanced over at the small green signs blurring past his window.

Marker 65

The strips were an expensive Stinger Spike System. He'd been reluctant to buy them at first, reading that some officers and deputies had been killed trying to deploy the damn things—struck by the very cars they were trying to stop—and Harp hadn't helped the cause by admitting that the Dallas PD had recently banned them.

But out here there was so much empty space, so much straight-line *nothing*, that you could chase someone all the way to El Paso or right down to fucking Mexico if you didn't have a way to slow them down.

So Harp had pushed and pushed for them, and in the end, Chris had agreed. *Caved.* That had become the defining nature of their relationship.

In fact, Chris had ordered *two* sets for each patrol truck, enough to cross both lanes. They'd proved easy enough to set up when his deputies had practiced it out in the department parking lot, but so far they'd never been used—not in *real life*, not like this.

Marker 66

Almost there.

Chris backed off the gas and hoped those damn spikes worked . . . and hoped to hell that Harp was out of the way.

THE NISSAN'S TIRES GRABBED the pavement *hard*—spitting rocks and boiling smoke—as the driver locked them up, with both car and driver holding on for life as the Nissan started to slide sideways. It tipped ever so slightly *up*, catching air as the whole car shuddered, looking for one horrible second like it might roll and tumble down Highway 90 in a mess of buckled metal and broken glass, before straightening out and hitting the strips square at sixty miles an hour. The hollow spike tips punctured all four radials clean, and Chris swore he saw a dance of bright sparks beneath the Nissan—a July Fourth light show—as it plowed over the strips and kept going even as its tires died beneath it.

Chris drove off the shoulder into the scrub, giving the strips a wide berth and catching air himself, as Harp's truck roared to life and paralleled him from where it had been parked on the opposite shoulder. Harp *had* gotten clear from the truck, never even bothering to use it for cover in case the Nissan's driver lost complete control and plowed into it. Instead, he'd been crouched low with his Colt AR-15 aimed straight and steady into the other car's oncoming windshield. As it slid past, he'd calmly stood up and tracked it with his sights, before running back to his own truck.

Now, he and Chris were slow-rolling up to the Nissan, which had finally come to rest in the middle of the road, nose canted at an angle, the driver's door visible to both of them but still closed. The car sat wreathed in smoke, all of its tinted windows dirty. The car itself looked exhausted, worn-out, sporting an ugly metallic scar down the left flank—another one of Dale's bullets.

And Tommy's blood, which had been so bright and visible to Chris only moments before, was now lost to the dust.

Chris got out with his Browning A5 and positioned himself behind his engine block, while Harp opposite of him did the same. Amé rolled to a hard stop behind them both, and with his attention full on the Nissan, Chris felt rather than saw her join him at his shoulder.

She was breathing hard, her Colt 1911 resting over the hood.

"Son of a bitch," she said. *"Pendejo."*

"Exactly," Chris agreed. He stole one glance at her; hair in her eyes and those dark eyes narrowed and angry, trying hard to see beyond the Nissan's windows. And for the first time since he'd made her a Big Bend County deputy, he was regretting it. Not that she wasn't capable—she had more than proven her worth and was tougher than he ever could have imagined—but because of moments like this one, right now.

He didn't want to send her in harm's way and he knew that was exactly what he was going to have to do.

In two years as sheriff, none of his deputies had gotten hurt on his watch. It was like a run of cool, calm weather, or a desert rain. It couldn't last forever and maybe it wasn't supposed to.

But he was going to make damn sure it wasn't two in one day.

"SHERIFF, TIME *IS* WASTING." Harp's voice carried over the road.

His chief deputy was pushing, his idea of subtle. Harp always complained that Chris was too slow, too measured; *too goddamn deliberate . . .* just like their long debate over ordering the Stinger system. Even though he won more than he lost, the older man still liked to needle Chris: *It's all about action versus reaction, Sheriff . . . you can't finish what you don't start.* These were Harp's idea of *lessons*, freely and frequently given, and Amé Reynosa had already taken way too many of them to heart.

It didn't take much for Chris to imagine what his two deputies would think about his first impulse here and now: to keep them all safe behind their trucks and just wait the fucking guy in the Nissan out.

All afternoon if they had to; hoping against hope that he got tired and gave up.

Now *that* was goddamn deliberate.

But there was another of Harp's sharp lessons: *Chris, hope is not a strategy . . .*

Sheriff, time is wasting.

Fuck me.

CHRIS TOOK A LONG BREATH, turning to Amé. "Okay, I'm going to call him out. If we're lucky, there's only the one and maybe he's already hurt. I'm going to walk him backward between us, and when I stop him and tell him to get on his knees, you're going to go up, put him facedown, and cuff him. I'll stay covered on the car in case someone else is in there. I've got the best angle on it, so Harp is going to stay covered on *you*. If our bad guy so much as flinches, reaches for anything, even breathes too hard, Harp will take the shot. Got that?"

Amé nodded, already grabbing for cuffs and making ready to move down to the rear of the truck, near to where she'd have to expose herself. It wouldn't be much and it wouldn't be long, but it would be enough.

Chris put a hand on her shoulder. "You're angry, we all are. It's not personal. Just do it by the numbers. Wait till he's on his knees." Chris let her go. "You good?" he asked.

She smiled, grim. *"Bueno."*

Chris waved toward Harp to get his attention, raising his voice. "I'll call the guy back. Amé is contact, you're cover." Harp never took his eyes off the Nissan, didn't respond, but hitched up a thumb . . . *okay*.

In a perfect world, Chris would've put hands on the guy himself, but he didn't have faith in his bad knee. It had never fully recovered after he'd reinjured it at the Far Six. *You've never fully recovered.* He pushed that cold thought away. But fortunately Harp had spent almost three decades on the Midland PD, many of those years as part of their SWAT team. Even though he and Amé had spent a lot of free hours together at the makeshift range near Chapel Mesa, and Harp claimed she'd developed a hell of a shooter's eye, Chris still felt comfortable with Harp taking a tight shot more than anyone, far more than even himself. The chief deputy was the only person who had killed more men than Chris. That left Amé as the best choice, the only choice, to approach the driver if he ever showed himself.

Chris took another deep breath, steadied himself. He squinted past the shortened barrel of his A5 to the Nissan. Still there, still waiting.

Waiting for *him* to do something. Just like his two deputies.

"Driver, roll down the windows and throw out the keys. Then

extend your left hand through the window and open the door." His voice surprised him, too loud.

Nothing happened and the Nissan kept idling.

"Driver, roll down the windows and throw out the keys." *Or what, exactly?* Chris didn't want to send Harp and Amé up to the car to forcibly pull the driver out, there was too much open ground to cover and it was too naked, too exposed. And they sure weren't going to start pumping lead into it from here. Even if he made that threat, would the driver believe it? Could *he* even make it sound believable? Maybe he'd get his wish after all and they'd just sit here the rest of the day like Old West gunfighters in a duel, forever trapped at high noon; neither of them ever drawing.

Fuck me.

Sweat collected in his eyes. None of his options were good, all of them just different kinds of bad. His shirt stuck to him like a second skin—that high white sun hammering hard. It had been infernally hot for days, with no end in sight. The scrub all around was burned brown, skeletal, brittle and quick to turn to dust. Except for the yucca standing tall, crowned with its ivory flowers and marching into the distance toward the mountains, the world out here looked and felt lifeless. Like a hot breath would be all it'd take to set it aflame.

The air above the car rolled back and forth in waves, reflecting the engine heat back skyward, where it got lost.

Impatient, Amé started inching forward, moving beyond the safety of his truck's tailgate; too far away from him to pull her back. Just like he feared, she'd been listening to Harp too damn much.

"Driver . . ." He started again, angrier, but before he could call out anything else, the driver's-side window slid down.

Chris braced, found a point in the darkened interior and kept his A5 on it, realizing the engine had also stopped.

The car was now silent, still.

Long moments passed, everyone holding their breath.

Then keys tumbled out of the open window, jingling loudly, and landed on the asphalt.

Followed finally by a slim arm, grabbing the door handle as he'd instructed and opening the door.

A MAN GOT OUT.

No, that wasn't quite right; he was younger than that, early twenties, maybe, a Hispanic male in black jeans and a white T-shirt. His hair was slicked back and he still had sunglasses on—metallic, small frame, designer.

There was no sign of blood.

Chris put the A5 on him. "Driver, turn around once, and then lock your hands together behind your head and walk backwards . . . slow . . . until I order you to stop."

The kid—and that's how Chris saw him, even though Chris wasn't a whole lot older than him—did as he was told. The watch on his wrist was big and looked expensive. It caught all of that impossible, fiery sunlight, and winked it back at Chris and his deputies as he put his hands behind his head. They might have been shaking, too, just a slight tremble matching the kid's heartbeat. He started walking backward, trying to catch a glance over his shoulder.

"Look straight ahead and keep walking. Slow." Now that the door was open Chris could see all the way through the cabin. There was no one else in the front passenger seat, but that didn't mean there wasn't someone curled up in the back. He still needed to clear the car while Harp and Amé dealt with the kid.

He heard it then, tinny music echoing over the desert. Some popular rap song he might have dialed past once or twice on the radio. It was the same few bars, over and over again—*a ring tone*—a cell phone somewhere inside the car. Is that what the kid had been doing while fleeing, making a call? *Waiting* for a goddamn call back, while Tommy Milford bled out on the asphalt behind him?

By the time the driver backed within the arrow formed by the two trucks, the cell had stopped.

"Driver, take five more steps. Count them with me and then get on your knees. Keep those hands behind your head."

One.

Two.

If the kid was counting along, Chris couldn't hear him.

Three.

Four

Five.

The kid's knees had barely flexed when Amé was already in motion, clear of the truck, handcuffs carried like a church cross in her right hand, moving toward him.

Goddammit.

Impatient.

Chris shifted aim and tried to zero in on the black mouth of the car, the open door, scanning for movement. But he couldn't help keeping one eye on Amé as she went to put her free hand on the back of the kid's head, her hand over both of his, ready to push him facedown. And just like that, inches away, the kid turned to stare at her, quick as a snake. His chin was up, like he was looking her up and down and giving her a once-over. Even hidden behind his expensive glasses, Chris had the idea there was something important passing through the kid's eyes . . . *recognition* . . . and then he said something to her, lips clearly moving, but whatever it was, it was low and fast so that only she could hear.

She didn't respond, just pushed him down hard and straddled him as she cranked his hands behind his back to get him cuffed. *They look so young* . . . his deputy and her prisoner. It was easy to imagine them as kids roughhousing in the yard, a brother and sister with their matching dark hair. Without too much effort she pulled the kid to standing and started to drag him back behind their trucks, while Harp moved toward the abandoned car, his AR-15 sweeping left to right; smooth, steady, like the hands of a clock. Now that Amé was clear with their prisoner, Harp could work up the passenger side and Chris could move in on the open driver's door, so they could finish clearing the car and then figure out what the hell was going on.

But then the kid said something *else* to Amé. Louder this time, in Spanish, just before he flicked his tongue out—quick, again, like that goddamn snake.

The kid was still talking, fast.

Chris held up, now forgetting Harp and the car. As hot as it already was, the temperature seemed to boil up another few degrees, releasing sparks and turning the air around them all to embers.

"Amé . . . *no* . . ."

It was hard to read her face: anger, surprise, something else. Or nothing at all. She nodded, like she was considering whatever it was the kid had said or maybe Chris's warning, and then she hit the handcuffed son of a bitch anyway in the face as hard as she could.

2

It was hours later, the sun lost and the Chisos and the Santiago mountains gathering long shadows beneath them, when Chris stood on the porch of his unfinished house and polished off the first of what promised to be several beers. Stars were taking their time coming up, holding their breath, waiting—letting summer lightning play havoc on the low hills, chasing its own bright tail.

All that lightning and still there'd be no rain. There hadn't been any in weeks and none was expected.

Some folks thought it bad taste that Chris had sold his dad's place in town and bought this piece of land so far out, a sliver of the old Far Six ranch. Chris had grown up in Murfee and everyone knew he'd never shown much interest in returning home, much less owning his own piece of land . . . *this* land . . . but all that had changed over two years ago, when he'd nearly died out here. When he'd been shot three times and then killed three men himself. While those same folks who wondered about it wouldn't say it to his face, they did raise it to Melissa at Earlys—wanting to know as they mulled over their beers or whiskeys why he would want to *live* out here when it had almost killed him before, and why the hell she'd let him. But she always just shrugged, smiled, and asked if they wanted another drink. Chris didn't know if he could explain it—not easily—so there was no way she could do it for him. Maybe it was all about moments like this, watching the world put on a show just for him. Maybe it was because the land was dirt cheap and it got him away from the town itself, which had always felt too small even before the shootings and twice as small after, with people driving by his old house and pointing it out like they still did for Sheriff Ross's place.

Out here, in this vast empty land, he could see a car coming for miles. He could see everything.

Or maybe it was just because he'd bled on it, and figured he owned the land now or it goddamn owned him. Either way, he'd never had to explain it to Mel. She'd never tried to talk him out of it or questioned it; even now, when it meant long drives for her back and forth to town and to the hours she still kept at Earlys. He'd told her more than once to quit, but the truth was they needed the money and she never complained. He knew she smoked those long miles away, careful with her ashes so she wouldn't start a fire in the scrub and caliche, listening to the radio with her window down as she drove.

And it *was* beautiful out here on the outer edge of empty, a perfect wildness.

The house itself was another story, a continuing source of frustration. Most things worked, although not all at the same time. The septic tank had its issues and the electrical was balky and the wraparound porch wasn't quite even. Chris had tried to do a lot of the work himself, but eventually relented after Mel had made some jokes about it at Earlys, and Judah Canter and his crew had offered to come out and shore up the whole mess. Judah had squinted and clucked his tongue just looking at some of Chris's handiwork, afraid even to take a sip of the beer Chris had offered as if that, too, might be off-kilter, but he'd promised to help. Judah was as good as his word, and cheap—he'd been doing building and electrical in the area for decades—and he and his men had at least made the place habitable. Just recently they'd put in two large Vogelzang potbelly stoves, one for the kitchen and one for the study, but with the summer heat it would be months before he and Mel would have a chance to try them. At least with Judah having finished the work, it was likely they wouldn't fill the house with smoke when they did.

There was something good to be said about the lack of rain . . . it meant Chris didn't have to worry about what parts of his roof might leak.

MEL CAME THROUGH THE SCREEN DOOR, handing him another Rahr & Sons, the bottle still nice and cold even where her fingers had been. She curled herself up in the porch swing they'd brought with them from the other house; one of just a handful of things they'd kept. It had been his mother's and for reasons all her own, Mel had been just as reluctant to part with it as he'd been.

"So Amé hit him in the face?" she asked, picking up their conversation from a few minutes before.

"Yeah, a nice right hook. She rocked him right down to his knees. He spit blood."

Mel shook her head. "Jesus, what did he say to her?"

"Something about Tommy supposedly, something about running him down, at least that's what she said. To be honest, I don't really know."

Mel watched the slow and darkening sky. "What does Ben think?"

Chris shrugged, took a long pull on his beer. *What does Ben think?* had become a familiar question over the past year. Ben Harper had retired from the Midland Police Department planning to spend the rest of his life drinking and bass fishing with his wife Jacqueline out at Falcon Lake in Starr County, but Jackie had gotten sick—a sudden stroke—and passed just as suddenly. After Chris had formally been elected Big Bend County sheriff, Harp's name had been passed to him as someone who had a lot of police experience and might be willing to help shore up a department still in disarray after former Sheriff Ross's murder at the hands of his own chief deputy, Duane Dupree. When Chris had called Harp out of the blue, the man hadn't asked many questions, easily reading between the headlines and understanding there was a hell of a lot more to that story. But he'd still agreed to help Chris, who'd admitted that he'd been elected after Ross's death only because he was something of a local hero—*a known quantity*—and not because he had any goddamn clue how to run a sheriff's department. Ben Harper had forgotten more about law enforcement than Chris could ever have hoped to have learned in his one year on the job before getting elected, and he'd proved to be a steadying hand and a reassuring presence. He never questioned Chris openly, never used his long experience to press a losing point, but had no problem waiting until they were alone to share whatever was on his mind; giving plenty of suggestions and advice. *His lessons.* Chris had made him the chief deputy from day one and he'd become a mentor to the other deputies, particularly Amé, and had become a friend to Mel, as well. He kept a small apartment above Modelle Greer's garage in town and spent a lot of nights at Earlys, keeping Mel company at the bar.

Chris liked him and trusted him, they both did.

"Harp was closer and could hear the kid was talking in Spanish but not much of what he said." Chris turned the beer bottle in his hand. "No reason to doubt her. Harp asked her about it later and she gave him the same story. Doesn't matter, really. You can't go hitting a guy in handcuffs, no matter what he said or did."

Mel's look suggested she might feel otherwise. "You call the hospital again? How's Tommy?"

"Better than we could have hoped, and a helluva lot better than he looked laying out there on the asphalt. He was awake, even cracked a couple of jokes. Buck and Dale are there and will take turns sitting with him. He wanted a burger from the Hamilton and they brought it over. He's not even old enough for a beer, but I let them sneak him in one anyway. The injuries read like a goddamn grocery list. Punctured lung, bruised spleen, broken ribs. Bunch of other stuff busted up. The left leg is bad . . . real bad. He's not walking for a while. Not running again ever, maybe." Chris refused to glance down at his own leg. He knew a thing or two about bad injuries, ones where you had to relearn to walk a straight line and where a lot of things still weren't quite straight again no matter how many steps you took. He finished off the beer. "Harp *warned* me not to put those two out there together. He likes Dale but doesn't think he's got much sense, says he's watched too many movies. And he caught Tommy dry-firing his gun in the bathroom, speed-drawing in the mirror. It was just going to be for a couple days, babe, just to get Tommy up to speed. That was it. Harp can't be everywhere. He can't ride with everyone."

"And neither can you. It happened. It's going to happen again." Mel stretched out a leg, tapped him with a bare toe to get his attention. "You couldn't have known."

"Sure, but maybe I'm supposed to know better." He grabbed her foot, held it. "Dale is barely twenty, Amé not much older than that. Till Greer is what, twenty-three? Same for Buck Emmett. Jesus, Tommy turned nineteen *two days ago*. They're all kids, babe. Kids I'm putting out there to get hurt."

Mel laughed. "Says the old man of twenty-six. We just agreed that you and Ben can't be everywhere all the time. You two have to train them the best you can and then hope for the best. Hope they do the right thing, the smart thing. And you know what? Even then, sometimes it's not going to be enough. That's the job and you know that as well as anyone."

He let her foot go. "Harp always reminds me that *hope isn't a strategy*. But you're right. Hell, I know you're right. It's the goddamn job. Still, it doesn't make it any better. Maybe I don't know enough to show them what to do."

She got up and went to put her arms around him, following his gaze out to the summer lightning and the places where stars would soon appear, if they appeared at all. "You know plenty. After all, you've been spending a fortune on all those books, right?" She laughed again and this time he joined her. He'd been ordering book after book on law enforcement techniques, police psychology, professional leadership and management. Anything he could get his hands on to teach himself how to do his job. He kept them in his truck and by the nightstand, even hiding a few in his desk drawers at the department. Harp had seen them and never made a big deal about it, but a couple of months back gave Chris one of his own, a well-thumbed copy of Edward Conlon's *Blue Blood*. Chris hadn't pegged Harp as a reader, but the man had surprised him more than once. He hand-painted his own fishing lures and liked to play chess against himself, easily beating Chris the few times he'd challenged him, and Chris at one time hadn't been a bad player, either, having learned the game from his dad. He also knew an unfathomable amount of Old West history, could endlessly recite cowboy poetry, and listened only to jazz. He didn't even own a TV, instead keeping a huge collection of Art Tatum, Charles Mingus, and Thelonious Monk CDs on constant rotation in his apartment and his truck.

"Why did Tommy and Dale try to stop this guy? Who is he, why did he run?" She paused, stepping carefully before adding, "Drugs?"

That was a thorny subject, far too sharp, given Murfee's history and that of its former sheriff and chief deputy, as well as Deputy Amé Reynosa's own brother, Rodolfo.

"Just speeding, but they saw the Arizona plates and got curious." Chris didn't offer the *other* reason, the *real* one, he suspected. His two white deputies had caught a young Hispanic male driving a late-model car probably worth more than a year's pay instead of the usual rusted-out trucks with Ojinaga plates they were all too familiar with, and *that* had gotten their attention. *A wetback in a nice car* is what really had made them curious.

"He pulled over when they first lit him up, but when Tommy approached the car, he gunned it, went backwards, hit him. Maybe he was just as nervous as they were. Maybe it was an accident. Who in the hell knows? Right now, he's not talking. I'll be meeting with Royal in the morning and see where we are then." Royal Moody was the district attorney for Big Bend, Terrell, Jeff Davis, and a couple of other counties— a good chunk of the Trans-Pecos plus some—almost sixteen thousand square miles. Over half of which was patrolled by Chris and his deputies in Big Bend alone. Royal kept one office in Murfee and another over in Nathan.

"His license says his name is Azahel Avalos. He's twenty-three years old."

Mel put her face against Chris's neck, breathing soft against him. "Not much older than Tommy and Amé and the others."

Chris kissed the top of her head, held her tight, counting lightning strikes and listening for thunder that never reached them.

"No, not much at all."

Chris had fallen asleep, the sheets kicked off; his long, thin body pale and exposed. He'd never really gained back all his weight after the shooting, after the recovery. And if you just looked at him nowadays, standing against his truck or out on the porch like he was earlier, with his scars hidden beneath his clothes, you'd never guess all that had happened to him. You would have had to have known him *before*, to really see how much it had cost him.

How much of himself he'd left behind and lost—both good and bad.

Mel slid next to him above the sheets, the way he was. She'd put up two box fans in the bedroom and even with them turning full-blast the room was still too hot. Chris had on boxers but she was naked, trying to stay cool, wanting to lie closer to him yet feeling the heat coming off his body. He moved in his sleep, said something to himself, as moonlight touched his face.

It was hard sometimes for her to imagine how he'd almost died out here, somewhere just outside, maybe within sight of these very bedroom windows. She'd never admit to him how she was afraid to look out them when she was here alone; afraid she might see the ghost of who Chris once had been walking over the creosote and caliche, lost and unable to find his way back home. She knew he took some sort of strange comfort from being out here, as if he could reach out to that younger version of himself; maybe have a talk and remind himself of who he'd once been, even though that person was truly dead and gone. Everything that had happened at the Far Six, in Murfee, had changed him irrevocably. It had killed some parts and strengthened and *darkened* others, all made worse now by the constant stress he was putting himself under to run the department well and protect those who worked for him. To be *nothing* like the men who'd tried to kill him—Sheriff Stanford Ross and Duane Dupree. But she'd lost something, too, when he'd been attacked: a sense of security, an untroubled future. She needed him and it was a need that was as strong as ever, since any Chris was better than no Chris at all. But she'd always be afraid living out here, sharing space with the ghost of the man she'd first fallen in love with. The only man she could ever love.

It was the sort of fear that wouldn't go away with alarms and security lights, even though they had plenty of both installed in the house.

Maybe it was the sort of fear that'd never go away at all.

IN FACT, Ben had wanted her and Chris to get a dog, a couple of them even, to keep her company out here alone, and she knew he'd been out to Artesia this morning looking at some before the chase. He'd mentioned it a few nights back while nursing his drinks at Earlys, when she'd told him if anyone needed a dog, or a friend, it was him. Better yet, he needed a new woman in his life.

Mel wasn't sure if Chris knew just how much Ben continued to struggle with Jackie's death. How he barely slept in that efficiency above Modelle Greer's garage and was probably drinking way too much, even when she wasn't serving him at Earlys. She really liked the older man, who was still good-looking in a sharp-edged, cut-your-finger sort of way. He was too damn thin—always pulled tight like a wire—with his peppered hair shaved down to a memory and his eyes the color of a cold sky threatening snow; eyes that reminded her of the smoke and clouds streaking the oil fields of her youth. She enjoyed his company, trusting his wisdom and appreciating the help and confidence he gave Chris. She couldn't imagine Chris managing the department without him, but also couldn't imagine Ben Harper without the job of managing Chris. The two men appeared very different, true, but they were really just opposite sides of the same coin. Chris and Ben needed each other, even if they didn't know how much. Still, she worried about him, wondering about all his empty nights drinking alone and listening to his jazz music in his apartment. Dreaming—when he slept at all—about his wife.

She thought about Amé Reynosa hitting Azahel Avalos and smiled. Just like everyone else in Murfee, she'd questioned whether it was smart to bring the young girl on as a deputy. Even now, Mel still caught the occasional whispers about Amé's long-dead brother and her remaining family in Mexico. But Chris swore she was doing a damn good job and that hiring her had been a needed step forward for the Big Bend County Sheriff's Department. *A necessary one.* He trusted her, and told Mel that the young deputy reminded him of *her* when they met back in Baylor—that they both shared a hell of a temper and a mouth. Baylor seemed like such a long time ago, first seeing Chris standing on the sidelines with a football in his hand. He hadn't thrown one since the night he was shot, when she'd watched him throw ball after ball into the cold desert dark at the old house before heading out to meet Duane Dupree here at the Far Six. They'd been having troubles for months by then, arguing over stuff that didn't matter anymore and probably never did, but he'd been the *old* Chris for at least that night, laughing with her, kissing her, throwing his footballs before holstering his gun and walking out the door. After all their fighting, she'd felt like she'd just gotten him back that very night, only to find out that the man who returned from the Far Six—*survived it*—wasn't the same; but, then again, neither was she. There was no way she could be.

The Melissa Bristow Chris had met at Baylor was now a ghost, too.

Mel was turning thirty this year, and although Chris was older than all the deputies who worked for him except for Ben—always joking about "the kids"—she still knew they were both way too young to feel this way. They were scarred, true; but only bent, not broken. She wasn't sure what to do about it, but she didn't want them ending up together and somehow still alone, holding on to nothing but the memories of how they used to be.

She rolled over, watching him sleep. Wondered what he dreamed about. A few months back he'd started writing longhand on some yellow legal pads he kept for just the occasion, hiding them away in a drawer in the study. She had no idea *what* he was writing—stories or memories or just notes about things he wanted to change at the department—but he always had the same expression on his face when he did it, the same as when he'd thrown those footballs that night in the yard at the old house. Focused, completely lost in the moment—his body present but his mind somewhere else; traveling far away. He looked like that now, too, dreaming, with his eyes closed.

She kissed him lightly, not wanting to wake him, wishing him well on his journey, before closing her own eyes.

SHE WOKE SOMETIME LATER—panicked—to the sound of Chris's voice. He was sitting up on the bed, talking low on his cell. She'd never heard it ring, the sound lost behind the turning fans.

Something's happened . . . to Tommy Milford, or the kid they were keeping in the Big Bend jail. Maybe to Ben? She struggled upright, covering herself with the abandoned sheet, checking the windows where moonlight had been replaced by a different kind of glow, the hint of a dawn sun—that brief moment when a brand-new sky comes up all gray, like an old photo exposing. Chris clicked off the phone and was now looking out the window with her, right into that slow and rising light, pulling himself together.

Getting ready to leave, when he realized she was awake.

"What happened? Is everything okay?" she asked.

He shook his head. "That was Harp. There's a body, just found over in Terlingua, outside the Wikiup. That's a little bar there, been there forever."

"I've heard of it." Mel sat very still, holding the sheet close, holding it tight; cold now, even though the room was thick and hot. The last time a body had been found, Chris's attempts to discover its identity had been like a match starting a fire, leading to the death of one federal agent and the murders of drug-corrupted Sheriff Ross and Duane Dupree, and Dupree's house actually burning to the ground around his decapitated body. It had forced Sheriff Ross's teenage son Caleb to flee Murfee and fueled Amé's desire to join the department after they learned the body Chris had discovered out in the desert was her brother, Rodolfo—murdered because of his own drug connections. It had finally flamed out, with Chris nearly dying right here on the Far Six, but not before shooting three cartel killers himself. It sounded wild, improbable, like someone else's story, but it was every bit true and it was *theirs*—hers and Chris's. And if the thing with Tommy yesterday was bad, Mel was afraid another murder so soon . . . *another goddamn nameless body* . . . was going to be a lot worse. She searched Chris's face for clues.

"It's . . . Do we know . . . ?"

"Yeah, we know who it is, a river guide, Billy Bravo. He's been identified by his girlfriend. She's the one who found him. Doesn't look like an accident, but . . ." Chris let it go and stood up, and even in the dim, his white scars seemed to glow. "I'm sending out Harp and Amé. I have to deal with our prisoner today and meet with Moody."

"I'll start some coffee," Mel said, getting up as well. She was relieved Chris wasn't going to Terlingua and twice as relieved that *this* body already had a face, a name; that there was no mystery about it. Those were ugly thoughts, but true. People died all the time, *bad things happened*, and she wished they didn't all have to be Chris's sole responsibility, his personal burden; except maybe out here, they did.

"You don't have to, but thanks, babe. You know, when it rains, it pours," Chris said, still looking out the window into the light. It was growing brighter by the heartbeat, turning the glass copper and blood.

"But goddamn, it's going to be another hot one today."

3

Ben Harper couldn't count the number of dead bodies he'd seen; too many by his very own hand.

Between his decade in homicide and twenty years on SWAT, he'd gotten used to them all, except for one—his own wife laid out at the Jessup Funeral Home, wearing the dress she'd married him in. Her face had been dusted with too much makeup, the touch of the mortician's finger almost visible on her cheek, as if he'd brushed a tear from there. Her eyes had been bruised and closed but so much like sleeping; almost alive.

No matter how they died, the dead all had the same tragic beauty about them—a body in motion stopped suddenly; a snapshot, forever suspended, a well-aimed grace. The beautiful dead were trapped between clock ticks and heartbeats. It was their moment . . . *their place*. So goddamn small, but spanning a lifetime. It was a sanctuary where they'd never feel pain or be hurt again, unlike all those they had to leave behind.

No matter what people said, dying was easy, effortless. It was living that was twice as hard.

HARP SIPPED HIS COFFEE, glancing up from the body to Amé Reynosa, who was standing a dozen yards away with the woman who'd found it and who claimed to be the girlfriend. She was young, Hispanic, like Amé, her black hair one long thick braid tied up by different-colored bands. She was crying, moving her hands, and even if he could hear what she was saying, he wouldn't have understood it. They were talking in Spanish, fast. Every few words Amé looked over to him as if something might have changed with the dead man sprawled beneath the ocotillo.

Nothing did, nothing would again.

Amé had picked him up with two black coffees, both for him, and four aspirin, which he'd dry-chewed with a couple of wintergreen Certs on the drive down to Terlingua. She knew he'd been drinking since he drank pretty much every night, but she didn't make a big deal about it. She drove and he drank and chewed and neither of them talked about what they'd find out here as the sun slowly came up to meet them.

Sunlight that did nothing to make Terlingua look better, or give the old ghost town any more weight or substance. It had started as the base for the Chisos Mining operation in the 1800s after cinnabar—quicksilver—was discovered, but all that remained now were the capped ancient shafts with names that meant nothing to anyone anymore, like the Rainbow, the 248, and the California Hill. In the years since, Terlingua had become an out-of-the-way hideout for all sorts of drifters and artists and hippies. It had gained some notoriety for its November chili cook-offs, and Harp had been here once before with Jackie to experience it. They'd stayed at the Lajitas resort, but had spent one clear and blue afternoon not far from where he was standing now, trying rattlesnake and elk chili and drinking the coldest beers they could find, getting downright drunk. They'd made love later in the hotel room that was far too expensive, fumbling off their clothes, laughing. Her skin had smelled like pepper, her breath like smoke, and when she came she had said his name a handful of times, each one faster until they ran together into nothing. What were the chances he'd ever be back here again, this time without her? It seemed that everything led back to Jackie.

Everything started and ended with her.

Terlingua had also become a popular spot for rafting. Terlingua Creek fed right into the Rio Grande, what the Mexicans called the Río Bravo, and there were several outfits that arranged multiday trips that took you deep into the gorges and dunes and beneath the high cliff walls. You could still find petroglyphs there if you knew where to look . . . stories about a time and people who'd long passed, if you knew how to read them.

And that's where Billy Bravo came in, who, according to his girlfriend, everyone called "Bear." He'd been a river guide in Terlingua off and on for five years, working the Salt River in Arizona and Colorado's Green River before that. He knew the water and the geology and the wildlife and all about those petroglyphs and those ancient cultures. He'd been hard and tough; a big man who came by his nickname honestly. Whoever had killed him—crushing his skull like they had—had either been a pretty big bastard himself, or had caught Billy Bravo by surprise.

Harp knelt down, where the high, ripe scent of alcohol cut through all the blood. Bravo had been drinking, a lot, right up until the moment he died.

Caught by surprise was still very much on the table, so that didn't quite rule out the crying girlfriend herself, even as small as she was.

Bravo lay beneath an ocotillo, but he hadn't died there. Harp had already noted the drag marks, and that was a point in the Mexican girl's favor. All that deadweight, literally—Bravo would have been a hell of a lift for even a grown man. It was a pretty shitty attempt at concealment, too, although Harp didn't figure the killer had been too worried about that given all the blood still pooled in the sand where Bravo had actually been killed, about twenty feet away. He died within sight of the bar, the Wikiup, where he'd been drinking the night before. The name was a stolen Indian word for a domed Apache dwelling, like a little hut or house. And just like Bear, the Wikiup was perfectly named—a damn cave almost, half underground, built up from all sorts of flotsam and jetsam flanked by a couple of barbecue pits. Outside

there were hand-painted signs and a collection of weathered lawn furniture and row after row of naked lightbulbs strung through the
branches of some mesquites. There was also an old car sitting flat on its
axles that visitors had been scratching their names into for years, and a
bunch of blown-out cushions had been crushed into the open trunk so
you could lie back there and stare up at the stars, which way out here
would fill the sky end to end. It was said that Apache women could put
up a true *wikiup* in a couple of hours if the right wood was available,
and the bar carrying the name looked like it hadn't taken much longer
to build.

Bravo lay on his side, arms pulled above his head, dropped from
where he'd been dragged. His shirt was torn, hiked up around his chest
beneath his armpits, revealing old scars, monochrome tattoos—names
that meant nothing; some Latin script and numbers and a rough picture of a bear's head where his heart would be. His pants were undone,
unbuckled . . . maybe he'd been taking a piss, or had been about to. And
lying there, he looked for the whole world like a passed-out drunk, until
you glanced all the way up . . . to the head.

The right side of Bravo's face was *gone*, pieces of it matted into his thick,
black beard and spilled down the front of his shirt. There was no eye
there beneath the shaggy hair, not even an eye socket. It had all been
pulverized, turned to blood and dust. That entire side of the man's head
was a misshapen crescent moon, like something large and fanged had
taken a bite out of his skull. Standing up, facing him, the killer would
have struck left to right . . . a left-handed assailant, unless—like Harp
favored—Bravo had been surprised from behind. Either way, the attack
had been vicious, meant to end the man's life. *Mens rea* . . . intent . . . with
malice aforethought. It would take an ME to help determine if it had been
one blow or many, and they still might never know. There were pieces of
Bravo's skull, brains, lying back near the Wikiup. The murder weapon
might be around as well, something hard and flat—a rock, a piece of
rebar, a damn shovel—tossed into the scrub.

Harp stood up, catching the first buzz of flies. A few people were milling around, watching him and Amé, but most of Terlingua still lay quiet
under the early-rising sun. The heavy tropical odor of the nearby river
pressed down, but he couldn't see it, and rainbow-colored banners and
other flags he couldn't place hung limp and unmoving from posts, just
like a wooden windmill with all of its paint peeled off that refused to
turn. Morning light shined off corrugated metal from a few RVs parked
here and there. The entire place was sepia-toned, except for odd flashes
of man-made color: trash and other stuff people had brought with them
and left behind. A dog barked somewhere, joined by others, and then he
caught a glimpse of an impossibly thin man jogging up a trail road, shirtless, his skin baked dry as beef jerky. Turned sideways, you might lose
sight of him altogether, except for his tight, bright green shorts and the
pink water bottles strapped to his waist. His head was bare, hair in wild
corkscrews, and his feet were bare, too. He was running barefoot
through the low hills, past the abandoned mines, out into the desert. If
he knew he'd just passed a dead man, he gave no sign, and never slowed
down to look back.

It was a goddamn miserable place to die.

AMÉ WALKED OVER, leaving Bravo's girlfriend behind where she stood
holding her arms, rocking in place. The grief looked legitimate, but
Harp wasn't completely sold, not yet.

Amé cast one look down at the body and then ignored it. She had a
pad in her hand that Harp hadn't seen earlier, with notes from her interview with the other girl. America Reynosa was bright, a quick learner,
and if she got that damn temper under control (as if he had room to talk),
she might become Chris's best deputy. She probably already was. There'd
be some measure of hell to pay for that little stunt she pulled with that
Avalos kid, but Harp would let Chris handle it. She knew she was in the
wrong, and would accept the consequences. She was tough that way. She

was also one of the most beautiful women Harp had ever seen, distractingly so, but she never drew attention to it . . . never used it or leaned on it. She had a magical ability to ignore herself and the obvious effect she had on other people, men mostly. She had history with Chris, back when Stanford Ross had been the Big Bend's sheriff; when she would have been little more than a kid herself. But she never talked about that or the year she'd spent away from Murfee after Ross's death and the final identification of her dead brother. In fact, he knew very little about her beyond the time they spent together on the job. Otherwise, she was a mystery. She never talked about herself or her hobbies or whatever interests she had outside the department, if any. When she was riding with him and he put on some Mingus or Billie Holiday, she never complained, never even said a word until a song was done. But she *listened* damn hard, like she was turning each song over in her head, just like she did with everything he told her about police work. He admired her and they'd developed a damn good working relationship, even their own silent, secondhand language. Like the way she'd brought him coffee and aspirin this morning, and the way she sometimes called him at night to ask him a question—to get his ideas on something—when all she was really doing was checking up on him and reminding him he wasn't alone.

He nodded in the direction of the girl. "What'd she say?"

Amé bit her pen, checked her notes. "*She* is Vianey Ruiz. She works over in Presidio at a Valero and spends some of her free time here when Billy isn't on the river. They've been together *más o menos* two years. They were drinking last night and she got tired and went back early to his trailer." Amé stood high in her boots, pointed east. "Somewhere over there. He stayed behind at the Wikiup, still drinking. She woke up this morning, went to look for him, and found him. Here." She motioned down to Bravo's body with her pen.

"So he's a drinker?"

Amé nodded. "*Uno grande.* It wasn't strange for him to close down the bar. *Era un problema.*"

"You know I still don't speak Spanish, right?"

Amé smiled. "Learning it should give you something to do instead of sitting in Earlys with Mrs. Cherry, drinking. *Eso es un problema, mi amigo.*"

"They're not married."

Amé waved it away. "*Lo que sea.* They might as well be. And you understand me well enough."

Harp laughed, wondering if the handful of gawkers noticed the two of them sharing a joke over a dead body. He'd done it plenty of times before, once even at a triple homicide in Odessa—an entire family, mother and two young daughters, shot dead by the father, who then didn't have the decency to shoot himself. They'd found him sitting at the dinner table, shotgun still warm in his hand, dinner spread out all around him and his family's blood drying on the dining room walls . . . his face . . . the food itself. After they'd handcuffed him and walked him out, Detective Bruce Cooper had said the guy must have really not liked the fucking meat loaf, and they'd laughed their asses off while the crime-scene techs took the photos, lighting that horrible room up over and over again. Gallows humor was the nature of the work. You needed it or it all got into your head and you couldn't get it out again. Sometimes it did anyway, no matter how many laughs or how many beers you had. Cooper had put his own shotgun in his mouth three years ago.

"Okay, *niña*, so what do we do now?"

Amé turned serious again, stealing a glance back toward the other girl, Vianey. "I've got a list of names, people she remembered in the bar last night. We have to talk to them all, *todo el mundo*. Bar owner as well, and all the other raft guides he worked with." She took in Terlingua as if seeing it for the first time; covering her eyes with a slim hand, blocking out the sun. "We're going to have to find them."

Harp grunted, agreeing. "What do you think about the girl?"

"I think she's telling the truth. She doesn't know why anyone would want to hurt Billy. Everyone loved him." Amé chewed her pen again, the habit of a onetime smoker, unconvinced.

Harp grunted again. "Of course they did." He didn't have to tell Amé that was complete bullshit, just like he didn't have to tell her to look for bruising on the other girl's arms or the dark stain of spilled blood under her fingernails—the telltale signs of struggle. Amé had the instincts of a good cop who *knew* the world was full of bad people, full of *wolves*. If it wasn't, Harp wouldn't have seen so many dead, attended to them; stood over them as he now stood over Billy Bravo. On TV shows and movies everyone was concerned with the reasons and the motives for all the horribleness that people inflicted on each other, but he'd learned long ago there was never enough rhyme or reason to any of it. The reasons, if there were any, rarely mattered. John Delaney, the father who'd shot his family in Odessa, had never offered one. Maybe he'd heard voices or his wife was stepping out on him or he just really, really hadn't liked the fucking meat loaf that night, but who knew? Harp remembered the names of all the dead he'd met, but what he couldn't remember was *why* they'd all died. All that'd mattered was death *had* finally come for them—on its huge black wings and wearing so many shapes—and as always, too goddamn soon. That awful, dark menagerie: car accidents and bullets and knives and lightning strikes and heavy objects within reach; or something as simple and horrible as a goddamn fucking stroke.

Death took away everything that you loved; it was fucking ruthless that way. And it left you behind to struggle on, searching for answers where there were none to find, until it came for you, too.

Jackie had always calmed dark thoughts like these. A devout Catholic, she'd been able to read his black moods better than her Bible. She'd always understood.

How it all got into your head and you couldn't get it out again . . .

"Well, there was something," Amé continued, sliding her notepad into her back pocket. She had sunglasses hanging from the front of her shirt, and admitting defeat from the sun, she finally put them on. "Or a *someone*. Some new people that have been coming into town and drinking at the Wikiup. They're staying over at Killing."

Harp had heard the name but otherwise drew a blank. "What about them?"

"Vianey didn't like them . . . didn't like being around them. Lots of tattoos, ugly stuff. She said they talked bad about Mexicans, blacks. Tough guys, bad men. They were loud even when they weren't drunk. A few days ago Billy had words with one of them and I guess they didn't like him dating a Latina. But she said they bought each other beers after and it was all good again."

"Or it wasn't," Harp said.

"*No, no lo creo.*"

"Were they in the bar with Billy last night?"

Amé nodded, her face masked behind her big sunglasses.

Harp thought about that. He'd seen his fair share of racists in their various stripes—bikers, militants and militia-folks, plenty of out-and-out skinheads in Midland, like the Aryan Circle. Some Hammerskins even had a clubhouse there once, and he'd helped serve a search warrant on the place for weapons and drugs. Most of them hadn't been very old, little more than teenagers, but they'd been a definite breed, easy to spot. They brought with them lots of *little trouble*: drunk and disorderly, concealed weapons, terroristic threats, graffiti and drug dealing. But also lots and lots of fights . . . the kind that *might* just leave a man's skull crushed. He wasn't aware of any around the Big Bend, though, and being this close to the border should give them hives—it was practically enemy territory—but it was something to look into. A possible reason, that unnecessary motive. The world was full of bad men, even here, in one of the emptiest parts of it. It never took long to find them, and somehow it never took long for someone like Billy Bravo to run into them.

Death on its dark wings . . . no place was too distant.

"Bad men, huh?" he said, searching for his own sunglasses and reaching for his cell phone.

Amé nodded. "*Malos hombres. Muy malos.*"

4

The first thing I always remember about my father's funeral is the flags.

The dozens that were snapping at half-mast over the cemetery, but more important, the lone one draped over the coffin that they later folded and handed to my mother, who, crying and shaking, tried to give to me. But I wouldn't touch it. It looked heavy in her hands, impossibly heavy, and I was afraid I'd drop it on the ground. I left my mother clutching it to her chest, left her to carry all that weight all alone, while my father was put into the earth.

I was nine years old.

The second thing I remember is the gunshots, the salute. They came in rapid succession, and even though I'd been warned to expect them, I still jumped at each volley. Someone, I don't know who, put their hand on my shoulder as if they thought I might run away. They held me in place, held me down, as the shots rang skyward. It was probably a good thing, because I really might have bolted then—straight across the green, clipped grass of the cemetery, beneath a gray sky threatening a rain that never quite fell. Running and running until I found a quiet place; I might have kept running and never stopped. Later, in Wanat, when things got bad and then worse and I was so scared and the only sounds I could hear were the metallic pop and crash of RPGs and mortars and the thunder of Camp Blessing's 155mm artillery rounds, fired from five miles away—and still a thousand times louder than those rifles at my father's funeral—all I'd wanted to do was run again, but there had been no need to hold me back. There had been nowhere to go, nowhere safe. In Wanat, you couldn't get far away fast enough. You had to kill your way to a quiet place again.

So I did.

The last thing I remember from the funeral is the handshakes, one after another. Thick, calloused hands pressed into mine over and over again, sometimes with another hand patting my shoulder or placed on my head. I was told over and over again it would be okay, that things would turn out all right. One man knelt down and leaned over me so close I could smell the whiskey on his breath, and he looked right through me with eyes the color of the empty sky overhead and whispered, *"Son, we're gonna find the sons of bitches who done this thing and put them right in the fucking ground."* Then he cocked his fingers in the shape of an imaginary gun and pointed it at my heart before someone pulled him away; standing him up and walking him off unsteadily, the spurs on his boots scraping the ground. The man after him had winked at me to let me know he felt the same way, they all did, and that the drunken man's words were the Devil's truth, even if they all couldn't or wouldn't say it out loud. Finally, someone stood over me, a shadow there and then gone, and pressed a silver star into my hand, still warm to the touch from all the other hands it had passed through—so hot it was almost on fire. And although I had been afraid the coffin's flag might be too heavy for me, I didn't know *real* weight until that star sat in my hand.

I had no idea at all how heavy something could be.

T-BOB AND JESSE ARE STAINED in blood that's not their own.

T-Bob, like usual, is drunk—a fucking mess. But Jesse is cool and calm just like the first time I saw him in Lubbock, before I met his daddy, John Wesley Earl. Jesse's been drinking, too, but he's plenty sober, and he runs his hands underneath the outdoor hose to clean them, washing away blood, before stripping off his T-shirt and trying to do the same with that. Nothing's working, though, nothing is going to get that blood out, and all he's doing is making a mess. Then Earl himself walks out and raises hell and strikes his piss-drunk brother until he starts crying, kicking him a few times for good measure while he's down in the dust made all muddy by Jesse's hose water. It isn't unusual for Earl to dump shit all over T-Bob for the smallest thing, but he'd warned all of us to steer clear of both Terlingua and Murfee . . . to stay the fuck out of trouble. It found them anyway, like it always does—like steel filings to a magnet or water flowing to the lowest land. Now it's found me, too.

Earl doesn't say a word to his boy, though. He gives Jesse a wide berth; Jesse watches bored while his daddy beats his uncle and doesn't raise a hand to stop it. T-Bob is getting whipped for Jesse's mistake and we all know it, Jesse most of all, but none of us says a goddamn thing.

We're all defined by what we don't do.

Joker stands silent, tongueless, his eyes nothing but slits and his tattooed arms crossed. He could be a piece of carved earth, a sliver of a nearby mountain.

Lee Malady tries not to laugh, hiding a smile behind a can of Pearl, while his cousin Cole smokes a cigarette, flicking ashes to the ground and intent on the dying flame reflected in his crossed eyes. Cole's really not *there* anyway, not smart enough to understand exactly what's going on. He's got the wits of a fourth-grader, trapped in the body of a strong, brutal man five times that age.

Sunny's mouth opens—T-Bob has always had a bit of a thing for her even though she's Earl's old lady—but she decides against whatever's on her lips and closes it just as fast again, turning away to stare at the high yucca, focusing on something in the distance that isn't there. Maybe she's looking for a way out, like there is one, or just searching for the crosses that line the old cemetery on the other side of the hill, counting them in her head.

Little B, Earl's other son and Sunny's boy, hangs close to her. He orbits her like he always does. He won't look away and watches every single strike that falls on his uncle, his thin lips moving, as if he's doing some counting of his own . . .

And Kasper, Little B's already pale friend and wannabe musician—he most always has a guitar in hand—goes even whiter by the second, trying not to catch anyone's eye but mine. When he does I nod to him that it's okay, even if it isn't. It's so fucking far from okay that it might be my biggest lie of all. I've hinted to him a few times that he needs to get out of here, but he won't. A different kind of gravity keeps him here, and it has everything to do with Little B. Kasper doesn't even understand how strong that pull is . . . crushing his goddamn heart . . . but I see it in every glance he steals at Little B, in the *way* he watches Earl's boy, who doesn't suspect a thing. I suspect *for* him.

Kasper's hands are tight in front of him to keep them from shaking, and there's no guitar in those hands now.

As it winds down, Jesse orders his girlfriend, Jenna—who's been standing near me the whole time—to go in and bring him out a cold Pearl, and she gets too close as she passes . . . almost brushing against me . . . close enough I pray he doesn't notice. If he does, he doesn't say anything. When she comes back and hands it over, Jesse pops the top with his freshly clean hands, but they aren't really, not by a country mile, and then he downs the beer in one long gulp, his throat moving like a snake swallowing something live and whole.

When he's done, he crushes the empty and tosses it to me, along with his wet and still bloody T-shirt.

He tells me to burn it, bury it, whatever. We both know he wants me to have my hands on it, so I'll always remember that my hands are just as stained as his.

Earl is finally done with T-Bob, who's stopped crying and is lying still, and now he's studying both me and his older son, shaking the sting out of the right hand he used on his brother. The sun's been up for a bit but it's still too low in the sky, turning Earl into a shadow I can't see through.

He's a hollow place where a man should be.

I wonder what he sees when he looks at Jesse . . . at me. One his true son, and the other, what exactly?

It's been weeks now and is there something in my face he recognizes that I can't anymore?

Does he know?

I remember holding my father's badge—a silver star and all its damn weight.

And now, holding this dripping T-shirt darkened by another man's blood. A man I suspect—know—Jesse just killed, even though I'm trying hard to pretend I don't.

I've never had any idea how heavy something truly could be.

5

Él sabía su nombre . . .

America sat quietly and let Sheriff Cherry finish his phone call, pretending to look at her own phone, although there were no missed calls there, no messages. Nothing personal. Nothing to show it belonged to her at all, just the photos she'd taken out at Terlingua: the body and the long blood trails it had left behind on the cenizos and sumac. They might tell a story, though, might help explain what had happened in the dark the night before. She and Ben would have to go back out there today and finish talking to other drinkers from the Wikiup, and then tomorrow they needed to run down these men in Killing. By then, hopefully, Doc Hanson would be done with Billy Bravo and they might have a better idea of how and when he'd died.

A little bit more of the story . . . the ending.

Her papa had a saying, *un proverbio,* maybe it was from an old song, she didn't know—*Nadie sale vivo de este mundo.* Nobody leaves this world alive. She'd learned just how true that was after her older brother Rodolfo had been found murdered out in the desert, like Billy Bravo. She'd learned it again after she'd met the boy Máximo, who'd killed Chief Deputy Duane Dupree for her. After that they'd run away together as far as Houston, before she left both him and Texas behind for what she thought would be forever. Although she never saw Máximo again, she had come back to Murfee, which made her understand her papa's words in a whole new way.

There were places and things and people in this world—*in your life*—you couldn't leave behind no matter where you went or how far you ran or how much you tried to forget them. You never escaped whole. A part of what you were stayed behind, and a part of what had happened stayed with you always and forever.

Like her old memories of Rodolfo. And Máximo from Ojinaga, with his dark eyes and wavy hair that had smelled of ashes the night after Dupree died, and who'd shared the same sharp-eyed smile as the man she struck yesterday out on Highway 90—a dangerous, knowing-too-much grin. But most of all, Caleb Ross, who'd once sworn how much he loved her and had promised to save her. Who *had* saved her, in ways she'd never expected and ways he'd never know.

Leaving her wondering where he was now and dreaming of how his life might have turned out.

She wasn't sure if Sheriff Cherry still kept in touch with him. She knew all she had to do was ask, but each and every time she came close, she chose not to. The sheriff seemed to sense her unease, and never offered on his own to talk about Caleb or anything that had happened to them. She was thankful for that, because she was Caleb's past and wanted to stay that way. Since she had returned to Murfee—this place and life they'd both been so desperate to flee—that had become truer than ever. Although she didn't or couldn't believe it for herself, she hoped he had found some way to forget all that had happened here. She didn't call him or look for him, because she didn't want to be the thing that brought him back here, reopening those wounds and haunting *his* dreams as Rodolfo and others still did hers. If he had any memories of her, she wanted them to be of those few good moments when they'd felt like they were the only two people in the world.

Sharing cigarettes in the back of his truck, searching for *fantasmas* out at the Lights.

Sitting out on the bench or the bleachers at school, laughing.

Lying in his bed, feeling each other's heat, wrapped in each other's naked arms.

Wherever he was, she hoped those thoughts might bring a smile to his face, for just one moment, and then nothing more.

And that had to be enough for the both of them.

SHERIFF CHERRY HUNG UP the phone and turned his full attention to her, shifting back in his chair.

His office was small, too small, she thought, for the Big Bend County sheriff. She'd been told that the huge room upstairs, the one that took up most of the second floor and looked out on Main Street, had been used by the former Sheriff Ross, but when Chris Cherry took over he'd changed it all around, turning it over to his deputies. He'd claimed this smaller place downstairs for himself, near the hallway that led to lockup. Its only nice feature was a barred window with shutters that actually opened, like they were now, letting in molten light. Sheriff Cherry had the ceiling fan spinning fast above them, but it barely moved the papers on his desk; it felt like someone breathing on the back of her neck. The building was as old as Murfee itself, too cold in the winter and too hot in the summer. Even with the AC turned up as high as it would go, it wasn't enough, and it seemed to her that the sheriff kept his window open all year round anyway, the shutters pulled wide, no matter what the temperature. He was so tall, this old, cramped building probably felt *demasiado pequeño*. She guessed he liked having eyes on the real world outside, *his* way of escaping this place, even if it was only for a few minutes at a time and only by looking through bars onto the tree-lined street beyond.

"That was District Attorney Moody, who I'm about to walk over and see. We were going to meet first thing this morning but he got held up for a bit. I guess we all did, with Terlingua. Anyway, when I see him we're going to talk about our friend in lockup there, young Mr. Avalos. And somehow, I think that right cross you threw to his jaw is going to come up."

She didn't say anything, looking instead down at the phone in her hands; swiping away the pictures of blood that were there.

"Do you want to try and explain to me what happened? Take another stab at it from yesterday?"

"*Lo siento.* It won't happen again."

Sheriff Cherry sighed. "No, no, it won't. I know that. But it shouldn't have happened in the first place. It undermines what we're trying to do here, Amé, the whole damn credibility of this department and the badge we both wear. People have to respect us, trust us. That won't happen if we beat the shit out of someone in our care, even after what he did, or maybe mostly *because* of what he did. We have to be better than that. Azahel Avalos is our fucking responsibility. These slipups help guys like him go free. Goddammit, you know better." He pointed out the window. "Right now, there are still folks out there pining for the *good old days*, for Sheriff Ross and Duane Dupree. They're waiting for me, for you, to show we can't do this job, that we don't deserve it. They're looking for any excuse, any goddamn mistake. Don't give them the ammunition. Worse, don't load the gun and point it at your own head."

"I was wrong. I know that."

"Okay, I guess I'm done, then. We'll just have to see how it falls out." Sheriff Cherry shuffled the papers around on his desk, still not quite done, no matter what he'd just said. "I told you not to make this personal. You really lost your cool all because he cracked wise about Tommy?"

She sat still, her hands clasped in front of her. *Más que eso*, but she wasn't quite ready to tell him that. She knew it was wrong and hated herself for it, but she wanted another chance to talk to Avalos alone . . . to look him in the eye and make sure she'd *really* heard him say what she thought she had. Then maybe she could talk to Ben Harper about it first and figure out what to do after that.

She didn't want to lie to the sheriff, so she didn't say anything at all.

He continued watching her, waiting, leaning forward with one hand propped beneath his chin. His eyes were bruised, soft, the way eyes get sometimes when you try to sleep but not well, or not at all. She recognized them because those same eyes had stared back at her in the mirror this morning, after she got the call about Billy Bravo and Terlingua. She'd already been awake for several hours, replaying the thing with Avalos in her head, watching the shadows coil and uncoil on the ceiling above her bed.

She knew Sheriff Cherry didn't quite believe her, but he *wanted* to, and that made her hate herself all the more.

Finally: "Well, I'll take that as a yes. Now I really am done with it." He sat back up, unhappy. "All right, tell me about Terlingua."

HE'D HEARD MOST OF IT from Ben already, but she walked him through it again: the body, the girlfriend, the Wikiup. One of the county's two ambulances had brought Billy's body back to Murfee, and she and Ben had followed it so they could make some calls to his guide company, Trek River, who they hoped could give them some information for family notifications, but they needed to get back to Terlingua. They had the whole town to deal with; everyone was still a suspect. People drifted in and out of the place all day; some were already out on the river, others sleeping off the night before. Word of Billy's death would get around and they planned on spending the rest of the day there questioning anyone they could find. Ben had Till Greer patrolling TX 118 and the River Road, FM 170, between Presidio and Terlingua, looking for anyone who might be trying to get out of town for good, and Buck Emmett was handling the crime scene and Billy's trailer. *Al mismo tiempo*, Dale Holt was making some calls for them and checking in on Tommy and Avalos. They were so few to begin with, and spread so thin—there were a hundred things she and Ben needed to do—but still the sheriff had made a point of calling her in just to have this talk. He was angry about Avalos and wanted her to know it, and as much as Avalos *was* a problem she needed to deal with, she still wanted to take the lead on Billy Bravo's death. She was afraid that when the sheriff finally dismissed her he was also going to pull her off the Terlingua case as punishment for what she'd done on the road. Ben would argue for her, hard, but it might not be enough.

"What do we know about these folks over in Killing that Bravo tangled with? Bikers?"

"*Nada.* Just what Billy's *compañera* said. We don't even have names, *la chica* didn't know them."

"But they sure as hell stood out to her. I take it she'd recognize them again . . ." Sheriff Cherry said it to himself as much as to her, turning around in his chair to take in the big map behind him on the wall. It was dark paper, heavily inked and lined, and protected behind a thick wood frame and smoky glass. It was one of the few items he'd brought down and kept from the old office upstairs. There had been all sorts of other things, antique guns and photographs, but he'd sold them all off and used the money for charity and the department. He stood, tracing a finger over the glass. "Killing's another little ghost town that makes Terlingua look like Houston. I've never had a call out there. Not when I was a deputy, and not since. I don't think I've been through there in years. There's a few families hanging on, Raymond Joyce and his bunch, but not much else, or at least I didn't think so."

"We're going there tomorrow, *esta noche*, if we can." She hit the word *we* hard, letting him know that she *had* to be involved . . . that Ben needed her.

Sheriff Cherry turned back to her. "I may have to call in the Rangers on this, Amé. Royal Moody already told me they're offering to investigate Tommy's assault, and I'm guessing he's going to let them. Royal's just one more person who doesn't think a whole lot of our abilities, mine most of all. He may want them to work the Bravo murder, as well."

"We can handle this. Ben and I can."

Sheriff Cherry nodded. "Yeah, yeah, I know." He offered a thin smile, falling back into his seat. He looked so different to her from the man she first met two years ago in Mancha's parking lot. But the eyes were the same, even now, even tired. Sheriff Chris Cherry was a *good* man and his eyes couldn't hide that. They were mostly green, sometimes blue, but always, always, the brightest thing in a room. Caleb had had similar eyes—like hot sunlight on water—and for a short time, she'd thought they were the most beautiful things in the world.

"Okay, Deputy Reynosa, let's see how far you two get with Terlingua and Killing . . . then we'll talk again."

She stood fast, grateful. "Yes, sir." She wanted to go before he changed his mind.

"And Amé, please let's try not to hit anyone down there, all right?"

SHE WAS SUPPOSED TO GO MEET BEN, but she needed to do this other thing first.

Él sabía su nombre . . .

She had to do it *rápido* because she didn't want Sheriff Cherry to see her.

She came out of his office and turned to go upstairs, but once out of sight, circled back around the big copier they were always repairing and went through the metal door into lockup. It was like walking *forward* through time, this part having been added to the original building to create their modern five-bed jail. That had been Sheriff Cherry's doing, but since she'd joined the department, they'd never had more than a couple of them filled at any given time.

Right now, there was only one.

All six deputies were on a rotation for managing prisoners when the jail was occupied, but Sheriff Cherry had two custodians who also dealt with the day-to-day things: cleaning the cells, cooking food, dispensing meds. Dale Holt had jail duty today, but right now he was over at the Hancock Hill Regional Medical Center, visiting Tommy. That left only the regular daytime custodian, Victor Ortiz, whom she'd helped get hired, and the prisoner: Azahel Avalos.

She'd called Victor earlier, so he knew she was coming. He manned a small office filled with even smaller computer screens; one for each camera focused on a cell. He was sitting in the dark, his weathered face lit only by those monitors, drinking coffee. She'd known Victor since she was little, when he'd lived on the same street as her mama and papa, the same street she still lived on now. He'd run a little *paletería* for a while and after school used to slip her *mango con chile*, her favorite, never charging her.

Victor didn't say anything, just nodded at her as she went by, with light and shadows reflected in his bifocals. She could smell his coffee, black and strong, like the coffees she always brought Ben.

Azahel Avalos was in the first cell with a plastic tray across his lap, picking at the remains of his breakfast. His T-shirt and jeans had been replaced with a blue jumpsuit, his feet wrapped in dark socks. He looked up when he realized he was being watched through the plastic window on his door.

Smiled, when he realized it was her.

But the smile was different from the one he'd flashed yesterday; it was thinner now, like soft ice on the river. All for show. Avalos was truly and deeply scared. She didn't know if it was the weight of what he'd done and what he was facing, or something else altogether.

She was worried about what that *something else* might be.

He got up and walked to the plastic. His breath fogged it, so he drew circles in it with a finger.

"*Oye, chica, ¿me extrañaste?*"

She tapped at the plastic, ignoring his question, but spoke in Spanish, low, so only he could hear.

"Yesterday you said something to me. Do you remember that?"

"It doesn't matter. I'm not going to be here long."

"Are you sure? Because right now you're the only one here I see."

He shrugged, glanced down, not wanting to meet her hard stare. She could see not only the bruise on his face where she'd struck him, but also that his hand—the one that seconds before had been drawing on the plastic—was shaking. Whoever he'd pretended to be yesterday was gone. *That* person had disappeared like smoke, leaving only this shadow behind, thinner even than the shadows on her ceiling last night or those reflected in Victor's glasses. And just like she knew so much about Sheriff Cherry and Caleb Ross through their eyes, she could see beneath Avalos's hidden glances that he wasn't truly dangerous. He was no killer, no matter how much he'd tried to act otherwise on the road. She'd looked into true killing eyes—Duane Dupree and Máximo—and Avalos was neither of them.

She pushed. "You called me *the girl with the gun*." She repeated it. "*La chica con la pistola.* But you also said *my fucking name.* You know who I am."

Él sabía su nombre.

He knew her name.

AND THAT'S WHEN she'd hit him yesterday. When he'd looked at her and said . . . *you're the girl with the gun, America Reynosa.* She hadn't been wearing a nametag; there'd been nothing on her badge or her uniform that would give it away. But Azahel Avalos had known her even before she'd put the cuffs on him.

He'd said her name in surprise, but also in fear. The same fear that he couldn't hide now and that was coming off him in waves. There was sweat in his hair and it was staining the back of his jumpsuit as he turned away from her and went back to his cot.

He knew her name.

And he was afraid of her, and she didn't know why.

6

Royal "Roy" Moody was the law. He had two offices, one in Murfee and the other in Nathan, and whenever Chris needed to meet with him, he was always at the other one, which meant Chris spent a lot of time waiting around for him, like he was now.

Royal was down the hall in the bathroom and had been forever. Chris sat in his office, a place that looked only half *here*, like Royal himself. There were a couple of dusty prints on the wall, generic cowboy stuff, and a picture of a smiling wife and son that Chris would have sworn came with the black plastic frame. Everything else—what Chris assumed were law books or case files—were hidden in water-stained boxes, stacked on the floor and on bookshelves. The desk was empty save for the picture and a battered laptop. Chris had stood for a while by the two big windows that looked out over the parking lot and across the street to the Dollar General store. Even the lot was bare, except for Chris's truck. He'd counted flies long turned to rust by the sun on the windowsill, and wondered at a lone nickel winking among the dead—how it had gotten there, who'd held it last—before giving up and sitting down.

A toilet flushed and a few seconds later Royal strolled in, wiping his hands on his pants. Chris tried not to hesitate when Royal offered to shake.

"Sheriff," Royal said, sliding into the chair behind his desk. "Got a goddamn mess on your hands, I see. Now, two messes." He raised two fingers for emphasis and rooted around in his blazer, finding a single stick of gum that he unwrapped with one hand, popping it in loudly. Royal Moody was short, maybe five-six, sporting the only outfit Chris had ever seen him wear—a blue chambray shirt, bolero tie, black vest, and a dark blazer that was neither black nor blue but some color in between. He also had his Stetson Bent Tree straw hat set down tight, hiding a nearly bald head. Chris had been told Royal used to be a damn fine baseball player in Pecos, but that was hard to square with the small, uptight man he'd come to know. Royal had been a longtime friend of Sheriff Ross and had never gotten over his death, or the fact that Chris had taken his place. Their relationship was cordial, professional, but little more than that. He was a good lawyer, though, very good when he wanted to be, and that was enough for Chris.

"What are we looking at?" Chris asked.

Royal snapped his gum. "I'm gonna charge the Mexican kid with aggravated assault with a deadly weapon on a peace officer." He paused. "You know, the car being the deadly weapon." Chris nodded, got it, and Royal continued. "Anyway, that's a straight-up second-degree felony, and I'll ask for and will get a high bond, in the neighborhood of a quarter of a mil at least. We don't want folks running down our deputies. If he doesn't make it, and by all accounts he won't, you'll have ninety days . . . well . . . call it a little less than that, to do whatever you're going to do investigation-wise, before I have to get it all in front of the grand jury for indictment. Otherwise, we'll likely be releasing him on a personal recognizance bond, and then it's *adiós*, back over the river he goes."

Somehow, Royal made *adiós* sound like three words.

"Royal, he's not from across the damn river. He's got an Arizona driver's license. The car is registered out of Phoenix."

Royal popped his gum again. *"Right* . . . well, that's where we are with that." He picked at something on his vest. "What do you know about him?"

"At the moment, not much. He's got two phones. I'm going to want warrants to dump both of them." Royal raised his eyebrows, but didn't say no. "He had a small bag with some traveling clothes, not enough for a long stay anywhere, and about two thousand dollars in cash and an unlicensed gun beneath the front seat."

Royal raised a hand in the shape of a gun, pointed it at Chris. "I'll toss on the gun charge, too."

"Good. Fingerprints are nothing, and there are no wants or warrants out of anywhere, at least not on the name and IDs that we have. We're still running those down. He may not be Azahel Avalos, but if he isn't, I don't know who the hell he is."

"And no idea why he was hauling ass through the county?"

"No, he won't say much. He's made one jail call to a Phoenix number and talked only in Spanish. We recorded it and Vic Ortiz translated, but I'll get someone else to look at it, too. No one picked up the other end, so he left a message. Said where he was and that there was a problem, car trouble, and not much else. No one's called asking about him, not yet anyway."

"So we still don't know why he ran?"

"No, no we don't. Your guess is as good as mine," Chris conceded, which was probably true. Although if either of them had to guess, they'd probably both pick drugs. He watched sunlight track across the dust on the floor and picked out his own boot prints there, from where he'd walked to the window and back.

"And the car?"

"Late-model Nissan. We tossed it and didn't find anything. I talked to Harp about borrowing a drug dog from one of the Border Patrol checkpoints to run over it, but then this thing with Billy Bravo happened. We'll get it done sooner or later, unless Avalos talks to us first."

Royal reached into his blazer, pulling out a folded sheet of paper. He scanned it with a finger and then put it back in his coat pocket. "His initial appearance is at three o'clock, in front of Judge Hildebrand. I'm not sure who's next up on the defense wheel, but sounds like we'll need a Spanish speaker. Might get assigned Santino Paez, at least until Avalos retains someone himself. If he can, I hope he does, 'cause Paez is a goddamn pain in my ass." Royal tapped his barren desk. "Anything else?"

Chris shifted uncomfortably. "Yeah, unfortunately there is. One of my deputies got a little excited. Avalos said something to America Reynosa after she cuffed him. Some crude comment. Something inappropriate, something about Tommy. She let him have it."

"In cuffs?"

"In cuffs."

Royal blew through his nose, a loud, unpleasant sound. "Not good. Not good. If he sues her, and by her, I mean both *you* and the department as well, go talk to Grantham. I wouldn't say anything about it until then." Sue Grantham was the elected county attorney, the chief legal advisor for Big Bend. She represented the county and county officials, including Chris, in all civil cases—the sort of case Avalos could now pursue after Amé's little stunt.

"Well, he's not making a big deal about it now."

Royal waved it away. "And he probably won't. It's probably nothing. Who was out there, just him and your guys? This isn't the big city, where there are a thousand people with cell phones snapping pictures and making videos." Chris didn't stop him to mention the dashboard cameras that he'd mandated all his deputies use, just like the one that had been running that night two years ago when he stopped those two DEA agents out by Dupree's place. "Anyway, if you all agree to call it resisting arrest, it's fine." Royal pursed his lips, like he was biting down hard on his gum. "If you don't mind me saying, it doesn't surprise me, though. I'm not sure I'd ever have given that young lady a badge and gun in the first place."

"She does a good job." Chris knew Royal was really suggesting that Sheriff Stanford Ross never would have made someone like Amé—a female, and a *Hispanic* female to boot—a deputy. But there was something else, too . . . that subtle suggestion that Amé shouldn't be trusted because of what Royal and everyone else thought they knew about her and her brother. It was an old story and Chris had heard it all before, all the hints and accusations. He let it go. "Anyway, that's all of it."

Royal shifted, wiped at his forehead. "Like I told you on the phone, I think we should hand this over to the Rangers. Bring in Bethel Turner." Bethel was the Company E Ranger who covered Big Bend County. "One of your own was hurt, Sheriff, and no one expects you and your folks to be all that damn objective about it. Hell, I wouldn't be. And clearly, they *aren't*, if they're punching our lone handcuffed defendant. On top of that, you got that murder in Terlingua, and we haven't even started talking about that yet. Bethel and his boys are better suited to handle both things."

Chris had worked through this whole conversation on the drive over, trying out different responses in his head. "Look, I get it, and I'm not going to argue with you . . . much. Particularly over Avalos. We both know you have concerns about my department's ability to conduct these investigations. Hell, Roy, you have concerns about me." Royal didn't deny it, didn't say anything at all, just watched Chris over steepled fingers. "But I have Ben Harper looking into the Bravo murder, and you can't tell me he's not a good investigator. He worked homicide for ten years."

Royal nodded. "Harp's a good man. The best you got over there."

Chris ignored the jab. "Okay, so give him a week. Give us a week on both things, and if you don't like what you see or hear, we'll step aside and let Bethel handle it."

"Dammit, Sheriff, after a week you'll have made a bloody mess of it all. Bethel won't want to touch it after that."

"No we won't, and Bethel won't give a shit one way or the other. I'm asking for a week, Royal. Two weeks. That's all."

Royal spit his chewed-up gum into the trash can. "Hell, I'll think on it. Tomorrow send over everything you have on Bravo."

Chris stood and got ready to leave. "Will do. Harp's got it." He didn't mention that Amé was helping him. Before he walked out, he had a thought. "You ever get down to Killing? Heard about anyone new down there?"

Royal shook his head. "Killing? That shithole? No, why?"

"It may be that Billy Bravo crossed swords with some people staying down there, bikers or something, a few days before he died. I guess they had some strong opinions about his Hispanic girlfriend that he took exception to. The sort of opinions most people keep to themselves. It may be nothing."

Royal shrugged. "Well, they wouldn't be the first to have some opinions. Being fed up with all the Mexicans around these parts doesn't make you a bad person or a racist."

Chris laughed, but didn't smile, just to let Royal know he didn't think he was funny at all.

"Yeah, I'm pretty sure it actually does."

Royal measured him, blinking in slow motion. "You know, what I *have* heard is that Bethel might be thinking about running for *your* job. He's a good man. People know him and he's got lots of friends in Murfee and all around the county."

Chris grabbed his hat. "That's good to know, Royal. Goddamn good to know. And when the time comes, and he gets your vote, he can have the damn job, too."

Then he left the district attorney in his office, with his mouth still open, before he could answer.

7

It turned out that Billy Bravo wasn't the dead man after all.

His real name was William Haley, born in London, Kentucky. He'd played some football at the University of Pikeville, but dropped out short of graduation and drifted west, picking up odd jobs, most of them having to do with hunting or fishing. According to his older sister, June, he'd always been good—*at his best*—in the outdoors, working with his hands beneath big skies. But he'd also been pretty good at finding trouble—public intoxication, drunk and disorderly, aggravated assault, bad checks. You could plot the downward trajectory like a topographic map, tracing the long arc of the man's fall with your finger until he arrived in the Big Bend.

June Haley, now June Buford, e-mailed Harp the last good picture of her brother. It was taken right before he left Kentucky and she hadn't seen him in all the years since, hadn't had more than a handful of phone conversations in all that time. When she said his name she sounded like she was practicing it, reciting words she hadn't spoken in forever. The picture revealed a tall man, handsome, with short hair and only a ghost of a beard. He looked like any college-age kid, holding a beer can up high, standing out in a field surrounded by other people, and if one of them was June Buford, she wouldn't say. It was early summer, the grass still green from spring rains and the trees behind them thick and heavy with leaves. But one corner of the photograph was sun-blurred, lens flare nearly whiting out Bill Haley's raised arm, like he was just starting to fade away. Harp imagined if you stared at it long enough you might really see the man's whole image grow faint and vanish, leaving an empty space where he'd once stood all those years ago.

Disappearing from the picture, just as he'd disappeared from his life and family in Kentucky and from all the other places he'd ever lived.

Harp didn't offer to send June any of Bravo's personal effects, didn't need to send her a current picture to identify her dead brother. She never asked who might have killed him or why, or begged Harp to do everything in his power to find her brother's murderer. And if she was crying on the phone, Harp couldn't tell. When he raised the issue of the burial, she just said do whatever you do for people who don't have families.

He was about to tell her he was sorry . . . thank her for her help . . . but by then she'd already hung up.

THE SUN HAD TURNED the world to glass, reflecting all its light and heat.

Every bit of color was burned away, but the Chihuahuan Desert still *glowed*, a bleached white that was impossible to look at, the air above the asphalt bent sideways by the heat. Harp had the AC in the truck dialed up as high as it would go, pushing it hard enough to drown out Billie Holiday, but there was still sweat beaded all over Amé's face and across the smooth skin exposed by the open neck of her shirt. She was wearing her sunglasses, looking right into that colorless blaze, staring silently through the truck's window. She'd been that way since they'd left Murfee. They were supposed to be heading back to Terlingua but he'd decided to go ahead and check out Killing first. She'd talked to Chris but she hadn't said anything about it since getting in the truck. She hadn't said anything at all.

"Everything go okay with the sheriff?"

"*Sí, está bien,*" she said, shifting in the truck seat. "He was mad, but . . ." She shrugged, fell silent again.

"Did you tell him what Avalos said to you?"

"*Sí.*"

"No, what he *really* said."

Amé looked at him, before turning her attention out the window again.

"Look, I know that piece of shit said something more than just a word or two about Tommy. I don't know what it was, and I don't know why you won't tell the sheriff *or* me, but I'm only going to let it ride for so long, then you *will* tell me, got it?" He passed a wooden sign by the side of the road, the words scorched away, marking something that was no longer there. "Did you go see him in lockup?"

Amé flinched, a small movement, but it was enough.

He shook his head. "Old Vic didn't tell on you. Whatever's going on, get it straight in your head and then we'll get it figured out together if we have to. Fair enough? We all got our little secrets, but you owe the sheriff better. He'll go to the mat for you, always does, so don't make him regret it."

Amé nodded, resigned. "*Lo sé.* How did you know? How did you know I went to see Avalos?"

He laughed. "Because I'm a goddamn good cop, that's how."

THE FIRST THING that greeted them driving down the hill into Killing was the old Catholic church, a tilted collection of mismatched wood barely held up by the wind. It was the tallest building in town, rising above the other adobe and concrete dwellings. It was the only dwelling made of wood, one of the few *things* made of wood in the entire place, except for the crosses . . . dozens of crosses, scattered on the small hill behind the church, rising up into the rock and scrub.

The town sat in a bowl formed by the Chinati Mountains, along a finger of what was supposed to be the Alamito Creek, although with all the heat, the dusty, shallow course looked like it hadn't seen water in a long time. It appeared drained, wrung out, discarded: a snakeskin peeled and left behind. Like Terlingua, Killing was an old mining town whose best years had been in the forties. Silver, lead, and gold had been taken out of the hills, and Harp had caught the telltale sight of a mine shaft on an outcrop of rock just before they'd turned down into the town. Some science fiction movie had been made here back in the seventies, or so he'd read, and that had been the last time anyone had had any interest in the place.

It was damn easy to see why.

He nosed the truck down the main road, trying to do a mental head count of how many people might be here. There were old cars in front of a few of the adobe buildings but they looked nearly as old as the place itself. An ugly dog stood in the middle of the road, part shepherd and part something else, crouched down because one leg was twisted and bad. It bared yellow teeth and didn't give an inch, so he drove around it.

It pissed a dark stream onto the ground as he went past, staring up into the windows, gauging whether it could get in.

He'd had Buck Emmett talk to the Mex girl again to get a better handle on these men Bravo had had his run-in with. The first night there had been three of them, an older guy with salt-and-pepper hair, a younger one with a close-shaved head, and a third one that had been huge, bigger even than Billy. She couldn't remember their names except for the big one, who'd never said anything. The others had called him "Joker," but there'd been nothing funny about him at all. He'd never said a word, never cracked a smile, just stood with his tree-trunk arms crossed when he wasn't drinking his beer.

They'd caught each other staring, and he'd rolled out his massive lower lip at her, inked with a skull.

Only the other two had been there last night, showing up on their big bikes, and she hadn't stayed long after they'd arrived. She was tired already and she hadn't liked the men anyway; the things they'd said and the way they'd eyeballed her, mostly the younger one. The old man, with flame tattoos all up and down his arms and strange crosses on his neck, had more or less ignored her—more interested in drinking—but the other one had kept looking at her, his cold eyes crawling up and down her body, lingering here and there. He'd been wearing a white T-shirt with the sleeves rolled up, revealing sunburned skin and massive tattoos of guns on each forearm, like the ones she'd seen in Old West movies.

And that was what she remembered most—all his tattoos.

The word HATE across the knuckles of his right hand and the numbers 1488 on his left.

LIE OR DIE stenciled on one side of his neck, and GOD FORGIVES BROTHERS DON'T on the other.

A grinning skull in the palm of one hand and two bullets in the other.

Just like Amé had said: *Un hombre muy malo.*

THEY FOUND THE BIKES, two Harley Fat Boys plus a couple of Low Riders, parked in front of a rambling adobe ranch house, along with a Fleetwood Southwind showing rust, its big front windshield blocked with sheets or blankets. He and Jackie had once looked at RVs, contemplating spending the better part of the year on the road hitting the best fishing lakes, so he knew something about them, and this beast was a gas guzzler, probably a dozen years old. It sat like a great boat on a dry lake bed, tilted at an angle, with sand and tumbleweeds collected under it. But the tires still looked good, so it had arrived in Killing under its own power; it hadn't quite settled into the earth to rot and decay like most everything else in town. There was also a Grand Marquis parked next to it that might once have been green or blue but was now some other, hard-to-peg color. It was probably a surplus cop car bought up at an auction, and it looked like there were bullet holes along its flank.

He was going to tell Amé to take down the plates of both, but she was already on it, glassing them with the small Bushnells he kept in the center console, so he slowed to a crawl as they went past, giving her a chance to get them all.

More blankets and sheets covered windows of the ranch house, everything hidden by something else. The house had been expanded, spreading out in a slow creep toward a large hill or bluff rising behind it, the additions all tacked on with pitted concrete and cheap siding. Beer cans littered the ground—glowing hot spots in the afternoon sun—and broken glass shined like diamonds. There was a burn barrel with a tongue of smoke lolling from it, disappearing into the high desert haze, and then, just like that, there was a man smoking a cigarette and watching them roll by from the shadows of a side porch on the house.

Harp stopped the car, backed it up, as the man flicked his cigarette into the dust and ground it out with a boot. He shrugged his shoulders and came out from under the shadows to meet them as if he'd been expecting them all along.

He wasn't big, but rangy, and didn't quite fit any of the descriptions the Mex girl had given. He had a thick head of hair, going gray, slicked back and held in place by pomade and sweat. He wore dark jeans circled by a thick belt he didn't need, and a blinding-white T-shirt and black Justin boots. His arms were long, almost too long, ending in thick-knuckled hands. The sort of hands that had dealt out more than their share of harsh punishment—always bruised, always swollen and sore. But what stood out the most were the tattoos, just as they had for Bravo's girlfriend. This man's skin was a blue-green canvas from his wrists all the way to where it disappeared beneath his shirtsleeves. Crosses and skulls and playing cards and Nazi symbols and the entire length of a naked pin-up girl across his left forearm, sprawled backward with her arms behind her head, huge breasts almost three-dimensional on the skin. *Prison tattoos*, and he'd been in a prison a long time to have that much ink. Running around his throat was a knotted noose, and just visible at his sternum was a huge map of Texas wrapped in flames and inside that a four-leaf clover, with the thick letters ABT in the center.

Harp recognized the letters and knew what they meant . . . the Aryan Brotherhood of Texas, a longtime prison gang.

One hundred percent bad men.

Harp got out of the truck, as did Amé. She had her right hand loose, above her holstered gun; obvious, and with intent.

One cover, the other contact. Just like out on the road when they'd stopped Avalos, but this time Harp was going to do the talking.

The man stopped short of their truck and half raised his arms. Even beneath the ink, there were lines across his forehead, the crow's-feet deep in the corners of his eyes. The ABT was at least Harp's age, probably older. His eyes had the faded laziness of someone who was used to being outside in the Texas heat without sunglasses. The bright light didn't bother him; he could look straight into the damn sun forever. His years in the prison yard had given him eyes in the back of his head, too, and he probably saw everything without even trying.

"Damn hot," Harp said.

The ABT shrugged. "Don't bother me none. A little heat never did."

From behind her sunglasses, Amé scanned the sheeted windows, looking for movement.

Harp motioned to the man. "You got a name and something to prove it?"

"The first I got, the second not so much. I can't say I've driven a car in a while. I'm JW Earl."

"None of those bikes yours, that Marquis or the RV?"

He pointed at one of the older bikes. "That one there, but I'm what you call *naturally gifted*. I ain't got no license for that and never had one. My daddy taught me to ride and that was good enough for me. Rest of them's *with* me, but they aren't mine." JW Earl took in Amé with one look, then ignored her. "Gonna get my smokes and lighter from my back pocket if it's all the same."

"Go ahead." Harp came around the side of the truck, got within a few feet of Earl as he fished around in his jeans for his lighter. He lit his cigarette without cupping it against the wind and did it all with one hand, with practiced ease. "Where'd you do your time?" Harp asked.

Earl blew smoke. "Coffield, Dalhart, and Walls."

"Walls" was a common nickname for the Texas State Penitentiary at Huntsville, due to its bright red brick walls. Huntsville also housed the state's execution chamber.

"Long stints?"

Earl shrugged. "Long enough."

"Ben . . ." Amé interrupted, pointing to the front of the house where the door had opened and another man . . . *men* . . . had appeared.

The first two were quite a bit younger than Earl, closer to Amé's age. One was shirtless and whip-thin, his head completely shaved and his naked skin a billboard, like Earl's, and his dirty jeans hung low, revealing the white band of his underwear. The second was taller and just pulling on a black T-shirt. His whole right side, from his triceps to his shoulder and down his arm, was colored in: a giant eagle in mid-flight, talons raised; an American flag; a pair of crossed rifles. There were other tattoos here and there across his torso, but it was clear he'd done his time somewhere in the military before ending up in Killing. His head was cropped close but not bald, his blond stubble shining gold in the sunlight. His strong arms were veined.

And the last was *big*, a walking slab. He was shirtless, too, like the first, his entire chest dominated by a skeletal bird, the wings stretching up to his shoulder blades. It was perched on a swastika in a ring of fire, with the letters NLR half circled beneath that, stretching across his massive abdomen like a cliff face.

If Harp had to bet, this was the one called Joker. Bravo's girlfriend had put him at the Wikiup when Billy got into his argument, but not last night.

Underwear and Eagle took up positions beneath the side porch, as the one Harp had decided was Joker came and stood next to Earl, arms crossed, towering over him.

Harp turned back to Earl. "There was a problem last night at a bar over in Terlingua, a place called the Wikiup. Now a man's dead. I know some of your folks have spent some time over there."

Earl nodded, unconcerned. "Yep, they have, off and on."

Harp continued. "I also got a witness who says there was an argument a few days back between our victim and *him*"—Harp pointed at the big man—"as well as some others. Two of those same folks were in the bar last night. I need to talk to them."

"Well." Earl slapped the shoulder of the man at his side. "Joker here was with me last night, that's for sure, watching TV. As for the rest of 'em, you might be talking about my brother, T-Bob, and my oldest boy, Jesse. I think they was over in Terlingua last night. I mean, if you have a witness who says that and all, and we know a witness ain't never wrong."

"Depends on the witness, but it doesn't matter, I'm going to need to talk to your brother and son anyway." Harp pointed again at the man Earl had confirmed as Joker. "And this one here, too."

Earl laughed. "Well, hell, that's gonna be a damn short conversation. Ole Joker don't talk, not a lick. Cat's got his tongue, so to speak, hasn't even cracked a smile in ten years."

Earl poked at the big man, who slowly opened his mouth, revealing a black, empty cavern. There was no tongue.

Harp shook his head. "What about the other two I'm looking for? You cut their tongues out, too?"

Earl winked. "Naw, but your luck's still not so good. They're both out about now. But you leave a card and I'll send 'em up your way. And where'd that be?" Earl looked hard at the badge on Harp's chest. "Big Bend County Sheriff's Department, right? Up the road, in Murfee?"

While Earl was talking, Underwear slid down from the porch and moved toward them. He didn't walk so much as slouch, his hands down in his jeans pockets, pushing them lower. Once he got within orbit of Joker, he whispered something to the big man, but kept his eyes on Amé.

"You all been here long? Going to stay long?" Harp asked.

Earl shrugged. "Hard to say. My older boy is visiting some friends here, the Joyces, and others might stop by. Me? I'm probably just passing through. Not sure the locals are all that friendly."

"Until I talk to everyone, you shouldn't plan on going anywhere, how's that sound?" Harp pointed at the house "How many more you got in there? Mind if I go in and look around?"

Before Earl could answer, Underwear spoke up. His voice was higher, softer, than Harp would have first thought. It was a kid's voice, trying to play grown-up. He was still looking at Amé. "You let any little *señorita* around here carry a big ole gun like that?"

Harp turned and felt anger spark behind his eyes; gave his full attention to Underwear. "You watch that mouth, son. That *señorita* is the law here, just like I am. Yesterday she near knocked the teeth out of someone else *just passing through*, and now he's passing time in our lockup. You want to join him? You keep it up. Other than your name, I don't want another fucking word out of you."

Earl raised his hand, trying to pull Harp's attention back; trying to play peacemaker. "Don't pay him no mind, Deputy. That's my younger boy, Bass, but we call him Little B 'cause he acts like a little shit sometimes. He ain't got no damn sense and don't mean nothin' by it." Earl looked *through* his son. "Do what the man says, Little B, shut your mouth, or I'll goddamn shut it for you." Earl waved at the last man under the porch. "And that over there is Hero. Hero, why don't you get Little B inside now, while I finish this up? I think we're almost done here."

The one Earl had called Hero, whom Harp had thought of as Eagle, detached from the shade and came up on Little B, cocked and ready to grab his arm if he said more. The two didn't look that different in age, although Hero *seemed* older. Little B had hints of his father's face and eyes, but not half his composure. He was jittery, his eyes and hands all movement. When he'd worked patrol, Harp had rolled up on hundreds of kids like him hanging out in alleys and on street corners in Midland and Odessa. One of his old partners, Revel, used to call them *TV outlaws*, because the only thing they knew about being tough they'd learned from some damn show or movie or a rap song. They were mostly bark, no bite. No real threat at all if you smacked them once or twice in the mouth.

But not like Joker, or the one Earl had called Hero. Or even ole JW himself. Each was very different but all three had the same casual, dangerous air, and they were all capable of causing serious trouble if they had a mind to.

Earl was still talking around a mouthful of cigarette smoke. "Now, as for comin' inside, unless you got a piece of paper sayin' otherwise, I'm gonna have to respectfully *deecline*. I'm sure you can understand. I'm a free man, mindin' me and my own out here." Earl left it at that, smiling as bright and open as the sun.

But it was still a standoff all the same.

Harp nodded, realizing he was soaked with sweat. It was in his eyes, salty, stinging. And he was all of a sudden tired and damn heavy, like the dry ground itself was pulling him down.

Too little sleep, too much drinking, and too many thoughts of Jackie. *Getting too old for this shit.*

He felt ancient and worn-out and didn't want to keep sparring with Earl and didn't like where this was going anyway. Although he *did* need to talk to Joker and the others—Jesse and T-Bob and whoever else was holed up with them—he wanted more deputies here and wanted a better handle on just who these fuckers were and why they were in Killing. He couldn't guess at everything hidden behind the sheets and blankets and dust-fogged windows of the ranch house, but he *felt* there were eyes there, watching them. Maybe even a gun—with a finger on a trigger—aimed at his face or Amé's. Walking away now was bad police work, and he hated losing precious hours they'd never get back, but he hated his other choices more, as well as having to admit that right now he really didn't want Amé here.

There was a real threat of violence in this dead place, where the rocks were the color of long-dried blood and the sand was as pale as bleached bone. He could *taste* it, feel it thick on his skin, like the sweat that was going to take two cold showers to wash clean.

As real as this JW Earl smiling at him.

Harp wasn't scared for himself. He was calm and in some ways welcomed whatever might happen—even death on its dark wings, like the skeletal bird on Joker's chest. But Amé was standing next to him, trusting him, and he knew this wasn't the time or the place.

Check, checkmate.

He finally returned Earl's smile. "Fair enough. I guess we understand each other, then." He was about to reach for a card with his name and number on it, when Amé beat him to it. She slipped one of her own out of her breast pocket and took a step toward Little B, none of the others, and held it out to him. He looked at it like it might as well have been a live snake, but when she flicked it at him, he caught it, fumbling with both hands.

"There's a phone number on that card," Harp continued. "And an address. Use either, it doesn't matter to me, but I expect to hear from your son and brother. If I don't in the next day or two, I'm coming back, and I'll have that paper you were so concerned about. All legal, all real, and with a judge's signature. And if they or anyone else leaves before then, I'm finding them. Are we clear?"

Earl watched his son, who was turning the card over and over, moving his lips, reading it. "We're clear, Deputy. Like goddamn glass." He made an imaginary gun, cocked a finger at Harp, and pulled the trigger;

Harp thought he heard a whispered *bang*. "Loud and motherfuckin' clear."

"Goddamn . . . *America?*" Little B said, holding up the card for the others to see; they ignored him.

Harp waved Amé into the truck and she turned her back on the men without a word.

As they were driving away, watching the men behind them disappear in the rearview behind a wall of dust, Harp would've sworn the one called Hero—who'd never said a word—was trying to hide a smile of his own.

8

I killed my first person on my eighteenth birthday.

There was no cake and no presents that morning, no one singing "Happy Birthday."

Only Sergeant Wahl punching me awake before dawn, night already turning into a gray afterthought on the horizon.

I opened my eyes with him breathing all over me, his helmet at a funny angle because it was *always* at a funny angle. It never quite sat right, making his head strange . . . weird. I thought he was the end of a dream, until he told me loud and clear to grab my dick and my gun and get the fuck up.

But it *was* a dream, just the beginning, not the end, and a bad one. A dream I've had a thousand times since.

The sergeant swore to me he'd heard something.

And he must have had the ears of a goddamn bat or dog, because it came out in the after-action report that someone in the village had been pumping water from an irrigation ditch into a field the whole night before, just to hide the sounds of the insurgents moving up on our positions. Still, somehow Sergeant Benji Wahl, from Flint, Michigan, had heard them. Or maybe he'd fucking smelled them, but thanks to whatever sixth sense he had, we were both awake, looking east into the place where the sun would come up, when the attack came.

I was still struggling to stand when an RPG hit the mortar pit, taking out the 120mm and the mortar stockpile. It went skyward and all the way to heaven, with a light and a peculiar sound I had never heard before and have never heard since. The blast sucked everything inward, pulling anything not nailed down into its arms, before throwing it all up in the air again. That noise wasn't explosive, not like TV or a movie. It was high, almost musical. My mom, who got a lot more religious after my dad died, would have sworn it was the first trumpet blast, the beginning of the end, and for a half-second I thought the same thing. The TOW missile launcher went next, and then the observation post itself was hit. I was seventy meters away but still saw Stafford blown clear of his position, backlit against the rocks and tree he and the rest of the company had dug in under.

The insurgents had also taken the village's hotel roof and were using that to fire down into our post, as well as the patrol base itself. Our Bobcat had broken down the day before, so most of our barriers weren't to seven-foot spec, not even close. Everything topped out at four feet, and we'd dug out a lot of that, including our trenches, by hand. In some places we'd just laid out the concertina wire along the ground, where we left it spread out on the dirt like silver snakes, sunning.

It was a cluster fuck from the get-go.

I turned in time to catch Sergeant Wahl get hit and go down to one knee. That damn helmet of his had been knocked off and was rolling around on the ground between us, so I thought at first it was his whole head, until I saw him holding his throat, tight, looking surprised; looking right back at me and his eyes as wide as dinner plates. There was blood all over his hands even though it was still too dark for me to see that. *I know it, though*, because in my dreams I see it still—red from the heart that had pumped it, just turning black in the air.

The second shot took his legs completely out from under him and he fell face forward into our shitty concertina. He was like a bird trapped in all that wire, his wings broken.

Then there were men running in the darkness toward me.

I first raked my Minimi over the hotel roof, keeping heads down even though I didn't hit anybody. At about seven hundred rounds a minute, I turned most of the roof to dust.

My radio was screaming at me like a living thing . . . but it was just my friends, screaming on an open channel, scared and dying. Apaches and Predators were inbound and the big arty from Camp Blessing was starting to zero in on us, but for a while it would only be us . . . each man hanging on to another.

I was moving toward the sergeant when an insurgent crawled over a barrier. He was small and struggling with an AK nearly as big as him, and I had this weird thought how that gun was a lot older than him as well. He was just a kid, younger even than me on my birthday, and he was sweeping that gun in big arcs and firing off the odd round—not really *at* anything or anyone—just hoping to get lucky. He was a diversion, a sacrifice, so his buddies could continue dropping unguided RPGs into our position. I learned later the kid and a few others like him had also been chosen to run forward and throw rocks into the observation posts as they came—fist-sized rocks that in the dark and craziness looked exactly like grenades; turning end over end, dropping into the dirt. Just more diversions. But those rock grenades had forced our guys to retreat from their trenches, not wanting to get blown to hell, only to come under concentrated small-arms fire.

That had been the plan all along.

The kid was coming up on the sergeant and was going to trip right over him; I still didn't know if he was alive or dead. But I couldn't let him take another hit, so I brought my Minimi around on the kid until he disappeared behind my barrel, a darker shadow in the dark. He wasn't even *a person* anymore; just the hint of a thing, a memory of something else. It was still too dark to see his face anyway, or that's what I tell myself.

But in my dreams, like Sergeant Wahl's blood, I see it so damn clear.

Small, round, boyish. A mole beneath his right eye and a wisp of a mustache around a tiny mouth.

He was crying as he ran forward.

And like the hotel roof, I turned him all to dust.

I killed my first person on the dawn of my eighteenth birthday. It wasn't my last.

THE DEPUTIES LEAVE, and Jesse and T-Bob have questions, a lot of them.

T-Bob was ducked down in the Fleetwood and Jesse holed up in the house, but they were here the whole time, trying to catch a peek from their respective hiding places.

Earl knows they won't be able to hide forever, and that we're all going to have to deal with this mess they've left in Terlingua, even though Jesse and the others aren't about to leave, *period*, no matter what, until Flowers shows up. I know that Earl doesn't really care about Thurman Flowers and any of his racist church bullshit, or the plans that Jesse and Flowers have been mulling for years, but there is something around here he does care about.

There's a reason he came out here and is willing to wait it out in this goddamn desert.

None of this is what I expected or what I planned for. So far Earl's not what I expected, either, and now I'm trapped here with him, and it's like being in that observation post in Wanat all over again.

Flowers . . . this whole setup in Killing—these are nothing but *diversions* for Earl.

Just stones pretending to be grenades.

EARL TAKES THE GIRL'S CARD from Little B and tells him never to talk to that girl or any of those deputies again. If he does, he'll pull out his fucking teeth with a set of pliers. When Jesse tells his daddy to lay off and that Little B doesn't have to take attitude from a fucking spic, Earl gives him the look I've come to know—his eyes flat like a TV tuned to a lost channel. If the *sound* of static between radio stations has a color, that's it. Most times that's enough to shut someone up, even Jesse, even though it's rarely turned on him, but this is one of those times. There's this ongoing tension between Jesse and his daddy that hums beneath everything they say like a high-voltage wire. They don't openly fight, at least not yet—neither of them quite ready to grab hold of that wire—but we all feel it. It's been bad since I arrived, and given what happened between me and Jesse in Lubbock and how Earl's treated me since, it's only getting worse, particularly now that Flowers is on his way to Killing. But today—again, one more time—Jesse shrugs it off and tells his daddy it's no big thing, nothing to get mad about, and leaves it at that. But what happened in Terlingua is a *big thing*. We all know it, even if Jesse acts like he doesn't have the sense to see it. He's smarter than that, way smarter than Little B or Kasper or the Maladys or any of the others that he's drawn to him. He's smart like his daddy . . . a natural-born leader.

He probably would have been a damn good soldier, if he wasn't such a coward.

The whole thing breaks up, with Jesse and Little B going off with Sunny and Jenna, and the others finding something else to do to give Earl some space . . . some time. T-Bob, still bruised from his earlier beating, tries to speak, but Earl doesn't want any part of it, so T-Bob slides off as well, probably to get another cup of Maker's. His drinking is going to kill him, but not fast enough for Earl.

That leaves Earl and me alone in the front room; too hot and close. It's like the sun outside is trapped with us both inside, and I give him a second if he wants to say anything. Sometimes he does. There are these moments when he talks to me more than any of the others, far more than even his own two sons. He might ask me my opinion about something or tell me a little bit about Walls or the other places he's been locked up. He'll play cards with me, Texas hold 'em mostly, shuffling fast and fluid with his thick and dangerous hands and talking the whole time, never missing a beat. He can carry a story better than anyone I've met, and he'll leave you laughing with a joke or an observation even when he's not laughing at all. I don't know if he's still checking me out or if he actually *thinks* he likes me . . . whatever that might mean for a man like Earl. But I've had this image of him for so long, crudely put together from the things I wanted to believe . . . that I *needed* to believe to get me this far . . . only to find it doesn't quite square with the real thing.

He's weighing me out, like one more stone, and I don't know why or what that means.

Compared to Jesse, it's easier than I ever imagined *not* to hate John Wesley Earl, and I hate myself that much more for even thinking it. He saved my life, but he owes me so much more than that.

The time can't be counted on a calendar, although I've marked each day off in my head for years.

He doesn't want to talk to me now, though, and just keeps staring at the Hispanic deputy's card . . . *America Reynosa* . . . not reading it because he's already memorized it, tapping it in his hand.

I like how she dealt with Little B, how she didn't flinch or back down. I can guess how hard it is to be a deputy in a place like this, and figure it has to be twice as hard for a young woman like her.

She's even younger than me.

I hope she doesn't ever come back, though. I hope, for her sake, we never cross paths again, because I still don't know how this all plays out or how it ends.

Earl finally turns those static eyes on me and tells me to go on and get the fuck out, even though he does it with one of those half-smiles he sometimes shares with me that, like his stories, I can't quite interpret.

It's our secret, and I don't ever want to have too many secrets with John Wesley Earl.

So I walk out, leaving him there alone, flipping the deputy's card over in his fingers like it's the ace of diamonds, wondering what he's thinking, and if any of those thoughts are about me.

9

Earlys smelled like stale beer, polished wood. Mel had the ceiling fans turning fast but even this late it did little to make the air move or cool the place down. Chris sat with Harp at the bar nursing his first beer, the older man somewhere between his third and his fifth. It had been a long, shitty day and both men were tired and neither sure of what they'd accomplished.

Chris gave Mel a look, carried it on toward the coffeepot, so that she knew to start setting up Harp with mugs rather than beer bottles.

Harp had wanted to meet here tonight rather than in the morning at the office, which meant something was on his mind. When he'd showed up he still had Terlingua's and Killing's dust on him and needed a shower, bad, and Chris had noted as much when he sat down, but Harp had waved it off.

"They had the prelim for Avalos. Quarter of a million, just like Moody said. He's not going anywhere for a while," Chris said.

"No one showed up for him? Nothing?" Harp asked through a last mouthful of beer.

"No. You still going to call BP to get a canine for the car?"

Harp half nodded, turned his empty bottle in his hands. "I'll call the Presidio POE instead, have Bartlett and his dog, Big Max, work on it. I know Elgin Bartlett better."

"Doesn't matter, please just do it. Royal wants to take the Avalos hit and run away from us, and he wants to take Bravo's murder, too. He's watching us. He wants to bring in the Rangers, Bethel Turner."

"Fuck Bethel Turner . . . he can't find his own ass with a flashlight."

Chris chuckled. "Maybe, but Royal's going to give him one, if that's what it takes. A goddamn spotlight."

Harp looked into the mirror that ran behind the bar, staring down his own face there. "I said I'd do it and I will. I'll have Buck follow up. Fuck, though, the Avalos kid isn't going anywhere, you said it yourself. And Bravo's getting colder by the minute."

Chris raised his hands in surrender. "I can do it if you want."

"Goddammit, Chris, you're the sheriff, I'm the deputy. I'll take care of it." In the office, out on the street, he was *Sheriff Cherry*, but between the two of them, when they were like this, he was just plain Chris. Harp raised his bottle to Mel. "Darlin', you want to bring another for me and this lousy lay you married?"

Mel stepped over, sliding a coffee mug into his hand. She'd already worked eight hours; her hair was pulled out of the way and she was wearing very little makeup, and to Chris she still looked pretty damn good, beautiful. Mel pointed at him. "We're not married, remember? And how do you know what he's like in bed? I think you're spending too much time together." She patted Harp on the hand, sniffed. "You need a shower, Ben Harper."

"That's from hard work. Jackie liked my manly scent," he grumbled into the coffee, which he'd set aside without tasting. "It was a turn-on."

"And *that's* more than I needed to know. It's a good thing you were married to her for so long, because she must have been the only one—" Mel stopped, realizing what she was saying, and looked to Chris, desperate for help. Talking to Harp could be a minefield, always having to step lightly over the memories of his dead wife. Chris had also stumbled before and would do it again.

"Hey, babe, give him one more Rahr for the road. I'll make sure he gets back to his place. I'll take that coffee, instead." Chris slid over the mug Mel had given Harp, winking at her to let her know it was okay. He'd get Harp home and then swing back by and follow her on the long drive to the Far Six. She brought a new bottle for Harp, but before moving away to the far end of the bar to let the two men keep talking, she grabbed Chris's hand and squeezed hard.

He knew what it meant, full of all the things she couldn't say . . . *Take care of him . . . Don't let him get worse tonight . . . Don't leave him alone if you think it's bad.*

She let go, and Chris drank the coffee that had been meant to sober Harp up—hot, black, no sugar—ready to get him talking again about something else.

"Okay, so what about Bravo?"

Harp shook his head, like he was shaking away the sight of something only he could see; something other than his own face in the mirror. "You mean William Haley, aka Billy Bravo, aka Bear? Rough man, hard life. I don't need the forensics to tell me how it ended." Harp took a long pull from his fresh bottle. "*Badly.* Beat to death . . . it'll probably be two or more days before I have something more definite."

"How about interviews? His girlfriend, all of that?"

"Cute little Mexican girl. Don't think it was her, but kind of wish it was. It'd make it a lot easier. Everyone else we talked to in Terlingua loved him. 'Course, that didn't stop someone from opening his skull anyway. Like I said . . . he was *rough*, and he had history. A history like that has a way of catching up with you, or *you* have a way of catching up to yourself. You can't outrun your shadows, those dark parts of what you are." Harp took another long drink, nearly finishing off the bottle, and Chris wondered if he was really only talking about Billy Bravo. "Anyway, there's more to do there in Terlingua, lots more."

"So people can't change? Someone can't turn their life around?" Chris asked, genuinely interested.

Harp made a face. "Not so much, no. Sure, you can hide for a bit, pretend maybe, but that's it. Fresh paint and wallpaper and fancy lights do not make a shitty foundation suddenly strong. Remember that, Sheriff, as you continue to build that money pit of yours out there at the Far Six." He pointed his beer bottle at Chris.

Chris laughed. "Advice noted. What else?"

"Best timeline we got is Bravo closed down the bar with a person or persons unknown. It wasn't unusual for whoever was tending the place to leave before the last customers, popping the top on the final round of beers and heading out. Hell, you could even grab one yourself and leave your cash on the bar. All you had to do was pull the door shut behind you. We know Billy Bravo was one of the last people at the bar last night, but after that, it gets all muddied. Those boys from Killing were probably still there with him, but no one knows exactly when they left. It doesn't help that I'm asking a bunch of full-time drunks, and nobody knows who was where or when. The Wikiup makes Earlys look like the goddamn Mirage in Vegas. You don't go there to be seen, you go there to be forgotten. To forget."

Chris took another slow sip of coffee. "Amé told me before she headed out tonight that you all stopped at Killing."

"Yeah, and that's what I wanted to talk to you about. Here, away from the department, away from . . ."

Chris finished it for him so Harp wouldn't have to. "Away from Amé . . ."

Harp nodded, slow, uncomfortable. "It's no place for her down there, Chris, no goddamn place at all. I want you to pull her off this thing and give her something else to do."

"C'mon, I'll be fighting Royal every day as it is just to hold on to the damn case, and now you want me to tell Amé to let it go? I need more than that. She deserves better than that. You know I can't let her mess with the Avalos thing anymore after she lit him up. You should see his eye." Chris was ready to take another sip of coffee but then put the mug down. "You don't think she can help you?"

"It's not that, and you know it's not. She's smarter than Till and Buck and Dale put together, maybe the both of us." He looked at Chris over the lip of his bottle. "Someday she might have *your* job . . ."

Chris laughed. "That's the second time today someone's talked about wanting my job . . ."

"It's not about her anyway. It's about those men at Killing. I thought Terlingua was something else, until I saw that place. Killing's a snake pit."

"Just a bunch of bikers, right?"

"More than that." Harp pushed his beer away for the first time that night and pulled a couple of folded sheets from his jeans, spreading them out flat on the bar. It was an NCIC printout stapled with some other papers. "They're ABT, Aryan Brotherhood of Texas, or at least they used to be, and that's not the sort of club you just up and quit. The Brotherhood's a prison gang all tied up in drugs and extortion and murder. From his tats alone I think the big mute one, the one they call Joker, is a Nazi Low Rider. Now, the Low Riders *are* hard-core bikers, but they're also errand boys for the ABT. They're the muscle out on the street and outside the prison walls. All the bikes parked out in Killing come back to nobodies, clean criminal records, which is bullshit, and which also means they're smart. *Too smart*, like our Amé. The only full name I had to start with is the one I talked to face-to-face, this SOB . . ." Harp tapped at the papers in front him, stained now with spilled beer. "John Wesley Earl. This is just the first couple of pages, 'cause the rest of it was too big to haul around."

Chris pulled the pages forward and tried to read them in Earlys' dim light. John Wesley Earl was in his mid-fifties and had gone to prison the first time in 1980, when he was twenty-one years old, for burglary and assault. Additional assaults and drug possession crimes in prison added time and kept him there until he was finally released in 1993, thirteen years later. After that he was tagged for a handful of misdemeanor offenses that dotted his record through the years—domestic violence, bad checks, drug possession. He went in again in 2000 for attempted murder of a biker outside of Abilene, and stayed there until May 2015, when he was paroled. That was just a couple of months ago.

Chris did the math. Earl had spent almost half his life behind bars.

Harp tapped at the pages. "I imagine what's there is only part of the story. I put a call in to Walls, where he did his most recent time, so hopefully someone there will get back to me tomorrow, day after at the latest. There should be a prison intelligence unit that tracks gang activity. I have a hunch that Earl was not just an ABT spear carrier. I think he was someone important, very important." Harp shuffled the papers around, held up one sheet where he'd written some notes. "He talked about a brother, T-Bob, who I figure is this character, Thomas Robert Earl, who's the registered owner of their RV. And JW apparently has two sons, Jesse and Bass. There's nothing much on the uncle, just misdemeanor stuff, and the younger kid, Bass, is completely clean. But the older one has some terroristic threats, a couple of possessions with intent to distribute, and other petty stuff. I'd also put my money that he's neck deep in gang and white supremacist shit, too, just like his daddy, but I'll know more in a few days. I made some other calls, and Texas DPS has their own gang intelligence index. Maybe there's something there, maybe not. Billy Bravo's girlfriend puts the uncle and Jesse in the Wikiup with Bill Bravo last night."

"And this John Wesley just got out on parole? For murder?" Chris shook his head. "Did he get time off for good behavior? And what the hell is he doing in Killing? There's nothing out there."

"*Attempted murder.* But . . ." Harp pulled the papers off the bar, refolding them and putting them back in his jeans. "Maybe there's *going to be* something out there soon, like a biker clubhouse or a goddamn vacation time-share for racists. Hell, I don't know. They're supposedly renting that property from Ray Joyce, and when I spoke to him about it, he wasn't all that friendly or talkative. He's a piece of work, that one.

Anyway, maybe he's scared of them or wired into whatever they're doing, but my gut tells me they're going to be there awhile. So now we have this JW Earl and his clan and a whole bunch of other fucking racist skinhead pricks . . . moving in right next door."

Chris thought about that, turned it over. "Maybe."

Harp shrugged. "Ever the cautious one. Look, even if they had nothing to do with Bravo's murder, which I seriously fuckin' doubt, they are going to be a problem, an ongoing problem. Men like this always are. We can't wait around to see what they're going to do, Chris—"

Chris interrupted him. "Yeah, I got it. Action versus reaction, we can't finish what we don't start . . . he who hesitates . . . et cetera, et cetera. I've heard this all before, in all its variations. You should write a book. And you know what? I've been looking into this since you talk about it all the time, and some studies have actually shown—" Chris stopped, reading the hard expression on Harp's face; he wasn't smiling or laughing along with him. "Okay, okay, never mind. But what do you want me to do, evict them? Smoke 'em out?"

"Look, Chris, I know what you read in all those books of yours, all that kinder, gentler policing stuff. But *that* world exists only in those pages. That's the only place it can exist, because in *this* world, where a man like John Wesley Earl gets to walk free, it falls to poor bastards like us to deal with him and put back together everything and everyone he breaks. And he will, because that's all he knows how to do. He was born that way and no one like him changes that much."

"No better than new paint on a shitty house, huh?"

"Exactly. I'm not going to be around forever and you don't have forever to figure this out. I'm doing my best to open your damn eyes."

Chris nodded, feeling the heat of Harp's words. It was more than just too many beers and too little sleep. "I know, I really do, and I'm not trying to be a smart-ass. I hear everything you say and I'm not blind, either, to the way the world really works. I haven't been for a while." He didn't have to say Sheriff Ross's name for Harp to understand. "But you're going to outlive all of us, anyway. *That* I'm not worried about."

"Okay, well, hear me out now, 'cause we're right back where I started with all this . . . these are *not* the sort of men Amé is prepared to handle. She'll only be fanning the flames. Let me deal with them and Bravo. Let me figure out why they're here."

"You don't think she already gets her fair share of racist bullshit here?"

"No, I don't. It's not the same at all. Not even close. A couple of ranchers mouthing something stupid underneath their breath when she pulls them over is abso-fucking-lutely *not* what I'm talking about. Look, you're going to catch hell from Amé, I get it. I'm going to as well, 'cause she'll figure out I put you up to it. If I didn't think I was right on this, I'd save us both the misery. But you brought me here to help you, advise you, and that's what I'm doing right now."

"Goddammit, Harp . . ."

Harp rubbed his eyes, and even the bar's weak light was enough to reveal every one of his fifty-seven years. They circled his eyes, lined his face. All those years were in the spider's web of veins on his rough hands. Chris had thought of John Wesley Earl as an old man, but realized Harp and Earl were almost the same age.

Harp sat back on his stool, resigned. Then he sat up straight again, as if he'd decided on something. "All right, I'm going to tell you a story, and then you think about it. But don't take too goddamn long." When Chris nodded, Harp continued. "In 2010, a young black kid joined the department by the name of Andre Lawson. Former Navy, he got through college on the GI Bill and decided he wanted to be a cop. We used to joke with him that Midland was a helluva long way from the ocean. He laughed and took it all in stride, but he was smart . . . probably should have been a lawyer."

Harp looked over Chris's shoulder to where Mel was pouring a beer, and pushed ahead. "So, he'd been on maybe eight months when he and his partner get caught in the middle of a robbery in progress at a place called Dooley's, Midland-Odessa's version of a 7-Eleven. Right off, his partner, Brian Cox, takes one here"—Harp pointed at a spot on his chest, near his heart—"the slug working its way beneath his vest. One-in-a-million shot. Goddamn outlaw luck, right? Sort of shot only bad guys ever make. Anyway, Andre is trying to pull him away when the perps grab them and drag them both back inside. Now they think they have a couple of hostages, although Brian soon bleeds out all over the aisle where they keep the chips and soda. He had a daughter. She graduated from the University of North Texas maybe a year ago, and I sent her a card."

Harp started peeling the label off his empty beer, letting the thin strips pile up on the bar wood.

"Chester Peltz and Charles Elley were the guys who took Andre Lawson hostage. Pieces of shit, both of them. Peltz had done some time at Dalhart and Mineral Wells, and he was the smarter of the two, which wasn't saying much. They stayed in there for about three hours, making all sorts of crazy-shit demands. They wanted two large pizzas from Nino's, and helicopters. They wanted to read some sort of manifesto to the news. They were meth heads with almost no options, making shit up as they went along, but every now and then they put Andre on the phone so we'd know he was okay. But he wasn't. Not really at all."

Most of the bottle was naked now, peeled down to the glass. "I was on the SWAT entry team, number three on the stack, when we finally got the green light to go in. If it had just been those two in there we might have tried to keep talking them out. Goddammit, we *still* might be trying to talk them out, but with one dead and Andre trapped, we weren't going to wait forever. Plus, the negotiators who'd heard Andre on the phone, who'd tried to talk to him . . . well . . . trust me, those two fuckers had more than enough time to hurt him, *torture him*, and they did. You'd be surprised at all the ways you can break a man, Chris, if you really put your mind to it, or if you're already out of your fucking mind. And we allowed it to happen. We never should have waited even half as long as *we* did, but it wasn't my call."

Harp set aside the bottle, swept up the torn label into his hand and dumped it into the ashtray. "Anyway, we flash-banged it going in, and when I saw Chester Peltz through the smoke, eyes shining like stars and mouth open and his hands almost raised but *not quite*, I shot him in the chest, double-tap, and then one more in the head as he went down. Elley, however, tried to make a run for the back but slipped over the spilled beers he'd been drinking, and that's where the rear entry team found him . . . flat on his face, soaked in shitty beer, with Andre Lawson's blood still wet on his fucking hands." Harp stopped, caught his breath, like he was seeing that day, that moment, all over again, but after all the years still couldn't find the words for it, and Chris didn't want him to. "Right after I shot Peltz I found Andre, and he fell into my arms, and the weird thing was, the flash bang should have knocked him silly, too, but he was already gone, Chris, like nobody was at home. I'd never seen a person's eyes like that, and never have since. They were glass, mirrors, and I was reflected in them a thousand times over. I could have rolled sand off them and he wouldn't have blinked."

Chris was unsure what to say, if there was anything to say at all.

Harp looked straight at him. "I put Andre in Ricky Mumford's arms, gentle, to keep him standing because I wanted to make damn sure he was going to walk out of that place, and then I went over and leaned in close to Charles Elley so he'd get a good look at my face, and I shot him where he lay sprawled on the floor, crying and trying to wipe Andre's blood off on his goddamn shirt. It had some sort of smiling cartoon character on it, like a little kid would wear, and I'll never forget that . . . that bright yellow shirt, stained all red. The official report read that he died during the entry, resisting arrest, and every single man stood by it. We never talked about it, never planned it. But I lied, *we all lied*, and I've never said a word about it again until tonight. And Andre Lawson never wore a badge and gun again."

"Ben . . . Jesus . . ." Chris started, but Harp stopped him, leaning in close.

"Look, I know what you're thinking . . . check that, I know what *you think you should* be thinking, and what *I'd* be thinking right now if I was you, but we aren't exactly the same, and maybe that's not even a bad thing." Harp smiled. "Brian had it easy in some ways, they just shot him dead. Quick." Harp snapped his fingers. "But while we waited around too goddamn long to do anything about it, we left that other poor kid in there with those two fucking animals. They did those things to him and when it was over I held him in my arms. He *let* me hold him, like he never wanted me to let him go.

"So I guess they killed him, too, in their way. A part of him anyway. Andre Lawson died inside that store. I don't know who it was who walked out."

Chris looked away, uncomfortable, not wanting to catch his own face in the bar's mirror. A man he liked, that he'd come to trust more than anyone else, had more or less just admitted to murder, to killing a helpless defendant . . . a prisoner. And only hours earlier Chris had read Amé the riot act over striking a handcuffed Azahel Avalos. He wanted to hate what Harp had done, it went against everything he was trying to do in the department and all those shadows of Sheriff Ross he was trying to banish, but if he imagined something like that happening to Amé, or to Mel, he couldn't quite hate it enough.

I know what you think you should be thinking.

It scared him, and his thoughts must have been easy to read.

"I get it," Harp continued. "That struggle. But they were fucking animals. There *are* wolves in the world, Chris. These criminals . . . outlaws . . . bad men, whatever you want to call them, they're pure predators and everyone to them is prey, and that's how we have to think of them. That's how we have to treat them. Don't forget that. Don't *ever* forget that."

Harp straightened up, looked back toward Mel and gave her a brief wave, a thin smile—his way of saying good night.

"And sometimes *we* gotta be the wolves, Chris. Sometimes we just do."

He stood and stretched. "Okay, how about you give me that lift home you promised?"

10

For the second night in a row, America watched the darkness, eyes wide open, counting her own breaths.

If you stared into the dark long enough, you could pick out colors, even there. Different shades of black and blue, rolling like ocean waves. She'd left Murfee to see the ocean, had traveled to Miami and stayed for months in an expensive hotel on the beach—all bright glass and chrome—just like she'd always imagined. She had spent her days on the sand, beneath a sun not quite as hot as the one hanging over her Chihuahuan desert, but hot enough, and at night she'd sat on her balcony with the salt wind in her hair, her sliding door open, watching the night touch the open water, trying to pick out where one began and the other ended.

She'd paid for that hotel, all those nights, with the money Caleb Ross had taken from his father. Money that had been stolen by Sheriff Ross from the cartel called Nemesio—which her brother, Rodolfo, had worked for, and which some people in town wanted to believe she worked for now as well. It was the same money that had brought the boy Máximo over the river from Ojinaga and that had left Sheriff Ross and his chief deputy, Duane Dupree, dead.

It was the same money that she still kept locked in a suitcase under her bed.

She wondered if all that money was cursed and destined to only bring bad luck.

Sheriff Cherry knew *something* about the money, probably guessing it had gone east with Caleb to disappear forever, but he knew nothing about Máximo or the part America herself had played in Dupree's death—how Máximo had gone to the chief deputy's little house out beyond the pecan grove and killed him for her, setting him and the house on fire.

How Máximo had come back later to her with all those ashes in his hair, smelling of smoke.

Smiling.

How she had almost shot Dupree herself with her brother's silver gun.

Avalos had called her *la chica con la pistola.*

And he knew her name.

Azahel Avalos had known exactly who she was the minute he'd put eyes on her, and if he did, that meant others did, too; others, maybe, from across the river.

Others like Máximo . . . like Nemesio.

So they might also know the truth about the money, the whole truth. And they might be ready to come and get it back.

She'd been quiet and careful with how'd she spent what had remained, moving into a tiny house in the same neighborhood where she grew up; not flashing a lot of it at any one time, and definitely not since returning home. She wasn't necessarily afraid, refused to be, because she'd lived like that once before and had made a hundred promises to herself she never would again, but she was cautious. Her parents had returned to Ojinaga after she'd left Murfee, and she'd spoken to them a handful of times when they'd begged her to come visit them, to stay with them, but she wouldn't. That was the one promise she'd made to her brother that she had kept and always would keep—she would never cross the river. There were still men there that Rodolfo had been afraid of, and that she knew she *should* be afraid of. She remembered the things her mama had said about her own brother, Amé's uncle—a man mysteriously called Fox Uno—and her other *familia* scattered throughout Camargo and La Esmeralda and Maijoma. She'd once wanted to believe Rodolfo had been recruited into Nemesio by a pretty woman he'd met at a bar, but knew in her heart it wasn't a stranger who'd approached him. It had been someone he'd trusted from the start . . . *la familia.* Although she was sure there was nothing for her over the river, that didn't mean something, or someone, couldn't come looking for her over *here,* and that brought her back to Avalos. She needed to say something about it sooner or later to Sheriff Cherry and to Ben; it wasn't right, or safe, to keep them in the dark about her. She just wanted a better idea of exactly *what* all those shadows were, and who hid within them.

All those different shades of black.

AMERICA GOT UP AND CHECKED the duty-issued Colt she kept on her nightstand. She padded through the house in just her T-shirt, looking through the blinds covering each window.

Looking for a car in the street or someone standing outside smoking a cigarette, pretending not to watch her house.

Esperando.

But tonight there was nothing, just a high moon lost in clouds. A faint silver circle, like a ring you might wear on your finger.

With Avalos still sitting in jail, she guessed she had a little time, just not how much. He'd made at least one phone call, so when she came home earlier tonight, after her long day with Harp at Terlingua and Killing, she'd had a cold dinner of leftovers, and then she got ready.

In the kitchen, she'd dumped out a drawer holding some of her mama's old forks and replaced them with a Beretta Storm she'd bought out of a pawnshop in Galveston.

In her hall bathroom, she'd duct-taped a S&W Governor revolver to the inside door of the medicine cabinet, along with three stacked moon clips where her NyQuil bottle once sat. She'd taken that gun from a man in Savannah who'd tried to rob and probably rape her. She was pretty sure both the Beretta and the Governor were untraceable.

She'd stabbed a matching set of Spyderco Ronin 2 knives blade-down into the thick soil of her potted orchid cactus, hidden by the leaves.

And last, she'd put the Winchester Model 12 shotgun she'd bought from the Walmart in Odessa underneath the coffee table in the living room, facing the door. She'd had a friend of Victor's cut it down for her to make it a little more manageable.

Now, she took out the shotgun, cradling it in her arms, and sat cross-legged on her couch, knowing that just like last night, she wasn't going to sleep for a while. She cut her blinds open a bit to let in that watery moonlight, letting her count all the shadows up and down the street. A car passed, slow, but it didn't hit its brakes, and then it was gone.

For the first time in a while, she wanted a cigarette—a way to pass the time, to watch and wait. A lifetime ago she and Caleb Ross had shared endless cigarettes, waiting.

She thought about Killing and the men there. *Los hombres malos.* But one of them, the one they'd called Hero, had smiled at her after she tossed her card at JW Earl's son. And it hadn't been a smile like Azahel Avalos's, half menace and half fear. It had been something else altogether.

Respect.

Ben had probably seen it, too, as they had driven on to Terlingua in silence, but she knew what he'd been thinking anyway. He didn't want her around those men. He was worried what they might say to her, what they might try to do. But she'd been dealing with men like that her whole life and there was nothing they could say or do to bother her.

Such men meant nothing to her anymore.

She aimed the Winchester at the place where the car had gone by, scanned once, and put it back in her lap.

She'd made a hundred, a thousand promises to herself.

No, she wasn't afraid. Not anymore. *Nunca más.*

But she was ready.

La chica con la pistola.

11

Harp was as surprised as anybody when they showed up un-announced at the department before noon, both dressed in jeans and identical black long-sleeve Sturgis T-shirts despite the unholy heat. Trying, he guessed, to hide as many of their tattoos as they could. They stood together outside and shared a cigarette, laughing, watching the thin traffic slow down and drivers stare before passing them by on Main.

The car that dropped them off—the Grand Marquis with the bullet holes—went by twice before sliding into a spot of its own farther down across the street, windows down. Harp thought the driver was that kid Hero, sitting way back in the car's shadows, watching the department with his face hidden behind sunglasses, but there was no way to be sure.

As Harp watched and waited, the two men, John Wesley Earl's brother, T-Bob, and his older son, Jesse—two of the last people to ever see Billy Bravo alive—finished their cigarette and got ready to walk in. While T-Bob ground out the butt on the cement with his silver-tipped boots, Jesse Earl glanced back once at the Grand Marquis, like he was studying the car, or its driver, but whatever he was thinking was impossible to tell from the expression on his face.

. . .

HARP WANTED TO START WITH T-BOB, and didn't want to wait.

Chris was at Hancock Hill visiting Tommy, and Buck and Till and the others were scattered to the wind, so without wasting a shitload of time getting one of them back to the department, there was no way for Harp to keep Amé from helping him with the interviews. And he *really* didn't want to waste any time with these two, or give them time enough to have second thoughts. He'd handle the questioning and she could take notes, which wasn't strictly necessary, since Chris had updated the department's lone interview room with recording equipment, but if he told her to hang back and watch through the remote, she might punch him the same way she'd hit Avalos. And she'd already seen T-Bob and Jesse walk in, so she was circling Harp like a hawk, working tighter and tighter spirals, getting closer to the ground and making ready to land on him. She knew as well as he did that Chris had mandated that even with the video system, there always had to be two deputies present in any interview, for safety as much as anything else, so if Harp tried to do it alone, Amé would probably 911 the sheriff and raise holy hell.

Claws out, hiding a thin victory smile, she had him, and they both knew it, so he gave up without a fight but with a whole lot of cussing under his breath, and told her to get the goddamn interview room ready.

The room itself was a sterile affair, all military gray, with a small table and uncomfortable chairs and the video camera tucked up high in the corner; just another kind of hawk sitting on a pole surveying everything beneath it. There was also a No Smoking placard in both Spanish and English on the far wall, right in the sight line of the person being questioned, and at odds with the small black ashtray from Earlys on the table. If a man got suddenly nervous, like he had something worthwhile to say and was just searching for a way to do it, Harp would let him smoke to his heart's content if he asked; he long ago had learned that a confessing man, like a movie actor, needed something to do with his hands while he spun his story. But if people were difficult or stone-walled, Harp would just lean back and point to the placard, with that empty ashtray still there to taunt them, no matter how many times they asked for a smoke.

He left Jesse Earl out in the waiting area, flipping through a *True West* magazine, and got T-Bob a small coffee, noticing the man's hands tremble as he handed it to him. Not nerves, but the shakes of a chronic drinker. T-Bob probably hadn't had a sip since leaving Killing, and his body was already yelling at him about it. For a moment, Harp almost changed his mind—starting with Jesse instead, so he could lock the pair into what should be a more solid, coherent story, or at least a damn good lie, before picking it apart with T-Bob. But he was already steering T-Bob, who was badly listing to port, toward the interview room, and he didn't want to waste any more time. *You can't finish what you don't start.*

Harp had also grabbed his own spiral notebook and pen, even though he wasn't going to take notes or write down anything at all.

He just needed something to do with his hands, too.

ALTHOUGH HE DIDN'T STRICTLY NEED to do it, not yet anyway, Harp Mirandized T-Bob, slipping it in casually and trying not to make a big deal about it. If the man started to bury himself and was willing to write out a statement, Harp might do it again, but he hoped the first warning, captured on camera and witnessed by Amé, would be enough.

But talking to T-Bob proved as hard as catching bait minnows in your bare hands—the words were all slippery, kept jumping around and never staying still. Yes, T-Bob had been to the Wikiup to drink; in fact, he'd been there several times. No, he'd never had any trouble there. Yes, he'd met Billy Bravo, but no, he didn't know anything about Billy and Jesse having words with each other. And yes, they were there that last night with Billy, but no, he couldn't remember exactly when they'd left. Only that when they had walked out, *both of them*, Billy had still been there at the bar, healthy and happy, throwing 'em back.

That he was very clear about. It was the only thing he remembered good and sharp.

Burned out . . . that was the phrase that came to Harp's mind. The thin old man, with his grizzled hair and the flames tattooed on his torched, sunburned skin, was like a used matchstick. He hadn't done any real time, and claimed he didn't know much about the Aryan Brotherhood or any prison gangs like that, even though the ink peeking out at the wrists and neck of his T-shirt told a slightly different story. He said that was all of his brother's doings, John Wesley, so they'd have to ask him about it. But even as he said it, he stole a glance in Amé's direction, and seemed uncomfortable with her there. And when Harp asked why he and his brother and all the others were in Killing to begin with, it was the first time T-Bob seemed purposefully evasive. More than just the drunk shakes, he talked faster, those fish really jumping, without saying much of anything at all. Listening to him made Harp's head hurt.

There was one last thing, and that was the bruises Harp noticed on T-Bob's forehead, spreading around his right eye. When asked about it, T-Bob admitted his brother had done it to him. They'd gotten into a fight about a whole lot of nothing, and it wasn't unusual for him and his brother to settle up arguments like that with their fists. *You know how it is, family and all,* is how T-Bob left it, with a shrug of his shoulders. And as much as Harp wanted those marks to have been made by Billy Bravo's hands, it was the one thing T-Bob said he actually believed. Being family with a man like John Wesley Earl probably brought with it a whole host of burdens and bruises.

He had Amé take a close-up picture of them with her cell phone camera all the same.

And just before they wrapped up, when T-Bob asked about a

cigarette, wondering if it'd be okay if he slipped a quick one, Harp pointed at that sign and closed his blank notebook.

JESSE EARL MIGHT HAVE BEEN GOOD-LOOKING, if not for the Texas stars inked all around his neck, circling the words LIE OR DIE and GOD FORGIVES BROTHERS DON'T; or the small dark tombstone cross underneath his left eye. An eye that was a startling, serious blue. Jackie might have called it *movie-star blue*, and she had loved her movies, as well as the magazines about them, filled with stories about her favorite Hollywood stars. She'd flip through them, maybe breaking down to buy *just one*, while checking out with their groceries and humming whatever last Eagles song she'd heard on the radio. Harp didn't like much in the way of modern movies or music, but he'd never minded the Eagles. He still had Jackie's iPod in his apartment, along with a stack of magazines he'd picked up for her when she last went into the hospital. He'd bought every one he could get his hands on for a week straight—*National Enquirer, OK!, Us Weekly, People*—driving in the middle of the night as far as Big Spring and Lamesa and Pecos and even Hobbs, New Mexico, just to see if the stores there had new or different ones. Knowing it was foolish, just to give his hands and his mind something to do. Now they were all in a taped-up box by his bed he couldn't throw out but could never bring himself to open again. He'd read them a hundred times right after she was gone, holding the pages the same way she once had, also listening to all of her songs over and over again, but it was those damn magazines that were always going to haunt him—the dates on their fading covers forever fixing the time of her passing.

Jesse slid back in the chair his uncle had been perched in only moments before, taking it over, with his hands spread out in front of him. Not afraid to show off the other tattoos that Bravo's girlfriend had remembered: the word HATE on the knuckles of his right hand, the

numbers 1488 on his left. Harp had looked up the numbers and knew
the fourteen stood for the "Fourteen Words" that made up the Neo-
Nazi belief: *We must secure the existence of our people and a future for white
children.* The eight was the eighth letter of the alphabet—H. Stamped
twice, it meant *Heil Hitler.* Harp wasn't sure about T-Bob, but pegged
Jesse as a true believer. Not just because of the Nazi crosses and lightning bolts all over his skin, but because of those damn blue eyes. They
were a different color from his daddy's, brighter by a few degrees, but
they held the same, indifferent, killing stare. Like the way he kept looking *right through* Amé, who watched him right back, unblinking. He
regarded her the way you might a dog you were going to put down.

Harp knew his first instinct had been right all along, and after today
he needed to keep her away from these men—all of them, but this one
most of all.

Harp tried the same Miranda game, but Jesse and his hardened eyes
knew better, so he let it go.

Instead Harp backed up, starting again from a different angle, pointing to the edges of large, identical tattoos just visible on both wrists.
"What's that on your arms?"

Jesse smiled wide; slowly, proudly, pulling up both sleeves on his
T-shirt to reveal the huge tattoos of six-shooters on the inside of each
forearm, the twin muzzles pointed across the table at Harp and Amé.
They were just as Billy Bravo's girlfriend had described them, right
down to the skull in one palm and the bullets in the other. "I got these
when I was sixteen. They're Colt .45 Peacemakers, just like Jesse James
used to carry."

"Your daddy name you that? Name you after him?"

Jesse nodded, slow. "He was around long enough for that, before he
went up for a piece."

Even in that small exchange, Harp caught something buried deep,
anger masked as indifference, when Jesse mentioned Earl. "What about
your brother?"

"Little B? His Christian name is Bass."

"Like Sam Bass?" Harp laughed. "So you're Jesse, and your daddy is John Wesley? I guess right there we've got ourselves a family of outlaws."

Jesse smiled again. "You could say that, yep."

Harp tapped his pen, as if a thought had just come to him. "You hate niggers, Jesse?"

The smile flickered. "Come again?"

Harp leaned back, relaxed. "It's okay, son, we're just talking, shooting the shit. No offense meant. But I'm just wondering if you hate niggers . . . kikes, Chinks. Beaners, wetbacks . . . you know, whatever?" Harp pretended to consult his spiral notebook, empty, without notes. "That's what all that white power shit all over your skin means, right? It means you hate people that aren't white, that aren't like you." Harp leaned forward again. "Like Billy Bravo's girlfriend, maybe."

Jesse glanced toward Amé and back again. "Shit, I don't know nothin' about that."

Harp looked again at his notebook. "I got people who say you do, Jesse, a whole bunch of folks. They all saw you at the Wikiup, you and your uncle and that other fucking retard, what's his name, Joker? They say *you* had some words with Billy about his girl. That you were going on and on about her being a wetback. That would seem to fit, right? *Heil Hitler* and all that shit."

"I can't remember what that was all about. It was whiskey talk. Barroom bullshit. It was nothin'. Shootin' the shit, as you say."

"Okay, so why don't you tell us what all that *shit* was about? Why don't you tell me and Deputy Reynosa here exactly what you said to Billy Bravo about his Hispanic girlfriend?"

Jesse spun the ashtray in front of him in circles. Those blue eyes danced. "Well, *sir*, I *might* have said something about her having an awful nice pair of tits. Just like this here Deputy Reynosa," Jesse continued, looking Amé up and down and giving her a wink. "You can still be a wetback and have nice tits."

Harp looked to Amé for a reaction, but she was as still as stone, as if she'd never heard the words. He hadn't meant to draw Jesse's attention to her, but he was down that rabbit hole now. He *had* been purposefully prodding the son of a bitch, trying to get him angry, trying to get him to slip up, because anything he revealed now might prove important later. And he was mad at himself for giving Jesse even this small opening at Amé. However, just like he'd argued with Chris, she was smart enough for the both of them. Her face said it all: she wasn't going to compound his mistake by pulling another Avalos.

Interrogation was an art, not a science. He'd always been good at it, having a natural knack or a feel for slipping into whatever role was needed to get someone to bury themselves, to admit to whatever horrible shit they'd done. *Father, friend, priest.* But that was before he found himself constantly distracted by stray thoughts of Jackie, before he started finding himself tired and slow, like he had at Killing.

Maybe I am getting too old for this.

Jesse was still talking. "You say you been hearing from folks about me? Well, I been hearing some stuff, too. Like how half this damn town is *wet*. What's that they call it around here, Beantown? Right over the tracks, back there." Jesse thumbed in the air behind him. "We passed it coming here, *smelled it*, in fact." He focused on Harp, but was really talking to Amé. "Is that what you're into? Little spic girls, like Billy?"

Harp clenched his notebook and held his breath for a ten count, wondering if he was going to be the one this time around to punch someone's ticket. Once, another, younger Ben Harper might have thrown this boy's ass out of the chair and across the room, just to get his point across and get his attention, but he wouldn't do that now, not in front of Amé. Instead he said, "You and T-Bob were at the Wikiup the night Billy Bravo died."

Jesse shrugged. "If you say so, if all these mysterious folks you keep talking about say so."

"Yeah, well, they do. I do. And so does your uncle, as a matter of fact. See, he's already admitted you were both drinking that night at the bar, and then later that same evening, someone goes and busts Billy's head in. Leaves him to bleed out and die in the desert . . ."

"That's a damn way to die, to be sure."

Harp agreed. "But you don't know anything about that, do you?"

Jesse stared at him. "I already said I know nothing about that. *Nothin' at all.* Less than I know about this here beaner's tits. But ask me that again, and you might be askin' it to my lawyer. The one I'm due, like you was goin' on about at the beginning."

"Do I need to do that, Jesse? Get you a lawyer? You want one? Need one?"

Jesse shrugged. "Just sayin', I watch some TV."

"Watch closer. You walked in here to see me, son, all on your own. All I did was ask."

Jesse stood, slow, and stretched, aiming his tattooed guns at the ceiling. "Well then, I guess I can walk right the fuck out again."

Harp hesitated. *Art not science* . . . They were at a line in the sand . . . cross it or not? If he told Jesse to sit the fuck back down—that he wasn't quite free to leave yet—then they were dealing with a full-blown *custodial* interrogation, and Harp probably would be getting the mouthy SOB a lawyer before his ass hit the seat. Without a doubt Jesse would shut the hell up then . . . he *had* seen enough TV to know that. Or his daddy had done enough time to teach him.

Harp could hear a clock in his head, ticking away—it seemed like he heard it all the time now—while Jesse waited for Harp or Amé to open the door.

But before Harp could say anything, it was Amé who spoke first. Soft, but steady and firm.

"Her name's Vianey . . . that *beaner* you keep talking about. I know she means nothing to you. But what if I said someone came back to the Wikiup later that night after Vianey first left the bar . . . a lot later? She was worried about Billy, so she called up one of his friends to go back and help him home. He was a big man, and there was no way she could do that herself." Amé kept her eyes on the paper in front of her, writing something while she spoke.

Jesse looked down at her, head cocked to one side, face unreadable.

"If she had done that, what do *you* think that person . . . Billy's friend . . . would have seen?" Amé asked.

Jesse hesitated. Opened his mouth, closed it again, like a fish. "A *friend*, huh? Another one of your mysterious folks, right? You know, I got no idea."

"*Yo creo que sí,*" she said, finally looking up at him.

"What did that bi—" Jesse started, but stopped himself. His eyes shot back and forth between Amé and Harp. He pointed at her, but addressed him. "What did she say?"

"Well, I'm not exactly sure, since I don't fucking speak Spanish, but I'm pretty sure she said you're a lying piece of shit. She also said we're probably going to get a warrant for your blood, Jesse. You see, Billy put up quite a fight before he died. Lots of blood under his fingernails, that sort of thing. Blood, DNA. *Just like you've seen on TV.* She said she thinks the two of you squared off that night and you killed him, and so do I." It was a pure bluff, doubling down on Amé's suggestion that someone in Terlingua might be able to place Jesse at Billy's body at the time he died. It was less than nothing, but for the moment, it was all they had.

Silence ticked on, and it was during *this* moment that guilty men most often got nervous, all edgy; this was when Harp could usually tell if they were going to start talking or not.

He looked into Jesse Earl's shining eyes, searching for something, anything, moving behind them.

Then Jesse laughed, that moment all gone, blown away like smoke, and he reached in his pocket for a lighter and a cigarette. But he didn't make any move to light it. "*Well*, okay then, *a fight*, huh? I think if this friend of that beaner girl was out there and had seen anything worth a damn, we might be having a different talk. So you go ahead and get your fuckin' warrant. You know where to find me. I ain't goin' anywhere for a while."

Harp stood, glancing at Amé's notes as he did so, at the handful of words written there. "Why are you and your family down in Killing? Why here, why now?"

Jesse put the unlit cigarette between his lips. "Just meetin' some friends, that's all, sort of a family reunion . . . call it family business."

"Who's outside waiting in the car?" Amé asked. "*¿Tu familia?* Maybe we should go talk to them about Billy Bravo?"

"Who? Oh, that's Hero." Jesse pulled out the unlit cigarette and spit on the floor. "He's got nothin' to do with nothin'. He's a damn chauffeur, nothin' more. Guess ole JW don't trust me out all on my own." Jesse laughed, but it was clear to Harp he didn't think it was funny at all. It was the second time he'd mentioned Earl, and both times it was like he was chewing on glass. "And you met him already, anyway. Last time you and the spic here was down our way." Then he walked straight between Amé and Harp.

"Don't get too comfortable, Jesse. We're going to see you again real soon," Harp tossed at his back.

Jesse raised a hand goodbye. "Not if I see you first, Deputy." Then he turned and aimed another long, last look at Amé. "But, come to think of it, since I ain't so welcome in that shithole bar in Terlingua no more, maybe I'll start comin' up around here." He winked right at her, pointed his cigarette at her chest. "And maybe I'll have another chance to catch up with *you*."

Harp gripped the handle, but finally opened the door and let Jesse go, as Amé stood and followed them.

On her way out, she crumpled her notes into a small ball that she tossed into the trash, but Harp had already seen the words she had written to herself.

Muy malos . . .

Jesse Earl *had* been in Killing when they were first there, either hiding out in the house or that old RV, just as Harp had suspected. *Those eyes on them the whole time.* Watching.

But there was another thing they'd learned, even more important . . . and that had been Jesse's relaxed reaction to Harp's alleged "fight." Jesse knew there hadn't been a real fight outside the Wikiup because *he'd been there.* Most likely, he'd jumped Billy from *behind*, and the man had never had a chance to defend himself.

Jesse had gotten the drop on all of them, and Harp was going to make sure that didn't happen again.

Not if I see you first.

12

Just before things got bad with Sheriff Ross and Chris's life changed forever, Chris took a phone call from a number he didn't recognize and a man he didn't know.

That man, who later visited him in the hospital after the ambush at the Far Six and showed him pictures of the three men Chris had killed there, was Joe Garrison, a DEA supervisor from El Paso. Two of his agents had been watching Murfee for weeks: watching the sheriff and Duane Dupree, even Chris. But by the time Garrison finally made that call to Chris, Dupree had hunted those agents down in the desert outside of town, killing one, Darin Braccio, and burning the other, Morgan Emerson, alive. Garrison had wanted . . . *demanded* . . . answers, and he came to Chris looking for them.

In the two years since, they'd stayed in touch, but it was a stretch to say they were friends. In some ways, both too much and too little had passed between them. Chris never fully explained that last night in Murfee that left both Ross and Dupree dead—could never quite find the words for it—and Garrison never fully got past the night Darin and Morgan were attacked. Like Harp's Andre Lawson, Morgan Emerson did survive, but she also never carried a badge or gun again, either.

In the end, the burns were too bad, the scars were too deep.

Maybe that was true for all of them.

It would be easy to point to the night at the Far Six as *the* moment that had changed Chris's life forever, or even the night he'd confronted Sheriff Ross in his own office—the big room upstairs where his deputies now all sat—and nearly bled to death all over the sheriff's massive mahogany desk. A desk that he'd since ordered Buck Emmett to chop down and use for firewood.

But the real moment was when he took that call from Garrison. When Garrison had angrily asked: *Who do you trust, Deputy Cherry?* And Chris had hung up, not knowing how to answer that at all, knowing even less about the voice on the phone that had asked the question.

Now, for the second time in his life, he found himself taking such a call; listening to a man he didn't know, telling him things that were tough to fit together and asking questions he couldn't really answer. So even after he hung up, he had to stand there for a long time, staring down at his phone, like he expected it to ring again, or because he'd left too many things unsaid.

Maybe he needed to stop answering the damn phone.

FINALLY, CHRIS PULLED AWAY from his silent phone and already summoned Harp and Amé into his office. Jesse and T-Bob Earl had been gone a couple of hours, and they'd been waiting to talk to him about their interviews. He'd been back from visiting Tommy for a while, but had been trapped on that strange call most of that time.

Harp started in right away, not giving Chris a chance to say anything, talking even as he came through the door.

"I actually didn't think they'd show up here, Sheriff. My guess is they don't want us poking around whatever they're doing in Killing. But it's going to be Jesse Earl or the uncle. It's got to be." Harp sat down, while Amé followed him but remained standing, leaning against the wall.

"Those racist pieces of shit got into it with Billy Bravo over his girlfriend and killed him."

"And they said all that, in there?" Chris pointed out his office door back toward the interview room.

Harp shook his head. "Hell no. They only confirmed they were there, but I didn't expect them to lie about that. They'll alibi each other, but we'll find someone who can definitely nail them down as the last people drinking with Billy. We'll talk to the barflies again, make sure we have them all. There's got to be someone." Harp sat back, talking as much to himself as to the others in the room. "I think Jesse followed Billy outside the bar and jumped him in the dark. Billy probably never had a chance." He looked over to Amé. "I was bullshitting when I threatened Jesse with a DNA warrant, but there still might be something to that . . . it might be worth a shot. If nothing else, it keeps the pressure on him." He focused a stare on Chris, thinking out loud. "I'm sorry, I thought about it too late. I should have let the fuckin' uncle smoke. If he'd tossed the cigarette, maybe I could have pulled it from the ashtray. The one they shared outside at the curb is too tainted now. And T-Bob never drank any of that coffee I gave him either, so that cup is also worthless. I don't blame him, though, since Miss Maisie made it . . . but damn, I had it right there in front of me, staring me in the face. Jesse and that cigarette in his mouth. He's a smart son of a bitch." Harp slumped. "I imagine Moody won't give me one, unless you push him into it."

Chris nodded. "A warrant? No, I imagine he won't. And I don't think any amount of pushing from me or anyone else is going to make a damn bit of difference." Chris paused, trying to work out how to say something he knew neither Harp nor Amé was going to want to hear. "Don't beat yourself up over it, it's over. Look, I know you two are working hard on this, and maybe you are right about those two. Hell, I'd bet money on it. But it doesn't matter, not now. I just got off the phone with the Rangers . . ."

Harp waved his hands, cutting Chris off. His face was dark,

thundering. "Goddammit, Chris . . . *Sheriff* . . . I thought you'd gotten Moody to give us more time. I just need a little more time. I told you Bethel Turner will fuck this up—"

Chris raised his own hand for Harp to stop. "It wasn't Bethel, Harp. It was Major Carl Dyer, from Region C. He wants to meet with us and have a sit-down about the Earls. About a lot of things."

Harp was searching for the name, coming up empty. "But that's not even this region. Why would this Dyer care about this? Hell, how does he even know about it?"

"I think your calls to the Department of Public Safety or back to the Midland PD rattled a few cages. And not just with the Rangers, but the FBI, too." Chris slowed down, trying to explain it the way Major Dyer had explained it all to him. "It seems that one of those bikers down there in Killing might actually be a cop . . . or at least *was* one, not all that long ago. And to make matters worse, another one of them is a federal witness, a very important one. Dyer didn't say a whole lot, but what he did say was, well, complicated, and that's a goddamn understatement."

Harp stood. "It's bullshit, that's what it is."

"Yeah, and it looks like we've stepped right in the middle of it." Chris rubbed his chin, feeling stubble. He couldn't remember when he'd last shaved. "Did either T-Bob or Jesse Earl mention someone named Flowers, a Thurman Flowers?"

Harp shook his head. "No, nothing." Chris looked over to Amé, who had remained silent with her arms folded the whole time. She shook her head as well. The name hadn't meant anything to Chris, either, when he'd heard it from Dyer, and he hadn't had the chance yet to run it down. But it was important.

"Okay, so you both know what I know, and that isn't much. Harp, you and I will drive up to Lubbock in a few days and meet with this Major Dyer, as well as someone from the FBI. Hopefully, we'll get some answers. But until then, Killing is off-limits. The Earls and anyone associated with them is off-limits." Chris looked straight at Amé again, pinning her down and making it clear. "Is that understood?" She nodded, a slight movement that was hardly a movement at all, and continued to say nothing.

Chris knew Harp wanted to argue, keep pressing the point, but instead, his chief deputy turned to Amé. "You need to call that girl, Vianey, right? Tell her to stay with family or someone in Presidio. She needs to keep the hell out of Terlingua, just in case."

Chris glanced back and forth between them. Although Harp had put the question to Amé, it had been squarely aimed at him. Like a gun. "Why, what for?"

Amé must have known it, too, because she stepped in before Harp could answer, trying to steer them all clear of a fight. "Her name came up in the interview, that's all. *No es un problema, voy a cuidar de ella.*"

Chris: "Is there an issue here?"

Harp shrugged, staring up at the ceiling. "Not unless one of the Earls wakes up one morning and decides that it is. She's a potential witness. She can put the Earls and Billy together. So far, she's the only person who can. She knows they were arguing in the Wikiup, about her. *Motive.* And to push on Jesse, we might have suggested she knows even more than that. But hey, Billy's murder doesn't mean shit anymore and the Earls are off-limits, so . . ."

"Goddammit, do not put words in my mouth, and do not make this harder than it has to be," Chris said, feeling his anger rise like the day's heat. "That's not fair, and I'm not the one who put a target on this girl. That's on you two. What the hell do you want me to do? We'll clear it up in Lubbock. We'll ask all the damn questions you want then."

Harp pulled his eyes down from the ceiling, fixing them on Chris. "You're *the goddamn sheriff*, you can goddamn do what you want, what needs to be done. You don't need anyone's permission. Don't worry, we'll look after this girl Vianey, but it is what it is. We both know nothing that happens in Lubbock is going to make it any *clearer.*" Harp started reaching for the door, even though Chris hadn't dismissed him. "Are we done here, Sheriff?"

Chris almost ordered him to sit his ass back down, but with Amé watching the both of them, thought better of it. This was the closest Harp had come to questioning him, arguing with him, in front of another deputy, and he didn't want to make it worse. Not now. Once Harp cooled down and could see it clearer, Chris would talk to him about it again. He dismissed him with a nod. "Yeah, we're done."

Harp turned his back on him and walked out without another word, leaving the door open for Amé, who wouldn't look at Chris when she fell in step behind the older man.

She shut the door quietly behind them both, leaving Chris standing alone, staring down again at that goddamn phone on his desk.

13

I'd been with Jesse for about three weeks when I nearly died, and finally met the man who killed my father.

We'd gone to a skinhead party in Terry County, just outside Lubbock. It was at an old Hammond single-wide trailer, where the blue siding had long ago faded to the color of asphalt, and it was spray-painted with rough approximations of what were supposed to be Confederate flags, with red wooden letters as wide as your outstretched arms—SWP, for *Supreme White Power*—nailed up by the front door. The trailer sat on a couple of acres bordering cotton fields, and I could see the orange tarpaulin tops of cotton modules marching into the distance; could hear the wind whipping off them and stray cotton turning end over end like snow, slow enough to catch in your hands. The property was surrounded by a chain-link fence hung with dead birds and cat carcasses and old trick-or-treat pumpkins filled with rainwater, those cheap orange plastic ones, along with a small fleet of rusted cars on rims. All of it was screened from the road by a row of battered wind-block trees that reminded me of Halloween skeletons and scarecrows, or maybe the big wind turbines back home in Sweetwater, and the wind through the branches made the same sort of sound. Like a heart beating, far away.

The place had been a skinhead crash pad for about a year, changing hands between a few different Aryan groups, but it was no different from the merry-go-round of shitty apartments and motels where I'd found myself in McKinney and Tyler and Ballinger. Skins use the crash pads until they are run off or evicted, leaving hollowed-out shells littered with pamphlets and graffiti and used condoms and broken beer bottles and windows. They're places for skins on the run to hole up for a few weeks, places to act out mock lynchings and beheadings and to kick off their "city walks" where they cruise looking for enemies, but mostly they're places to hold recruiting parties. Older skins are always on the hunt for *freshcuts*, like Little B's friend Kasper—any lonely and lost teenager they can draw in with free beer and music and a sense of community. That's the thing most people don't understand, the *real* reason these gangs continue to grow and spread like cancers—that at the beginning, it has very little to do with hate, and everything to do with love. In their own fractured way, the gangs provide a family, a home, *a place to be something or someone*, for kids who don't have anything or anyone else. It's like joining the military, but the war is every day and right here at home. That love, that acceptance, is a high as strong as any liquor or any drug and it holds on twice as long, and many of these kids get their first taste of it at the parties, like that one in Terry, where they'd even brought a band out of Austin called Hate Storm, and floated several kegs of beer in a cracked, leaking baby pool. By the time we got there, driving through blowing cotton and arriving well before midnight, the yard was already filled with a handful of wide-eyed freshcuts and more than a dozen lifer skinheads and their girls, all tattooed head-to-toe and somehow still fish-belly pale beneath the bulbs strung up on ladders.

THE TATTOOS ARE THE STORIES, their brands. Getting openly inked with their hate and their symbols marks them and makes them different. It draws a line that is hard to recross, a way of never going back. At some of these parties I've watched a newer skin getting inked in front of a crowd like it was a hazing, an initiation, so that right after the piece was finished, the other skins could circle in and punch and slap the raw flesh, singing loudly, spraying blood.

I know because it's happened to me.

Tattoos are also a way to sort everyone out. The Aryan Brotherhood favors their "patches" or "shields," massive tattoos like a coat of arms. And you can tell a Hammerskin from an ABT and an Aryan Knight from a Nazi Low Rider just by reading their skin; someone like Joker, who has a skeletal bird riding atop the letters NLR across his chest. There are outlaw bikers like the Low Riders and "true" skins like Combat 18 and the Confederate Hammerskins and then all the various Aryan prison gangs: Peckerwoods and PENI and the Dirty White Boys and the ABT and the Aryan Circle. There used to be greater differences between skins and the prison gangs, roughly where one might draw a line between pure ideology and just straight-up dope dealing and murder, but that's not even true anymore. Those lines are now blurred, and there's no better example than Jesse Earl, who was born in the shadow of his daddy's prison gang, the ABT, but grew up drifting through the wider white resistance movement, right into the arms of Thurman Flowers. And his own inked skin reflects that, covered with ABT flaming patches, the Aryan Nations' crowned sword and shield, and the skull and roses of Flowers's own Church of Purity.

That's why the tattoos are important. *They tell stories.* Who you are and where you come from.

What story does my skin reveal now?

And with all those skulls and crosses and nooses and gravestones, they often tell you how your story is going to end.

THE TERRY COUNTY PARTY STARTED SLOWLY, like an awkward high school dance, until the beer and booze got working, until the three members of Hate Storm started hammering out the only two chords they knew, screaming until the veins in their necks stood straight up. Then the moshing began, bodies throwing themselves against one another, some yelling *Rahowa* and *Burn nigger burn*, and that was just the warm-up before the real fights started. In that scene, everyone always wants to prove how tough they can be, how hard-core and serious they are. Jesse is mostly past all of that, he's not that sort of warrior anyway, instead using the parties like business meetings, a way to make connections and recruit for Flowers and his Church of Purity. But Little B is all punk, still trying hard to be a meaner, crueler version of his brother or his daddy. And then there's Kasper, who was with us that night because he had nowhere else to be and no one looking out for him, except maybe for me. Even now he still talks about starting a band with Little B, but that's not what brought him to that party in Terry County or down to Killing and it's not what keeps him here—the real draw is Little B himself, and nothing good can come out of that. I can't help but feel sorry for him, watching him constantly circle Little B and struggle with a whole different type of addiction, one that's just as difficult to break. No matter what, if he keeps it up, everything good about him is going to get killed, little by little, and if I don't get him away from the Earls and Flowers, in a few months he'll be in jail or truly dead, too.

If he's really lucky, maybe he can still go back to whatever shitty home he left, but at least he'll be alive.

Jenna was with us that night, too, in tight jeans and a barely-there leather top, her faded butterfly tattoos taking flight across her shoulders and seemingly out of place in a sea of everyone else's skulls and Celtic crosses. She's originally from California and got into the skinhead scene there with a group called Fuck Shit Up, out of Huntington Beach. I didn't know it then, but she also had some family here in Texas, the Joyces, and that's how Jesse learned about Killing in the first place and aimed us here. At that point, she and I hadn't talked much, because Jesse was always draped around her, but she was watching me all the time out of the corner of her eyes. Like Kasper, I want to get her away from all this, but I can't afford any friction with Jesse and his daddy, so I've stayed clear of her. I can't risk another Ballinger, but she doesn't know anything about that. None of them do. I was originally vouched to Jesse by a Volksfront skin out of McKinney, a snitch working off a two-year assault-and-battery charge, and I had a different name in Ballinger, so my cover is strong and back-stopped, but back then—that night in Terry—Jesse was still pushing me hard; wary, feeling me out and not quite trusting me. He didn't accept me, not yet, and in all the ways it matters it's even worse now, but I knew if he didn't take me in there was no way I would ever get close to his daddy. It didn't help that Jenna reminded me so much of that girl in Ballinger, and still does.

That seems like someone else's life, a lifetime ago.

Over the last two years I've met enough of these skins, these so-called white *supremacists*, to figure out that it's a lot of smoke and mirrors. They're just lost souls like Kasper or Jenna, running from something or just plain running in place. They talk tough and a few of them even talk smart, but they're mostly hollow, empty. *They're pretending, just like I am.* They drift in and out of the scene unless someone like Jesse or Thurman Flowers gets ahold of them and fills them up. But that doesn't make some of them any less dangerous, particularly when they're together. I've seen it again and again.

They draw strength in numbers, like a pack of dogs or wolves. Piranha.

In Terry, it was a big Confederate Hammerskin that started the fight, and the flashpoint was Kasper. Kasper had bumped into the Hammerskin's girl, touched her somehow, and even though he would have been the last one at the party interested in that girl or any other, he was suddenly pinwheeling over the ground in front of me, spitting blood. He's thin anyway, small and delicate, so it would take little more than the back of a hand to drive him to his knees, but he took a shot full to the face and never saw it coming. He's less of a fighter than Jesse, doesn't have the reflexes or instincts for it. He doesn't know how to hurt people and doesn't dream about it or wake up with his hands clenched and his palms bloody from the half-moons of his nails after throwing punches in his sleep . . .

But I do.

THE HAMMERSKIN WAS SHIRTLESS, his head uncovered and bald but scarred enough you could count his age on them like rings on a cut tree. He wore an iron chain tight around his neck and had crossed hammers on display across his torso, and 55/HFFH inked in red across his forehead. He had Kasper by about seven inches and more than a hundred pounds, and although he had a couple of inches on me, too, seeing Kasper nearly broken in half on the ground and Little B swinging wildly at anyone nearby gave me the opportunity I thought I needed, my chance to gain Jesse's trust.

I hit the Hammerskin low, then started working high, using the inked hammers as my first target. He was faster, or a lot more sober than I gave him credit for, and the right cross I aimed at his eye went wide. He ducked under it, got his arms around me and lifted me up, spinning me high, trying to take me down to the ground in one move, but I hooked his leg for leverage and all we did was dance a tight circle. Holding each other close, his sweat on me and his breath on my face, I shot an elbow into his exposed ribs and then followed with two Krav Maga knee strikes, the second one breaking something important with a sickening crunch. When he howled and let go, taking a crazy, loose-limbed backhand at my head, I dipped under his flailing arm, threw a crossing elbow to his jaw and brought another one backward across his face, and as he started to go to his knees, helped him along with a straight-razor hand to his throat.

He threw up dark blood and beer and his eyes showed all white, slick and hard as exposed bone.

People were yelling, although I couldn't hear them. We were standing in a darkened circle and all the light was around us, so it was like we were trapped together in a dark, dark hole. But there was a small part of me *outside* that hole as well, just above it, looking down along with the crowd as I beat this man to death. I've experienced this at other times and places—moments where I am unmoored and lost and where I'm desperate to find myself again.

Like my father's funeral . . .

Like Wanat, when I killed that boy running at Sergeant Wahl . . .

Or like Ballinger, where I beat a man senseless for a girl I barely knew. She'd begged for my help, but her final words—screamed over and over again at me—were *Not like this, never like this.*

I tried to tell her there was no other way. *This is how you stop a man's heart.* But no one was listening anymore.

And maybe there will come a moment like that in Killing, too. Soon, because as each day goes by, I'm less sure of who I am or what I'm doing anymore.

But after putting the Hammerskin out, I was able to get a deep breath and find a way to focus, pulling myself hand over hand back to sanity. I was even about to reach down and help him up, when all of his friends hit me from behind.

Like I said, they draw their strength in numbers, dogs and wolves.

I went down with hands all around me, dragging me over the grass and pushing me face-first into the baby pool where I'd seen some skins pissing into the water and ice earlier. My head hit a keg, and my mouth filled with that water. There was a flash of something bright and sharp—a knife—and fingers searching for the softness of my eyes while still holding my head down, and I had time to catch one glimpse of Jesse standing at the far edge of the yard, so far out of the fray it might as well have been the edge of the world. Jenna was hanging on his shoulder, pulling at him and pointing in my direction, but he turned away and I lost him in the shadows thrown by others.

More hands were at my throat and a boot was in the small of my back. My lungs were exploding and it felt like the whole party was standing on me, all to make sure I stayed under that water.

And then, even though there was no way I could see it or hear it, I sensed in the rolling movement of bodies around me and the sudden silence falling over all of us like a sharp intake of breath that someone had pulled a gun.

I was crushed beneath a pile of people and the water and piss were cold in my mouth and I was alone.

I fought harder to stand, still choking, still waiting for the shot I was sure was coming, when all the hands released me. I pushed away from the pool on my knees, covered in drifting cotton, and spit out what felt like an ocean of water, a deep black sea, to find an old man pointing a huge Ruger revolver—nearly as old and rusted as him—at the crowd. There was another man at his shoulder who I later learned was Joker, and he had a long knife pointed at the face of a skin he'd just pulled off of me. Joker wasn't smiling, wasn't moving, and didn't even appear to be blinking. He just kept that knife steady and still and a breath away from the skin's eye. He'd already helped Little B to his feet; he was wiping at his bloody mouth with a shaking hand. He'd never landed a punch, but at least he'd tried.

Kasper, whose face was already going black and blue, smiled at me, thankful in ways he'd never be able to say, and then passed out into Jenna's arms.

The old man wore a stark white wife-beater that showed his tattoos. He had clean and pressed Dickies, and his gray hair was pomaded back. There was a long chain from his belt to his back pocket, and it shined so bright in the naked bulbs it hurt my eyes. All of the Hammerskin's crew, who moments before had been trying to kill me, still circled us, but they wouldn't approach *him*, and it wasn't just because of the gun or Joker's knife. He stared at me curiously as Jesse returned and hovered nearby, and the old man couldn't hide the look on his face when he caught sight of him. A look that was there and gone again, but I saw it plain: disgust, disappointment. Jesse had stayed clear of the fight the whole time.

Then the old man shook his head and turned back to me and I knew who he was before he even said a word.

"I guess you're some kind of goddamn hero, huh, takin' on all these peckerwoods yourself? But I like it. That's some goddamn big balls right there, ain't it, Joker?"

And Joker with the knife didn't say anything at all.

The old man continued. "Yep, a real hero. A real badass, not like some pussies 'round here." His eyes slid over to Jesse and back again. "Hero, you're gonna have to tell me where you learned to fight like that. I bet that's a damn interestin' story." I knew then he'd been watching the fight right from the start, letting it play out to see how I handled myself; or maybe just to satisfy himself that Jesse wasn't going to handle it at all.

He then slipped the gun into the front of his Dickies, where it was still visible and he could get to it fast . . . where it could still be dangerous. Just like him. Always.

I learned it that night and I try never, ever to forget it.

"Howdy, son, I'm JW Earl."

And then John Wesley Earl reached out a hand to help me up.

I WAS WAITING IN THE CAR for T-Bob and Jesse, just like Earl asked me to. He ordered them to come here to Murfee and answer the deputy's questions because he doesn't want any more trouble down in Killing, but he won't come into town himself. He's hiding, laying low. He made me drive them, which pissed Jesse off to no end, and told me to keep one eye open and another on his son and brother, but there's more going on than that, because with Earl there always is. *I don't know whose lies to believe anymore, his or mine.* He's like a movie set, but so am I. Nothing we show each other or anyone else is real. There are the faces we present and then nothing but our own empty hallways and rooms behind them. Our own ghosts move there, up and down the corridors, restless, always haunting us.

JW also asked me to draw a layout of Murfee for him: all the main buildings and streets, the sheriff's department and the bank and the fire station.

Like a map to buried treasure, or something else.

The others are waiting in Killing for Thurman Flowers to arrive, so they can start building his Church of Purity, another Elohim City or Hillsboro or Hayden Lake. They have all these crazy plans and Jesse believes every one of them, but Earl doesn't believe in anything, other than himself. He doesn't give a damn about Killing or Flowers or any of that, even his own family. He's always standing off by himself on the big bluff behind the house, staring at the sky, always on the phone.

Who is he talking to and what is he talking about?

Other ghosts, maybe; telling stories he won't share with us.

Whatever he's waiting for isn't out in Killing and never was. That's all Jesse's doing. I think whatever Earl is looking for, whatever he wants, is right here in Murfee.

But when T-Bob and Jesse first got back in the car, it was Jesse who was fixated on Murfee, ranting on and on about the damn beaner deputies in the town. That Hispanic deputy, America Reynosa, must have gotten under his skin, the same way she did with Earl and Little B. And Jesse knows now he's not going to be able to get out from under what happened in Terlingua, neither those deputies nor Earl will let him, for whatever reasons of his own. Jesse muttered something about blood and a fight and Bravo's girlfriend, someone named Vianey, before lapsing into a cold silence. He still wasn't ready to let it go, though, or ready to face his daddy. So we've been driving around Murfee since then. For almost two hours. *Just circling.*

Now, though, I decide on my own that we've all had enough, and I get us away from the town and back out in the desert and the mountains. He doesn't stop me or say anything at all, and instead looks at the receding people and buildings with eyes dead and quiet and still as graves.

Eyes so much suddenly like his daddy's. But where Earl is impossible to read or predict, everything about Jesse is an open book. There's nothing subtle or measured about him at all, but it doesn't make him any less of a threat to someone who crosses him.

Like father, like son.

In 1999, John Wesley Earl killed *my* father, gunning him down in the middle of the night on a road outside of Sweetwater. Despite all the promises made to me at my father's funeral, Earl was never tried or convicted for it, never put down for it, and I've been waiting over fifteen years to look him in those grave-like eyes of his and make him say it, so I can pull that trigger myself, only to find now that I can't. I *want* to believe it's because I need to find out what he's doing down in Killing and in Murfee, but I don't wear a badge anymore. This isn't my town and none of these people, including Jenna and Kasper, are my responsibility, even if a part of me still wants to pretend I'm a cop and can't leave them to the mercies of Jesse or Earl when I know they don't have any.

But I *know* this is a lie, too.

I should have killed Earl that very first night I met him in Terry. But he saved my life and continues to treat me, day after day, *almost like a son.* Better, in most ways, than his true boys. Which should mean nothing to me since the man killed my father, yet somehow has come to mean everything to a kid who hasn't had anything, or anyone, for a long time.

So I make myself look in every mirror, at my reflection in the car window as we drive back to Killing, just to remind myself *I'm not that kid anymore.* That boy died, I died, the same night my father did. Whatever I see there, whoever is looking back at me, it's not that nine-year-old boy, but that's the biggest damn lie of all.

Because I've always been just another lost soul, too; as hollow and empty as Kasper and all the rest of them, just waiting all these years for someone to fill me up.

Maybe it wasn't that I always wanted Earl dead, as much as I just wanted a father back.

MURFEE REMINDS ME OF SWEETWATER, but it's a lot prettier. Almost like a movie set, too, all the houses and buildings just pretty fronts without backs, spread out in perfect squares beneath the shadows of the mountains. By the time I left Sweetwater, the horizon had just started to disappear behind the turbines of the first wind farms. Now, as far as you can see, there's nothing natural or beautiful anymore—there are no mountains or trees—just those damn turbines, turning and turning and turning. I've been back a dozen times to the place where my father was shot, to stand beneath those spinning blades and to touch the ground where he bled out, and there are always more of them, and soon they'll block out the sky.

My father was on his back when he died, looking straight up, and for years I tried to imagine that the last thing he saw was a fresh night sky filled with a million new stars.

It's a nice thought, but I need to let it go.

I need to remember, always remember, that the last thing my father *really* saw before he died was John Wesley Earl staring down at him, right before he pulled the trigger . . .

Like father . . . like goddamn son.

PART TWO

HOMBRES MALOS

We're peckerwood soldiers, down for our cause
Texas convicts, soldiers, and solid outlaws!
The rules we live by are carved in stone,
Awesome and fearless, bad to the bone.

In joints all over and from around the ways
People try to down us with each passing day.
The strength we have when we go to war
Was passed on to us from brothers before.

We'll go to war with our heads held high
Knowing some of us will get hurt and die.
None of that matters while the battle is on
We will fight to the finish, till all strength is gone.

Our bodies are solid, blasted with ink,
Warbirds and bolts are all that we think.
In times we turn cold, ruthless and hard,
The price we pay to survive in the yard.

We are peckerwood soldiers down for our cause.
Texas convicts, soldiers, and solid outlaws!

—Popular Peckerwood poem, credited
to the Aryan Brotherhood of Texas

14

He killed his best friend, his only friend in the world, with fire.

Setting it up had taken months. Gettin' the matches was easy, but smuggling in the lighter fluid—enough of it—had been the fuckin' hard part. Sunny had been able to slip some in for him, and Mack Doty's old lady had as well, passing it to Doty mouth-to-mouth in tiny condom balloons as they swapped hot spit over their one allowed kiss during visitation, which Doty later shit out in his cell. The Family moved all their drugs that way, too, and John Wesley Earl had come to learn there were a lot of things a man could keep hidden up his ass, if he were so inclined or desperate enough. It was like a goddamn magic trick, but instead of pullin' a rabbit out of a hat, a man could make a six-inch metal shiv appear out of his asshole, almost out of thin air.

Now *that* was a fuckin' trick.

After he got the lighter fluid, he stored it all in a tied-off rubber glove he'd pinched from the chow hall. When the time came, he brought Doty with him, and they cruised by George's cell to find him calmly sitting there—all three hundred pounds of him—knitting. It was George who had shown Earl the value of knitting, almost like meditating; a way of concentrating hard and floating free at the same time, moving past the bars and over the walls into the wide world beyond.

Earl had dropped the knitting in favor of his own kind of meditating, the phantom motorcycle rides he'd take in his head, but it was George who had also vouched for him as a prospect nearly twenty years ago, and who'd later made him a general. Together they'd helped run all the activities of the Family—the Aryan Brotherhood of Texas—for over five years. They were two-fifths of the Wheel, the Family's "steering committee," and they called the shots over several state prisons and one federal pen and answered to no one but each other. Earl didn't know how many men's names they'd put into the hat together, Family slang for ordering a hit, but if all those dead men stood up at one time, there wouldn't be much elbow room left for a living one. They'd had a helluva ride together, but now it was over.

Blood in. Blood out.

You had to spill blood to earn your patch, and the only way you ever left the Family was in a body bag.

George "Big King" Chives was sitting there, garter stitching a potholder, when Earl sprayed his face full of lighter fluid. He'd punched a hole in the thumb of the rubber glove so it made its own little nozzle, and when he squeezed it one-handed, nearly every bit of that thick fluid hosed down George's eyes, right into his open mouth and down the front of his shirt. It soaked that shitty potholder that no one was ever going to use, and George was just standing up, about to yell, when Earl hit him with the lit match Doty had handed him. It *felt* like the very air between them caught fire, and George was suddenly breathing flame as he lunged at the bars, the inside of his skull lit up like a carnival. He tried to say something but his tongue was already melting.

Big King was wearin' a goddamn crown all right, when the fire circled his head.

Earl tossed the wadded-up glove into George's face, sparking another dark explosion of embers, and although he'd wanted to stay and see the end of it, he and Doty had kept walking, fast-casual the way only inmates can, as thick smoke started to seep through the bars like blood.

In about twenty more seconds the block would be in a full uproar, but by then they'd be down on the next level and would be halfway toward the yard, sharing a cigarette and laughing and cutting up without a care in the world. He'd have to wash the lighter fluid off his hands, but that was just for the guards and all the questions that'd come after. All the true peckerwoods in Walls would know what he'd done, and that was part of the reason for makin' it so damn hard on himself. It would have been far easier to just stick a shiv or sharpened guitar string or hacksaw into George in the shower and be done with it, but he'd wanted it done *this* way. It was a statement, a blazing bright show that everyone could see and would never forget, and one of the first things George had taught him, all those years ago.

They have to believe you'll do anything, JW . . . that there's no line you won't cross, because there just is no line. You're only as strong as how much they fear you, and strength is the only damn thing anyone in here respects. That's the way you'll hold on in here, and I reckon that's the only way to hold on to anything, anywhere.

That had proved true over and over again. George had been a great teacher and a better friend, and if setting that friend (and a high-ranking member of the Family) on fire in the middle of his cell on a fine October afternoon wasn't a statement—loud and clear—then Earl couldn't imagine what would be.

If *that* wasn't a show of strength, then goddamn nothin' was.

EARL STOOD IN THE ENDLESS SUN, turning Hero's hand-drawn map of Murfee this way and that, looking it over. It was military precise, the writing neat, which squared with the time Danny Ferro had spent in the army, and Earl hadn't expected any less. Earl had taken to calling him "Hero" from that first night they met, but the boy *had* done some serious superhero shit over in Afghanistan or Iraq or some other raghead place, so Earl knew the kid could handle himself. Hell, he'd seen it firsthand in Lubbock, watching him damn near fight that whole skin-head party himself, while his older son, Jesse, had stood and watched with his dick in his hand. Danny had come back from over there *not quite right*, got himself a head-case discharge or something like that, but had sworn to Jesse he still had plenty of friends in the service that, for the right price, could get their hands on grade-A military weapons, even explosives, so Flowers could arm his goddamn Church of Purity for the comin' race war. And that truly *was* serious shit, even if Earl wasn't convinced Danny really would follow through on all those big promises. Danny was weird in his ways and hard to pin down, always slippin' and slidin' around everyone, like he was trying to hide some-thing behind his back (and he wouldn't be the only one), but he was also whip-smart and there was no hidin' that. He was smarter than both Jesse and Little B by a country mile, which meant he had far too much sense to ever be sucked in by Flowers and all his bullshit.

But here he was in Killing all the same, talkin' that nonsense, and why? That was a question worth turnin' over.

Fortunately, neither Jesse nor Flowers had a pot to piss in or a win-dow to throw out of. Not now, and if Earl kept Jesse out of his business, not ever. But if Danny did get ahold of a bunch of grenades and shit, the best thing to happen for everyone involved would be for Flowers to blow himself sky-fuckin'-high with 'em.

Earl folded the map back up and lit a cigarette, blowing smoke over Killing. He was up on the bluff behind the place Jesse had found for them, high enough that he could pick out the white steeple of the church and all of its little grave markers, and the few roads that spoked out into the scrub behind the town like parts of a broken wagon wheel . . . like a little kid's drawing in the dirt. He'd come up here where the reception was best to call that half-breed prick Manny Suarez, and the conversation had been short, brutal, simple.

It figured . . . after all of their years of doing the business together, where most of their contact had only been through coded jail letters and passed messages, when they finally *could* talk openly, there wasn't a helluva lot to say, anyway.

For more than a decade, they'd made each other rich with only a handful of words.

And now, although Manny and his people were willing to accept a certain amount of responsibility for the current pile of neck-deep shit Earl was standing in, Manny had made it clear—in as few words as possible—they weren't gonna help him dig out of it. Not right now and not near fast enough.

So yes (or *sí*, as Manny that motherfucker put it), although they all could agree that their man (actually Manny's *own* boy, Miguel) had fucked up—and royally—it was now only Earl's problem, since he was the one who'd insisted on this particular godforsaken place to celebrate his Christmas in July. And Manny *had* warned him again and again about the risks of doing it here, how they'd needed agreements and promises and money to change hands even to consider it, since Manny's people had no sway in this shitty little corner of Texas, no *strength*. It wasn't even like Earl hadn't understood all the problems, either, because he'd seen that firsthand in prison, where all the gangs—the Black Guerilla Family, the Mexican Mafia, the Texas Syndicate, the ABT—had built their own invisible walls behind the real ones so that *everyone* had to pay something for the privilege of crossing their little empires. But in the end, since Earl had never really had a choice, neither did Manny or his people, and after a lot of wetback pissin' and moanin', Manny had honored the request and come through just like he'd promised, only to find that now he and his boy were the ones paying the price. So there was really nothin' more Earl could or would ask of him, and it wasn't like he could honestly explain the *real* reasons why this fuckin' flyspeck of a town had been *the only choice*, and how it had fucked them both.

But none of that mattered anymore, what was done was done. And Manny's people were now, for the moment, content to let things shake out on their own time, even though time was something John Wesley

Earl most certainly did not have. For a man who'd spent so many years locked up, where time itself was near meaningless—where it had no shape and seemed like it could stretch on for a thousand of these hot Texas summers ass-end to ass-end forever—even he had to laugh at his sudden concern over it. But Manny's last words had been clear: Earl's present was still wrapped, so far still safe and untouched, and just waitin' for him where they'd left it. But it wouldn't stay that way forever. Someone would eventually find it. So if Earl still wanted Christmas to come early, it was all on him now. He should probably start plannin' to celebrate alone . . .

Otherwise, he could sit tight and go fuck himself.

And that was why Earl was glad he'd sent Danny into town this morning with Jesse and T-Bob: to have someone he could rely on and trust (as much as he trusted anyone) put first eyes on this place Murfee, so Earl could figure out exactly what he was dealing with and where to start.

So he could start that holiday plannin' . . .

Jesse last told him that worthless snake-handler Flowers was only a week away, maybe not even that long. And Jesse liked to say that when Flowers got to Killing, things *were* finally gonna change, and fast, making it out like it was some sort of promise, or worse, a goddamn threat. Earl was even fine with some of that smart mouth, if it meant Jesse wasn't the yellow coward Earl was afraid he was. But Jesse had also been slow-pissin' on him about *what he was due* for weeks, as if that was Earl's concern, and that just showed that his older son didn't know him at all, not really. In fact, none of them *knew* John Wesley Earl, not Sunny or T-Bob or the rest; none of them had any idea of what he was truly capable of when his back was against the wall, like it was now. He'd kept that hidden, tucked down deep. He was a shark of a cardplayer, and that was his ace in the hole.

They didn't know *there was no line*. But they would if it came to it.

That dead man in Terlingua had brought Earl a whole new set of problems he hadn't seen comin' and hadn't prepared for, and the stink of it was now carryin' all the way to the sheriff's department in Murfee. He couldn't wash it off the way Jesse had tried to with a damn hose. Yep, things were gonna change and change soon, no doubt about that, but not in ways Jesse or any of the others could imagine.

HE STAMPED OUT the first cigarette and shook out another. He'd been out of prison for a little while now, but still lived on yard bird time. It's like the bars and walls and regimen had followed him, stayed with him, everywhere he went. He sometimes sat in his room for the same hours he would have sat in his cell, waiting for an invisible guard to come and tell him it was time for chow or time to walk the yard or time to take a shit or whatever. He was free and still as locked up as he'd ever been. Even Sunny, who'd done a small stint of her own for extortion and passing Family notes, couldn't understand why he still woke up at four-thirty a.m. every goddamn day when there was no one to order him to do it. But there was somebody, she just didn't see or hear them.

Some mornings before the sun was fully up, he took his big Harley out on the back roads; the '87 FXLR Low Rider with the fireball and black candy finish that flashed grinning skulls in the right light, and that Sunny had kept cherry for him while he was locked up. The last time he'd been on it before goin' up again had been right after the trip to Corpus, and he still didn't like to think about *that* much. But he still loved that damn bike, the feel of pushin' it hard, as fast and far as it could go. He'd fight that bitch through the tightest curves with his eyes closed, just so he wouldn't have to watch the world go by or face the fact he was still just goin' around in goddamn circles.

Not really going anywhere at all, no matter how fast he went.

But that was gonna change, too.

He looked south, toward scrub and mesas that reminded him of broken plates, all stacked up; past sawtooth mountains blocking the horizon, where Mexico would be. The land was wide and open and as pale as a skeleton; the dust as dry as ash, as fine and loose as talc. It took nothing for the wind to throw handfuls of it high in the air, where it spun wild like the damn Devil himself.

Free.

His daddy had loved that old Johnny Rodriguez song "Ridin' My Thumb to Mexico." Johnny Rod had sung about headin' on down to Mexico for a little change of atmosphere, and Earl had sold out everyone and everything he'd ever known for his own change of atmosphere, too; his one good chance. And he'd burned his best friend to death to clear the way. He burned now, too: a fire that'd only been getting more furious by the years, scorching away everything inside him, leaving only scar tissue, twisted and black.

So he had no problem burnin' down Killing and Murfee and the whole damn world if he had to. Just like the damn Devil himself.

He looked at his watch. It was time to check in again, as bad as the old nightly two a.m. cell checks in Walls, and in some ways, worse. But when all this was finally over, he was gonna take this watch and throw it in the cold deep of the ocean, where maybe the water would finally put out all the fires inside of him, too, and where he was never gonna have to worry about the fuckin' time for anyone else, ever again.

He bent down and pulled out a second phone from his boot, one none of the others knew about, not even Sunny. Twenty, thirty years ago, he'd have kept a knife down there, five inches of stainless steel; more than enough to get through a man's ribs and cut deep into something vital behind them. Nowadays, you could hurt a man twice as bad with a simple phone call, or just by talkin' to the right people. He knew that as well as anyone, and it was one of the few lessons he'd learned beyond what prison or ole Big King or even Manny Suarez had taught him.

He'd truly learned that from FBI Special Agent Austin Nichols, the man he was about to call.

Blood in . . . blood out.

Earl took the phone and turned his face to the desert and dialed.

15

Things were frosty between them for the first part of the drive, but started to thaw somewhere just outside Odessa, where they stopped to grab some coffee and stretch. Chris didn't say anything about the Earls or Billy Bravo, and Harp didn't, either. It was like they'd made a silent pact not to discuss any of that again until after their meeting in Lubbock, and Chris was fine with that.

Since Harp didn't bring it up, Chris figured his chief deputy was okay with it, too.

WHEN THEY ARRIVED, no one asked them for their guns, but Chris and Harp had to show a bored security guard their badges and their driver's licenses. The address Chris had been given was a bank building, a four-story in downtown Lubbock. It was a newer Bank of America, and the lobby was an expanse of black-and-green-veined marble dominated by a pyramid fountain that made the open space smell like a cave. After a twenty-minute wait, they were escorted past the fountain and a glass-walled maze of well-lit suites into a sterile set of offices on the third floor.

There were no books on the shelves, no pictures on the walls. The modular furniture was by and large empty, except for some computer monitors turned away from the windows, feathered in dust. Even the trash cans looked unused.

Chris had no idea if it was a fed or state operation. It didn't feel like it existed at all.

They finally settled in a conference room that *did* look used: numerous folders spread out on the table, a few iPads, cups of coffee, and a selection of cell phones from the men who were waiting on them. Major Dyer was a big man, matching his voice on the phone, and same as the lieutenant he introduced as Stackpole, he was dressed in the standard Texas Ranger uniform of white collared shirt, blue tie, khaki pants with Ranger belt, Stetson Rincon Vented straw hat, and boots. They both had their silver stars high up on their shirts, and Dyer's hair was pushed back even higher on his head, a wave of gray that looked almost blue beneath the overhead lights.

With them was the owner of most of the phones and folders on the table, an African-American man in an expensive lightweight suit named Austin Nichols; an FBI agent out of Dallas. Chris had a hard time imagining Nichols was much older than him, and he had the air of someone who always left everywhere early but still was fifteen minutes late to the next place he had to be. Chris figured he'd been the president of his fraternity at whatever college back East he'd attended. In his life, he'd probably been the president of a lot of things; was used to it. He was slim and good-looking, like someone you might see on TV, and he was on one of his phones and looking at his watch when Chris and Harp walked in.

"Nice to finally meet you, Sheriff Cherry. Bethel Turner speaks highly of you," Major Dyer said, shaking his hand firmly and pointing them to any of the numerous free chairs. Harp shook Stackpole's offered grip and a brief look passed between the two men that Chris barely caught and didn't understand. Dyer continued, "I was at Sheriff Ross's funeral and memorial. He was a friend of the Rangers, a living legend. I'm not sure they make 'em like him anymore."

"No, no they don't." And Chris left it at that.

Dyer looked like he, too, was going to add more, but didn't, either. "Thank you for coming up here to meet with us. I know this is highly unusual. I've been doing this a long time, and I don't think I've been involved in anything quite like it." Major Dyer stared at all the folders on the table, uncomfortable. "Anyway, it's probably best I let Agent Nichols take it from here." While the major was talking, Nichols had finished his call and had pulled one of the folders in front of him, opening it up to reveal a thick stack of photos. He was placing them on the table in some exact, specific order that made sense only to him. The pictures were all turned to face Chris and Harp, who was already leaning forward to look at them.

It reminded Chris of another set of photos he'd been shown in the hospital by Joe Garrison, after the shooting at the Far Six. They'd been of the men Chris had killed. He kept his gaze steady on the agent, not on the faces staring up at him from the table's expanse.

When Nichols was done arranging the photos, he sat back, proud of his work.

"Okay, gentlemen, who do you recognize?"

HARP IMMEDIATELY SET FOUR ASIDE.

"Yes, that's James Wesley Earl, his brother Thomas Robert, and his two sons, Jesse and Bass," Nichols said, lining them up.

Harp kept looking, before pulling out another. "This one, too, no doubt about it."

Nichols glanced at it, nodded. "His name is Larry Wayne Hasse. They call him Joker."

Harp stared longer and was about to give up, when he paused, tapped one more photo, and slid it from its place. He picked it up, brought it close to his face, and then spun it back across the table to where it came to rest in front of the agent. "Him," Harp said. "His hair is shorter now, but I saw him in Killing, and I think he drove the other two up to Murfee when we interviewed them."

Nichols was about to take up the picture, but Major Dyer got to it first. He looked at it for a long moment himself, and then turned it around to face both Chris and Harp again. "That's the photo they take when you join the Texas Department of Public Safety, the Criminal Investigation Division. That'd be the same one on his credentials, if he carried those anymore. But he doesn't. Not his badge, either." Dyer put the photo facedown on the table.

"His name is Danny Ford, and up until seven weeks ago, he worked for me."

AGENT NICHOLS TALKED WITHOUT NOTES. Even with all the folders and papers he'd brought with him, other than the pictures, he didn't refer to anything at all.

"John Wesley Earl has spent the better part of his life in prison, most recently for attempted murder. And let's be honest, there really isn't any 'better part.' He's a violent and dangerous bastard and always has been. He probably came out of his mother that way.

"However, he's far from stupid. I've seen the prison psych reports, and in fact, he's quite intelligent. During his years locked up, more than twenty-five of them altogether, he successfully crawled his way to the top of the hierarchy of the Aryan Brotherhood of Texas. The ABT is one of the most violent white supremacist gangs in this country, and one of the largest. They are distinct from that 'other' Aryan Brotherhood, the white prison gang that got its start in California in the sixties and is now prominent throughout the federal prison system, but they aren't any less violent or dangerous. The ABT's constitution reads that it was founded *upon the sublime principles of White Supremacy, no pretense is or will be made to the contrary. The ABT remains and always will remain a venerable all-Aryan organization.* When you join, you have to go through their study course, which focuses on the 'Fourteen Words': *We must secure the existence of our people and a future for white children.* It's a slogan we've seen again and again with other white supremacist groups. Nowadays, though, the ABT isn't just a white supremacist gang. They aren't even principally white supremacists. They are, in fact, a highly organized criminal organization involved in a plethora of illegal activities."

Nichols opened another one of his folders and pushed it forward to Chris. It was filled with dozens of photocopied newspaper articles. Chris thumbed through a few, offering them to Harp, who shook his head. All were about ABT-related murders and criminal cases throughout Texas, very few of which seemed to have occurred behind prison walls. One detailed an FBI operation called La Flama Blanca—The White Flame—which had culminated in the arrest of more than two dozen ABT members in central Texas, all for meth distribution. The article had a color picture of Nichols standing at a lectern, pointing at a board full of head shots not much different from those he'd brought with him to this meeting.

Chris closed the folder and slid it back.

Nichols picked up Earl's picture and put it front and center. "John Wesley Earl was part of what they call the Steering Committee, or the Wheel. He was a general, as powerful as they come, and he was heavily involved in some of those ABT 'illegal activities.' Specifically, he ran *all* drug distribution for the ABT throughout the entire Texas prison system, and a couple of federal facilities as well. He had the connections and spearheaded that little ABT profit-making enterprise, along with another general, George 'Big King' Chives. Together, Earl and Chives made themselves and the ABT a lot of money, and Earl was probably responsible for more crime, more murders behind bars, than he was ever charged with on the outside." Nichols stood and moved the photos around with his slim fingers. The only ring he wore was some sort of signet or class ring. "However, a little less than a year ago, like clockwork, he was due for another of his mandated parole hearings. And he would have been denied again, like every other time before that, but this go-around he wanted a thumb on the scales in his favor. He decided to do something he's never done during the two-plus decades he's been locked up. He wanted to deal. He agreed *to talk.*" Nichols sat back down. "He wanted to become a cooperating informant."

"Bullshit," Harp said, almost laughing.

Nichols shrugged. "That's what I thought, too. In fact, he was already being looked at for the recent murder of one of the few ABT generals that had as much, maybe even more, clout than him, that man Chives I just mentioned. Word was that Chives had brought Earl up through the ABT, but that didn't stop Earl from burning him to death in his jail cell. No honor among thieves, I guess. Anyway, there was nothing we could prove on the Chives murder, so when Earl offered to talk, we listened. And I'm glad we did. After a few months of running his mouth, Earl did more to undo the ABT than either the FBI or state or local law enforcement has been able to accomplish in years." Nichols pointed to the folder with the newspaper articles. "He gave it all to us on a silver platter."

Chris asked, "And so you paroled him. But why talk now, after all this time? What did he really want?"

Nichols steepled his hands in front of him. "Well, it seems he got disillusioned. It's hard to imagine that with someone like Earl, and God knows I tried, but he claimed he didn't like the in-house decisions being enforced by all the newer, younger gang members working their way up the hierarchy. He said they were too violent, had no respect, and he didn't like the fact they were targeting kids and girlfriends on the outside. Even for a bunch of murderous psychopaths, family is supposed to be out of bounds." Nichols paused. "Personally, I think he just got tired, worn-out. He's a big-time cardplayer, so maybe he was sick of the shitty hand life had dealt him, and decided to do something about it. He's been locked up a long, long time and didn't want to spend his last few healthy years behind bars. He doesn't believe any of that white racist bullshit anymore, and it's a hard life to stay on top for as long as he did. Look what happened to Chives."

Chris shook his head, reluctant and unconvinced. "No, look at what he *did* to Chives. But whatever, there has to be more to it than that, right? Does someone like John Wesley Earl really wake up one morning with that sort of conscience?" Chris glanced at Harp, who was nodding in agreement, as if he was glad that Chris was finally the one to say it first and not him. "I'm not sure, not if what you've told us about him is true."

Nichols smiled, but it was thin, barely there. "Me, either, and maybe you're right . . . maybe he wasn't just suddenly nostalgic about the good ole days in the gang . . . but this is where his son, his older son, Jesse, enters the picture, as well as a man named Thurman Flowers." Nichols pulled Jesse Earl's photo front and center. "Despite all that ABT nonsense, Earl is really no more of a racist than your garden-variety cracker redneck." Nichols avoided looking at Harp or Dyer. "He doesn't *believe* any of that *Heil Hitler* shit, at least not anymore. It was always a matter of convenience for him, jail survival. Trust me, right now, the ABT *is* more of a criminal organization than anything else, and the Wheel isn't about to order up cross burnings and lynchings. That's bad for business when your business is moving drugs, both inside and outside of prison, and increasingly, more of the latter. I saw that firsthand in La Flama Blanca. Where do you think the ABT is getting all that weight? Not from a bunch of hotel and bathtub meth labs run by some Nazi Low Riders, but instead straight from the source, the Mexican cartels. *That* was Earl's strength, his forte. He brokered those deals. Jesse Earl, though? That's a whole different story. While Earl was away doing his time and building his little business empire, Jesse got himself neck deep in the *ideology*, white race purity. He's a true convert, a zealot. He's ready for a race war, and wants his finger on the trigger when it happens. He'll fire first."

Harp looked up, smiled through his teeth. "He's got guns tattooed on his arms."

"Yes, yes he does." Nichols pulled out another photo from the ones on the table, and held it up. "*This* is Thurman Flowers. Although Jesse's been half raised by his uncle and the mother of Earl's younger son, a woman they all call Sunny, whose real name is Mary Deshazo, it's been this character, Flowers, who's really been Jesse's father figure while Earl was locked up. They've met in person maybe a dozen times, and they've kept in constant touch for years. He's Jesse's mentor, his teacher. There's nothing original about Flowers at all, he's simply following a trail already blazed by the old guard of the white power movement. But that doesn't make him any less dangerous. A drive-by shooting of a federal prosecutor in Terrell, a shooting in a traditionally black church in Georgia, a young black man beaten to death in Arkansas by some Hammerskins, and most recently, a bombing of a Jewish community center in Oregon, all have Flowers's fingerprints on them. He's the one standing in the shadows, urging others like Jesse Earl to do his dirty work. He's trying to build something bigger than the Aryan Nations. He calls it the Church of Purity, and calls himself *Pastor* Flowers, but all he preaches is hate and terror and violence. The Southern Poverty Law Center has a whole bookshelf on him, and he's on every domestic terrorism watch list. He created some that didn't exist before."

Chris took the picture. The man was nondescript, with thinning hair and cheap wire-rim glasses; the eyes behind them muddy water. His Adam's apple seemed too big by half, and in some ways, all of them bad, he reminded Chris of Duane Dupree. He turned the photo so Harp could get a good look, and the other man shrugged and shook his head.

Chris put the photo down. "I've never seen him in Murfee, and apparently Ben didn't see him when he was in Killing."

"No, I expect not. But you will, and soon. Jesse and his group have been on the move for months. We wouldn't have had any idea that they'd finally camped out in Killing if it wasn't for John Earl. Our information is that Flowers is on his way there, too. He dropped off the radar after that bombing in Oregon, but we've been monitoring some Internet chat groups, and our best intel is that he and Jesse are planning to meet up in Killing and turn it into another all-Aryan settlement, like Elohim City or Hayden Lake, or Leith, North Dakota. Flowers put out the word to his followers to come there and start their new world order with him." Nichols studied the ring on his hand. "Back in the sixties there were these places, these 'sundown towns,' that excluded African-Americans and other minorities. They had signs up . . . *Nigger, don't let the sun go down on you here* . . . that sort of thing. Of course, most of those are all gone now. Or at least you can't see the signs anymore."

Harp put his hand solidly on the table. "Be careful, Agent."

Chris waved him off. "No, it's okay. Look, Agent Nichols, Murfee and the other towns around the Big Bend have the same racial issues any border community does, and I'm not going to pretend we don't. Still, I don't think anyone around our area is looking to join up with someone like Flowers."

Nichols shrugged. "No, probably not. But he's going to bring plenty of his own with them. Trust me, eventually they'll come. And he's coming now."

"And Earl is going to somehow help you stop this?"

Nichols started pulling together all of his photos. "Flowers is the real prize. He's been talking about blowing up a courthouse, another Oklahoma City bombing, among other things. He's actively looking for money, weapons, explosives. Earl is going to find out the how, the where, and the who, and in exchange for his cooperation and testimony, we've agreed to work out a deal for both of his sons, mainly Jesse. He doesn't want Jesse to spend years locked up the way he was, not over Thurman Flowers's fantasies. Once Flowers is in hand, we'll unseal all the pending RICO indictments we have on the ABT, again thanks to Earl, and then roll everyone up. After Earl works through several months of open court testimony on both the ABT and Flowers, he goes into witness protection."

Harp laughed. "A lifetime of causing shit and misery, and now he walks free? Must be a nice job if you can get it."

"WITSEC is not a walk in the park, Deputy." Nichols hit the word *deputy* hard, and kept going. "He'll spend the rest of his life being monitored. Plus, he's already done over twenty years behind bars. He's walking free now, and yes, I helped make that happen, but it's always been a two-for-one deal, the ABT *and* Flowers. He could have told us to fuck off and he would have been denied parole *again*, but who knows? In two or three years, maybe he would've been granted it anyway, only then we'd have nothing to show for it. Just another 're-formed' criminal on the streets. Right now he's on a leash, a tight one, and when this is over, he'll still have a collar on his neck. I think the ends justify the means."

Nichols paused, collected himself. "You know, the ABT and most of the current prison gang problems are remnants, relics, of the old building tender or trusty system, when the job of guarding and disciplining these inmates fell to other prisoners, so-called inmate trusties. It was cheaper to run and manage the prison that way, but it also set up a brutal hierarchy. The most trusted were even armed, the 'trusty shooters.' They had the full authority of prison guards and controlled the lives of their fellow inmates. Many times, it was a white trusty overseeing black inmates. It was de facto racial segregation, and it flourished in these prisons. Federal rulings abolished most trusty systems in the seventies, but Texas held on all the way into the eighties. I didn't create the system that gave birth to men like Earl, but I won't shy away from using him and the current system if I can."

"Is this personal for you, Agent Nichols?" Harp asked.

"Are you asking me that because I'm African-American? No, of course not. It's purely professional."

Harp shook his head. "Well, you know, for most cops, I think it helps sometimes if it *is* personal. If nothing else, at least you can be more honest with yourself. It provides a moral clarity of purpose. If this was personal for you, I'd understand it better." Harp turned to Chris, ignoring the others. "Because this is where he tells us our Terlingua murder takes a backseat. He doesn't want us spooking those folks in Killing or running Flowers off before he even shows up. He said the ends justify the means, and that means getting his shot at Flowers is worth letting Earl get away with another murder."

Nichols sat silent for a moment. "That's one way to put it. But JW Earl didn't kill anyone in the Big Bend. You know it and I know it."

"Well, I'd say that's the *only* way to put it," Chris offered. "This so-called leash of yours must be pretty damn long, because you're sitting here and he's way out there, outside my town, my home. But you are talking to him, right? What did he really tell you about Terlingua, about Billy Bravo?" Chris pressed. "Harp's right, that's why we're here, isn't it?"

"Yes, Earl did. He told me there was a homicide in Terlingua and that your department wanted to question his brother and Jesse regarding it. I directed him to have Jesse and T-Bob cooperate, and he followed through on that. That's why they came and met with you, and maybe the only reason they did, so you can thank me for that. Consider it a peace offering, a sign of good faith. Concessions had to be made to even make this work. He lives with these people. He's with them twenty-four hours a day. He's taking great risks, and there's no way to keep eyes on all of them, all the time, but I'm in daily contact with him. Earl's not going to jeopardize his deal."

"Daily contact? On the phone? You should know, Agent Nichols, that cell reception is bad down in the Big Bend. He might not always answer right away, or at all. Maybe you won't hear him quite right even when he does," Chris said. "And would he really tell you if he did know anything about Bravo's murder? We're talking about his son, his family. The same son he's supposedly doing all this for. Do you really trust him that much?"

"He doesn't want to go back to jail. He's got a lot on the line . . . I believe him," Nichols said.

Harp: "No, you *have* to believe him, or you're fucked. He's out there running around on your dime. This only gets better by the moment. That piece of shit gets to call his FBI friends to tell *us* to back off."

"And we're talking about a homicide," Chris added, "not an unpaid parking ticket." He shook his head. He needed another coffee after the long drive here—a drive that was going to feel a hell of a lot longer going back. "You're asking a lot, maybe too much."

Nichols tapped the table, as if the decision had already been made. "I get it. It's an uncomfortable situation for all of us. But all we need is for Flowers to show up, which should be any day now. Earl knows the minute he does, he has to close the deal and it'll be over. Then I'll personally squeeze Earl over what happened in Terlingua. If his brother or Jesse had a hand in that, they'll have to stand for it . . . all the way, no deals. I promise you that. Until then, all you have to do is stay out of the way and out of the picture."

The room was quiet, all of them looking down at the table. Somewhere deep in the building, an air-conditioning unit kicked on, making the room hum around them, but not any cooler.

"Of course, that means I have to believe *you*," Chris said, shaking his head. "This is happening right here, right now, in my backyard, and if it wasn't for what happened in Terlingua, you never would have come forward and said a thing about it. Not about Earl, or Jesse, or Flowers. They're all down there plotting God only knows what, and in the meantime, you're putting my town and my deputies at risk . . . your fellow law enforcement officers." Chris pointed at Nichols. "You keep talking about *we* and *us* a lot, but right now, as far as John Wesley Earl goes, I only see *you* sitting at this table. So if this goes south, you're the one who's going to have to stand for it, *all the way*." Chris shook his head one last time, realizing how he sounded like Harp. "And I can promise you that. It seems to me Earl is *your* damn trusty shooter. I hope you're comfortable with that."

Then Chris turned to Stackpole and Major Dyer, both of whom had sat still as stone throughout the long conversation with Nichols.

"Okay, so what does all this have to do with your man Danny Ford?"

16

They'd left for Lubbock earlier that morning without her. The sheriff had apologized for not taking her, but really, she was okay with it. As much as she liked both Sheriff Cherry and Harp, she didn't want to be cooped up with them for the eight-hour round-trip journey.

Besides, she had plenty of things of her own to get done.

SHE CHECKED ON AVALOS when Victor brought him his lunch—a bologna sandwich with one swirl of yellow mustard, a bag of potato chips, and a carton of milk. Another day locked up, and Avalos seemed paler, smaller. He was falling in on himself, reminding her of a *pescado* that had been left out in the sun. She and her papa had fished together many, many years ago at a place where a lot of the locals went—a hard jumble of rocks and river grass at a bend in the river below the Puente Ojinaga. One morning when they went there she found *un pescado* that someone had forgotten to free back into the water the day before. It was lying there on the rocks, not much bigger than her child's hand; the scales that had once been bright as silver pesos and that had once reflected rainbow light were dirty and dry and flaking away. Its eyes had sunk in, disappeared, and there was a bit of frayed fishing line running from the rusted hook that had twisted in its mouth. She'd cried hard at seeing it, at how it must have twisted and flopped while trying to get back into the water to its mama and papa, and her papa had told her, *sí*, it was a sad thing, but the water was *muy mágico* and it would soon bring the *pescado* back to life again. He'd then slipped it beneath the cool, dark water, where it had floated alone until it dropped away and she lost sight of it. She knew her papa had lied to her, but was glad he did, and after catching a dozen big shiny *pescados* of her own, she gave it no more thought. The tiny one had been too small to keep and too easily forgotten.

Whoever Avalos was waiting for still hadn't come. Not yet, and maybe never, and other than her stopping by to look in on him, his only other visitor was his appointed defender, Santino Paez. The lawyer's visits were brief, necessary, leaving behind the pepper and orange scent of his aftershave, and leaving Avalos mostly alone, except when Victor was there to keep him company. Sometimes Avalos talked to him in Spanish, questions about the town and the people in it, but other than that, said little. Victor told her all of this and shared everything Avalos said to him, but none of it was much use. None of it explained why Avalos thought he knew her or why he was in Murfee.

She watched him eat his bologna sandwich but he wouldn't look at her, and when he was done, she took away what he hadn't finished.

SHE THEN MET WITH PAEZ in his small office by the Hamilton, where it smelled like burgers outside, and that orange and pepper aftershave of his on the inside. The office was filled with fake plants, too bright and green, almost like a jungle. Paez was smaller than she was, with equally small, manicured hands, and his fake plants towered over him. His hair was slicked back tight against his head, gleaming with oil, and his suit was dark and creased sharp. He sat across from her with his fingers spread flat and a bright gold watch circling his wrist.

He apologized there was nothing he could say about his client, raising his hands as if in prayer. *Estas cosas son lo que son.* It was all a horrible mistake, tragic for everyone, but Mr. Avalos would have his day in court, and everyone would understand his side of it.

She asked Paez if Avalos had any serious interest in talking; maybe there were some details he could provide that really would help everyone see his side of it, without the need for a trial. Deputy Milford wasn't dead, after all, and nothing that had happened couldn't be *undone*. She was willing to bet one or more charges could be dropped in exchange for just a few words explaining *why* Avalos—the young man from Phoenix—was in Murfee, Texas.

What had brought him here . . . what was he doing?

Paez sat back, eyes narrowed. She had seen him wear these silly glasses before: thin wire-rims where the lenses were nothing but clear glass. She knew he could see perfectly well without them, the way he was seeing her right now. He brushed at something invisible on his desk with his thin fingers and their gleaming white nails, and asked her point-blank if Royal Moody knew about this visit; if, in fact, the district attorney was *officially* offering a deal, of if *she* was, all on her own. They both understood that anywhere other than a small town like Murfee such a discussion wouldn't even be taking place, but this *was* Murfee, and she and Paez and Avalos shared language and cultural ties that extended across the river at the town's back; the same river that more than half of Murfee's citizens went back and forth over every day.

She shrugged, letting her silence answer for her. Paez stood up, smoothing out his tie with tiny gold suns on it, and said he'd think about it. He'd speak of it with his client and let her know.

Veremos . . . we'll see, he said, raising his hands skyward again.

He walked her to his office door, opened it for her, and asked if she might be interested in going out for a drink in the coming days. There was a new place in Artesia, a bar that was supposed to be quite good . . . *for Artesia*, he added with a laugh. She knew he had gone to law school in El Paso, but he acted as if he had been away to Houston or Dallas or even New York. He had no idea of the cities she had visited.

As she slipped on her sunglasses, she thanked him for his time, and asked him if his family in Presidio and San Angelo was well. When he mentioned the bar in Artesia again, a touch more insistent, she just smiled again . . .

Veremos . . . she finally said, as she walked past him and left him standing in the doorway.

SHE THEN WENT AND SAW TOMMY at Hancock Hill, and as she walked in, caught him trying to slip a *Penthouse* beneath the sheets. She'd brought him more books and magazines and cold beers, and sat with him for a bit, filling him in on the Bravo case. All of the deputies had been taking turns visiting him every day, so she really wasn't telling him much he didn't already know, and she could see that he was tired and listless and anxious. He was supposed to be discharged in another few days, but it'd be months before he could truly walk again, and maybe never quite the same. They wouldn't know until he started rehabbing his leg. Still, he was glad that she visited, and she held his hand while she talked to him, and when there was nothing more for either of them to say, she told him he could get back to his dirty magazines. He ogled her and raised his eyebrow up and down, told her she was hotter than any of the women in there, and that left her laughing as she left.

Finally, unable to avoid it anymore, she went and picked up Billy Bravo's body.

IT WAS LATE IN THE AFTERNOON when she left for Terlingua to meet Billy's girlfriend, Vianey. She had called the girl the day before to make sure she was staying out in Presidio, telling her it was safer for her to be with family and friends while they continued to look into Billy's death, but there was one more thing they could do together in Terlingua. *Two things.* The department was done with his trailer, so if there was something personal from it she wanted to take, that was fine. And they were also done with the body, so if she wanted that, it was hers as well.

Despite what Ben had threatened to Jesse Earl, there wasn't much hope they'd find any evidence on Billy. There wasn't a whole lot to suggest he'd ever put up any sort of fight. Still, his clothes and his nails had been scraped and a thousand pictures had all been taken, until Doc Hanson had said there was nothing left he could do with the body. Whatever story it might tell was finished, and he'd write it all down and let them know. Billy had been cremated at Pearl's Funeral Home, and she'd picked up the small box wrapped in plastic before leaving Murfee.

She rode with it in the front seat next to her and tried not to look at it, or the small brown bag next to it, while driving.

When she got to Terlingua, Vianey was already sitting outside on the stoop of Billy's place, smoking a cigarette and looking up at all the words people had spray-painted on the trailer. The little yard, what there was of it, was filled with upright beer cans and bottles, pushed hard into the dirt; standing tall at attention, like *soldados* on watch. There had been a party last night in Billy's memory and the people in town who knew him best and the other river guides he'd worked with had come out and toasted the life lost, writing remembrances on the skin of his home.

She'd passed a similar display where his body had been found, the ground now sporting a hundred bottles like dark flowers, half filled with the last of the day's sun.

She and Vianey stood together outside for a minute, silently reading the words people had sprayed there: *We love u Billy . . . Cross the next river . . . Follow the sun brother . . . See ya soon Bear . . .*

They didn't say much more, either, when they finally went inside the hot trailer.

For the next hour they looked through Billy's things, and although she'd found and set aside a Nike shoe box if there was anything Vianey wanted to keep, nothing went into it.

Still . . .

There was Billy's collection of arrowheads he'd found while out on the river, and a small ashtray of blood-dark musket balls.

There was a bunch of small notebooks of his sketches. None of them were particularly good, just good enough that America could make out what he'd intended—a butte or a mesa lorded over by a perfect round sun; a long-legged *pájaro*, head dipped down toward the water; a bear peering through broken grass; a girl who was not Vianey with a tattoo of a dragon over her shoulder.

There was a Mason jar full of old concert and movie ticket stubs, crushed together like a hand squeezing dry leaves, many over ten years old.

A dream catcher with blue and purple feathers hanging just over the bed.

A knife without a grip, just a naked blade still bright.

A small gift wrapped in Christmas paper, long faded and never opened.

There were dozens of old pictures of people neither of them knew, in places they didn't recognize; one of a small boy, hair a mess, standing on a carpet of green grass, holding a fishing line that dangled a catfish. The boy was half trapped in shadow, the legs beneath his shorts tan, and the arms gangly and sticking out at angles from the sleeves of a thick-striped T-shirt. Because of how his face was split by sun and shade, it was hard to see if he was smiling or not. Someone had written something on the back of the picture, but the words were long ago smudged away.

And last, there was a more recent photo, of Vianey, her arms raised toward the camera, hiding the full, naked curve of her breasts; her head thrown back, laughing. The image was spotted with drops of sunlight, like drops of rain, and it was a good picture, natural. The girl in it was far more beautiful and alive than the girl standing next to America in the trailer. Vianey looked at it for a long time, as if seeing herself for the first time, before slipping it, along with the photo of the small boy, into her jeans pockets.

America took the rest of the pictures and the notebooks and dumped them into the box she'd set out and carried it outside, where she poured it all into Billy's grill, and Vianey lit it on fire with one of her endless cigarettes.

And then, just like before, when they'd read the words on the outside of the trailer, they stood silent together, watching those things burn.

Vianey may have been crying, or she may not.

Ben liked to go on and on about how people never changed, or couldn't change—not for the better, anyway—but America wasn't so sure. Maybe she *felt* like she needed to believe otherwise, because Azahel Avalos was sitting up in the Big Bend County jail, acting as if he knew something about what *she'd* been and the things *she'd* done. And she didn't really want to accept that Billy Bravo had died because of his past mistakes—few people deserved to die like he had outside the Wikiup—and in the years since he'd settled in the Big Bend, he'd worked hard to be a better person in spite of that past. The words spray-painted on his trailer seemed to prove that. Had he done enough? *Y ¿qué importaba de todos modos?* Maybe you could never completely leave your past behind, but if that was true, it was just as true that there were things you could never quite take with you, either.

Arrowheads and musket balls and dream catchers and old presents.

A picture of a boy catching his first fish.

Someone like the girl standing next to her, watching sketches and pictures and memories burn.

Y ¿qué importaba de todos modos?

She thought about Duane Dupree and the money under her bed and Azahel Avalos, while she waited for Billy's things to become ashes and embers. And after those went cold, she scooped them into the shoe box.

Then she and Vianey got into her truck and followed Terlingua Creek down to where it met the river.

. . .

THEY PARKED AND GOT OUT with both boxes and the brown bag, walking until they found a place where the reeds were pulled free—a curved patch of sand like the moon, where people slipped canoes in and out of the river. The area was wide and flat, the sun slanting low and orange against it, and the drought-low water of the river moved like a snake, thick, its skin brown and pebbled.

Crickets filled the silence, making the air tremble and hum, and big *libélulas* in a thousand colors hovered as still as the water below them.

She asked Vianey if she wanted to say something and she nodded. She gently took the box holding Billy's ashes and held it out over the water . . .

Santa Muerte, te convoco. Santa Muerte, te invoco. Dame justicia, justicia contra mis enemigos . . . justice against those who hurt and harm me. Santa Muerte, hear my cries, punish my enemies, as only you can punish them. Santa Muerte, you know that I am not an evil person, this is a problem only you can fix. Use your scythe to cut down my enemies, as they had me pushed down to the ground, and you gave me a hand to stand back up. Cut them to the ground, Santa Muerte, thank you for your protection, thank you for your help, thank you for hearing my cry . . . Amén.

It wasn't the Catholic prayer America expected or knew from her own childhood, it was instead a plea to Nuestra Señora de la Santa Muerte, the female skeleton wrapped in robes and carrying a scythe, the woman called Saint Death. Even in Murfee, her worship had increased over the years, brought over the river from all the small towns like Valverde, Nueva Holanda, Potrero del Llano. She was popular with the poor and the narcos because they believed in her ability to grant miracles and to ensure a path to the afterlife. America didn't know much about it, but the prayer Vianey had offered had nothing to do with Billy's soul.

It was a prayer of protection . . . and revenge.

After she finished, Vianey shook open the original box and watched Billy's ashes spin and scatter over the river, held aloft by a slight wind. America did the same with the shoe box of burned photos and drawings, and for several seconds all of it mingled together in the air, a white cloud drifting down into the water below.

America then took the brown bag and opened it, revealing a small black and silver revolver: a Taurus 85 .38 Special. When she and Ben had originally searched Billy's trailer, they'd recovered several guns, all makes and models and spanning decades, most of them unregistered or unlicensed. All of them were still locked away safely at the department, except this one.

Last night, America had checked and double-checked the .38, cleaning the barrel and the cylinder the way Ben had shown her, and taping the plastic grip so it would be even easier to hold.

She gave it to Vianey, making sure she understood how it worked so she wouldn't blow her hand off. She'd almost replaced the original rounds with the federal hollow-points the department issued, but had thought better of it. She told Vianey to carry it with her for a while, just to be sure. She also reminded her again to stay out of Terlingua and stay close to Presidio, or even cross the river, and wrote down her personal number. She made Vianey promise to call her if she had worries about anything . . . *cualquier cosa.*

It was in that moment, awkwardly holding the gun in one hand and America's phone number on a business card in the other—looking out over the brown water going black with the sinking sun—that Vianey's tears finally came. America hadn't been sure before, but she was now.

She left Vianey there and walked back toward her truck.

And the whole time they'd been standing on the riverbank, she hadn't seen a single silver flash of *un pescado* in the water.

THE VERY FIRST STARS were hanging on the horizon as she drove away from Terlingua, many of them caught on the mountain peaks. Other than a quick text from Ben letting her know they had gotten to Lubbock, she hadn't heard anything else from him or the sheriff. She didn't think that was good . . . there was no way it could be. If nothing else, it meant they weren't getting home until very late tonight, maybe tomorrow.

She toyed with the idea of driving into Killing, but both Ben and the sheriff had been very clear about not wanting her down there, and although their concerns were silly, *tonterías*, she didn't want to hurt the investigation. But if the sheriff was right, and if the Lubbock trip was going as bad as she was afraid it was, there might not be an investigation anymore, anyway.

She didn't know what she thought about that. Much like the question of whether you could change or should even try to, she wasn't sure what she was *supposed* to think about it. She didn't know if there was a right answer, or if there ever could be one, but she didn't feel ready yet to let Billy Bravo's murder go that easily.

She'd heard Vianey's prayers by the river. She'd made similar prayers of her own when Rodolfo had disappeared, and right or wrong, they'd been answered.

However, she did slow down at the turn-off for the old mining town, just for a heartbeat, but that way was deeply shadowed, already lost beneath the mesas and the setting sun. She passed by a flood gauge sign, a familiar sight across the washes and low areas of the Big Bend, this one set to measure the rising water from Alamito Creek if it ever rained again and the creek filled, but it was dusty as the dirt it stood in. The wooden sign had two ragged bullet holes in it, at the three-foot and five-foot mark, and the dying sun winked at her through them.

Almost like eyes, watching her.

And if there were lights already on in Killing, she was too far away to see.

17

It was Dyer who talked, slow and steady, while Stackpole sat next to him, looking at nothing.

"I knew Danny's daddy years back when we came up through the ranks together. Robert Ford was a good man and a damn fine Ranger, a legend in his own way. Back in the summer of '99 he was investigating a bank robbery in Roscoe, Nolan County, and putting the squeeze on a wannabe biker named Daryl Lynch, who owned a strip club outside of Sweetwater called the Aces High. Daryl had snitched for Bob before, and word was he could put names and faces to the Roscoe robbery. One of them was supposed to be John Wesley Earl." Dyer waved at the spot where Earl's picture had rested on the table.

"Bob Ford was shot down on a highway outside of Sweetwater. Left there to bleed out, leaving behind a wife and his young boy, Danny. Me and a bunch of others worked the hell out of it, but came up empty. It didn't help that the Aces High burned down a week after Bob's shooting, with Daryl Lynch inside it. We all figured Earl for the whole mess, the shooting and the fire, but he got sent up first on that *other* attempted murder beef Agent Nichols here talked about, so for most of us, it was done. It had to be."

"But not for Danny?" Harp asked.

"No, not for Danny." Dyer looked at a spot on the floor. "Imagine you're a nine-, ten-year-old boy, and you gotta deal with that? You need to figure out how to wrap your head and your hands around it and make sense out of it. Some do a fair bit better than others." Dyer breathed hard, like he was clearing dust out of his throat, and Chris thought about Jesse Earl, growing up the same as Danny without his father, for pretty much the same reasons. "So, you know, things were hard for him and his mom, Catherine, real hard. Danny joined the army as soon as he could, got some waiver to get in the second he turned seventeen. He had his mom sign off on it, and then just like that, he was gone. He went over to Afghanistan and did real well, if you can say such a thing about a place like that."

Dyer took a sip of water. "When he got back he joined DPS. He eventually wanted to be a Ranger, like his daddy. He worked his way up fast to the Criminal Investigation Division, and got himself assigned to a multiagency state task force created to crack down on these Aryan gangs and racist skinheads. That task force was a big deal, very high-profile, and Danny was right in the thick of it. He was shipped off to Tyler and then McKinney and then Ballinger, working his way into these groups. Danny was a born natural for undercover, and since all these wackos were always on the lookout for guns, the bigger the better, that became Danny's story, his *in* . . . that he was just out of the military and could still get grenades and rifles, that sort of thing. Like I said, he was a natural, and very, very good. Too good. He even got himself tattooed just like them, and then inked over later whatever he'd done. It was like writing and then erasing his damn skin, over and over again. I took issue with that, and said as much." Dyer's jaw clenched, like he was biting on something hard. "But it wasn't my call, and they bought him hook, line, and sinker, every damn time."

"And he knew all about Jesse Earl, right? Who he was, but more importantly, who he was related to?" Harp asked, before Chris could.

Dyer nodded. "Let's just say it came up, more than once. If you want to think that's why Danny pushed so hard to work that task force to begin with, I'm not going to argue with you. Even though CID has its own command, I still felt responsible for Danny because I brought him into DPS, and because of everything that had happened with Bob. I tried to keep an eye on him, even talked to his immediate supervisors, but it didn't help much, honestly. Then before he ever got close to Jesse, they had to pull him out anyway. Things went bad for him in Ballinger. This young pregnant girl was being used as a punching bag by some skinhead piece of shit she'd taken up with. Danny took exception to *that*, and put the man down, *hard*. The girl ended up going back home to her family in Austin, so I guess you could say Danny saved her and all, but still . . ."

"And the skinhead?" Chris asked.

"Well, he breathes okay, so long as you don't trip over any of his wires. It's fifty-fifty whether he'll ever wake up again, and those odds are going south every day. Danny was put on admin leave so that it could get sorted out. I made some calls and pulled some strings and took him in for light duty, had him filing paper in my command. The truth? We needed to get Danny sorted out. You lay in the gutter with folks like that, listen to them say that shit they do, all day every day, and you're going to get dirty. It's going to take more than a shower to wash it off." Dyer looked over at Nichols, weeks of long history passing in one glance. "Anyway, he would have been okay," Dyer kept on, almost as much to himself as to the others, "we'd have gotten him over what happened in Ballinger, and eventually, one day, he would have made the Rangers."

Chris could hear the sound of Dyer trying to convince himself of that. "Then why is he down in Killing now?"

Dyer look pained. "Because I had to tell him that Earl was getting out. That against all sense, that sonofabitch had made parole."

You need to figure out how to wrap your head and your hands around it, make some sense of it. Some do a fair bit better than others.

"But you didn't know Earl had cut a deal, did you? You didn't know anything about that at all." Chris turned back and forth between Dyer and the still-silent Stackpole, then Nichols, who was looking down at one of his phones. "Then Danny hears his father's killer is now a free man and—"

Dyer stepped in. "Like I said, he didn't *hear* about it, hell, I told him. He needed to know. And right after I did, he turned in his badge and gun that day. Two weeks later I get word from that task force that he's in Lubbock, trying to get in with Jesse's bunch again . . . this time all on his own."

"And he did," Harp finished for him.

"It seems he did, hook, line, and sinker. Earl's testimony, the RICO case, this thing now with Flowers, is all federal. We had nothing to do with it and didn't know anything about it, at least I didn't. That only came out to me later." Another long glance in the direction of Nichols, who was holding his phone and stared back without blinking, without any emotion at all. "As far as we know, Danny still doesn't know a damn thing about it."

Harp shrugged. "And now he's not taking your calls. I get it. But he's been with Earl for a few weeks now, and if the boy isn't over his daddy, why hasn't he just put a bullet in him and be done with it?" Harp looked to the other men at the table as if that was a perfectly acceptable solution.

And there was a lot Chris could say about *revenge*, how it could be as strong and cold as the ocean's tides, and so much worse when it involved the lightless and deep mysteries between some fathers and their sons. How then it truly was unfathomable, unknowable. He'd caught only the very end of Caleb Ross's struggle with Sheriff Ross, but that had been going on for years before Caleb had decided to end it with a bullet. John Wesley Earl was not Danny's father, but what was it like to finally stand in the presence of the man who'd taken away the only father you'd ever known?

"We never proved that Earl killed Bob Ford, and during all the long

talks he was so eager and willing to have with Agent Nichols here"—
Dyer pointed at Nichols, who had put his phone down but didn't seem
inclined to add anything—"I guess it just never came up. I'd bet all my
money and yours, too, that Earl was the shooter, but *knowing* isn't the
same as proving it. I expect Danny wants to hear it from Earl's mouth
himself. No matter what he's been through, or what's going through
his head now, Danny's decent. He isn't a cold-blooded murderer."

"And when, or if, he hears some sort of confession or admission from
Earl, then what?" Chris asked. "Is that when he finally decides it is okay
to shoot him? Are all of you just hoping you don't find yourselves tripping over Earl's wires in my hospital?"

"Well, he's no murderer," Dyer said, and gave Nichols a raw smile.
"But he's no saint."

Nichols finally joined in again. "So you can see, Sheriff Cherry, like
I'm sure the major relayed on the phone . . . it's complicated."

Chris laughed. "It appears, Agent Nichols, that *you're* the one making
it complicated. You have a serious problem being forthcoming. You do
like your secrets. You didn't tell anyone in DPS about your deal with
Earl, and you didn't tell me about the little operation you're running in
my county until you absolutely had to." Chris waved at the files and
folders. "What are you calling this thing, anyway? I'm sure it has a
name, like the others you showed me. I might as well know what I'm
getting myself into, or is that a secret, too?"

"It's not about secrets, Sheriff, it's about operational security." Nichols thought about it, and then shrugged, relenting. "But if it matters to
you, we call it Sol Blanco. White Sun."

THEY TALKED for another hour, maybe two.

Chris started to see it slowly, like something ominous taking shape
out of early-morning fog, or surfacing from that ocean he'd been imagining a few minutes before. They weren't actually talking about Billy

Bravo's murder in Terlingua anymore; that had been set aside as a distraction and a nuisance. Center stage now was this never-ending argument between the Texas Ranger and the federal agent, and Chris and Harp were the audience—bystanders—or even worse, the tie-breaking votes. Dyer wanted to rescue Danny a second time, *pull him out* again, like he'd done in Ballinger. He wanted Danny to know that Earl was untouchable, and that made Nichols understandably nervous, since Danny might take that knowledge and just go ahead and pull the trigger then anyway. After all his hard work, Nichols had to live with the fear that this Danny Ford was going to upset all the knives he had spinning above his head. The agent had probably contemplated a hundred ways of spiriting him out of Killing, few of them feasible, and none that didn't run the risk of scaring off Jesse Earl and Flowers. He'd probably even turned over the idea, more than once, of just outing Danny to Earl, but couldn't bring himself to do that without first having Flowers in his sights—because no matter what he said or how sure of himself he pretended to be, Nichols didn't quite trust the old outlaw, either. He had no idea what Earl would do if he did figure out Danny was recently a cop, and more important, the bitter son of a Texas Ranger he may or may not have murdered.

Chris even sympathized with Major Dyer and his concerns for Danny, but as much as he didn't like Nichols or his secrets or his juggling act, he also didn't envy the responsibility and the calls the young agent was being forced to make. Day by day, almost minute by minute, and all the people he had to answer to who *weren't* in the room, although their presence was heavy and just as real, as real as the phones Nichols had in front of him and kept constantly checking. Chris couldn't help wondering if Earl was on the end of one of them, too.

At the end, Nichols showed them more photos, gave them names of other people who should be in Killing with Earl, and made sure that Chris had several cell numbers to get ahold of him anytime, day or night.

And then it was over.

But when they got up to leave, breaking into their own groups with Nichols left standing alone, Chris wasn't sure what, if anything, had been decided. Nichols wanted Chris and his people to leave the Bravo investigation alone if it pointed toward Killing, and keep him in the loop about any of the Earls' movements if it brought them into Murfee. But for the moment, it was still simply a request, a professional courtesy he'd been reluctantly forced to extend. It could become an order, though, one with sharp teeth. That was easy, and all it would take was a call from one of those phones.

That was the only damn thing that was really clear.

Major Dyer finally had Stackpole, who in all the time still hadn't said a word, walk them out.

No one shook Nichols's hand, and he didn't offer it.

THEY'D CLEARED THE BUILDING and were walking to their truck with Stackpole still in tow, when Harp suddenly turned toward the Ranger.

"Dammit, Rodney, it's been a long time." For the second time that day, Harp grabbed the hand of the other man, who smiled back wide.

The Ranger nodded. "Don't I know it? I knew you had left Midland PD, and then I heard about your wife, right? Damn shame, I'm so sorry about that. Word was you were down in Murfee, but I had trouble believing it. Then you were calling around from down there about John Wesley Earl, and that stirred things all up, and when the major said we were meeting with Sheriff Cherry here, I figured you'd come along. I told the major you'd be here, and I was right. I also told him all about you, that you were good people. One of us."

Chris stared back at Harp. "You two *know* each other?"

Harp grinned. "Yeah, Rodney and I worked together before, back when he was CID like Danny Ford." Harp released the Ranger's hand but clapped him on the shoulder, glancing back to the bank building, as if to make sure Nichols wasn't standing at a window, watching them. "I recognized him straight off when we walked in, but thought I would let it play out."

"I'm glad you did," Stackpole said. "Nichols doesn't know we have history, and the major won't tell him. But he wants me to ask your help in getting Danny out of there. Whatever you have to do, just get him out."

Chris stepped in, pointing at the lieutenant. "You sat there and didn't open your goddamn mouth for hours, and this is what you're saying now?" All that fog back in the room suddenly cleared away, burned off by the late afternoon sun above them.

Stackpole looked pained, and turned to Harp for help. "Sheriff, I get it, I do, but it's the major. He and Danny go way back, and he can't just stand by and let it go down bad for him. Sooner or later, Earl and Danny are going to make each other for what they really are."

"Or Nichols is just going to up and tell Earl," Harp added, echoing Chris's earlier thoughts. "Nichols can't risk his golden goose getting a bullet behind the ear from Danny, but what can he do? He doesn't want Flowers to slip through his fingers, either."

Stackpole agreed. "Nothing good can come out of it either way. Nichols doesn't see Danny as a lawman anymore. He's a civilian. An obstacle, a problem."

"But he *is* a civilian. He quit. He walked out, nobody walked out on him," Chris said. "You do understand he may not want to be helped?"

Stackpole reached into his pocket, pulling out a DPS badge—round and gold with the state of Texas in the center—not the "star in the wheel" silver badge of the Rangers. "This was Danny's. According to the major, it *still* is. All he's got to do is get out of Killing and leave Earl and the rest of them to the feds. He needs to come home. You know how it is, once you pick it up, you can't ever put it down again. Not really. Please give it to him and remind him of that. That you're always a lawman, no matter what."

Harp touched Chris's arm. "Danny doesn't know he needs our help, but we do."

Chris hesitated, took it, let it weigh out in his hand, and thought about Harp, who had taken up a badge and gun again to work for him, *to help him*, long after his duty was done. And how a year ago he'd stood outside Duane Dupree's burned-down house, under a hot and heavy sun . . . *sol blanco* . . . not much different from the one above him now, and put a similar heaviness into Amé's hands.

He'd done it several times since: for Dale Holt and Tommy Milford and the others.

Always a lawman . . .

Chris closed his fist around the badge, but didn't put it away. He didn't have an answer for Stackpole, not yet. He wanted to hold on to it for a while, on the whole drive back to Murfee. Instead, he turned to Harp.

"Let's go home."

18

Chris came in late. Mel had told him he could stay in Lubbock for the night—that she was okay with it—but she knew he didn't like leaving her alone out at the Far Six, and the truth was, she didn't like it, either. So she was still awake, watching TV and not really reading the open book in her lap, when he walked through the door looking tired, run-down. It had been a long day and only part of it had anything to do with the drive. He said Ben had bothered him the whole way back about getting her those damn dogs, or that maybe it was time to have a child or two running around out here, so she'd have some company . . . someone to take care of.

She told Chris she already did.

EVEN GETTING IN at the hour he did, he woke up before her, when dawn was still just a bleeding edge on the horizon, so that she found him later sitting out on the porch, writing in one of those yellow pads of his. It was his black coffee that had finally roused her, the hard, smoky smell of it, and she poured herself what was left in the pot and came out to join him. Something was bothering him, and there was a time, not all that long ago, when he would have kept silent about it and held it all in. But that time had passed, just like Sheriff Ross and Duane Dupree, and she knew he'd share it if she was patient. She stood back and waited for the sun, waiting for *him*, when she realized Chris had put his pad down and was bouncing something in his hand . . . a doorknob.

"Came off in the bathroom, got to get it fixed, I guess. Goddamn, babe, just one more thing." He tossed it to her and she caught it one-handed, not spilling her mug.

She turned it over, gave it a good look. "Oh, Chris, I can fix this, don't worry about it." She slipped it into the pocket of her robe and went back to sipping her coffee. The porch boards beneath them creaked, the only sound at all, since what little wind there might be for the day hadn't woken up yet, either. Something, maybe an owl, turned on a wing and circled down into the ocotillo ahead of the rising sun, and the whole of the sky was empty and clean, momentarily colorless, unmarked by man or anything else. Chris looked like he might reach for his pad again, but thought better of it.

"Babe, I think I got a bit of a mess with this whole Terlingua thing . . . Billy Bravo's murder. And I don't think my meeting in Lubbock helped. In fact, I think it made it a helluva lot worse. Harp warned me that it would, and by God, if he wasn't right." He was looking out toward the mountains, where it was still dark, where it had the look of a place that could stay dark forever.

She waited a few heartbeats and took another sip of her coffee. Then, putting a hand on his shoulder, "You want to talk about it?"

And he did.

He told her all about Danny Ford and John Wesley Earl and the FBI agent Austin Nichols, who, from the sound of it, she wasn't sure she'd like if she ever met in person. He told her about standing in the bank parking lot with Lieutenant Stackpole and the badge Chris still had in yesterday's jeans, draped over the old leather chair in their bedroom. He told her about the drive back with Ben and the debates they had about what they were going to do, if anything.

She heard enough to know that when all was said and done, Chris had an idea in his head of what he *wanted* to do, he just wasn't sure he should go through with it. And *that's* what had gotten him out of bed so early in the morning, and had probably kept him up most of the night. It was probably that frustration more than anything else that had really pulled that silly doorknob free . . .

She didn't say much until he was done and had lapsed into another silence. He'd talked long enough that his coffee had gotten cold, and he poured it off the porch into the caliche.

"We both know you aren't going to let it go, Chris. You aren't going to let that young man hurt himself or anyone else. Not after what you did for Caleb Ross. It's not in you." It was the first time she'd said Caleb's name in a year, and she knew she didn't even have to. Caleb was already, always, on Chris's mind.

"It's not my problem. It's Dyer's, and Nichols's. Hell, they created it."

"Chris Cherry, you're not really trying to convince yourself of that, so don't try to convince me." She poured out the last bit of her coffee, too. "You once stood out here before the house was up and said *as far as the eye can see, that's my responsibility*. Now, maybe you said it to impress me, or to get me to agree to live out here with you, or just because you were hoping to have a little fun that night, and I guess two out of three ain't bad." She laughed. "But those were your words, not mine." She caught him smiling. "You believed them then, and you do now. If you can stop something bad before it gets a whole lot worse, isn't that your responsibility, too?" She didn't have to add her own words: *before you get a call about another body*.

"Maybe I need to put a star on you and make *you* a deputy." He shook his head, tired and frustrated, but smiling at her all the same. "But we did have a whole lot of fun that night, didn't we?"

"Yes, Sheriff, we did." She put her arms around him and pulled him out of his chair. "Let's have some more . . ."

SHE TOOK HIM BACK INSIDE, slid her robe off with nothing underneath, and let him have a good long look, before she pulled off his T-shirt and peeled his shorts down to the floor. They fell together into their bed, which, like their coffee, had gone cold, as static lightning played on them beneath sheets that drifted cloudlike over their heads, settling softly against their skin. She guided him into her and said his name and rolled beneath him to give him everything and to let him know there was no part of her he didn't know, that he couldn't have if he wanted it, and she put her face into his chest and shoulder and moved along with him. He was slow, still tired from the long day before and the longer night that had followed, but she felt his strength return as he stayed tight against her, and when the sweat broke free on their skin and he was finally saying her name, over and over again, both bodies arching, she ran her hands all around him and held him as tight as she could so as not to lose a single drop of him, not afraid anymore to have her fingers brush against the bullet wounds that were still there and always would be.

Just like she would . . .

She thought at some point that the sun would finally come up, that dawn light would heat up their room even more than they had. But as they lay against each other after they were done, Chris finally falling back asleep, the moment remained blessedly dark, as if the sun was kind enough to wait just for them . . .

WHEN SHE GOT UP SOMETIME LATER, Chris was just coming out of the shower. He'd laid out new jeans and a shirt and badge and gun on that old leather chair.

He bent down to kiss her, dropping water from his still-wet hair onto her face, onto her eyelashes, and the sun that had waited on them before was out in full force, burning holes into the bare wood floor.

"I need to get in to the office and call Royal Moody for a favor. I hate doing it, and he'll raise hell about it, but . . ." Chris trailed off, letting the rest of that thought go. He put on the fresh jeans. "You think this heat's finally going to break?" he asked. He didn't say anything more about what they had talked about before the sun had come up. He was done with it, whatever it was had been decided, and there would be no more talking about it or second-guessing it. That was the new Chris, who had survived the Far Six.

"I saw something on the weather yesterday. We may get some rain in a week or so."

He buttoned up his shirt over his scars and looked down at his badge, before clipping it onto his belt.

"Well, we're going to need it, a real good thunderstorm to wash all this damn heat and dust away."

19

I'm trying to hide a gun when Jesse walks up on me.

I've been doing this for a couple of weeks now, slipping a piece here and there around the Killing property. Earl really doesn't want anyone other than himself walking around with a gun, although they have more than they can keep track of; T-Bob mostly, and it's one of his old S&W 929s that I took out of the RV, wrapped in burlap, and am now wedging beneath a span of rusted car hood on the bluff behind the house. It's the same spot where I always see Earl standing, smoking, and making phone calls because the reception is good, and I'm curious about what he's doing up here. *What does he see?*

Wondering, maybe, if he's hiding things like me.

With no rain, his boot prints are still visible, thin and ghostly in the dust. Not much walking around, just standing, looking south, toward the mountains. He takes his bike out there early some mornings, but the ground's not good for a Low Rider like his. That's hard riding and there's nowhere to go anyway, or at least nothing I've found.

I hear Jesse and smell his cigarette before I see him, so I'm already standing up when he calls me out.

"Danny, what you doin' up here?" he says to my back, because I still haven't turned around. I'm counting the possible number of steps between us in my head and how fast I can close that space if I have to.

When I do turn, he's not staring at me at all, but down at the old car hood. It looks like a Bonneville, like the rest of the car sank right into the dust and this pitted piece of metal is all that's left to see, but he doesn't comment on it. I still don't like the way he's looking at it. "You're getting to be like my daddy, creepin' around, keeping to yourself. Makes me nervous." He flicks ash and kicks at the dirt.

"It's nothing, Jess. I just get cooped up with everyone all the time. You know how it is."

"Yes, I s'pose I do. That's why you shoulda been coming into Terlingua with me and T-Bob when we had the chance. Getting a drink, getting outta all this, at least for a little while." He waves his hand with the cigarette at the empty desert circling Killing. I don't bother to remind him there will be no more trips anywhere. His daddy will put a stop to that, if he has to chain Jesse to the bumper of the RV parked out front.

Jesse smokes silently for a bit, looking back between me, the car hood, and the mountains. He's got his father's brains and his eyes so I wonder what he got from his mother, though Jesse doesn't talk about her, and Earl doesn't, either, for that matter. There was nothing about her in all the police files I read. Jesse's brother, Little B, is Earl and Sunny's boy, and I do know quite a bit about her. She's got a decent criminal record and did some time of her own, and has been hooked up with Earl off and on for over twenty years. She had Little B in that window between Earl's two stints behind bars, when he also found the time to kill my father, and she and T-Bob raised him; Jesse, too, more or less, who also spent a lot of time bouncing around on his own. T-Bob has this thing for Sunny and he gets nervous when Earl treats her bad, the same way he does with how Earl treats his sons. He won't raise a hand against his brother, though, and turns to the bottle instead. It was through T-Bob that Jesse somehow first heard of Thurman Flowers, a man he now considers more of a father than Earl himself.

The strain between Jesse and his daddy is like grit in my mouth; dry, so thick I sometimes think I'm going to choke on it. For the last couple of years, Jesse's had his own thing going, trying to build something with Flowers. Most of those down in the house are supposed to be *his* people, but then Earl made parole and showed up. Now we all know where the real weight is settled.

Earl is like gravity, a black star; bending light . . . *bending us.* Hard and unforgiving and pulling everything toward him.

Earl is the only one keeping me around now, although I tell myself I have a choice in the matter; trying hard to convince myself there's some greater good in me at work. I can't escape Earl's gravity, even though I could walk out of Killing at any moment. None of them would raise a hand to stop me, least of all Jesse. Maybe the friction I feel isn't even between Jesse and his daddy, but between Jesse and me. Maybe he's caught Jenna staring at me, or still resents that brawl at the skinhead party that went down in front of Earl. But I really think it all comes down to his daddy, that black star we're all falling into. The more Earl relies on me and confides in me, the less Jesse wants to, and the more he looks to pick fights with both of us. It doesn't help that the big guns and ordnance I've promised haven't come through, and he's beginning to realize they probably never will.

We both know I'm lying about it, he just doesn't know why, and that's worked its way under his already thin skin. His suspicions about me and my relationship with Earl are probably the only thing keeping me alive, but it's also what's going to kill me in the end. He's going to be washing *my* blood off his hands, like the morning after Terlingua.

Jesse blows smoke. "I spoke to Thurman. He and Clutts will be here in three, four days, on the outside."

"That's good, real good," I say. Clutts is Marvin Clutts, Flowers's right-hand thug. I only know him from intelligence reports.

"Things are gonna be different then, you know that, right? Thurman will have his folks . . ."

"Like Clutts?"

Jesse stares at me, like he's sizing me up for a hole in the ground.

"There will be more than Clutts, a lot more, soon. We're gonna buy all this up, acre by acre, make it ours."

This is a familiar story. I've heard it all before, and I'm not in the mood for one of Jesse's white power rants today, but he's not going to let it go.

"We've got plans, Danny, Thurman and me. What's that they say, build it and they will come? You can't hide out here on this hill away from it. You don't get a pass, no one here does. No matter what my daddy says, he can't give you one . . . and he don't get one, either."

"Then you better take it up with him, I guess. I said I'm working on it. Men I know are stationed up at Fort Bliss in El Paso, just like I said. They're going to get you what you want, it just takes time. If you can do it faster on your own, then go ahead. Either way you're going to need money. A lot of it."

Jesse nods, slow. The money is a sore point with him and it comes up again and again in his arguments with Earl. Flowers is pushing him about it, too. They both believe Earl's got money stashed away from his time in prison, or even from before that, maybe from the bank job my father was investigating that cost him his life. "Okay, Danny-Boy, okay. You say you're working on it? Keep working. But unless you have that shit buried out here, right now, you're just wasting time. *My* fuckin' time."

He hits a little too close to home. "I got it, Jess, loud and clear."

Then, surprising me, he takes a few steps toward the car hood and me. Jesse is not one for a face-to-face fight. It's not his way. "Guess this place reminds you of being over in that shithole on the other side of the world, right?"

I tense up as he moves closer, pretending to look out toward the mountains; the wide desert and a small switchback road cut into the scrub that I've seen Earl churn into dust with his bike. Jesse steps through my shadow, keeps coming. "Well," I counter, "*that* shithole was a lot nicer than this place. You sure picked a helluva spot to build your king-dom on earth."

Jesse flicks away his cigarette and bends down where I was kneeling moments before, like he's going to search around for whatever I was doing. He grins. "Location, location, location, right? Land is cheap, Danny-Boy . . . land is . . ."

His hand reaches out . . .

"I wouldn't do that." I cut him short and point to the ground around the hood. "I thought I saw a rattler a second ago, curled up under there, heard it, too. Sounded big."

He laughs, but holds up, his hand suspended and still. "Sounded big? You can tell that, huh? More of that high-speed army training shit?"

"No, but I had family in Sweetwater, where they hold the largest damn rattlesnake roundup in the world every year. I've seen a few."

Jesse is still hunched over like he's almost hanging in the air. I'm unsure of what he's going to do, and maybe he is, too, until we hear Earl walking up the hill, calling out for us. *Both* of Jesse's hands are now out, reaching right toward where I slipped that 929, but he pulls them back and acts as if he was always just fishing another cigarette out of his shirt pocket.

He stands, lights up, and looks back toward his father walking toward us.

"Guess we don't want anyone to get snake-bit out here, do we?"

WE'RE STANDING TOGETHER, silent, as Earl comes up. I can tell by the way his neck is corded he's pissed, grinding his teeth together in his skull, chewing on whatever's angered him. He's wearing a button-down shirt that's come all undone, untucked, and it flaps open like wings, revealing the ink all over his chest and stomach. So much of it, you can't even tell there's skin underneath. That stomach that's always been strong enough for killing is starting to sag, and the once powerful prison muscles slabbed over his chest are falling in, too, giving him a small set of tits. Beneath the harsh lamp of the sun, his face is deeply lined, and his slick-backed pompadour is showing all of its flat gray. More than any other moment since I've been with him, Earl *looks* old. Killing is making him older. Every damn one of his miserable years is there for both me and his son to see.

Jesse's smiling at him, fake-curious. "What's got you all spun up, JW?" It's the question of someone who already knows the answer.

Earl stands clenching and unclenching his fists. "I just talked to Jenna and she says you got a call today from that sheriff in Murfee? Is that right?" He looks at me as if I knew it and hadn't said anything, but Jesse hasn't breathed the word *Murfee* since I drove him and T-Bob back from town.

I never even told Earl how Jesse had me circle the place, just staring at it.

"Yeah, when we was up there a few days back, they wanted a way to contact us. You said to be cooperative, right? You said don't give 'em no reason to come back down here, so I gave 'em Jenna's number and forgot all about it. But I'll be damned if one of 'em didn't call today. I think it was the sheriff himself, leaving a message that he had that warrant for me an' T-Bob . . . for our damn blood or something. They'd threatened that when we first talked to them and I thought it was all bullshit, but I guess it wasn't so empty a threat after all. He was polite, though, the way he asked us to come up again to take care of it."

Earl goes very still, but his neck is tense, his teeth clenched. "So, were you gonna tell me this?"

Jesse takes a long draw on his cigarette before answering, enjoying Earl's anger. "Well, I *was*, but I guess I don't have to now. Goddamn bitch can't hold her tongue." He points at his daddy with the cigarette. "*You* were the one told us to go up there in the first place. *You* told us to talk to 'em, make nice, and be all helpful. Now look what it got me, more fucking shit. So there's no cause to be all pissy about it."

Earl pops his neck, then his knuckles. "Dammit, boy, it's what it got *us*. You know why I said that. The guns and the other shit we got down here, not to mention a houseful of felons and peckerwood ex-cons? It's not gonna take much to throw me back in, or stir up a shit storm for you and everyone else. You want all that, with your friend Flowers on his way?"

I'm still here, but neither are talking or looking at me anymore. It's like Earl's arguing with a younger ghost, the man he used to be. Arguing with himself in a dark mirror.

"Well, first off, you ain't in no position to call me *boy*, and haven't been in a while, *Daddy*." Jesse spits the last word and flips his cigarette end over end. "Second, if you are all so worried about it, you don't have to stay. No one invited you, remember? You just fuckin' showed up one day, and ain't none of us was waiting for you. You been dead and gone for twenty years in that hole. You're only here 'cause I let you be, and 'cause I'm fine with it. But you keep telling me what to do and not do, and I'm not gonna be fine with it much longer."

Earl smiles, all shark teeth. "That's right, I forgot, you're all grown now."

Jesse smiles back twice as hard. "Have been for a while."

Earl laughs in his son's face. "Okay, okay, here's what's gonna happen. I'm gonna think on this for a day or so, but I'm guessing you and T-Bob *are* gonna have to go and do this thing. You're gonna do it, and then you're gonna pray when it's done they don't find your goddamn blood or whatever it is all over that spic lover you got sideways with—"

Jesse yells, his voice echoing in the emptiness. "We already did it your way. You said it would go away and it hasn't, so now we're gonna do it how I want to."

Earl goes on, not missing a beat or drawing a breath. "You even know who that sheriff is? Sheriff Chris Cherry? He's some kinda hero, was in the paper for gunnin' down a bunch of beaners and damn near died in the process. Make no mistake, he is the goddamn law around these parts, so you're gonna honor his warrant and we're all gonna hope they don't find anything, because if they do, the last thing you'll have to fuckin' worry about is the law." Earl's calm again, his eyes flat, featureless, like most of the desert around us. It feels like a storm blew in and then blew out again, just as fast, leaving electricity in its wake. "I'll burn this whole place to the ground, Jesse. By the Devil I swear I will. I ain't goin' back in for your stupidity. I ain't havin' it. Not now. I gotta take my share of the blame for how you turned out, but I ain't takin' the blame for this."

Jesse breathes through his nose, mouth open. "That's fuckin' rich. Goddamn rich, coming from you. That supposed to be a threat?"

"No, boy, that's just the way it is. The way it's gotta be. You listen to me now and things will be okay. I promise. But if you don't . . ." Earl shrugs, leaving the rest unsaid.

Jesse spits on the ground. "Fuck you, old man. Fuck you to hell. You keep talking and talking. Something happened to you down in that hole. It was too damn long. The world's done passed you by. You shoulda stayed there, where you was still somebody. Out here, you don't mean shit, not anymore." And then, just like that, if there's any more fight in Jesse, it's gone now, too, like Earl's passing storm. He takes one last look at me, then back to his daddy, and turns his back on us both.

Earl watches him go and shakes his head. We're alone again, like the other morning after the deputies first came to Killing. He reaches in his own pocket and pulls out his matches and cigarettes from a crumpled soft-pack. He offers me one and I take it, and he lights it for me off of his own.

He holds up his cigarette, breathes on it, daring the end to brighten and burn. "There was a time inside when these were worth something, everything. A damn fortune. Trade 'em for just about anything." He puts it to his lips, draws hard, and the end turns to ash before it flares again. "Even a man's life."

I don't say anything, as we both watch Jesse make his way down the bluff. What is there to say? I'm standing beside the man who killed my own father, sharing one of his cigarettes. I can return the favor right now and walk off this hill like Jesse, but in the other direction, out toward that switchback road and the mountains.

Out into the desert, far away, and never look back.

I've had more than a few moments like this—where it's just me and him and no one else. No one close enough to stop me or make a difference. I can do it.

My muscles clench.

He's looking away from me, toward his real son.

The gun I was hiding is only an arm's length away . . .

I can make it . . . I can make it . . .

Breathe . . . relax . . . aim . . .

He speaks up, sudden. "I may need more of your help, Danny. No, I'm definitely gonna need your help, 'cause there's no one else around here I trust." He looks me right in the eye then, searching for something . . . for what, I don't know.

That stops me, shakes me.

"It's not just about me, you gotta see that. And you will see it. It's about all the rest of 'em. The girls, that boy Kasper. You're always talkin' to him, I know he looks up to you."

I reach for some words, something to say, so he won't keep looking me in the eye. "What do you need, JW? You want me to drive Jesse and T-Bob into town again for those warrants? Keep a watch on them?"

"Well, yeah, that's likely part of it," he answers, but that's not really what's on his mind, not at the moment, and whatever it is, he doesn't share. He turns back to where his son's disappeared, lost in the shade of the house, staring there, as if he's still looking for him.

When he does speak again, it's odd, unsettling. Like the stuff about the sheriff and Murfee and the maps he has me draw; a hint of things only he knows. And even in the heat, I go cold.

"If we don't do something, that boy is gonna be the death of you all . . ."

20

Jesse Earl often thought about his mama.

Not that he had any real memories or pictures of her, or anything at all to remind him of what she'd truly been like. His daddy had always called her *that whore* and left it at that, even if the words never quite matched the softer way he'd said them. But that left Jesse free to imagine her any damn way he pleased, so he did. Sometimes the life he dreamed up for her was good and clean and bright and a thousand miles away, just like a commercial or one of them reality TV shows Jenna liked so much, and that hurt like hell. But other times it wasn't much different from his shitty day-to-day, and that hurt, too, just in a different way. In *that* life, she was holed up in some rusted trailer in Beaumont or Waco, way too fat or way too thin, strung out or deep in the bottle like T-Bob, with someone else's shitty kids and a whole shitload of that someone else's problems to boot. But no matter what he dreamed, there was always a moment when he got to stand right up close to her and look her right in those eyes he didn't remember, and ask her what he, but more important, *his daddy*, had done so wrong to make her up and leave them in the first place.

He would never say that Sunny and T-Bob hadn't tried to do right by him; they'd done what little they could. And Flowers had always been there, too, a presence like a hand on his shoulder, eager and ready to listen. He'd had more talks with Thurman in the last fifteen years than he'd ever had with his daddy. But if he'd thought that was going to change with his daddy's surprise release from Walls, well, JW had quickly set him straight on that score. His daddy had no more interest in him or even Little B now than during all those years down that goddamn prison hole, when they'd never received so much as a letter or a phone call. It was like *they* didn't exist, like they'd been the ones who'd done something wrong and been sent off to serve the time, when Jesse knew they had done nothing more than have the bad fuckin' luck to be born to a man like JW. Their biggest mistake was being a couple of *his* mistakes—too much booze one night or fuckin' the wrong woman, *that whore*—which is why he wasn't gonna stand around now while his daddy and Danny talked it up like old friends on the bluff. Like father and son, and probably about *him*, too. Fuckin' Danny was about the only person in Killing his daddy didn't seem to mind so much, 'cause he was the only one who didn't remind JW of all the mistakes he'd made in his miserable-ass life, and that only pissed Jesse off all the more. It made no sense, or worse, it made all the sense in the world, but either way, there it was . . . all the fuckin' same.

Just like it made no sense that JW was the broke-ass nigger he pretended to be. Jesse *knew* he had money hidden around somewhere, and Flowers knew it, too, and their plans here for Killing were built on that belief. His daddy had been *someone* inside for a long time. He'd called shots, made shit happen, held other men's lives in his hands. It was like this shit with the Murfee sheriff and his deputies, that old man and that little wetback bitch. Not telling JW the sheriff had called for him had been partly spite, a way to give his daddy a little of his own medicine. But it had also been about fear, real fear that he'd fucked up royally this time. As long as those deputies weren't gonna let Terlingua go, JW wasn't going to let it go, either. There was a time when his daddy would never have let fuckers like these push him around. He never would have jumped just 'cause they called . . . he would have made them regret just raising their voice to him . . . but that man was either dead or had been left behind in the hole. His daddy, the man he was here and now, was scared of his own shadow, acting like a big pussy. And although JW liked to make it out that Jesse was the one who was stone-cold yellow, a big fuckin' coward (mostly, but not only, because of that damn fight in Lubbock), Jesse thought it was his daddy who was finally showing his true colors.

He wasn't sure if he actually hated the man or was just disappointed at what he'd become and all the things he wasn't, but some days that hate was strong as poison and today was one of 'em. Soon, though, Thurman was gonna show up and help set things straight; he felt just as strongly that it was JW who *owed* Jesse, and that it was finally time for JW to do some paying up.

And if JW couldn't afford to give Jesse the time of day, and there was no way to pay back all those years he'd been gone down that hole and the years Jesse had lost right along with him, then old JW could settle up in the cash he had hidden around. It wouldn't perfectly pay off Jesse's shitty life up to this point, but Jesse liked to think of it as a *down payment on his future.*

He'd heard that on one of Jenna's TV shows and had written it down.

There was another part of it, too; something Jesse would never admit to anyone, least of all Flowers, who wouldn't understand it. Jesse figured his daddy's debt started adding up the minute he ran off Jesse's mama, and the meter had been running ever since.

His daddy owed him for *that* most of all.

JESSE PAUSED AT THE BACK DOOR of the ranch house, taking one look back at his daddy and Danny still up there on the bluff. It didn't seem like they were talking at all, just staring out into the desert, standing almost shoulder to shoulder. From way back here, it looked like Jesse himself standing up there, but it wasn't. Danny had showed up weeks ago talking a big game and promising guns and shit, but all that had fallen to the wayside once JW had come into the picture. It was like Danny had just been looking for his own damn daddy all along.

Jesse knew that goddamn feeling.

He shut the door on 'em both.

Then he went to go look for Kasper and Little B. Shit was getting serious, and it was maybe time to find out exactly what that little wetback girl from the Wikiup knew . . .

21

Harp was sitting in his own car, not his department truck, watching Main Street and sipping a Coke with just a touch of Firestone & Robertson.

It was still *Jackie's* car, that's how he saw it. That's how it still *felt*. There were all her old grocery lists still in the center console, and in the glove compartment there was a lost earring—a hoop with a gold shamrock—that had never found its companion. The car still smelled like her. He couldn't help thinking of all the times she'd sat right here in this seat, taking another damn call from him; how something had come up at work, how he was going to be late . . . again. He imagined her talking to him on the phone but looking at herself in the rearview mirror, her hazel eyes getting older, wondering where all the years they were supposed to spend together were going. All those days, all those hours, forever lost behind her and disappearing in that mirror like whatever road she was driving on.

They'd never even owned a second car. There had never been a need, as long as he'd had a department patrol car or unmarked to drive.

He'd promised again and again that when he retired things were going to be different for them.

He'd promised her that.

He took another long sip.

Things definitely were.

BRIGHT AND EARLY the morning after they got back from Lubbock, Harp had caught Chris in his office reading up on the Aryan Brotherhood of Texas and Thurman Flowers and his Church of Purity. There was nothing church-like about it; it was just another dime-a-dozen white-power hate group. The sheriff had found videos somewhere online of Flowers's speeches or sermons, all sorts of things he'd written, and had gone through them all. Despite everything Nichols and Dyer had told them, Chris had checked and double-checked it all himself, trying to understand exactly who they were dealing with in Killing, and what Danny Ford had gotten himself into.

After Chris had finished with it, he'd left it piled up for Harp on the middle of *his* desk. But he hadn't looked through any of it. He didn't need to read that shit to know what sort of men Flowers and Earl were.

Harp had just about decided everything with the Earls and Danny was going to end right there, with a bunch of papers on his desk, until yesterday, when Chris had walked in while Harp was drinking a coffee and bullshitting with Till Greer and added two final pages to the top. Chris had tapped them, hard, and told Harp without smiling he might actually want to read these.

Harp had pulled them off the stack to find they were signed and sealed DNA warrants for T-Bob and Jesse Earl.

CHRIS HAD LATER EXPLAINED his reasoning like this: assuming someone in the Big Bend County Sheriff's Department decided it was worth meeting with Danny Ford, the only realistic chance was to get *him* away from Killing. They had no cell phone number for him, no easy way to contact him directly, and he might not even take their calls if they did. But maybe, just maybe, they could get him to come to them again, and not even realize it. That's what had gotten Chris thinking about those DNA warrants Harp had asked about before they went to Lubbock. If Jesse and T-Bob were forced to come back to Murfee, Danny might be the one to drive them a second time, like he had the first. And while the other two were inside the department getting their DNA swabs, there might be a few minutes to get him alone. If he wouldn't listen, so be it. But at least they could say they tried.

Chris had admitted the whole idea was a Hail Mary toss, but Harp also knew the sheriff had been a pretty damn fine quarterback in college. He didn't know what had moved Chris to make the decision, whether it was the sour taste they'd both had after the meeting in Lubbock, or listening to a few of Flowers's so-called sermons, or just his own fears about having Flowers and Earl and the rest of them so near to Murfee, but Harp knew it hadn't been easy for him.

It had required Chris's calling Royal Moody and begging for a favor Harp knew he didn't have and somehow still pulled off. Worse, it also meant facing the wrath of Agent Nichols, who'd been burning up the phone lines for the last twenty-four hours. It had obviously taken no time for Earl to yank his agent-on-a-leash and scream bloody murder about how his son and brother were *still* being harassed by the local yokel cops. Chris had avoided the calls, but after another long, ugly recorded tirade from Nichols, he'd told Harp not to be surprised if the agent showed up in Murfee with an arrest warrant for Chris himself. Knowing there was going to be fallout, even if he wasn't sure exactly *what* it would be, Chris had never considered letting anyone else put their name on the affidavits; he'd done it all on his own and sworn them out in front of Judge Hildebrand himself, and he was going to be the one to serve them. Harp respected the hell out of his young sheriff—he was doing right by Danny Ford and risking a lot along the way, refusing to expose anyone else to the trouble he'd brought on himself.

Unfortunately, Harp also knew that it didn't always work out like that, and whether Chris's plan succeeded or not, there *was* going to be plenty of trouble to go around, no two ways about it.

So now he was hiding out in Jackie's car, the AC turned way up, drinking his whiskey and Coke and staring at the street for what had come to feel like hours, because the Earls were late, very late. Amé was a little way down on the other side of the street in her own truck, also on lookout, since Chris had decided he wasn't going to let Harp approach Danny without another pair of eyes on them both. She was also the only other person in the department who'd actually put eyes on the Earls or Danny up close, not that it would matter if they never showed up at all.

He rolled a mouthful of whiskey around, let it burn his tongue, and scanned the sun-bleached street some more. No matter how hard he tried to look anywhere and everywhere else, his eyes were drawn to the little silver chain with the medallion that Jackie had left wrapped around the rearview mirror. The medallion was shaped like a badge, etched with the visage of Michael the Archangel, the patron saint of cops. Michael had led God's armies against Satan, fighting the good fight against all the world's monsters and wolves.

How many times had Jackie held that medallion in her fingers and prayed for him? Praying to keep him safe, to keep him alive?

And now here he was, and she was the one who was gone.

Like everything else in her car, he was afraid to touch it. Doing it would be like touching her skin again and that would be too much, too overpowering. It would blind him, turn him to dust, and as much as he might want that—and part of him *did* want that a little more each and every day, more than he'd ever wanted anything—he also knew he wasn't quite done here yet. All her prayers had to have been for something. He still had some fight left in him, and there were still wolves circling those he'd come to care about.

He finished the drink, rummaged around in his pocket for two Certs and started chewing them.

The Earls might come alone, or in a different car. They might have their own countersurveillance. They might show up on those damn motorcycles of theirs or they might not show at all. Agent Nichols may have even told Earl they could ignore the summons, because whatever happened in Terlingua didn't matter anyway, just like the law out here in Murfee didn't seem to matter much to him, either.

Nichols may have gone as far and told Earl all about Danny, and one or both of them were already dead.

There were a thousand ways this wouldn't work, and only one that it could.

Chris's Hail Mary pass and Jackie's Hail Marys; all of her prayers for him . . . that's all they had.

How often did either actually work?

Harp checked his watch for what felt like the hundredth time, and was about to call Chris and Amé to suggest they pack it in, when the gun-shot Marquis came sliding down Main Street.

But behind the sun's glare, he couldn't tell who was inside it.

BUCK EMMETT WAS A BIG MAN, reminding Chris of himself once. Buck had been the first deputy he'd hired after he was officially elected sheriff, and he'd been a constable before that and also did a stint with the Pecos Sheriff's Department for a bit, but had a brother in Murfee who worked at the Comanche Cattle Auction, and so was more than eager to come back to the Big Bend to be near him. The two hunted and fished together whatever the season allowed almost every weekend, and Chris thought the man would have been just as happy spending the rest of his life outside, instead of cooped up in buildings that probably always felt small to him.

Chris knew the feeling.

Buck had brought Chris the DNA swab kits, and his big hands dwarfed them, threatening to crush them.

"Just go put them in the interview room, Buck. If those boys do show, I'll do it in there."

Buck nodded, squinting down at the packages in each hand. He'd never used one. "So Harp says these are some bad folks down there in Killing . . . that these two showing up are some of the worst."

I don't know about the worst.

"Let's put it this way, they are a little rough around the edges," Chris said. "But this will go easy. I don't even need Doc Hanson here. Just a quick swab on the inside of their cheeks and then I'm done." In truth, Chris hadn't done one of these, either, and he'd watched a video on the Internet just to be sure he had it right. The buccal kits were commonplace now both in state and local departments and with the feds. For years many states had been collecting involuntary DNA samples from sex offenders and violent criminals, even probationers and parolees, and dumping them into the National DNA Index System, until the Supreme Court had ruled that law enforcement could collect those samples from *anyone* arrested. Civil liberties lawyers were still howling about it, but it was the policy now in a lot of places. However, if you didn't have enough probable cause to even make an arrest, which admittedly was a pretty damn low threshold, getting an involuntary sample still took a warrant, like the ones he'd wrangled out of Moody and Judge Hildebrand. Although Doc Hanson *had* gotten some skin and hair from underneath Billy Bravo's nails, it was just as likely to be his girlfriend's as anyone else's; more likely, in fact. So he and Moody had fought about it for hours, with the DA arguing Chris might as well pull samples from everyone in Terlingua, until Chris had finally threatened to do just that.

Although Chris didn't need much to throw handcuffs on either of his primary Bravo suspects, he needed more than what he had—some eyewitness hearsay and Harp's intuition—and he refused to arrest them just as a pretext to get to Danny Ford. He wasn't willing to push Nichols that far, either. He could make weak but plausible arguments for the search warrants—at least ones he could live with—and with some promises and concessions and begging had finally even won Moody over on them. But just hauling T-Bob and Jesse into Murfee and locking them up? That was stepping over a line he was afraid he couldn't step back across.

Because *that* felt far too much like something Sheriff Ross would have done. And maybe Chris was drawing a line where there wasn't one, desperate to split hairs as fine as those under Billy's nails. But that's all he had, even if it left him with dark thoughts he couldn't quite shake, as he looked uncomfortably at the signed warrants on his desk.

Buck was still standing there, mesmerized by the little boxes he was holding, when Chris's phone buzzed. He checked it, thankful it wasn't Nichols again. He didn't know if it was funny or not that the kits had been provided to the Big Bend County Sheriff's Department with fed money to support the FBI's Combined DNA Index System.

Maybe one day he and the agent would laugh about it, but he didn't think so.

It was a text from Harp. Chris read it, and folded the warrants.

"Well, Buck, let's get on it with. It looks like they're here."

T-Bob and Jesse Earl had walked into the building two minutes ago, and Ben still hadn't approached the car.

The driver was sitting in it, but America couldn't see if it was the ex-soldier, now ex-cop, Danny Ford, or someone else.

Ellos no iban a tener mucho tiempo. The sheriff could stall inside, but not forever, so she wasn't sure what Ben was waiting for. She glanced back and forth between the old Marquis and the front door of the department. The car looked out of place, like it didn't belong. It seemed to take up the whole street and cast no shadow.

There was talk of rain soon, but the sky was so clear, as sun-glazed and as empty as the earth beneath it, it was difficult to tell the two apart.

The sheriff and Ben had told her all about Danny Ford: who he was . . . *who he'd been* . . . and she tried putting those different uniforms on the man she'd seen in Killing, but it was hard to look past the tattoos and the harsh white blaze of the sun that had been over them that day. A sun that was still overhead, like it was going to hang there forever and would never dim or set.

But she thought she had caught a glimpse of the real Danny Ford when he'd smiled at her. The sheriff had tried to explain to her how or why someone like Danny could end up with the Earls, but he'd really just been trying to make sense out of it for himself. *Ella ya sabía.* Anger and loss had led her to many dark places and then all the way back to Murfee again to join the sheriff's department. A need for vengeance demanded hard choices; it was a wish for *sangre. Y sangre exige sangre.* No different from Vianey Ruiz's prayers to Santa Muerte on the riverbank; if they were answered, it was always with a price.

Siempre había un precio.

No, she understood Danny Ford a lot better than the sheriff or even Ben ever would.

She was about to call Ben and ask him what he was waiting for, when she saw him finally walk down the street toward the Marquis.

WHEN HARP GOT to the car door and leaned down to look in, he thought at first he'd fucked up, made a mistake. *The car was empty.* His hand left a clear print on the roof where he braced himself, joining the tracks of a dog or coyote or wolf that had recently run across the dirty hood, bounding onto the car and standing sentinel on top of it, keeping watch over the desert around Killing.

The clawed tracks were the only evidence of its passage. Leaving its mark, like Harp.

The engine was still ticking, making noises, and he was about to back away, when the passenger window rolled down to reveal Danny Ford looking up at him.

Something played behind his eyes, recognition, from their encounter in Killing.

Danny shook his head. "What's the problem, Deputy?"

BUCK STOOD BY, silent, arms crossed. He refused to let Chris be alone with the Earls.

Chris had let them sit for a few minutes before getting the uncle, T-Bob. The old man had smelled like dirt and whiskey, his splotched hands dancing a drinker's waltz. He must have been told by Earl to keep his mouth shut, because the only time he opened it was when Chris did the buccal swab.

Jesse Earl was a whole different story.

AMERICA COUNTED OUT the seconds as Ben lingered at the car door, staring down at his hand for some reason, before he started talking to someone through the window.

He looked like he was just going to walk away again, but then he opened the car door, or it was opened for him, and he disappeared into the Marquis.

Ben was supposed to get Danny to drive around the block, away from the department, but the car was stubbornly *not* moving. It remained as immovable, as dead and fixed, as that first day she had seen it in Killing surrounded by tumbleweeds.

She bit her lip, drummed her fingers on her steering wheel, *willing* it to move.

When it didn't, she got out of her truck and walked toward it.

. . .

HE'D MADE NO ATTEMPT to hide his tattoos, like Harp had said he'd done last time. He wore faded jeans with black lace-up boots and a thin, sleeveless T-shirt, and the exposed skin shined blue, green, and a handful of other colors. The red eyes of a lion glowed hot from his rib cage, just visible beneath his arm.

Jesse Earl smiled at Chris, addressed him by name.

"Well, you're Sheriff Chris Cherry. *The* Sheriff Cherry. Pretty damn famous. My daddy told me about you. I did some asking around, too. I should shake your hand, for those damn beaners you killed. A few less makes this world a better place."

Jesse stuck out his hand, aiming one of the guns tattooed on his forearm at Chris, but he ignored it, so Jesse kept on.

"Well, maybe when we're done here, I can leastways buy you a beer, one for each of 'em you put in the ground. I hear there's a good bar around here, a cool place where a man can get a drink. Like I told that busted-up ole deputy of yours before when I was here, I guess I'm not much for going back to the Wikiup anymore."

I hear there's a good bar around here . . . did some asking around, too.

Chris was sure Jesse was hinting about Earlys. He looked at him a long time before answering. "I don't drink to men I've killed, whether they deserved it or not."

Jesse shrugged. "Guess it depends on the kinda man. What kinda man are you, Sheriff? Shoots a beaner one day, puts a badge on a little beaner girl the next?"

Buck leaned forward, jamming a thumb at Jesse with his bulk shadowing him. When he spoke, his words were deep and slow; syrup. "None of your damn concern. Stop running your goddamn mouth and let the sheriff do his job."

Jesse turned on Buck, chuckled. "You his dog? Bark when he tells you to?"

Chris shook his head at Buck to stand down, and rapped on the table to pull Jesse's attention back to him. Jesse's eyes were bottomless.

"Let me tell you the sort of man I am. The sort who doesn't let another man get beat to death and turn a blind eye to it, the sort who doesn't take kindly to threats, subtle or otherwise. And as the sheriff here in Big Bend, the sort who doesn't have to put up with you, understand that?"

Jesse, mercifully, stayed silent.

"So, as my deputy said, do me a favor and stop running that damn mouth so I can do my job . . ."

SHE COULD TELL it wasn't going well.

She slipped into the backseat, where it smelled like hot leather and old beer, with both men turning to look back at her, their mouths open. Ben's hands were raised like he was trying to show off the size of something, something too large to fit in the car, and although she had no idea what he'd been saying, it was clear from Danny Ford's face it wasn't moving him.

And it wasn't making the car move, either.

Danny was shaking his head, like he was about to push Ben back out of the car and into the street, and only America's sudden appearance had stopped him.

She focused on him. "We don't have much time. I know you remember us from Killing, and we know who you really are. We know a lot about you. We just need to talk with you, that's all. I'm sure Deputy Harper told you to drive, so do it, *por favor.* Just give us that, and then we're done."

Danny looked back and forth between her and Ben, as if wondering where these crazy people had come from.

"It's about you and your *padre*," she said, and she put a hand on his shoulder. *"Drive."*

He did.

.   .   .

HARP TOOK A DEEP BREATH as Danny pulled out onto Main and left the department behind.

Then he started again, and told it all fast—all about Special Agent Nichols and Major Dyer and the meeting in Lubbock. How they knew what had happened to his father in Sweetwater, and everything about John Wesley Earl and the rest of them in Killing.

He ended, finally, with what he'd suggested back in Lubbock. "If you're still pissed off about your daddy, then shoot the son of a bitch and be done with it. But Earl is a free man and he's protected. He cut himself this deal with the FBI. If you kill him, it's straight-up murder and there'll be no mercy or understanding for it. Your daddy's death doesn't count for anything right now."

Danny wouldn't look at him, just gripped the wheel harder. "You're telling me that Earl's doing all this to protect *Jesse*? That's utter bullshit. Earl doesn't care about his sons, either of them. He doesn't care much about anyone other than himself, and Jesse's no better. If anything, he's worse. There's no love lost between those two. *None.* Whatever reason Earl is helping this FBI agent, it's got nothing to do with saving Jesse from Thurman Flowers."

"And you're betting your life on that?" Harp asked.

Harp saw that Danny caught Amé's eyes in the rearview mirror, before focusing again on the road ahead. "I'm positive. Some days, he and Jesse are practically at each other's throats. Jesse is pushing me for guns and Earl for money so he and Flowers can wage their little race war. Everyone is on edge, anxious how things will play out once Flowers arrives. And it's more than that . . . I know it sounds crazy because I'm living it, but Earl trusts me more than anyone else. He's had me casing Murfee both of these times I've been up here, drawing him maps and stuff." Danny reached into his jeans with one hand and pulled out a sheet of paper, folded into a tight square, and gave it over to Harp.

Harp turned it around a couple of times to orient himself to the drawing. It was a map Danny had drawn of the town, and he handed it back behind him to Amé.

"Looks like one of those army maps or something. Maybe you should have been an architect or a city planner. You know, you could have just used Google Maps or whatever. I'm old and even I know that."

That brought a reluctant smile to Danny. "Yeah, but you aren't *prison old*, you haven't been locked up for more than two decades. He barely trusts that stuff and thinks everyone is monitoring it. Checking out Murfee is the main reason he's had me babysitting Jess and T-Bob, it's why I'm here. He's always on the phone, too, but he can't be talking to that FBI agent all the time. There's got to be something else . . ."

"Even if there is, what's your plan, Danny? What happens now? Are you going to play detective all by yourself?"

"I don't know what's going to happen when Flowers arrives, and I know even less what Earl's got planned for Murfee, but right now, I'm the only person in place to see or stop any of it. And some of those down in Killing are just kids. They don't have any fucking idea what they're doing or what they've gotten themselves into."

"There's an argument here that you don't know, either. You went there to confront this man, kill him, and now you're talking about saving—"

Danny shook his head. "Not him, never him."

Amé spoke up quietly from the back, where she was still holding the map. "But you don't hate him, either. Not as much as you thought you did. Not enough to finish what you started."

"No . . . I still do . . . I don't think I can explain it. I've had my chances. Plenty of them. One minute I think I have it all clear in my head, and then I get afraid I've got it all wrong. Fuck, he saved my life . . ." He didn't say anything more about that, and he didn't have to say what *it* meant, as his hands stayed tight on the wheel, holding on to it like he was trying to hold on to all those years of hating the man he'd always believed had killed his father, but now maybe he wasn't so sure. "As bad as he is, it's not even Earl I'm worried about. *It's Jesse.* Earl is dangerous, but Jesse's out of control. You're investigating that Terlingua murder, right? He came back that night from the Wikiup with blood on his shirt. He burned it."

"Goddamn," Harp said, although he didn't feel as vindicated as he thought he would. "But it doesn't matter, none of it. It's not your concern. We'll handle it." Harp motioned to Amé. "We're still the law around here. You? You're just making our fucking job harder, almost as bad as one of them." Harp didn't mean it, not a word of it. It hurt him to say it, and the look that it left on Danny Ford's face, like he'd been struck, didn't make him feel any better. But he needed the boy's attention. He wanted him angry enough to see clearly.

"Fuck you," Danny said. "I didn't ask for this. I didn't ask for you or her to get involved in any of this, or with me."

"No, you're right, instead you just drug it all kicking and screaming to our front door." Harp pointed to a free space on the curb. "Pull over here for a second. We're almost done." Harp reached into his pocket and took out the badge that Dyer had given Chris, who in turn had given it to him. He held it up where Danny could see it, right in front of his eyes. "This is for you, to remind you."

Danny kept his hands on the car's wheel, not letting go. "Remind me of what? I still have one. My father's, from his funeral."

Harp bounced Danny's former badge in his hand, watching it catch sunlight. "Sooner or later, FBI Special Agent Nichols is going to tell Earl who you are, and you're going to end up buried in that desert. He's got everything invested in that murderous bastard and not a goddamn thing invested in you. Your daddy's badge isn't going to save you, but this one"—he raised his hand—"just might. You want to shoot Earl because of your daddy and be done with it? Do it today and walk away. I won't stop you and I'm not sure I'd even try hard to talk you out of it. Otherwise, you need to let that go. And you think you can save those folks down there? Not this way, Danny, not when you can't even save yourself. But if you want to be a full-time cop again and help us with the Terlingua case, and work with us to figure out what Earl is so fixated on here in Murfee, then take this badge right now and come with us. Dyer will give you your job back. This lone undercover bullshit, though, without any help or support? That is just going to get you dead."

Amé leaned forward, put a hand on Danny's shoulder. "And it's too late now, Danny. We *are* involved. *Escúchame*, I've been down this path, I know what I'm talking about. Ben makes it sound like if it's blood you want, just revenge, that it's easy and that you can do it and walk away. But he's wrong. You don't leave it behind. Blood demands blood. *Sangre exige sangre*. The price is high and you end up paying it forever. *Puedo verlo*. It stains you. This FBI agent isn't going to have to tell Earl who you are, because he's going to see it himself soon, or Jesse will. You are in danger, and you're putting in danger the very people you say you want to help."

Harp had no clear idea what Amé was talking about, but whatever it was, it was having a deeper effect on Danny than anything he'd said. Maybe it was the words, or the way she'd said them. Maybe it was just *her*, but for the first time since getting in the car he thought Danny was really listening.

He was hearing them.

"*Blood in, blood out*. That's an ABT saying, something I've heard Earl repeat a hundred times," Danny said. "You only leave the Family when you're dead."

"*Sangre exige sangre*. Not so different, Danny Ford."

Harp's phone buzzed, interrupting them all. It was Chris texting him he was done with the Earls. Their time was up. Harp pulled out an old Certs wrapper with his cell number already written on it and put it on the dashboard.

"That's my number. Call it if you change your mind. We've said our piece and did what we told Dyer we would do. Our sheriff risked a lot on your behalf. Don't let it be a waste."

Amé had torn off an edge of the map she was still holding, and put her number down on it as well. She pushed the small scrap into Danny's hand before Harp could stop her. "Just in case."

Danny looked down at it, and then through the windshield. "Reception is shitty down there, and it's hard for me to talk. Near impossible sometimes, but I have a Boost phone with some minutes left . . ." He trailed off, but then, unasked, started reciting his own number so Amé could write it down. "I appreciate what you're doing. Just a little bit more time, then it will all be over."

Harp opened the car door, letting in a heavy blast of heat that hit them all like a hammer. As he got out, he realized where Danny had parked.

Jesse is pushing . . . Earl for money . . .

"Goddamn, I think I know what Earl's up to."

"What? What is it?" Danny asked.

"Amé, hand me up that map before you give it back to Danny." When she did, he turned it around, and put a finger on a spot. "Your daddy was investigating Earl for a bank robbery, right? That's what started all this?"

"That's what I was told. In Roscoe, small-town stuff. A Star Texas bank."

"And Earl's had you casing *our* small town, checking it all out?"

"Yeah."

Harp handed the map to Danny, tapping at one of the hand-drawn buildings. Then he looked back over his shoulder, staring past some stunted lemon trees to a pale marble building.

Goddamn.

Both Danny and Amé saw what Harp had pointed out on the map, and then followed the older man's gaze across the street.

The Big Bend Federal bank.

22

It's déjà vu. I've been here before.

But this time, we're not going to drive around aimlessly for two hours. This time, Jesse knows exactly where he wants to go.

He's not even mad when he gets in the car, not throwing sparks like he was last time. Instead, he's silent from the start, still, and that's somehow a lot worse. Now I'm the one humming like a high-tension wire as he sits where Deputy Harper was only moments before.

Jesse keeps rubbing his jaw, his cheek, as if the swab they did was still there, lingering.

I turn on the radio, wanting something to fill that silence between us other than my sudden nerves, which I know Jesse can see, most likely feel, right there on his own skin. He watches me long and hard for a while, and tells me to cut that fucking radio out, before asking T-Bob if he feels like a drink.

Jesse spits into the floorboard. "See, that shit left a bad taste in my mouth. What say we have Danny here drive us over to that place, Earlys? That's what old Joyce was talking about. We can each get us a cold one before we get on the road. I'm buying."

In the backseat, T-Bob's head bobs up and down, eager, although a part of him knows better. That smarter part of him hesitates, but his voice sounds far away. "I dunno, Jess, your daddy told me he'd have a big ole bottle of Texas Crown waitin' for me back at the ranch as long as I didn't fuck this up."

I agree with T-Bob. "Earl said for us all to come right back."

Jesse glares down his uncle, but directs his fury at me. This is all about me. "He also told you to be waiting for us, but you was just pulling up when we walked out. So what were you doing?"

"A truck blocked my sight. I went around the block a bit."

Jesse turns as if he's going to search for the mysterious truck, but we're already too far down Main Street, backtracking toward the bank, where I left the two deputies on the corner. "Here's what I say to that . . . fuck the both of you. You two just gonna play house niggers now for JW? I said I wanted a cold one, and that's what we're gonna do." He hits me hard in the same shoulder Deputy Reynosa touched as she talked to me, but he doesn't have half the strength she did. "He told *you* to drive me, so you go ahead and be a good nigger and do just that." I feel his eyes cut me but I keep my own straight ahead. "And if you don't want to, soldier boy, we can put your ass out here and I'll take the wheel. Maybe you can hitch a ride back with that truck you was going on about." He leans in close, so close I feel his breath on my face.

I hear his heartbeat.

"And that'd be just fine with me, *Hero*, just about goddamn fine with me. Some might say long damn overdue at this point. You better start making yourself more useful than playing cards with my daddy."

I don't answer. I don't give him the satisfaction.

I just drive.

23

Mel guessed who he was the minute he walked in, in his T-shirt and tattoos. There were three of them, but he was the leader. One of the ones Chris talked about . . . those men holed up in Killing. He was good-looking in a rough, uncut way, reminding her of all the wildcatters she knew growing up, but it was hard to look past the ink that went all the way to his throat. That was what most defined him; that colored him in and made him whole.

She wondered if you erased all that ink if there would be anyone at all underneath it, or maybe you'd only find a little boy, and his tattoos were like playing dress-up in his daddy's suit and tie.

He stopped at the old Rowe CD jukebox in the corner and slipped in a quarter, and the sound of Whiskey Myers's "Headstone" followed him as he walked up to the bar, smiling right at her, while the other two found a table near the door.

The place was near empty this time of day, the sudden music too loud, with just Javier Cruz holding down one end of the bar, flipping through yesterday's paper and drinking a Lone Star and a coffee. She'd come in early to fill out Tammy Landgraf's hours, so Tammy could take her mom to an oncologist in Nathan for some tests. Normally, Mel would still be at home, getting ready to come to work. She'd been about to call Chris to see how his day was going and maybe see about grabbing lunch together when the men walked in.

The smiling one slapped his hand on the bar. "Goddamn, you're a sight for sore eyes. I don't know which is nicer, you standing there looking good, or the three cold Pearls you're gonna set up for us."

"Flattery gets you nowhere around here," she laughed, keeping it light while fishing in the big cooler behind the bar for the beers.

"I dunno about that. I've found flattery gets me just about everything, everywhere." He draped himself on a stool, leaning forward to look over and down the front of her jeans. "Yep, damn fine. I could also use two fingers of whiskey for my uncle back there, lady's choice."

She slid the beers over, trailing ice. "My choice is going to be expensive, cowboy."

He laughed, but like his smile, it didn't quite hit his eyes, falling somewhere just south of them. "Well, I reckon a woman like you, it would be. Hooked up with a famous sheriff and all, I bet your tastes run fine."

At the mention of Chris, she realized that Javy Cruz wasn't turning the paper's pages anymore. Instead, he was looking down the bar at the other man, his snow-white hair gleaming under Earlys' always-on Christmas lights. Cruz was even older than Ben Harper, but decades of ranch work and the cattle auction had kept him similarly thin. A couple of years ago he might not have come into the bar, but after Chris was elected sheriff, now he did all the time. He owned about six hundred acres right on the edge of the national park, and out-of-state hunters paid him well to be their guide. He knew his land better than his own well-worn hands.

The man also noticed Cruz staring at him, and returned the look twice as hard. "Keep your eyes in your head, old man, this don't concern you." He spun back to Mel. "My name is Jesse."

Mel folded her arms. "I figured. And is that your idea of flattery, Jesse? Anyway, you heard about me and Sheriff Cherry, and I've heard a little about you, too. I guess that makes us even."

Jesse popped his Pearl open and took a long, loud drink. "No, I don't reckon it does, not at all."

One of the other men who had walked in with Jesse came up to the bar. He was around Jesse's age, with cropped hair, and good-looking, too; better-looking even, by a fair bit. If Jesse Earl reminded her of the men working the oil rigs, this one reminded her of some of the boys from college. If she had to guess, this was Danny Ford, but she wasn't completely sure.

And if Jesse was flaunting his tattoos to be someone he wasn't, the other man also looked like he was just borrowing another man's skin, too—pretending to be something he wasn't, saying and doing things he'd never be quite comfortable with. She'd seen that look before with Chris, and knew it all too well. At a glance the two men in front of her were similar in so many ways, but her intuition told her they were nothing alike.

"Thank you for the beers, ma'am. We'll finish these up and be on our way."

"I'm still waitin' for T-Bob's whiskey," Jesse said, standing firm.

"Why, that's right, you are." She reached back to all the bottles lined up tall and straight behind her, pulling down Balcones Brimstone. She poured a full glass of the dark liquid, reflecting red, like she'd poured real flame into the highball, and pushed it to Jesse.

"You said lady's choice."

"Damn right I did, and too damn nice to waste on my shitheel of an uncle over there." Jesse took it up and swallowed it back. "Goddamn, that's fine. *Hot.*"

She put the bottle back up high and started wiping down the bar. Javy Cruz raised a finger to her, just an inch. "The beers are on Mr. Cruz down there, and the whiskey is on the house." Then she took out a couple of wadded bills from her jeans and slipped them into the big pickle jar they used for tips. "And the tip's on me."

Jesse looked into the bottom of his empty glass before putting the highball down hard and loud. "My money ain't good here? You gonna take that fuckin' beaner's money and not mine?" Jesse thumbed down to the other end of the bar in the direction of Cruz.

"It's not that. You just can't afford anything in here, cowboy. I'm doing you a favor."

"Goddamn . . ." Jesse rose from his bar stool. "I don't have to take that mouth from you."

The other one, the one she thought . . . *hoped* . . . was Danny Ford, put a firm hand on Jesse's shoulder. "That's enough, Jesse. The lady's being nice, and we need to go."

"Danny's right . . . *that is enough*. You're done." The voice came loud from the front door, louder over the music, where Ben Harper was standing, backlit, with Amé Reynosa at his shoulder. His gun was pointed at the head of the uncle, T-Bob, who had his shaking hands raised.

Amé's gun was out, too, aimed toward the floor.

"Shit, Ben, it's okay . . . we're fine here," Mel said, trying to restore sanity and grab hold of a moment that had slipped through her fingers. She'd provoked Jesse, at least a little bit, and she didn't want him getting shot because of it.

Jesse took another drink of his beer, left his can on the bar, and pointed at Ben. "What, you gonna shoot my uncle 'cause I gave this bitch here some attitude? What the fuck sort of hick town is this?"

Ben shrugged, and then carefully and slowly re-aimed the gun at Jesse, while Amé focused hers on T-Bob. They moved together as if they'd practiced it. "I guess the sort that doesn't take kindly to a prick like you giving anyone attitude. You call that woman a name again and I'll knock it out of your mouth." His hard glance took in the two other men. "All of you. You want to test that, push me?"

Danny stepped past Jesse, putting himself in front of Ben's gun. "No, Deputy, we were just leaving. T-Bob, get out."

Amé stood aside to give him some room, but her pistol stayed on him.

T-Bob walked out the door, angry. "Shit, and I never got my beer or my whiskey."

Danny had a hand on Jesse's shoulder, steering him that way, too.

Jesse shrugged off the arm, but kept walking. He looked back at Mel and blew her a kiss. "Nice to meet you. I reckon we'll run into each other again." And as he and Danny moved past Ben and Amé, he leaned in close. "And you two? We're definitely gonna have our moment . . ."

Then he was out the door, gone.

Ben watched them go, then walked up to the bar and popped open one of the Pearls that had never made it to T-Bob. He raised it to Javy, who had gone back to reading his paper. Mel saw that the old ranch hand was also slipping something long and sharp back into his left boot.

Amé remained by the door, watching the street to make sure the others were truly gone, as the song Jesse had chosen finally ended, leaving a welcome silence.

"So those were the wonderful Earls?" Mel asked.

"Some of 'em," Ben answered, as he finished up the beer.

"Charming," she said. "I appreciate it, Ben, but I had that handled, it was okay."

Ben crumpled up the beer can and put a couple of dollars in the tip jar. "You don't *handle* men like that, not for long," he said. He grabbed her hand, squeezed it, and then turned around to go.

"Sooner or later you have to put them in the ground."

24

Chris was as mad as Harp had ever seen him.

"You're telling me this now? And I guess Mel wasn't going to say anything at all?"

Harp got up to shut Chris's door, although this late in the day, the department was nearly empty; mostly shadows and faded sunshine and the sound of desk fans and air conditioners. Miss Maisie peeked in their direction at the raised voices, but she already had her purse over her shoulder and was ready to walk out. Harp waved at her, smiled and shooed her on, before sitting back down to let the sheriff finish.

"I'm sure she's going to tell you tonight, when y'all get home. I just didn't want her blowing it all out of proportion."

"Blowing it out? Jesus, Ben, you're telling me you pointed a gun at a man *inside* Earlys today. In the bar where my wi—" Chris almost said *my wife*, but stopped short. Harp couldn't figure out why they just didn't go ahead and get married. It would make it easier for everyone. "Where Mel works."

"Look, it sounds bad when you put it that way, but you met him, Jesse Earl is not the sort of man you reason with. But the business end of a gun? Trust me, he understands that just fine."

"Dammit, if I didn't know better, I'd think you're trying to provoke them. You're hoping one of them gives you a reason, or you're damn close to making up one of your own." Chris took a deep breath. "Amé was there with you. She respects you and watches everything you do, and she's learning from you. What the hell are you trying to teach her?"

"Stuff she'll need, Chris, sooner or later."

"Sooner if you keep pulling stunts like that. Do you really want to start a war with these people?"

"You can try and tell yourself they rolled into Earlys for the hell of it, but Jesse and his daddy were sending *you* a message. So I sent one of our own."

"But Danny was there?"

"Danny's hanging on by his fingernails. He's got no more control over what the Earls do than Nichols does."

Chris thought about that, shook his head. "And you really think Jesse went there just to see Mel, because of *me*?"

"I know he did."

Chris looked defeated. "Maybe, it's possible, I guess. He more or less suggested it . . ."

Harp popped in a Certs and an aspirin, chewed them together. "Exactly. Who else lives down in Killing, the Joyces, those fucking inbreds? Didn't we pick one of them up on a D-and-D outside of Earlys a while back? They're probably no friends of yours, Chris, and you're almost sorta famous. I know you don't want to think so, but in these parts, you are. If for no other reason than you stepped into Sheriff Ross's boots and those were pretty damn big boots to fill." Harp offered his last Certs to Chris, who shook his head. "But yes, I absolutely think he went there to fuck with you. That's what someone like him does. He's a dog worrying at a bone. He doesn't know any better and couldn't stop himself anyway." Harp took another aspirin and changed the subject. "You finally talked to Nichols, right?"

"Well, I wasn't going to dodge him forever. Right after I finished with T-Bob and Jesse. I let him scream and holler a bit. I should have told him *you* made me do it. If he wasn't scared of everyone knowing

what the hell was going on with his little secret operation, he'd probably already have taken a bite out of Moody and Judge Hildebrand as
well for giving me those shitty warrants. He's not finished with it yet,
though. There will be plenty of hell to pay, somewhere down the line.
You call Dyer?"

"Yeah, I told him we met with Danny today. That he looked good,
okay for now. I told him I didn't know if we'd made a difference or not."

"Did we?"

They'd covered some of this earlier, but Harp could tell Chris wanted
to go through it again. He wanted to convince himself that the misery
with Nichols was worth it. "He's confused, Chris, and hell, he's been
undercover for a long time, long before Killing and John Wesley Earl. It
can mess with you. Maybe he doesn't know how to do anything else."

"You ever do anything like that?"

"I worked narco for a while, but it was in-and-out stuff. Vice, too,
chatting up hookers. Nothing like what Danny was doing, staying
under for days or weeks at a time. He's been *living* that life, with those
people, nearly twenty-four/seven. I don't know if you forget who you
are, but I can see where you definitely forget what you're doing sometimes, or *why* you're doing it. These people you're supposed to despise
are laughing and telling jokes and sharing their problems and you're
hearing about their kids or their wives or whatever. Their dog dies and
you see them cry all over it and it plays hell with your compass, here"—
Harp pointed at his head—"and here." Harp tapped his heart. "No way
it doesn't. I had an old narc tell me once that the secret to undercover
work is not so much the lies you tell, but how much truth you're willing
to reveal. The best lies start with the truth, so I just don't know. Honestly don't. But I think Amé made a lot more headway with the kid than
I did."

Chris ignored Harp's last comment. *"Amé?* She talked to him, too?"

Harp *hadn't* mentioned that before. "C'mon, what the hell was I supposed to do? She walked on over and hopped in, and honestly, I'm glad

she did. She did better than fine. Maybe it wasn't even *what* she said but how she said it, because I'm not sure she was trying all that hard to talk him out of shooting Earl between the eyes, and I know I wasn't. But he understood her. He *believed her.*" Harp hesitated, rubbed his jaw. "We did the right thing, Chris. We tried, anyway. And no matter how it ends for Danny, I do know how it ends for the Earls. The way it always ends. The only way it can end."

"You really aren't making me feel any better about the two of you trying to save this kid's skin." Chris shook his head, like a man watching a barn burn who couldn't do a damn thing about it. "But I need you to hear *me* for once. I don't care about dealing with Nichols, I'm fine with that. And although I don't want either you or Amé in the Earls' crosshairs, that seems to keep happening no matter what I do, so I have to own that. But I cannot . . . *will not* . . . risk Mel right alongside you, so for God's sake, don't put her there. Not like you did in Earlys. Danny isn't worth that, not to me."

Harp wasn't sure how much Chris meant it, but he got the point anyway. "You know I'm not going to let anything happen to that woman. You know that."

"Yeah, yeah. You're my hero." Chris took a drink of the same cup of coffee that had been sitting on his desk all day; that Harp had brought him before the Earls had showed up. "You really think Earl is casing our bank?"

"Yeah, I do."

"But Earl's *working* with the feds. He's got a deal with them . . . it's all squared away. They're looking over his shoulder all the time. It doesn't make sense."

"No, Chris, *we're* the ones looking over his shoulder. Nichols is just hoping and praying. He's blind, only knows what Earl is telling him. It's like what Danny said about Earl's relationship with Jesse. Those two nearly hate each other, and either Nichols doesn't know it or doesn't care."

"But what about you, are you okay? This thing with the Earls and Danny has gotten to you."

Harp rubbed his eyes. "I guess. I'm tired, just tired, more each day." There was no point avoiding it. "And maybe I'm slipping, too. Little things that I never would have forgotten, that I would have *seen* coming. Some days it feels like everything around me is moving too fast or I'm just too slow. Maybe you do reach a point where you have to hang up the gun and spurs before they hang you."

"You've done enough for me, for the department. God knows I've needed you, but these aren't your fights anymore and I understand that. You can walk out of here tonight and I'll never ask you to stay."

"And I'd never do that. Not with all that's going on. You need me now, even if you don't see it, which is how I know I'm right. Let's get past the Earls. That's what I need to finish, what I need to see to the end."

What was it Danny Ford had said? *Just a little bit more time, then it will all be over.*

Chris said, "Fair enough. Anyway, I'm done talking about Danny Ford and the Earls, at least for tonight. Remember I have to go to El Paso in a couple of days for that damn HIDTA meeting. I'll meet with Garrison and run this whole Nichols operation by him then, see what he says. I already gave him a heads-up."

Garrison was another federal agent that Chris knew from a ways back. He was a supervisor in the DEA office in El Paso, and although Harp wasn't sure exactly what their connection was, it had something to do with Chris's shooting. Chris talked to him every now and then and seemed to trust him, even if he didn't exactly consider him a friend.

"And if Nichols calls you anymore, put him through to me, I'll handle that righteous prick." Harp laughed and stood up, then added, "But I do think about her all the time, Jackie, I mean. It's hard, so goddamn hard. Harder than I ever imagined."

"I know," Chris said.

But Chris didn't, not really, and Harp knew there was no way that he could. "Okay, get on home to that wife of yours. She'll tell you herself all about that nonsense at Earlys. Just remember, it wasn't half as bad as she's gonna make it out to be."

"And that makes both of you liars. And you know she's not my wife."

Harp wanted to tell Chris how much he wanted to have someone tell him that . . . *get on home to that wife of yours* . . . to even have that as a choice anymore.

How important it was . . . how *needed*.

But he worked hard to keep the bitterness out of his voice as he got up and walked out.

"Well, by God, she damn well should be."

25

It was two days after Jesse and T-Bob came back from Murfee that Thurman Flowers finally showed himself.

And it took only one look for Earl to know he'd been right about him all along.

He arrived in an old van filled with white power DVDs and books and boxes of clothes and a hot plate and other shit, so it looked like he'd been livin' in it and he probably had. A man named Marvin Clutts was following behind in another car, a Jap sedan with Washington plates that was also full up of crap. Flowers wore dark pants and a white button-down shirt that had long gone yellow under the arms, with his hair slicked over to one side, held down with somethin' that glistened beneath the Texas sun. He had a small mouth and tiny eyes behind frog glasses that didn't make those shifty eyes any bigger, and he reminded Earl of a warden he once knew in Dalhart. That man had been vicious, a real prick, to both the inmates and his own bulls. He'd bullied out of fear and weakness, not strength, and he'd died hard from throat cancer, rotting from the inside out. First he lost his tongue, then his whole lower jaw, and then it went straight on up to his brain and that was that.

After he was gone no one said a word about him; didn't talk or tell stories about him. No one remembered him and it was like he'd never existed at all.

Flowers was just that sort of man. He thought of himself as too damn important, controlling everything, and he looked at the world through those glasses like it was his own damn prison to run; to do as he pleased. He didn't—*couldn't*—understand the real secret that all smart bulls and wardens soon learned: that they didn't really run the prison at all. It was an illusion that they had any control of the place, a bit of dress-up and pretend made fancy and *almost* real with their suits and guns and rules and walls. None of that was really needed because none of it mattered— all of that shit appeared to work only because the inmates pretended right along with it. For the most part, the world inside those walls was nicer and easier than anything they had to deal with outside of them, so most of 'em were never trying that hard to get out anyway.

And eventually, when Flowers was gone, he'd be no more missed or remembered than that warden from Dalhart.

He'd never really been needed at all.

THE MORNING AFTER FLOWERS'S ARRIVAL, after he'd made the rounds the night before, meeting everyone he'd only heard about from Jesse, he came up to Earl last, sitting outside smoking beneath the porch with Sunny and Little B. The boy hovered around both him and his mama, always underfoot, waiting for Earl to talk to him. Flowers, too, had his own fan club—the man Clutts staying right at his shoulder, and Earl guessed Flowers didn't go very far without him. Flowers wanted you to think *he* was dangerous, but Earl could tell with one glance that Clutts was the one you maybe had to watch out for. He wanted to be menac- ing, like Joker, but at about a third of the size. Clutts weighed maybe a hundred ten pounds soaking wet, most of that his big lace-up boots. He had a scarred-up face and big teeth—too big for his mouth—that made

Earl think of a rat. His dark eyes moved up and down over Sunny, detoured back to her tits, before flashing those big fucking teeth at Earl.

Sunny pretended not to pay any attention, drinking a sweet tea and swirling the last of it around a Disney World glass.

But Flowers *was* looking, licking his tiny mouth and adding and re-adding her measurements in his head. Earl flicked a spent cigarette past him, just to make him duck and break up his figurin', and started up a fresh one.

Flowers pulled up a chair and looked across Killing like he owned the place already.

Playing at goddamn warden.

"It's good to sit down with you, John. Jesse's told me a lot about you, and I'm glad we're finally meeting face-to-face. Particularly here, in Killing. This place is going to be good for us, a new start for me, for Jesse, even for you. More importantly, for our race. We're going to build something here."

Earl laughed, waving a cigarette at Killing's sunken buildings and blowing dust. "This shithole? This is where you're going to build your white empire? You do know there are more beaners per square inch here in this part of Texas than about anywhere else. And that"—he pointed back over his shoulder to the mountains—"*is* fucking Mexico. You're surrounded by wetbacks here. This place isn't yours and never will be. It's enemy territory, Preacher. Hell, we're just leasing."

Flowers pulled his glasses off, rubbing dust off them on his dirty shirt. He also took out a folded handkerchief and touched it to his mouth. "I assure you, I'm well acquainted with Texas history. We took this land from the mongrels, we're not giving it back." He settled his glasses on his nose, but kept out the handkerchief, wiping his mouth a second time. "At least there aren't many niggers, isn't that right, Marvin?" Clutts laughed, slapping a hand lightly on his leg at a joke he'd probably heard a hundred times. "Anyway, Killing *is* the place, and God saw fit to lead us here."

"*God?* God ain't got nothin' to do with it. It so happens Jesse's girl is related to some folks who live down this way. He learned about it from her. It wasn't God talkin', it was Jesse's lucky dick."

Clutts started, "Pastor Flowers . . ."

But Earl shut him off with a cool, long stare. "And *you*, you can shut the fuck up. This here's adults talkin' . . ." He looked Flowers up and down. "More or less."

Clutts was reduced to glaring, waiting for Flowers's next order. Flowers coughed into his hand, nodding toward a silent Sunny like he was apologizing that the two of them were the most reasonable on the porch; the only reasonable people. "And that's what we need to do, John. Talk. Talk about the way forward now that I'm here, maybe just the two of us."

Earl wanted to see where this was going. "Anything you want to say, you can say in front of Sunny and the boy. It's no skin to me."

Flowers shrugged, and motioned with his kerchief for Clutts to stay as well. "Okay, if that's what you want. And you're right, there's no need for secrets here. More like-minded people will be coming. We've put out the word and have been for months, and we're going to build a haven here on the principles of racial purity and freedom. We're going to cut it right out of this earth, free from the government, free from interference."

"With a van of shitty DVDs and homemade magazines? That ain't much of a start."

Flowers started talking with his hands. "No, you're right, it's not. We're going to need a lot more than that. We have to buy up the land, make improvements. Protect this home we're making. We're going to set up my radio show here, and we need a meeting hall. We need to be fully funded and self-sufficient and we're going to . . . well, I have a lot of plans. Everyone is going to pitch in and do what they can . . . give what they can." Flowers hesitated, fumbling with his glasses again. "And Jesse said you might be in a position to help us with that . . . that you—"

"*Jesse said?* You're barely here a sunrise and you already got your god-damn hand out?"

Flowers went slow, testing each word. "I understand you were very important in prison. You had a lot of friends and made a lot of friends, and always took care of your family while you were inside. You're a good businessman, influential, *profitable*. We need that knowledge and expertise, and if I were to assume that your business didn't come to an end when you got out . . ."

"You don't know shit about me or what I was doin', in or out."

"I see, and it's possible that I have misread you. I understood from Jesse that you were with us on this, John. That you believe in what we're doing and want to be a part of it." He folded his hands in front of him, like little birds coming to rest. "If you don't, then why are you here?"

Earl wanted to yell at him, *So I'm not rotting away in a five-by-nine cell while mousy little fuckers like you strut around*, but instead he flicked ash. "For my boy, for my family you was goin' on and on about. But like I already done told Jesse, there ain't no money. And even if there was, fuck that if you think I'd give you a thin nickel so you can sit down here and blow up courthouses or kill cops or lawyers or whatever the hell other ideas you've been putting in my boy's head."

"Jesse's a man, John. He grew up while you were away. He has his own ideas, and plenty of them."

"You are about to walk onto dangerous fuckin' ground, *Preacher.*"

Flowers stood and took a step back closer to Clutts, as if he were already standing on that bad ground . . . within striking distance of Earl. He held up his hands, offering peace. "I was wrong to approach you like this, so soon. It was inappropriate and rude. I'm just anxious to start this project that Jesse and I have talked about so long. In so many ways, I've been in exile and now I'm home." He frowned, as if thinking hard about something unpleasant, before turning a smile at Little B but still talking to Earl. "It's a hard thing to face, that moment when our kids are up and grown. We see the final sum of our choices and mistakes, the good and the bad. We have to face our mortality."

Earl worked his cigarette, wondering if he'd underestimated Flowers. Not about him being a mostly worthless piece of shit, because he was every bit of that, but he couldn't help appreciating the man's one talent: his way with *words*, that hellfire preacher in him. In the right time and place, Flowers could pull those to him who didn't even know what they were looking for until Flowers told them what it was. It was no different from when he'd first been approached by George Chives in the yard at Coffield, a meeting that had turned him into a prospect for the ABT. And it was no different from how he himself had approached others, turning their path in his direction. In another time, another place, he might have made use of a man like Flowers, or killed him first.

"Mortality? That's a damn big word just to say I'm a short way from dyin'. We all are. But I've been so bad, hell might even send me right back."

"So I've heard," Flowers said, his eyes invisible behind glasses that were still dusty, no matter how many times he cleaned them. He wiped his hands with his handkerchief before putting it back into his pocket.

"Men like us, John, making the world the way we want it, there's always bound to be some blood on our hands."

FLOWERS AND CLUTTS WERE GONE and he'd sent Sunny and Little B back inside, so that left Earl alone, walking back up to the high hill behind the house. *His hill*, he still thought of it, even though he'd found Jesse and Danny snapping at each other up here like pissed-off dogs. It was bound to come to a head between those two, but that was a problem he didn't have the time or energy to solve. Besides, that meant coming down on one side or the other, and he didn't like where that had to go . . .

Flowers had said: *It's a hard thing to face, that moment when our kids are up and grown. We see the final sum of our choices and mistakes, the good and the bad . . .*

Yep, that sounded about right.

Earl lit a cigarette, held the smoke in his mouth till it hurt, and then blew it away on the still wind. He'd spoken again to his ole business *compadre* Manny yesterday, just before Flowers arrived, and the only thing that had changed was Manny's people had finally decided to take care of *his* son, so Manny had told him (again) everything he needed to know about his Christmas present and how to get it unwrapped, and all the problems he was gonna face doing just that. Manny had promised his people still weren't gonna go anywhere near it, and they sure in the hell didn't care how Earl got his hands on it, but Earl wasn't sure he actually believed him. Manny might not out-and-out lie to him, but Manny didn't call all the shots, either. *Compadre* or not, it was too fine a prize for them to completely walk away from.

It was just business, after all.

So if Earl didn't do *something* soon, Manny's people certainly would later.

Flowers had talked about how important Earl had been in prison; how he'd had friends and influence. That was true, no doubt about that, but that was also the past. He'd been cuttin' loose those so-called friends for months, burnin' all his bridges. Jesse had told him, *Out here, you don't mean shit, not anymore,* and that was even truer than the boy could ever know. Earl couldn't complain too much now that he was gettin' his wish.

He'd been ordered to let Nichols know the minute Flowers appeared, but he still hadn't made that call, not yet. Flowers's presence meant that Nichols would be all over his ass to bring this thing to a quick close, now more than ever, since that tall prick was spun up over Sheriff Cherry and his bumbling deputies. That business with the warrants had been a damn surprise to everyone, but Nichols hadn't tried all that hard to shut it down, leaving Earl to figure the nigger probably *wanted* to hold that murder beef over Earl, find some way to pin it on him, so when all this was over he'd be able to keep his hands on him. The agent tried to hide it, but he was all raw nerves, losing his patience and wearing out Earl's as well. Maybe the ass-chewing Nichols had said he was gonna give those dipshit locals would be enough to keep their heads low for a while, but Earl thought they might just decide to keep on pushin'. They seemed to have a mind of their own on the matter, and the pressure from Nichols might not be enough to get 'em to change it.

What would Nichols do if Jesse's blood was all over that dead fucker in Terlingua? What would someone like Sheriff Cherry *have* to do?

It was like playing Texas hold 'em where you not only couldn't see the other players' cards, you couldn't see the other fuckin' players at all.

Earl guessed he could measure out the time he had in hours, a day or so. No more than that.

But he'd had an idea forming from that first moment yesterday when Flowers and Clutts had arrived. It was like the idea itself had rolled up on wheels with them, and in some ways, it had. He'd since discarded everything else and hadn't come up with anything half as good; nothing, at least, that didn't risk showing his hand before he had a chance to play it out, and after his last talk with Manny yesterday, there just wasn't enough time to come up with much else. His hole cards sucked and he was bluffing with practically nothing, bettin' all in on the turn before the river, but he'd won plenty of pots on bluffs like that before.

Never one this big, though, or this important. There were a whole lot of goddamn chips on the table.

Everything.

He swallowed more smoke. He'd been lining Danny up from the get-go, but now it looked like he was gonna need a little more help.

Now it was time to talk to the little faggot.

HE WAS ABLE TO GET HIM AWAY from the others and take him out front by the RV and the cars, where Flowers's van and Clutts's sedan were also parked. In two days they were both already covered in pale dust; it took almost no time for everything in this place to disappear beneath the fine grains of it.

Like a shroud, hiding the dead.

He brought them each a beer, opened them, and handed one to Kasper. Earl figured he got his nickname because he was electric pale, just like the dust, his bone-white skin prone to burn and peel. While the others' tattoos were open and in your face like Earl's own—swastikas and skulls and white power slogans—Kasper's were subtle, more acceptable. He had a few Celtic crosses and runes and the Valknot here and there, and a spiderweb spread across one elbow, but his face and neck were clear. It was like he was saving himself for a day when he could walk away from all of this and go back to whatever life he had before. Kasper had a shitty guitar he tried to play that sounded like a cat dying, and he'd bonded with Little B over bands like Hatebreed, Blue Eyed Devils, and Warfare 88. He was also close to Danny—a fact Earl was now countin' on—who'd been the one to mention the faggot had gone down for a few months for auto theft. Earl didn't care that the boy had cow eyes for Little B, practically walkin' around half the time with his dick hard. He personally had no more interest in fuckin' a man than he had in fuckin' a dog, but he didn't hold that against Kasper. After all, Earl had to admit that pussy had caused him no end of troubles throughout his life; if he'd just stayed away from it, he wouldn't have most of the damn problems he had now.

But this was gonna be the first time he and Kasper had actually talked, and for Earl it was just like approaching a new prospect on the yard.

"Thank you, Mr. Earl," Kasper said, sipping at the beer like he was afraid to drink too much at once.

"Don't mind all that, call me JW," Earl said, taking a long gulp of his beer and wiping his mouth with the back of his hand. "What do you think about all this? You glad to be out here?"

Kasper nodded along with another sip. "Yes, sir, I am." Then added, "I got no place else to be."

Earl laughed and raised his beer. "Hell, I'll drink to that." He finished it off and threw the empty out into the dirt. "Now that Pastor Flowers is here, I guess things are really gonna start movin'. This place will start to liven up . . . more people comin' . . . maybe even some goddamn women. God knows we need more than two sets of tits around this place."

Kasper hid a smile, embarrassed, even though they both knew he didn't care about women or their tits. "I'm glad the pastor is here. I'm glad Little B and Jesse let me come with them." He looked at Killing, convincing himself. "It's going to be okay here."

"Yes, it will be. It'll be fine." He paused, as if a new thought had just occurred to him. "Say, I see you hack around on that guitar all the time. Pastor Flowers says you want to start a band, so maybe you'll get to do that soon. You gotta real knack for it. Me, I can't do shit with my hands, no talent."

Kasper stared down at his long slim fingers holding the beer can. "I'm just all right, but I'm getting better. It's these hands that got me in trouble to begin with."

"How's that? Fightin'?"

"No, sir, stealing. I started when I was little. First it was just gum and magazines from stores, then later beer and smokes for my friends. After that, car stereos and stuff . . . that sort of thing."

"The whole car, too, the way I hear it," Earl said, tone casual.

"Yeah, I got pretty good at that. My mom and I lived up in the Third Ward, and I used to boost cars from student parking at the U of H. I looked like just another guy on campus."

"Fast, huh?"

Kasper flashed that embarrassed smile again. "I guess, better with a car lock and an ignition than a guitar. My mom used to always say that thing about hands and the Devil's playground. Finally figured she was right."

Earl pointed over to Flowers's van, and then to Clutts's car. "What about those? I bet you could get into those and be up and moving pretty damn fast."

Kasper took them both in with a long, curious glance. "Yeah, nothin' to it." He fumbled with his beer, wouldn't look Earl in the eye. "Sir, you don't want me to steal those, do you?"

Earl laughed, took the can from Kasper and finished it off for him and walked over and sat it on the hood of Clutts's car.

"Hell no, kid. Not these pieces of shit. Not these at all . . ."

Sunny watched them through the dirty window, Earl and the boy Kasper, sharing a beer and laughing it up without a care in the world. Earl didn't seem to sleep much, but somehow she was the one bone-tired; all the time now, with each passing day in this godforsaken place.

Shit rolls downhill. That was something her mama used to say, and it was something she thought about each and every time Earl went out back and walked up the long slope to make his calls, to that one spot higher than everything else around it, where the reception was good. She had no idea who he was calling all the time, and asking would get her a smack across the mouth so that she'd be tasting blood for a day or more. It could be another woman, a hundred of them, but even that wouldn't get her half as pissed as watching him play daddy to Kasper now, right after dismissing *their* son, Little B. The problem was goddamn *time.* Earl kept going on about it, worrying about it, acting always like he was too damn hard-pressed to share it, but somehow still found enough of it to ride that big Harley of his all mornings, or spend afternoons on the hill on his phone and smoking. He had all the time in the world for everything else when it suited him, but couldn't spend more than ten minutes all added up with Little B.

He didn't treat Jesse much better, and that ate at Jesse bad, too. He had to watch his daddy make nice with Danny, treat him like he was an equal . . . *like real family.* She and T-Bob had raised Jess up as much as anyone, and she hurt for him almost as much as she hurt for her own boy. She couldn't understand why Earl was pushing all of his own away now, not when they needed him the most. Especially with that shifty son of a bitch Flowers here, talking around all in circles but still not saying a goddamn thing.

She had herself partly to blame. Earl had told her to abort Little B, and he'd nearly beat that baby out of her when she wouldn't, but she'd held on for dear life all the same. It was the only time she'd ever stood up to him, and if it had surprised him, it had surprised her, too. And he'd made her pay for it every day since.

She wondered if that's how he'd run off Jesse's real mother, by telling her to kill the best thing they could ever have between them, and then punishing her when she wouldn't.

Still, Earl hadn't completely abandoned her and Little B. In the past, men had come, most often Nazi Low Riders or Aryan Circle or ABT on their big Harleys, once even a goddamn wetback, to drop off a Target bag or a 7-Eleven Big Gulp or a bent-up Nike shoe box still smelling like high-tops, all hiding a tight roll of bills, some thicker than others. She'd never talked to these men and they'd never talked to her, she'd let T-Bob handle that, but the money had come from Earl—from his businesses inside the prison and his private little bank outside of it. She'd never questioned him about it, because that would've definitely earned her a hand across the face. But Jesse knew all about that money, though, even if Sunny didn't give a damn about it. To Jesse, his daddy *owed* him a piece of it for all those years he was away, and unlike Little B, that's *all* he wanted now; he'd all but given up on Earl being an actual *daddy* to him. But her boy still wanted Earl's attention. Although he looked up to his older half brother, he even more desperately needed Earl's approval. He *wanted* to earn it, if Earl would only give him half a chance—if Earl would just give him the damn time of day.

She'd been with John Wesley Earl for more than twenty years. She'd had one son by him and helped raise another, and she still wasn't sure she knew him at all. There were whole parts of his life she'd never been a part of and couldn't understand. He'd always been with other women when he wasn't behind bars—Earl was a grade-A pussy hound and she'd had to accept that—but she sometimes wondered if he had another family tucked away somewhere; a real wife that he treated nice and respectful, and another set of sons that he was actually proud of. She imagined tall boys going off to college, ready to be accountants or doctors. She imagined a house, too, painted green and white, with palm trees out front near a beach. *That's* where all the money Jesse expected and wanted had gone—to that family, to that house, that life. And she wondered if it was that *other* family he was talking to all the time on his phone up on the hill, telling them he was finally coming home.

Sunny's own daddy had died on a sweltering June night in 1979 in Sparks, Nevada, right outside their apartment, within sight of the big lights of John Ascuaga's Nugget Casino Resort. Sunny was eleven years old at the time, when one of the big attractions at the Nugget's Circus Room was the elephant Bertha and her baby Tina. Her daddy had worked nights at the Nugget until two men put bullets in him in the parking lot beneath Sunny's bedroom window. She saw it, *heard it*— those shots, steady; one right after another—while across the hall in her mama's room the Bee Gees were singing "Love You Inside Out" really loud, so loud she couldn't make out if her daddy had yelled or begged when they put the guns right up to his face . . .

But it damn sure *looked* like he had, right up until she'd turned away and couldn't watch anymore.

Her daddy had died on a stretch of dirty concrete ten steps from her window, and afterward cops came and got the body and took some pictures and tossed their cigarette butts on the place where he'd drawn his last breath, leaving behind only a yellow chalk outline. It had been an ugly, empty thing, making her daddy seem like he'd been nothing, too.

Impossible angles and curves, and all of it empty on the inside.

But she remembered how he took her a dozen times to see the elephants Bertha and Tina; how he used to sing *You are my sunshine, my only sunshine* when he put her on his shoulders, and how he'd smelled like cigarettes and Aqua Velva and Royal Crown. He'd been so much more than that ugly, empty chalk sketch that she'd stared at every day until it was gone, finally fading away under the footsteps of people going on about their business.

That's *all* she had of her daddy: that damn outline and some memories to fill it in, and that was still a hundred times more than Little B had from Earl.

Outside, Earl put an arm around Kasper and pulled him close like he was telling him a secret. She didn't have anything against Kasper, but damn, it wasn't right.

Sunny, born Mary Grace Deshazo, although she hadn't let anyone call her that since the summer of 1979, turned away from the window.

Again.

26

She aimed for the head, even though that's not what Ben had taught her.

Two to the chest, center mass, and keep firing, until the threat stops. That was always his lesson.

She found a spot between the eyes anyway, and pulled the trigger.

SHE WAS PICKING UP HER SPENT BRASS, hunting for it gleaming in the dirt, when she realized Sheriff Cherry had walked up to the makeshift range. He was standing there looking through her spent targets, the ones she'd held down with the boxes of .40 caliber ammo she'd brought with her, counting her good shots. The targets weren't QT bottles or black and white circles, they were paper people . . . exaggerated criminals pointing guns straight at the shooter or holding knives, one even wearing a ski mask; their middle sections squared away with additional lines to separate out center-mass shots.

Most of her targets were clean in the middle, the paper untouched. All of her shots were clustered around the head and neck.

The sheriff was still wearing his ear protection, the sound of gunfire carrying loud and far out here in the desert. He'd probably heard the shooting when he drove up, his window down, and had walked all the way through Chapel Mesa's shadows with them in place. The range had been bulldozed out of the hard earth four or five months ago, little more than a messy trench with a high berm in the back and a few rusted target stands. There was a thick tangle of tarbush along the berm that refused to give up, along with some red yucca that looked like drops of blood hanging in the air. It wasn't much, and there was a nicer indoor range in Nathan, but the department used this one all the time; she and Harp most of all.

She waved at the sheriff with a fistful of brass to let him know she was done, and he took off his plastic earmuffs.

He raised a faceless target. "Nice group. I had no idea how good a shot you'd become."

"It's okay," she called back, dropping her brass into a bucket.

Sheriff Cherry held it up some more, looked through the holes. "I've seen targets used by DHS, their Tactical Training Task Force. They're printed up like zombies, and they say the only shots they count are head shots. I guess it's their idea of humor." He put the target down and slid the ammo box back over it, walking up to her. He bent down and started helping pick up brass. "So if the zombie apocalypse comes, you're clearly ready. Harp would be hurt that you didn't invite him out here with you. This is your guys' favorite place."

She smiled. "He's taught me a lot out here."

Sheriff Cherry bounced some brass in his hand, then leaned over and tossed it in her bucket. "Between the two of you, I may have to increase our budget for training ammo. I sometimes wonder if Till Greer even knows where his gun is, while you and Harp go to sleep with yours under your pillows."

She pretended to look for more brass, the sheriff's words hitting too close to home. With all the guns she had staged around her house, she didn't have one under her pillow, but damn close enough. If the sheriff noticed, he didn't say anything. He had other things on his mind.

"Look, we haven't had a chance to talk much since you and Harp met with Danny Ford. If I didn't know better, I'd think you were avoiding me. Harp told me about the things you said, how you handled the whole thing better than him. He doesn't know if it changes anything for Danny, but . . ." The sheriff trailed off, deciding what to say next, how to say it. "I want to tell you I'm glad you tried. I think I'm supposed to say that, even if I'm not sure that's how I feel. What I do want to say, what I want to make sure you understand, is that Danny Ford is not your brother. He's not Rodolfo."

"*Lo sé*. They don't look the same at all."

The sheriff laughed, picking up the last bits of brass and pretending to dust them off, clean them, as if it mattered. "You know what I mean. We don't talk much about what happened with you, me . . . with Caleb." He turned a spent casing over, reading the little words etched on it. "Or Sheriff Ross and Duane Dupree. I guess *I* don't talk much about it, because I've always figured, what's the point? It's done and over. But we can talk about it, and we will, if everything that happened back then is affecting your judgment now. *Danny Ford is not Rodolfo Reynosa*. This is not a second chance to save your brother."

She raised her head. "I didn't think that. Is that what Ben said?"

"No, not so much. He's worried about you, all of us, but for his own reasons. He doesn't think this thing with the Earls is going to end well no matter what we do." The sheriff watched the red yucca bend and wave in the hot breeze. "Maybe he's right."

"I won't do something foolish, if that's what you're afraid of. Both of you told me to stay away from Killing and I have. I will."

Sheriff Cherry nodded, satisfied, as if he just needed to hear her say it out loud.

America remained silent for a long, long time, the only sound the jingle of brass in her bucket. Finally: "Do you really believe what happened to us can ever be over?"

Sheriff Cherry shrugged. "It has to be."

She stared down into the bottom of the bucket. "Ben doesn't think so. He doesn't think people can change. He says they can't get away from the bad things they've done, and that's why the Earls will always be trouble for us, always *hombres malos*. I've made mistakes, too, but I want to believe I left them all behind. I just don't know."

"First, you didn't do anything wrong or bad, Amé, and second, you *have* changed. You're not the same girl I saw outside of Mancha's, not the same girl that Caleb told me needed my help. You were tough then, but you were also still afraid . . . very afraid, and for good reason. Fear makes a lot of people weak, but not you. In the end, it made you twice as strong. You're here, now, doing a job that a lot of people didn't think you could do and that most wouldn't have even given you a chance at. But you're my best deputy, and you know it.

"And look, Harp cares about all of us in his unique ways. My father was not much of one to say *I love you*. He wasn't affectionate like that. But if I ever mentioned I was looking for a certain book at the library, somehow, some way, it would appear on my dresser. If I said I needed some new football cleats, he'd make a special trip and get them before the next practice. When he noticed a broken lightbulb in my room, he'd always fix it before I even knew it was out. My dad showed me how much he loved me in all the little things he did, even though he never said it out loud much at all. Harp's kind of the same. When he's telling you and showing you things, he's doing it to keep you safe. He's showing both of us he loves us."

The sheriff tossed a spent casing end over end into the desert. It caught light and seemed to burn up in the air before it hit the ground. "Maybe Harp is right and we can't just run away from the bad things we've done and the shitty choices we've made, but that's because we're *always* going to carry those scars and the lessons we've learned with us. We're supposed to. That's called surviving. And I have to believe it's not our mistakes that define us, it's how we go on living after we've made them, for better *and* for worse." The sheriff smiled at her. "And you, America Reynosa, are a survivor."

America thought about that, and about Billy Bravo; the entire weight of his life—the good and the bad, but most of all, how light he'd been at the very end, when she and Vianey had tossed his ashes into the river.

You didn't do anything wrong or bad, Amé . . .

But Sheriff Cherry didn't know about the boy *sicario* Máximo. He didn't know about the money in her house and the guns she'd hidden there to protect it and herself, and she wondered if today was the day to tell him about it. What would he say, and what would he think of her then?

She was still deciding when the phone on her belt buzzed. She stole a glance down, where it took her a long second to recognize the number. It was Avalos's lawyer, Santino Paez. He'd never called her before and she couldn't imagine why he'd be calling her now. He had talked about going to Artesia for dinner, *but* . . . it could have something to do with Avalos himself. She'd asked Paez to work on him, to get him to talk to her, and maybe, finally, he was ready.

"Do you think about him, miss him?" the sheriff asked her, putting his last handful of brass in the bucket and wiping his hands on his jeans.

"Rodolfo? Some days *sí*, some days no. It's less every day."

"No, not your brother. I mean Caleb Ross. You know, since we're now talking about the past and all."

Pero no todo, no hoy . . . not now, not until after she talked to Paez. After that, she'd tell the sheriff everything. She promised herself.

As she hefted her bucket and started walking back to the truck, she knew she was about to lie to the sheriff, again. Even after all of their talk about choices and mistakes and learning from them, she didn't miss a beat when she finally answered.

In her life, how much could one more secret, one more lie, truly weigh?

"No, I don't think about Caleb at all."

27

Mel caught sight of Ben's truck coming down the long gravel drive, throwing up a plume of rocks and dust behind it, so she was already standing on the porch waiting for him when he pulled to a stop. It still seemed to take a long time, and even in the shade, heat had collected under the porch, so she was sweating through her T-shirt. She'd have to take another shower before getting ready for work.

"What brought you all the way out here? You could have just called," she asked.

Ben was fumbling around in his truck, pulling out a bottle and a large box. He had a grin on his face.

"Well, if I'd called, you might have said no."

"No to what?"

Harp put the box on the ground, tipping it over with his boot.

"To this . . ."

IT WAS ABOUT FOUR OR FIVE MONTHS OLD but still large, all white, with almond eyes and dense fur. It ran around in circles, barking at something only it could see, and then tumbled up the porch to sniff and lick Mel's bare feet.

"Goddamn, Ben Harper, it's a puppy." She laughed, bending down to rough up its fur.

"Don't act like you've never seen one," Ben said, following the dog up the stairs, the bottle still in his hand.

"Not one like this." She picked it up, discovered it was heavier and bigger than it first appeared, trying to get a good look at it. She stared into its liquid eyes and it stared right back at her, unafraid, and licked her forehead.

"Well, set us up with some glasses and I'll tell you all about him." He raised the bottle, and she could see around the dog's bobbing head that it was Balcones Brimstone. The same whiskey she'd served Jesse Earl.

She carried the dog with her when she went inside.

HE'S A KUVASZ, a type of Hungarian livestock dog. Useful, if you had any livestock." Harp raised his full glass to the empty scrub around them. They'd settled into chairs on the porch and the dog was lying beneath her legs, head on its paws, watching the distance.

"You couldn't have just got a shepherd or a miniature dachshund or something?" she asked, feeling the dog's breath on her skin.

"Well, I looked around and just came across him."

"There is no way you just came across this dog. You shouldn't have gone to the trouble, Ben. And it had to have been a lot of trouble. He's beautiful, but you shouldn't have."

Ben sipped the whiskey, skinning back his lips at the burn in his throat. "I told you I was going to do it and I did. Now it's done. Besides, he's perfect. He's all guard dog. He'll look after you and your kids, when you get around to that. As a breed they're incredibly loyal, always alert. They're gentle with a family but damn cautious around strangers. I read they're barkers, but out here, I figure that's more a blessing than a curse. He'll be good for scaring off the coyotes and wolves. He'll take lots of attention and training, but he'll be worth it." Ben took another sip. "You know, though, you really might want to buy some cows or sheep or something to give him something to do. Or you can take him to the bar with you, let him hang out there."

"Ben, I haven't seen a wolf out here, *ever*, and I'm sure in the hell not going to see one in Earlys. That's just what I need, for him to bite a customer." Even after she said it, she knew what he was really getting at.

Ben raised his eyebrows. "Some customers might need it."

She reached down, ran her hand over the dog's fur. It felt electric, charged. She needed to go in and get him his own bowl of water. She'd never owned a dog, and wasn't sure if Chris had, either. "So you're still worried about that thing at Earlys?"

"I'm a cop, I'm paid to worry. It's sort of the job description."

"Yeah, Chris was madder than hell about it. *Worried.* Almost made me quit my job, and now here you are with a dog. I'm sure that's just a coincidence."

Ben ignored the last of it. "I don't think that man makes you do anything. It's not in his nature, or yours."

"No, I guess you're right." She considered the dog at her feet. "What do you think will happen with all that, with Danny Ford and the Earls?"

Ben shrugged. "Don't know . . . still hard to say, just like I told Chris." And he left it at that, focusing on his drink. But she knew with all the things he didn't say, whatever he thought was going to happen, it wasn't going to be good.

She took a mouthful of the Balcones and tasted fire and sugar and oak. It rolled through her, made her shudder. Her lips were pins and needles.

"I'm going to get a bowl of water for the dog and some ice to cut this." She raised her glass and stood up, and the Kuvasz stood up with her, tail wagging. "Does he have a name?"

"Nah," Harp said, pouring more into his empty tumbler. "He's all yours now. You can name him whatever you want."

.   .   .

WHEN SHE CAME BACK, she thought Ben might have snuck another two, or even three, glassfuls of the whiskey. He was standing and his eyes were bright and it had nothing to do with the sun, and the whole porch smelled like the Balcones. Like a campfire—like fruit and pepper and smoldering scrub.

"You're not already leaving? You just got here." She put the bowl down and the dog stuck his head in it, seeking out the water. "And, you know, it looks like there's at least half that bottle left."

"Chris has to go up to El Paso for that meeting tomorrow and there's some stuff we need to get done. I think Tommy's going to be released today, so I need to be getting back." He tracked her eyes to the bottle on the porch. "And yes, before you ask, I'm fine to drive. Hell, there isn't shit out here to hit anyway."

She put a hand on his arm, holding him back. "But are *you* fine, Ben Harper? You're worried about me, about Chris. Who's looking after you?"

He picked up the bottle from the porch and tucked it under his arm. She was afraid he was going to drink it all the way back to Murfee, and wondered how hard it had been for him to get it out here unopened, untouched.

"At Jackie's funeral, the priest, Father Murray, comes up to me afterwards and tells me how things are going to be okay, that I'll make it. How I'll be *fine*." Ben held the bottle under his arm tighter. "Now, he really doesn't know me, since I wasn't much of a churchgoer, not regular, but he knew Jackie, because come every Sunday, she was sitting right up front in her pew. Sometimes I was working, other times I just didn't go with her, but what it all comes down to is I just wasn't there that much. All that extra time I could have had with her, and I let it go."

"Ben . . ."

He stopped her. "No, it's okay. Let me finish, please. So Father Murray, who probably thought I was a shitty husband anyway, still tells me with a straight face that I'll be okay. That my Jackie will always be look-ing down on me, looking after me, taking care of me. And maybe it was complete and utter bullshit, since we both knew I didn't deserve it, but at least he knew the sort of woman that she was, the heart that she had, so that was enough for me. It was then, and it still is now. That's enough and it's all I need."

Ben started to take a step off the porch, and the dog rose like he was going to follow him. His muzzle was wet, dripping, from his bowl of water, but after he looked up, back and forth between Mel and Harp, he settled back down again in Mel's shadow.

"See, even the dog here agrees. I'm good."

"If she's up there, do you think she likes what she's seeing? What you're doing to yourself?" Mel could have pointed to the bottle, but didn't.

"She didn't like it when she was here, but she was a forgiving woman, and she always knew me, understood me. Like no one else before and no one ever will, warts and all." Ben coughed, looked away, so Mel couldn't see his eyes and what might be in them. "The way you and Chris know each other. That's special, don't ever forget that. Hold on to it, hold on to each other, goddamn tight. Even if you don't understand why, just do it for this old man."

She bent down and picked up the dog and held him. He was still in her arms, unmoving, watching them both. But she could feel the beat of the dog's heart against her own.

"I will, Ben. *We will.* And thank you for the dog. Jackie would approve. His coat is so white. I've never seen anything like it. He's beautiful."

"Wait until he's full-grown . . . just wait. And there's a reason they were bred for white coats like that, although it has nothing to do with beauty."

"Why is that?" she asked.

"That white color helped those Hungarian shepherds tell their dogs from the wolves . . ."

28

They met at the bar he'd mentioned before, the one in Artesia. America arrived before him as the sun was setting—the sky going blue to purple to black—but it was still too hot to sit outside on the porch, even with fans and misters. She found a tall table inside the bar itself and waited with a water, the ice inside melting as she watched. He finally showed up without his suit, just jeans and boots and a button-down shirt the color of morning fog. He'd left his gold watch and his glasses behind as well and his hair was not quite as slicked back, as if the Santino Paez she had met in his office had been replaced by this new one; similar in a lot of ways, but not quite the same.

And somehow, in the dark and nearly empty restaurant, this one looked so much more real and so much more natural than the other.

THEY TALKED ONLY IN SPANISH.

It had been a while since she'd talked so much, for so long, in her native tongue. She'd gotten in the bad habit of starting her sentences and thoughts in one language and then finishing them in the other, and Ben liked to joke about it—how he needed a damn Spanish dictionary just to hold a conversation with her, and how she always seemed to have one foot on the other side of the river. Maybe that was also true for Paez, the two sides he showed the world as different as the clothes he chose to wear. It would be nothing that Ben could understand, so she didn't blame him, but perhaps she and Paez were not so unlike as she'd wanted to believe.

He ordered for them both, got her a glass of sangria and a *michelada* poured with a Pacífico for himself. His drink showed up cold and dark and bloody at the table, smelling of salt and tomato and lime. He drank it slow, letting the foam settle and spiking it with a little extra pepper, talking about everything *but* the reason he'd asked her to meet with him: his years in law school, some of the cases he'd worked, his last trip to San Antonio. He told her how someone in his family owned a small place in a village outside Mazatlán, La Noria, and how he used to go there in the summers. He used to fish in the sea with his cousins, and once saw the eyelike spots of a massive manta ray only an arm's length away as it cut beneath their small boat. On the water one night he'd also heard the call of blue whales, or so his cousins had claimed, an eerie whistling and cry that had made them turn down their little radio so they could hear only that. He was sixteen years old and they'd sat silent and shared a bottle of tequila and the sea itself was as large as the world and warm as blood.

She told him she had spent some time living by the ocean, and once you'd heard the sound of it, really *listened* to the surf and the tide, you never forgot it. It was like a massive heartbeat, reminding you of how small you would always be.

They clinked their empty glasses to the sea and he ordered them another round.

Perhaps not so unlike after all.

"Azahel Avalos knows you," he finally said. "He knows *of* you."

"He told you this?"

Paez shook his head, pushing his empty salted glass away. "Not in so many words. He's heard about you from the people he works for. And they are powerful people. He's afraid of them, and I think he probably should be."

"Should I?" she asked.

"I don't know. Should you?" He looked at her close. "You'll have to ask him that yourself."

"Because he's willing to talk?"

"Yes, at least for the moment." Paez folded his napkin over and over again. "But there is a problem."

She laughed. "There is always a problem."

Paez didn't join her, just kept folding his napkin smaller and smaller. "You need to understand this is not an official proffer. He will never, ever do that. Anything he tells you is *not* in exchange for consideration on his charges, and the district attorney cannot be present. He's willing to talk, but only to you."

"Why? If it's not to help with his case, what does it matter?"

"Mr. Avalos is under the impression that you are someone important and that you are in a unique position to help him. That you, and only you, will understand his situation. He feels somewhat abandoned, and that certain people have not taken a greater and immediate interest in his problems." Paez put aside his folded napkin and revealed a tired smile. "I imagine he is not very impressed with his current lawyer."

"I don't understand," she said. "I'm no one . . . just a deputy."

Soy la chica con la pistola.

"No," Paez said, trying to get the waiter's attention for the check, "I don't think that is true at all."

THEY STOOD IN THE DARK next to his car. Away from the restaurant's lights, it was difficult to tell what kind it was, although it reminded her of the Nissan that Avalos had driven, just several years older. Lawyers in the Big Bend did not make much money, and a defense lawyer made even less, maybe even less than a deputy. In the distance there was lightning, then a soft roll of thunder, moving away.

"They say it will rain this week, but I'm not so sure," Paez said. He hadn't reached for his keys yet. "There is more to what I said inside. I received a call this morning from someone who is going to help Mr. Avalos. I am no longer just his court-appointed attorney, I'm on full retainer. I'm going to make more money than I ever have, and tomorrow my client will also, surprisingly and suddenly, be able to make his very expensive bond, all of it. He will be out."

"It's a quarter of a million dollars."

"I know," Paez said.

"Who was it?" she asked. "Who's hired you?"

"Come now, you know I can't tell you that. This conversation already risks far too much."

"Okay, but you just said Avalos felt abandoned, that no one was coming to help him?"

"True. But I said *I* received this call. He's not aware of it yet. It seems our mutual employer has a strong distaste for talking on jail phones. Unfortunately, I've been a bit delayed in telling Mr. Avalos about his good fortune. Call it a family situation"—Paez smiled at her—"or a prior engagement. Anyway, first thing tomorrow I *will* have to meet with him and make arrangements to post his bond. I can't in good conscience wait any longer. He is my client after all, but . . ."

"But tonight I can speak with him?"

"Tonight, yes, you have a small window, closing fast. He's afraid of these men we both now work for, but he's also desperate. They've been cautious and patient up to this point, but I think they fear their caution and his desperation might drive him to cut an unacceptable deal, which is why I got that call this morning. Whatever Avalos tells you will never be admissible in court, and he will likewise never acknowledge he's talked to you after he's bonded out." Paez looked to the night sky.

"These men are also not the type to come forward, ever, and I can and will deny this conversation took place, or that I was aware you even approached my client. So whatever it is you think you need to hear from Mr. Avalos, for tonight, it will be yours alone to hear. Whatever secrets he has, you have this one chance to get them."

"Why help me, Santino? Why put yourself in this position at all?"

He leaned back against the hood of the car. "I wasn't exactly lying when I talked about a family situation. My mama is Zamantha Barriga Paez, her papa is Manuel Barriga Rivera, and his brother, my great-uncle, is Octavio Barriga Rivera. He's in his eighties now, married several times, and was always very popular with women. He had a gift in that regard, I think, and a wonderful singing voice. But all the cigarillos over the years—his favorites were Te-Amos and Mocambos—made that voice disappear, like a bird flying away. One day it just never came back." Paez snapped his fingers. "He now has one of those tanks to help him breathe, and he lives in Presidio, where some of his many sons and daughters, his great-great-nieces and -nephews, can look after him. They bring him McDonald's cheeseburgers and the dirty magazines he likes and Don Julio tequila, and even the occasional Mocambo, although he should never have one of those again. There's one who sees him almost every Sunday. She makes a rice dish he likes, and she's looked after him better than all the rest."

"You're talking about Vianey Ruiz," she said.

"Yes, Vianey *Barriga* Ruiz. Her mama is Donatella Ruiz Alamo, one of those many women my uncle married, but not for long. He was sixty-eight and she was forty-two. She's passed now, a hard illness, but she was a good woman, or so I've been told. Octavio is going to outlive all the loves of his life.

"Anyway, like me, like you, Vee often shortens her full family name."

America didn't have to say anything, they both understood. Hispanic names and surnames were always a problem for American driver's licenses and official records, particularly criminal history checks, and some of the other Big Bend deputies like Buck Emmett and Till Greer still hadn't figure out how they were constructed. Most of the Hispanics living and working in Murfee had Americanized their names, dropping a part of their family, their history, along the way.

"I had the chance to talk to Vee after Billy Bravo's murder. She told me how you helped her, the interest and concern you took in her. I appreciate it."

America waited to see if Paez mentioned the gun, but he didn't. "I was just doing my job," she said.

"I think it was more than that. But sometimes here, in this place, for someone like Vee, even that's enough."

"Like you're doing your job for Avalos."

"More or less," he agreed. "And I'm not happy about this thing with Avalos. When I started as a lawyer, I thought it would be . . . different, somehow. I imagined I'd be helping more people, *our people.* I wanted to right all these wrongs, balance out all of these injustices and protect the innocent. But I've found that there aren't many truly innocent people left in the world. Most everyone has dirty hands, even bloody, in some cases." He pulled away from the hood and fished for his keys. "So it seems all I do is help wash it all off. I make it all appear clean, at least for a little while, and try not to look at myself in the mirror because I know I won't like what I see."

"I still don't understand why Avalos wants to talk to me. If it won't help his own case, what's the point?"

Paez opened his car door, his face barely lit by the dome light. Whenever she blinked, he was here and there and then gone again. "There was a reason he came to Murfee, Amé, something he was sent here to do. And he seems to think you'll help him finish it, and it has nothing to do with the law or the courts or you being a deputy."

"Then what?"

"He believes your hands are already dirty, too, just like his." Paez hesitated. "You know what the people whisper, what they say about you and your brother. I want to believe he's wrong, because I've seen how you work and I know what you've done for Vee. What you were trying to do. *I need to believe he's wrong*, but I guess we'll only know after you talk to him. And then when all this is over, I hope we both can look at ourselves in the mirror."

Then he reached into his car and pulled from the floorboard the gun she'd given Vianey Ruiz, and put it carefully in her hand.

Paez was gone, but she was still sitting in her truck, thinking.

The truck she'd bought with Nemesio's money.

He believes your hands are already dirty . . . when all this is over, I hope we both can look at ourselves in the mirror.

Still holding the gun she'd stolen from the department, which Paez had returned to her.

She searched for the lightning from earlier but it was gone. Now the whole of the sky was a glossy black, like a curtain hiding the possibility of brighter light somewhere behind it, and it reminded her of the photo Duane Dupree had sent to her phone, hours before he'd died.

The last message she'd ever had from him: A picture of the black hole out in the desert he'd buried her only brother Rodolfo in.

She put the gun away in her glove box, and found her phone and called Victor Ortiz at the jail, to let him know she was on her way.

And she tried not to catch her reflection in her rearview mirror.

29

He came home to find Mel trying to put his papers back together, a mess of them in her hand.

He'd left some work on the nightstand, the rest piled on the floor by the bed, and the new puppy had gotten into it. Most of it had been the research he'd printed up and brought home from the department on the ABT and the Aryan Circle and other white militia and hate groups; Southern Poverty Law Center reports and newspaper articles about Thurman Flowers and older stories about Elohim City and the Christian Patriot Defense League. He'd also been reading about the National Decision Model, a risk assessment process designed to deescalate confrontations between the civilians and police that some departments were implementing. It had become the model for policing in the UK, and was slowly making its way to the States.

The rest had been some handwritten notes about changes he wanted to make in the department . . . and last, a short story he'd started. He hadn't gotten very far with it, just something that had come to him on the long drive home one night. Chris had loved books and stories for as long as he could remember, and his literature classes at Baylor had been his favorite, but Caleb Ross had been the real writer and Chris still daydreamed about catching his name on the cover of a book at the Barnes

& Noble in Nathan. Maybe Caleb's picture, too, something black-and-white and serious-looking on the back flap of the dust jacket. It'd be good to see how he'd turned out, the man he'd become.

Chris knew that Mel would remind him, *You gave him that chance.*

However, he still couldn't guess what sorts of things Caleb might write about, what stories he'd want to share. He'd read Caleb's early journals, now destroyed, but couldn't bring himself to believe Caleb's first book would be about a corrupted father and a wounded deputy and the futile search for a boy's missing mother.

To the few who knew that story—how it all came to be and how it ended—it still barely seemed real, the truth of it far stranger than any fiction. But Chris still thought about Evelyn Ross all the time, and how he'd never discovered the truth of what had happened to her. How no one had, and maybe no one ever would.

The handful of pages Chris had scribbled down near the back of his yellow pad was ruined, along with everything else. He'd lost the thread of the story anyway and had no idea where it was going. He never had an ending.

Just loose words and phrases scattered like the pages themselves on the floor, that didn't mean anything more.

Mel was upset, futilely holding the scraps in her hands while the dog Harp had given them watched them both with big brown eyes.

He told her it was okay and nothing to worry about, as he helped toss it all in the trash.

Now, HOURS LATER, he couldn't sleep, moving through his darkened house. He'd let the dog out to do his business, shutting off some of the motion-security lights out front because the dog's wanderings kept setting them off, and the dog had come back in only to follow Chris from room to room, close at his heel—uninterested in the pile of blankets and pillows Mel had piled at the foot of their bed for him to sleep on.

She didn't have a name for him and they didn't yet have a real dog bed or a leash or a collar or even dog food. Chris had to go to El Paso tomorrow for his meeting and to see Garrison, so Mel planned to head into Murfee early and get all of that.

But something had made the dog alert, anxious, and he cut from doorway to doorway, staying close to Chris but circling back to the front door, nose down.

Whining.

Growling.

Chris went back to the bedroom and checked on Mel, and then came back with his Browning A5, the shotgun she'd bought him, and went to the front door.

He'd wanted to be angry at Harp for getting the dog, but couldn't bring himself to be, not after watching how Mel had carried him around; how she'd sat on the couch petting him and tried to get him to stay in his makeshift bed. She put him there and surrounded him with blankets, just to have him immediately wiggle free and follow her into the bathroom or the kitchen. It had made both of them laugh, the new puppy proving as stubborn as both of them together. And he was beautiful, and would only be more so the older and bigger he got. Chris had no idea where Harp had found him or how much he might have cost, but he knew what he paid his deputies, and it wasn't much. He'd called Harp to thank him and the older man had said he didn't want to talk about it anymore. The dog was a gift, one they damn well couldn't give back, so they'd just have to figure out how to live with it now.

Harp had been drinking—it had been there in his voice—with his jazz playing a little too loud in the background. Chris had insisted that he was coming out to dinner over the weekend, that they'd grill some steaks, and Harp had tried to be noncommittal until Chris told him Mel absolutely wouldn't take no for an answer. That she'd drive to Murfee and force him into the truck at gunpoint if she had to. Harp had softened at that, even laughed a bit, and said he'd see about clearing his social calendar, before hanging up.

But not before he'd warned Chris never to cross that damn woman, ever.

Chris checked the side panes by the door, but still didn't turn on any porch or security lights, crouching down while his bad knee popped, opening the door from nearly a seated position. He couldn't keep a hand on the door, the gun, and the dog, so he expected the latter to bolt out into the night, but he didn't. He stayed close, scanning the darkness, moving forward only as Chris did.

Chris swept the porch with the shotgun, giving his eyes a chance to adjust. There was no moon, just stars, a few here and there flickering brighter in that way that stars sometimes did; trembling, alive. On a night like this, when even the Milky Way was lost in the sky, Chris imagined he could see all the way to the end of the universe. Driving home he'd caught some lightning in the east, but the promised rain was still far away or never coming at all. He could make out his Big Bend truck and Mel's older Ford, and found that darker line where the gravel gave way to the scrub, but the long drive up to the house was deserted.

He searched for cars pulled over in the dark, hidden by ocotillos, but if they were there, he couldn't find them.

The dog was low to the ground, his body taut as a wire, almost humming . . . tracking something in the night only he could see and smell.

Something or someone approaching the house.

Chris moved out wide onto the porch so he wasn't backlit by anything from inside. The ill-fitted planks creaked beneath his weight, calling out to the emptiness. The ugly noise carried far, echoing back only half as loud, but loud enough. He'd been anxious since coming face-to-face with Jesse Earl, since Jesse had approached Mel at Earlys, but still found it hard to believe the Earls would try something as foolish as attacking a sheriff in his home.

Harp refused to put it past them, though, and Chris had his own share of enemies. He'd killed men out here before.

Chris caught the licorice smell of creosote and the lighter tang of queen of the night, a cactus that bloomed heavy white flowers only on summer nights. Closer to the house was damianita, a shrub topped with a mess of yellow flowers that gave off its own recognizable scent when brushed against.

Like now.

Chris turned the shotgun toward the wide swath of damianita, the flowers moving with the slight breeze, or because of something else.

Maybe it was just a coyote . . . a wolf.

Chris reset the A5 into his shoulder, leaned hard into it, so when he pulled the trigger the recoil wouldn't throw him off balance. He also wanted to be up and moving so he could retreat to the house and get to Mel.

The dog inched forward, growling louder. He gave out one sharp bark and then relaxed. He sat up on its haunches and looked at Chris, as if to say: *It's okay, I'm here and there's nothing to worry about now.*

No, nothing to worry about at all.

CHRIS GOT BACK INTO BED, desperate to catch a few hours of sleep, the gun upright in the corner and within reach. Mel had woken at the dog's bark, but when Chris told her it was nothing, she'd rolled back over, even though Chris still couldn't relax. He turned again to Jesse Earl showing up at Earlys and Harp's warning about the bank. He'd met with Jim Hannant, who'd managed the bank for ten years, and who walked him into the steel-reinforced concrete vault that had been built around 1920, and which, despite its age, still looked impregnable. With its Diebold vault door and the time lock and security cameras, it just didn't seem feasible or worth the effort for someone like Earl to try to get into it, but he'd put Buck and Till on a rotation to swing by the bank a couple of times a day and night anyway, and was still left wondering if that was enough. *Was he doing enough? Was there ever enough?* He thought about America shooting round after round at her faceless targets and Harp bringing over the dog. Was Chris the only one just sitting around waiting for something to happen, like the rain that refused to come?

It had been foolish to creep around in the dark outside the house, with all the cameras and lights at his disposal, but he'd wanted to feel in control of *something*. Take the lead, make a damn decision. He didn't like worrying that everyone was in harm's way, except for him.

So maybe tomorrow morning before he went to El Paso he needed to pay a visit to Killing himself, to see this John Wesley Earl in person. He wasn't sure what it would accomplish, but it was something. It was better than nothing.

Like Chris, the dog wouldn't let the night go and refused to get back into his pile of blankets. He was up on his hind legs on Chris's side, peeking over the top, breathing and whining. Chris finally gave in and pulled him into bed and pushed him in between him and Mel. At some point he'd be too big, but for now, it was fine. Besides, he'd earned his keep tonight. Chris could feel him settle in, his large head up on a pillow, where he could see them both.

Watching over them.

30

Victor was there waiting for her but didn't say anything, just un-locked the door to let her into Avalos's cell. She'd slipped her gun from her holster and left it on Victor's desk, and told him to shut the door behind her and lock it again but stand by, just in case. If he heard anything strange, anything at all other than the low murmur of their voices, he was to call Ben Harper first, then the sheriff second.

Then she told him if Avalos tried in any way to get out of the cell, he was to shoot him.

FOR THE SECOND TIME THAT NIGHT, America talked only in Spanish.

Avalos watched her warily from his bunk, still rubbing sleep from his eyes, as if he wasn't sure she was really there.

"I didn't know if you would come."

"I'm here, so say whatever you have to say."

Avalos considered this. "In another time, another place, you'd think differently of me." He pointed at the jail cell. "It's hard to see past this."

"It's hard to see past the deputy you ran over."

"I did not mean to hurt him. My lawyer said he will live, but I will still be here, or someplace worse."

"Because you panicked?"

Avalos looked as if he was going to cry. "Because I was nervous, yes. Trust had been placed in me, the sort of trust that is given once and never again. My father wanted me to earn my place at his side. I know you understand this. You are the girl with the gun, the girl who avenged the death of her brother and then took *his* place."

At the mention of her brother, she hesitated. "I was young and foolish, as was he. Other than that, we are nothing alike."

Avalos shook his head. "No, they say you are tougher than your brother. I see that."

"Who says these things? I know nothing about what Rodolfo was involved in. *Nothing*. I was never a part of it."

"But your brother worked for Nemesio, because of your uncle, the one they call Fox Uno. He is a very important, powerful man, now more than ever. The wars on the border have weakened everyone, all the blood spilled over plazas and routes. They say there are not enough police for everyone to bribe and not enough foot soldiers to continue the fight. One day a man is raised up and the next he is cut down, and for what, a handful of pesos or a strip of road in the dust? Once we could all be rich, but no longer. There is one constant, however, and that is Fox Uno. Nothing happens here in the Big Bend without your uncle's knowledge. He is a *padrino*, and even in this crazy time, all the narcos listen to him. They seek his advice even if they don't work for him."

"So who do you work for?"

"Not Nemesio, but others. My father does. I could not have come here without Fox Uno's blessing. A payment was made in exchange for it."

America knew Avalos was talking about *piso*, the toll that the cartels allegedly paid each other to move drugs through their rival territories and to access their smuggling routes. For some reason she still didn't understand, someone had paid the *piso* for Avalos to come through Murfee and the Big Bend.

Avalos continued. "Ojinaga is still held fast by Nemesio, by your uncle, and that includes everything that touches it on both sides of the river. That includes Murfee, and *you*. He put out the word long ago that you are not to be harmed. Everyone on the border knows this."

He put out the word long ago . . .

And there it was, finally, the answer to a question she'd asked herself two years ago, when Máximo had showed up at her door. *Why?* At the time she'd foolishly thought it some kind of magic, as if she had summoned him. But it had been *blood* instead—invisible ties to a man she'd heard about and met only once, if at all, when she was too young to remember. Her uncle never crossed the river and moved between towns like Coyame and Delicias, where both her mama and papa now lived. Fox Uno was her mama's brother, one of six, and had always been just a name to America, nothing more. But Avalos assumed she'd been working for him all this time, just like Rodolfo, and it did make some kind of sense, even if it wasn't true. Maybe this Fox Uno had spoken it aloud enough times that she *was* helping him, moving his drugs and money across the border and claiming to everyone that she was one more badge in his pocket, that the lie had taken on a life of its own.

The girl with the gun.

Blood demands blood . . . sangre exige sangre.

He believes your hands are already dirty . . . that's what Paez had said to her, and that's why Avalos wanted her help. He thought she was *already* corrupted. That's what the people in Murfee and Presidio and in the towns on the other side of the river were whispering: that America Reynosa was now the right hand of this uncle she barely knew.

She'd replaced Rodolfo and was a narco, just like him.

All the things she had tried to do and the person she'd wanted to be—the person Sheriff Cherry and Ben Harper and the others *believed* she was—had come to nothing. She'd spent the past two years wondering and worrying whether it was possible to outrun your mistakes, and in one night Avalos had shown her just how foolish she'd been.

268 | J. TODD SCOTT

There's only what people are willing to believe about you. That's the only truth.

Avalos hadn't yet mentioned the money: Sheriff Ross's, Nemesio's, money. *Her uncle's money* that she'd run off with. He was looking at her, eyes clouded, now suspicious.

"You truly know nothing of this?"

"It doesn't matter. Tell me why you were sent here and what it is that you want me to do. Say it now or I walk away, and leave you to the men you work for. The men whose trust you've already broken."

Avalos hesitated, unsure. He stared at the four walls around him, the ceiling pressing down. All gray, again all the same, unchanging.

"You can help me finish what I came to do. I have dishonored my father, but after you help me, you can tell your uncle that I did not falter. That I did not trade for leniency, and eventually my father will learn that, too. Then, even in prison, I will be safe."

"They can hurt you in prison?"

Avalos nodded, looking at the ground. "They can hurt you anywhere. This you have to know . . ."

"Tell me," she said.

"My true name is Miguel Suarez, and there is money . . ." he started. Then he told her all of it.

31

There were all these things he remembered, things he could flip over one after another like the colored cards in a deck his daddy once gave him, the only present Mason William Earl had ever put in his hands.

His daddy had claimed it was an original deck of Civil War–era cards—Highlanders—and goddamn if they hadn't been a sight to see, fifty-five cards in all and no jokers, an ace of spades in faded blue ink with an eagle and thirteen stars, and a queen of clubs with a ragged black hole in the center that his daddy said had come from an actual bullet during a faro game gone bad. His daddy had also promised him that Billy the Kid had carried those cards in Lincoln County, New Mexico, and years later, even when a young John Wesley had figured out it was all bullshit and the cards were fakes, he'd still carried them with him everywhere. He'd had them during his first stint behind bars, flippin' 'em end over end into the trash can at the far end of his cell in Coffield.

He'd learned by then that if the cards really had been valuable, worth a damn thing at all, his worthless daddy would have taken them back and sold them off like everything else.

. . .

STILL HE REMEMBERED . . .

JACK OF CLUBS

Being fourteen or fifteen years old and riding in his daddy's big old Chevy, the engine knocking and banging, listening to some Johnny Rod and then Gordon Lightfoot's "Sundown" on cassette, his daddy drinking a bottle of Wild Turkey and sharing some of it with him and how it goddamn burned all the way down his throat right into his stomach; how it stayed on his lips for miles and miles as his daddy weaved lane to lane, cryin' or singing or both.

How they stopped somewhere deep in a stand of trees that smelled of standing rainwater and pine, and how his daddy made him sit tight even as he pulled a big ole Ruger Blackhawk revolver out from under his seat. There were lights out past the windshield, like fallen stars trapped beneath the pines; a house or trailer in the dark, but they'd left Beaumont miles behind and he had no idea where he was anymore. His daddy told him to get in the driver's seat and keep the engine runnin'; put the bottle of Wild Turkey in his lap and told him to take a big-ass swallow on each count of ten Mississippi, and just to wait . . . *wait*. He smiled, showin' gold fillings and a missing front tooth, and disappeared into the dark.

About the second or third Mississippi he heard the shot, then another.

Then he watched those stars go brighter, turn to flames, and smelled thick smoke blowing into his face.

His daddy turned back up with blood flecked all across his neck and hands, those bloody hands shaking. He tossed the still-hot Blackhawk into his boy's lap and grabbed back up the Wild Turkey and finished it in one long gulp, and yelled—but it came out a whisper—for John Wesley to just *drive, goddammit.*

And he did.

DEUCE OF DIAMONDS

His first day in the yard in Coffield . . .

Standing in dust that might once have been grass, as some big beefy white guys worked weights on one side next to the fence, while some niggers just kind of shucked and jived across the way. There were the bulls high up on the corner towers, their eyes nothing but big mirrored shades, sometimes taking an extra second to stare down their scopes at the inmates below them; just zeroin' their sights and smokin' their Luckies or their Camels and telling jokes. In a couple of years most of those bulls would work for him—they'd slip him packs of Camels for the sort of favors only he could grant—but not on that first day, not when he was a new fish.

Not as he walked around the yard in smaller and smaller circles, like water goin' down a drain. Too afraid to get close to any of the milling groups, too afraid they'd just suck him right down and he'd flat-out disappear.

One of the niggers peeled off from the others and made a line right for him; the tar baby's Afro spiked out all over his head and pushed up high with a dirty bandanna. Everyone's eyes were on Earl, weighing him, taking bets on what he'd do, as Afro just kept getting closer, his hands in his pockets, smilin', like they were both just standing on a street corner in Waco and he was going to bum a cigarette or ask directions. The rest of his time in Coffield came down to *this moment*—even the clanking of the weights had stopped—so he bent down like he just spotted something interesting on the ground, scoopin' up a handful of dust and rocks in one long move that he followed through right into

Afro's face, catching that nigger off guard. Afro made a noise and reached up to protect his dusted eyes, while Earl hit him in one of those watering eyes just as hard as he could, feeling something soft give way, and the man's spit all over his face, as Afro folded over and went down puking into the dust. That brought all the other niggers runnin', but he stood his ground with his fists balled up, ready for the fight or the shankin' or whatever, figuring that was better than the alternative; hoping the bulls might fire off a few rounds before one of those niggers straight up killed him. But no one laid a hand on him, as the weight lifters, *all white* except for their tats, rose up and surrounded him, so it all ended in a bunch of pussy pushin' and shovin' right until the bulls yelled over their bullhorns to stand down.

One of the young men, with a shamrock and the number 666 tattooed on his face, put an arm around him and said that was *damn fucking fine, just fine.* His name was George Chives, but they called him Nickel then for no reason that Earl ever knew, although that was eventually changed to Big King. And it was thirty years later that Earl set him on fire in his jail cell, burnin' him alive with a balloon full of lighter fluid. But on that day in 1981, George asked him his name and explained that everyone needed someone behind bars, everyone needed a friend, and that with one punch Earl had just made all the friends he'd ever need for life.

He'd been so afraid of gettin' pulled down into a group, but it had happened the other way around.

They'd come to him . . .

QUEEN OF CLUBS

Then there was Sierra . . .

She was a little dancer at a place called the Aces High in Sweetwater, although her real name was Phyllis. She was young, could have been his daughter, and he was twice a daddy already: Little B was five or six, and

Jesse probably twice that. Things were tough and he was movin' all around, sending Sunny a little money now and then, some of it even from that robbery in Roscoe that was bringing down all the heat. Daryl Lynch was telling him that a Texas Ranger was looking at him hard for that particular bank job, and had been asking about him and runnin' a lot of questions up the flagpole. This Ranger spent his free time and money at the Aces High, Lynch's place, and liked talkin' up all the pretty girls, and unfortunately Earl was learnin' Lynch was a bit of a talker, too—snitchin' out of both sides of his mouth. It was only a matter of time before all the money the Ranger was throwin' around might be worth more to Lynch than whatever threats Earl could enforce while on the run.

He once walked out of a Dollar General store and caught that Ranger sitting across the street in his truck, reflected in the store's front windows like there were two of them—both of them staring at him.

Then, to make it all worse, Phyllis told him she was pregnant. He had been fuckin' her for a few months and keepin' her up to her eyeballs in crank, all 'cause she reminded him so much of Jesse's mama. Same eyes, same hair, same way she said his name when he slipped inside her—the only woman he'd never put his hands on in anger. But he did hit Phyllis when she said she was having his baby, busted her up pretty good, and told her he wasn't having another goddamn kid, not with a cranked-out stripper like her, even as she swore it was his and he had no reason not to believe her. Actually, he had a hundred reasons—every fuckin' prick that had ever walked into the Aces High in the last four months—but he knew she was telling the truth and it was gonna be his. She was staying in that shitty little apartment just outside Sweetwater with two other girls and her tiny room was all done up with her high school stuff: cheerleading trophies and pictures of old boyfriends and magazine cutouts and even a pink stuffed dog from the 1989 Texas State fair on the bed, and although Phyllis had her problems—a whole fuckin' bruised-up armload's worth of 'em—being a lyin' piece of shit wasn't one.

And he knew that, like Sunny, Phyllis was gonna keep the baby no matter what he did or said. So he stayed away from her for a few days, trying to sort it all out, while Lynch kept at him about that damn Ranger; tellin' Earl also it was about time they made him a full ABT. Lynch was a pure peckerwood only good for errand-boy shit and little else, but Lynch thought different about it, figuring he'd earned his colors. So much so that every time he opened his mouth it was startin' to sound like a threat, and Earl didn't like being threatened.

It was all so much like a goddamn noose around his neck, that a year later when he was back inside, he had a noose tattooed there, just to remind him.

So he got a shotgun and a pistol from Mel "Krazy" Ketchum, who brought them all the way from Tyler. The weapons were stolen from the house of a federal judge up there six months before, and there was nothin' to tie them to Earl if it ever came to that.

Nothin' at all.

Next he told Phyllis he just needed her to do this one little thing for him, almost like a joke, but a little more serious. And when it was over, he was gonna take her with him to Corpus Christi, where they could go sleep on the beach for a few days and drink and fuck and talk baby names or whatever.

Then he told Lynch how it was going to be. How it had to be—*blood in, blood out.* If he wanted to be a full ABT, it came down to that, and it always did.

THAT NIGHT THE WIND was gusting hard, and he and Lynch were hunkered down in the tall grass next to the road, the grass bent nearly sideways, so they both felt like they were hiding behind nothing. Sittin' there so long he could barely feel his legs anymore, watching Phyllis smoke and get more and more nervous, until all three together saw the headlights comin' toward them.

The right headlights.

Lynch was breathing hard the whole time through that dumbass mask he refused to take off, but Earl had wanted this Texas Ranger Robert Ford, who'd been following him all around and eye-fuckin' him, to know exactly who'd done him in, so he made sure of it, when he finally walked up to the wounded man on the road and put his shotgun against his face.

He looked him right in the eye.

It wasn't personal, nothin' like that. *It was just business, after all.*

Some goddamn hard business.

And really, it was just unfortunate circumstances for everyone involved. He didn't know much about Bob Ford, if he had a wife and kids. Hell, he barely knew anything about the man at all, and none of that mattered anyway.

Howdy, Bob . . .

ACE OF SPADES

And finally, there was Phyllis again . . .

Her eyes flickerin' on and off, winking out like the lights in that trailer in Beaumont years earlier, but this time there was no fire to follow.

Just an endless black that she fell into and was gone.

THEY'D GONE TO CORPUS just like he promised, within sight and sound of the Padre Island Seawall Beach, so close there was salt and sand all over everything, dusting her hair, collecting later in her open and unseeing eyes. She'd been a mess since that thing on the road, so he set up the needle for her with everything he'd brought: a chunky mixture of pure white horse cut with a little powdered milk, and even purer, harder crank that Krazy Ketchum had cooked up for him, and she never once looked at it. Never even thought twice as he slid it in for her and held her arm tight to make sure she didn't try to pull out too soon, not that he really thought she would, not that she ever did. She took it all and the whole time she kept going on about the blood and the wind and how she hoped the baby was a boy, even as her eyes rolled up white and then flat black again in her skull like holes in the ground itself, and her breathing went as flat as the low tide outside their motel window.

She wanted to name a baby boy *Jeb*.

Afterward, he sat with her awhile, smokin' her last cigarettes, before he took her purse and everything else that said who she'd ever been and burned it in a trash can down by the beach.

Two days earlier, before they left Sweetwater, he'd also set up something similar for Daryl Lynch: a gas fire in the Aces High with Lynch inside, that damn mask he'd never wanted to take off taped across the eyes and mouth and held tight to his head with another half a roll of duct tape.

Blood in, blood out, motherfucker.

THE RETURN FAVOR for the guns that had killed Texas Ranger Bob Ford was helping Ketchum square a problem of his own: whacking a high-ranking Bandido in Abilene who'd been fuckin' Krazy's old lady. That was a tough hit that no one had felt good about unless Earl gave it the green light, 'cause no one wanted an all-out biker war over Krazy's ole lady, who'd been pretty busy fuckin' just about everyone in West Texas. But Earl owed the man, so he'd helped set it up, and after the Bandido ended up with three bullets but was still breathing—that was one tough motherfucker—a recording *also* surfaced of Earl talking about it, and that was all the bitch wrote.

Everything that had gone down from the start—the Ranger and Lynch and Phyllis—had all been about staying *out* of fuckin' prison, but when all was said and done, he was sent back up anyway. This time for the one attempted murder he'd had *almost* nothin' to do with, and not for the robbery in Roscoe or the killings in Sweetwater that he most certainly did.

BUT THAT WAS ALL done and gone now, and none of that bothered him too much, except for Corpus Christi.

Except sometimes, for Phyllis.

For months afterward he'd still felt her there in his arms, like she'd never left him. A ghost he was carryin' around. He'd close his eyes and there she'd be, sayin' his name, talking about their goddamn baby. He'd wake up in his cell and smell seawater and salt, brushin' at his face like the girl's hair was still there. Once he even found sand scattered around his bunk with no idea how it got there, and for a while he'd been afraid she was never gonna leave him alone, but over time she'd started to fade and fall back, just like everything else in his life he'd ever turned his back on and left behind.

Just another fuckin' card in the deck.

32

He left early like he'd planned, even though he never ended up getting much sleep. He kissed Mel and she kissed him back, saying his name softly once as she rolled over to face the fan, while the dog watched him with his head resting on her shoulder.

He holstered his Colt and grabbed his A5, not even bothering with a cup of coffee. He went out to his truck beneath a gray, diffuse sky, like the whole of their world was trapped in the long shadow cast by some distant, unseen thing. When he turned it over, the truck sounded muted, too, even in the desert's expanse. After he rolled down the long gravel drive and reached the edge of the Far Six, where the gravel gave way again to the blacktop, he didn't aim toward El Paso, but instead turned south, toward Killing.

CHRIS WAS SURPRISED when he nearly ran right into Earl flying toward him on Farm Road 12 on a big Harley; in black jeans—both shirtless and helmetless—his hair slicked back thick and hard so that even the wind didn't move it.

The sun was just now up, setting fire to the quartz edges of the low-slung mesas around Killing, and although Chris had planned to go all the way to the front door of the Joyce house to meet Earl, here he was instead, burning oil and leaving a trail of smoke behind him on an early-morning ride, not a care in the world.

Chris flipped around and dropped in behind the bike and rider, hitting his lights and sirens and following him for another half-mile, until Earl turned once to look behind him, and then backed the Harley down and pulled over.

He was already lighting up a cigarette as Chris walked up.

THE RESEMBLANCE WAS IMMEDIATE, not even counting the tattoos, although there was definitely that: LIE OR DIE inked in big letters, along with GOD FORGIVES BROTHERS DON'T, just like Jesse. His throat was surrounded by a hangman's noose, and Chris could make out a huge, flaming map of Texas with ABT in the center, spreading across his chest and sternum. HONOR and LOYALTY were stitched on one set of ribs, and a cross wrapped with a coiling nest of snakes covered the other. There were numbers and symbols written across every inch of skin, and there was something about the way Earl watched him, the way the older man remained stubborn and slouched on the bike seat but still tense, almost coiled, that reminded Chris of Jesse back in Murfee. Although Danny Ford might not think there was any love lost between father and son, they shared too much of each other for either of them to ignore.

Looking at each other must have been like looking in a cracked mirror.

Caleb Ross had always worried about how much of his father he would end up carrying with him. He'd never wanted Stanford Ross's legacy or that same dark and poisoned blood running in his veins, and Chris wondered if Jesse Earl ever felt that way, or if he had simply embraced his birthright and all that came with it.

Earl flicked ashes. "C'mon, Sheriff, it's early and I wasn't goin' that fast."

Chris nodded. "No, you weren't, and it is early. You got somewhere to be at this hour?"

"Naw, I just don't always sleep well, can't turn it off easy some nights." Earl tapped at his temple with the fingers holding the cigarette.

"Bad dreams?"

"Them, too, and some bad, bad thoughts." Earl chuckled.

"You're John Earl, right? I've heard a lot about you."

Earl tilted his head, out of the early sunlight. "Same here, Sheriff, same here."

Chris pointed up the road, to where it curved and disappeared around a jagged spear of rocks. "So where were you headed?"

"Just around, I like these early-morning rides. Helps clear my head when I ain't sleepin' anyway. When I was locked up, I used to go into the yard, lie on my back in the dirt, close my eyes, and imagine a ride just like this. The other peckerwoods and the guards thought I was crazy. Fuck it, maybe I was . . . being inside so long can do that to you. But I'd lay there like that in the sun and do two, three hundred miles in my head, easy. I'd think about all the places I'd been on my bike, remember each sign beside the road, each and every hill. I had these maps right behind my eyes, all perfect, even more perfect than seeing it for real."

"Did it really help?"

Earl offered Chris a cigarette and, when he declined, pushed the pack back into his jeans. "It did, for a while, but nothin' inside helps forever."

Earl's smoke turned and coiled in the air. In Lubbock, Chris had looked through one of Nichols's files, flipping through all the different booking and prison ID photos taken of Earl through the years. He'd started young, unblemished, but in each later one he'd been a little older, a little harder. More tattoos had appeared, and the lines around his eyes had deepened like scars, until you arrived at the man in front of Chris now. *That's* what being inside so long did to you—it changed you inside and out.

"Your son came in town for his DNA test like I requested. I appreciate that. I know you made that happen."

Earl didn't say anything one way or the other.

"I imagine he's not easy, Jesse I mean. He's not the sort who's going to do much of anything he's asked. Probably even more when he's told to do it."

Earl laughed, pointing his cigarette at Chris, dropping ashes. "Now, you got that damn right. He's headstrong, got that from his mama."

"Where is she now? They see each other much?"

"Naw, we was done forever ago. She didn't want much to do with either of us, least me anyways. He was mostly raised up by my brother and Sunny, too, my youngest boy's mama, while I was doin' my time. But c'mon, you know all that, right?"

"You know I do," Chris admitted. "I guess that was hard on him."

Earl's eyes narrowed, thinking. "Sheriff, life's damn hard on everyone." He knocked off some more ashes. "I'm not the real fatherly type. I don't come by it naturally, and I got *that* from my own daddy. Jesse's always had a mind of his own. Always will."

"Did he tell you he stopped in at a bar up in Murfee and had a few words with some folks there?"

"Your girl, right?" Earl shrugged. "It was brought to my attention."

"One of them, yes." Chris paused. "I don't know, but with everything that happened in Terlingua, maybe he ought to be staying out of bars. Any bars, anywhere, period."

Earl considered it. "Not the first time I've thought it, and not the first time it's been told to him. His uncle likes his drink, though, so that makes it hard. But I will pass your neighborly concern on to him. He'll still do what he likes, but I'll do my best."

"He listened to you before, you think he won't now?"

"Tough to say, sometimes he takes issue with his ole daddy's opinion. Someone told me recently that most kids do." Earl looked him up and down, trying to guess his age. "You and your girl have any?"

Chris shook his head. "No, we don't."

Earl nodded, stepped on some ashes with his boot, rubbed them away. "After Jesse and Little B, I knew I didn't want no more. Hell, between you 'n' me, I didn't even want those two to begin with. Like I said, I'm not fatherly." He winked. "Ask me today, and I'm still not sure I want anything do with 'em. They take everything, you know? Family does in general, but your damn kids most all. They eat you up, swallow you whole, and spit you out, if you let 'em."

"If you don't mind me saying, that's a pretty shitty way to look at it."

"Tell me somethin' different after you have yours, and you will. You got that look about you." Earl tossed his cigarette over his shoulder. "Anyway, I'm guessing you bein' all the way out here isn't just some coincidence, and you didn't plan this social call to talk about kids and shit. If you're upset about Jesse's little dustup in town, I'll try to keep him leashed."

"You seem to have some pretty odd ideas about family." Chris pointed at the ABT tattoos on Earl's arms. "Isn't that what all that's about? Solidarity, unity, family."

Earl glanced along the length of his inked arms. "Sure, right, gang and family, all the same. I believed all that shit for the longest time, until I learned it don't matter. You give and give and there ain't nothin' to show for it in the end. Like I said, it swallows you right up."

"Jesse doesn't matter?"

"He's my blood, so I have some measure of responsibility for him, but I don't have to bleed for him, if you get my meaning. I won't."

"So now it's all about you, I guess."

Earl shrugged. "Well, I reckon it's gotta be about something, ain't that right, Sheriff?"

Chris stared at Earl, who returned the look, not backing down.

Although he thought about saying Special Agent Nichols's name out loud, there was no need. He and Earl knew each other perfectly well enough now.

"Just remember those folks in Murfee are *my* family. I'm not going to let anything happen to them, you understand that?"

"And they feel the same about you? Are they ever gonna take care of you, the way you're tryin' to take care of them now?"

It sounded like a threat and Chris knew that Earl had wanted it to.

"It doesn't matter. It's not supposed to matter. I don't expect anything from them."

Earl smiled. "That's good, because you're gonna be damn disappointed. I think you always end up disappointed. All you can do is know who *you* are, what you're willing to do, and everything else don't mean shit. It's like this . . . all those years inside I thought I was makin' deals with the Devil just to survive, just to get by. But I was just makin' those deals with myself. That's all we ever do. And once you know that, shit, every other choice is easy."

"And I'm going to make this even easier. As long as you keep your folks and your sons down in Killing and out of trouble, I'll keep mine out of your way. This is just between you and me, no one else is listening. Finish up whatever it is you came here to do and then you're gone for good, are we clear?" Again, Chris didn't have to mention Nichols or Flowers or any of it. Earl understood what they were both really talking about.

Earl went to throttle back up his bike, giving Chris a little three-finger salute, his middle finger most prominent. "No worries there, Sheriff, everything here's about done, and then you won't be seein' me again. I can fuck-all promise you that."

Earl had to say it loud, over the revving bike.

"I've had enough of this shithole to last a lifetime."

33

Jenna is naked. It's not the first time, but it's got to be the last.

She's going to get me killed.

Somehow she knows I'm here and comes out of the bathroom with her towel open, nearly off. She's taller than me, her skin so pale like the moon, her hair slicked back wet. It's shiny, dyed a hard metallic blond; her face still beaded with water. There's a name, not Jesse's, written in script along the soft curve of her hip, drawing my eyes to the small, dark arrow between her legs. Her breasts are heavy, another tattoo over her right one—a dolphin leaping over invisible waves. She claims she used to surf and I wonder if she wakes up and asks herself how she ended up here, so far from the ocean, so far from any real water at all. Her areolas are large, several shades deeper than her skin, surrounding perfect, raised nipples. Her breasts are still spotted with water, like her face, as if she hasn't even bothered to use the towel that's barely wrapped around her.

If she turns around I'll see the butterflies on her shoulders and another tattoo, a field of flowers across her waist, rising up her back, in a thousand bright colors against her pale skin. But none of them are the same color, or even half as bright, as her eyes.

"I didn't see you there, Danny," she lies, making very little effort to do anything about her towel, her nakedness.

"I'm sorry," I say, standing aside and looking away, right into the face of Thurman Flowers, who is watching us both.

Jenna makes a face, pulls her towel tight, and walks past me and him. He watches her go and licks his lips, and then turns back to me.

"I think it's time we talk."

I HAVE TO SUFFER with him for another hour, sitting outside in the morning heat, listening to him talk about niggers and beaners and big-nosed Jews and all the other mud people he hates; the race war that is coming that only he can prepare for. He's a bad sketch of the worst kind of caricature—bullshit twice removed—describing a world we both know doesn't exist and a future that is never going to come to pass. If you're not in the middle of it, it's hard to believe that *anyone* swallows this poison straight, but I've heard it all a thousand times before. I heard echoes of it in Afghanistan and even in the halls when I first joined DPS. I heard it full-throated in McKinney and Tyler and Ballinger—in those shitty clubhouses and dirty apartments and out in the farm fields and parties like the one in Lubbock where the young skins jumped around and fought each other because there was no one else to fight. And of course, I've heard Little B and Jesse spout it, almost word for word, even though Earl long outgrew this type of blind, silly hate. He just doesn't like much of anyone, and it has nothing to do with the color of their skin. It's no wonder he despises Flowers and what his son has become.

But I listen to it all again and nod in all the right places and even throw in a *Heil Hitler* that makes Flowers smile, his teeth weirdly white, wondering how much of this shit even Flowers truly believes, and when he's going to get around to the real reason he wants to talk to me. It's even harder for me to concentrate now since I spoke with those deputies in Murfee, and not concentrating and focusing here is going to get me killed, just like Jenna.

America Reynosa's words circle like black birds.

You don't leave it behind. Blood demands blood. Sangre exige sangre.

It's at the very end when he finally gets around to what I know he wanted to talk about all along.

"HOW MANY SAND NIGGERS do you think you killed over there?" he asks, pointing over my shoulder, as if he's talking about the other side of the street, and not half a world away.

"I don't know." Although the real answer—the only answer—is *too many*. "I don't think about it that way."

"No, I'm sure you don't, Daniel. But you should. Ultimately, it's a numbers game, a math problem and a somewhat simple one, actually. Each one *less* of them means a little more for us and for our kind. The world is growing scarcer by the moment, space, food, water. Our world, our home, the one we're trying to build for our children, is being eaten away by these termites. They take and take and take. They weaken the foundation and make our home unstable, unsafe. And what do you do when your house is infested with termites?"

I don't answer. He takes off his glasses and cleans them with a handkerchief, grinning broadly before settling them back on his nose. It's unsettling, like watching a snake skull smile.

He puts a hand on my shoulder and it's weightless.

Sangre exige sangre.

Blood in, blood out.

"Why, you call a good exterminator."

Then he asks me about the guns. About the explosives and the weapons and when I can get my hands on them.

But more important, he also asks me about Earl's money.

LATER, WHEN I'M TRYING to find a moment to myself, when I just want to drink a beer even though it's not even ten a.m., just to wash away the taste of things I had to say to Flowers, Sunny catches me alone in the kitchen. Sunny isn't happy here and doesn't like the way Earl treats their son. Little B is weak, brittle, not even as strong as Jesse, and Earl probably hates it that the one son who *wants* to listen to him is the one he wants even less to do with. Sunny isn't blind to it, and she hurts enough for the both of them.

She helped raise Jesse but can't ignore what he is or how he acts; how in some ways, he's only the worst parts of his daddy. The same parts she's learned she can't stomach in Earl anymore, either.

She was pretty once, but those years on the outside alone were a lot harder on her than Earl's time inside was for him. She did a short stint, too, because of Earl, and all of it is etched on her face. There are deep lines around her mouth, at the edges of her eyes, which are always shadowed, too, like they're permanently bruised. It's hard to tell who she's looking at or exactly what she's thinking and she's gotten pretty good through the years at hiding her real thoughts, even if I can guess. Her hands are spotted; she's getting old and knows it . . . after all, she sees it in the mirror every day. And in the same way Jenna probably wonders where the ocean's gone, Sunny wonders where her years have flown away to, and if there's any way to get any of them back. She's lost them and Killing is the only thing she has left to show for it all.

Sunny and I don't talk much, because Earl doesn't like her talking to anyone, so I'm surprised when she gets me a second beer, opens it and takes a long drink herself, and then hands it to me.

"So, I guess JW doesn't know Jesse's got Little B and Kasper out looking for some little wetback girl from that bar, the Wikiup?"

I tell her I didn't know that, either, and it's one of the few things I've said in weeks that's not a complete lie. "You really think he knows about that? I can't believe that. What about Flowers? Have you talked to JW?"

She shakes her head. "No, it's not my business. You know that, and you know how he gets. We both have heard JW go on about it, and he isn't too high on these boys' out runnin' around, particularly down that way, and if he *doesn't* know, well . . . he's gonna be more than pissed when he finally does find out. Little B don't need that sort of trouble from his daddy, so I told him to knock it off, and if Jesse says different, he's gotta come say it to me. And honestly, I got no idea why that little creep Kasper has anything to do with anything."

But she has a perfect idea of what Earl's reaction will be when he finds out what Jesse is up to, and that's why she doesn't want to give him any reason to take it out on Little B.

Kasper, and even Jesse, are another matter. She's willing to give them up to protect her true son from Earl's wrath.

"So what do you want me to do about it, Sunny?"

She looks at me with those eyes that hide everything. "Well, *Hero*, sometimes I think you're about the only person JW will listen to. And I just kinda thought you should know. Someone needs to know what the hell is goin' on around here."

Then she takes back the beer she gave me and walks out.

I LIKE TO THINK I'm so fucking smart . . . all that bullshit I shoveled to Deputy Harper and Deputy Reynosa. All the lies I practice and the stories I tell, pretending I know the way Jenna and Sunny ask themselves how they ended up in this place, when I could just as easily ask myself the same damn thing.

Was it really my father's death out on that road that brought me all the way here, or was it something else?

Was it always just me?

Would all roads have led me here, one way or another?

I asked Sunny what she wanted me to do about Jesse, but we both knew the answer all along.

I FIND HIM out on the porch with Jenna, who now at least has some clothes on, but not much—tight shorts, tighter T-shirt. Flowers is out here, too, and his man, Clutts. They're all laughing about something Jesse just said, and he turns to me as I walk up, to see if I've heard it, too . . . to see if I'm smiling.

I am.

So he's completely off guard when I catch him with a hard right across his face, driving him out of his chair. That shot would put most men down. I put most everything I had into it, but to my surprise and his credit, Jesse rolls with it; comes up standing and swinging, blood blossoming from the gash I opened beneath his eye. There's blood on Jenna's face, too, Jesse's blood, and then she's screaming. Beneath that is the sound of metal on cloth, a gun being drawn, most likely Clutts. There's a barrel aimed at the back of my head but I don't have time for that. Jesse comes in low, fast, but I'm faster. He's not really fighting anyway, just stumbling, falling. But he's trying, maybe putting on a show for Flowers. I throw an elbow across his face, stand him straight up with a strike to his exposed throat, and then use his momentum to raise him up high, higher, spinning him so he sees the earth and sky in equal measure, and then toss him on a chair that explodes, throwing up dust and rotted wood.

He lays there gurgling blood. He threw up whatever he had for breakfast, and it's all over him, stinking. His eyes are wide and full of tears and his damaged throat is working, trying to catch his breath. He's staring up at me, mouth opening and closing, and if he didn't know it before, he knows it now: I could have killed him and still might.

I turn to where I know there's a gun, and I'm surprised to find that it's Earl standing there, pointing his Ruger at me with Sunny at his back in the doorway. He lit out earlier this morning on his bike and I never heard him come back. Now he's got the same Ruger he saved my life with in Lubbock pointed between my eyes. Clutts has a gun out, too, but he's lowering it, hiding it, and Flowers is standing behind him, eyes as wide as Jesse's.

Earl thumbs back the hammer on the Ruger. "Boy, you better have a good story for why you just beat the ever-livin' hell outta Jesse. Start talkin', fast."

I pull torn skin from my knuckles. "Jesse's got Little B and Kasper out searching for the girlfriend of that dead man in Terlingua. They're out *hunting* her, like no one's going to fucking notice, particularly if she ups and disappears. Is that what you want, JW? Are they doing that on your orders?" I turn to Flowers. "Or yours? We're going to end up with even more goddamn cops down here, looking around with good reason. Jesse got into it with that sheriff's girl up in Murfee and nearly got us all shot there. Now he's out hunting the one potential witness they might have." I bear down on Flowers. "Did anyone bother to tell you that Jesse is a goddamn murder suspect?"

Before Flowers can answer, Earl flicks the gun in his direction, silencing him, and then puts it right back on me.

"Nobody wants that. But you know this for sure? Who told you, Little B?"

I look at everyone and everywhere but Sunny. "I just know. But if you ask Little B, he won't lie about it. He's doing it because Jesse told him to, probably because he thinks that's what *you* want." I wipe Jesse's blood on my shirt. He's now sitting upright, Jenna kneeling next to him, but hasn't stood up. He won't look at me or his daddy.

"You"—Earl points the gun at Jesse for emphasis—"get inside and get yourself cleaned up. I'll talk to you in a bit." He glares at everyone else. "All the rest of you get the fuck outta my sight. 'Cept for you, Danny, you stay right the fuck here."

With the morning sun still rising in the sky, the porch is split, half in light, half in shadow. We each have our side, and I'm the one standing in the dark.

After he's sure everyone is gone, Earl decocks the gun and slips it into his jeans.

"How long did you know about this?"

"I just found out."

"And you didn't think to talk to me first? This how you decide to handle it?" He motions at Jesse's blood drying all over the dirty planks.

"I wanted to get his attention."

"Well, that you did . . . that you motherfuckin' did." Earl lights a cigarette. "And I thought you were the goddamn sensible one around here. I was kinda countin' on that, countin' on you. You keep it up, Jesse's gonna kill you, you know that, right? Not today, not tomorrow, but he will."

"He'll try," I agree. "But in the meantime, *you* better deal with him. You were the one saying we need to get a handle on him . . . *you* said he was going to get us all killed or thrown in jail."

"Right, I did at that," Earl says, long and drawn out, around a mouthful of smoke. "But you givin' the orders around here now, too?"

I rub the raw knuckles of my right hand. It should hurt, but it doesn't, not at all. "No, I was doing what I thought you wanted me to do. I've been babysitting that boy of yours, drawing your goddamn maps. I've been waiting, ready, for whatever you got planned, and none of it's going to matter if Jesse gets us all fucked first."

"No, I reckon it won't." He lets smoke build between us and looks at the blood going black on the porch planks. He studies it like it's a map. "But it's 'bout time now anyway. I had a little surprise run-in with the sheriff this morning. He ain't too happy with Jesse, or any of us . . . Time's runnin' out, so I gotta ask, are you all in with me, Danny? I gotta know where you stand."

I'm surprised to hear about Sheriff Cherry, but I don't blink; I don't show a thing. And I almost can't do what has to come next, can't say what I know I have to. Each word hurts, like swallowing a knife; like throwing fresh dirt on my father's grave. "Where the fuck am I standing right now?"

"Well, okay then," he says slow, looking up from his son's blood. "We ain't got no more time. We're gonna do this thing tonight, tomorrow mornin' at the latest."

I hesitate, wanting to push, needing to know for sure. "Flowers asked me about money. *Your* money, and I figure he thinks you're about to come into some. It's the bank in Murfee, right?"

Earl breathes more slow smoke. "Something like that," he says. "Let's just call it Christmas in July. Fuck Jesse and Flowers. No matter what they suspect, they can't know, hear me? None of 'em."

"Okay, I got it. But I need to know, JW. I need to know exactly what I'm getting myself into."

"Look around you, Danny. I think it's a bit late to be wonderin' that."

Earl crushes out his cigarette with a boot. "One other thing, you hit my boy like that again, embarrass him, and he *will* kill you. I reckon it's just for the one more day, but you gotta stay clear of him as best you can, because if it comes to it, I won't stand in his way. No matter what, he's still an Earl."

"He's blood and I'm not?"

"That's right, and that's a damn shame, too. You would've made a helluva Earl, son. But I ain't worried about it. You're a damn hard man to put in the ground in a fair fight, so keep those eyes in the back of your head, 'cause if he does find the belly for it, he'll not likely want you to see him comin'. That's one reason I like you, Danny, you're a hard man all the way around, kinda like me. And *that's* what I need."

They buried my father because he was shot in the back on a dark road. He never saw it coming, either. He never had a goddamn chance.

You would've made a helluva Earl, son.

A helluva Earl.

That's what he just said.

Son.

Earl reaches into his jeans and pulls out the Ruger with one hand and presses it into mine, and then walks past me and slaps me on the shoulder with his other hand.

His shooting hand.

AFTER HE'S GONE I stay out on the porch alone, out in the sunlight, glad to have finally stepped out of the shade.

There's a vulture up high in the clear sky, turning circles around and around—America Reynosa's words all over again, this time in the flesh—marking a spot where something has died. Another joins it, and then another, so that there are three of them. They're black marks against the blue, the only things scarring the sky, and I wonder why they spin around like that, why they wait so long to claim the dead thing that is already theirs.

There's a short bark of laughter back behind me in the house, someone watching TV.

I've been telling myself all along I want to help Jenna and Kasper, even Sunny, but maybe the deputies are right and there's nothing I can do for any them, if I don't do something for myself.

In the end, it's always just been one more lie I needed to believe . . .

But I can warn Deputy Reynosa and Deputy Harper about the girl in Terlingua, and I can tell them what I know about Earl's plan for tonight. Maybe it's the bank or maybe it's not, but whatever it is, I can get all of us ready.

The sky is now empty and unmarred again, and the vultures are all gone.

34

This is a dream . . .

They are out on the lake and she's sitting in the front of the boat, her hair pulled up, laughing at something he just said. The water behind her is blue, capped white, catching the sunlight and sending it back skyward. Everything is bright and she has on her sunglasses so that he can't see her eyes and her head is thrown back and there is light playing on her throat and her skin shines like a new day dawning . . .

There is wind between them, drying the water that falls against them as quickly as it lands, as if it never touched them at all.

There's a radio somewhere playing the Eagles, her favorite song, and she's singing along with it.

And he wishes he could see her eyes . . . goddamn wishes he knew what he just said to make her laugh like that, so he can say it again, forever and always. He can't take his eyes off her shining skin and wants to take her up and hold her and feel that shine with his own hands . . . hold her tight . . . so they can both glow together. But he is darkness and always has been and always will be and he's ashamed that he exists only when reflected by her, by stealing her light.

It doesn't matter to her, it never did. She never thought he was stealing what she was willing to give . . .

*She says something to him but he can't hear her, the wind snatching away
the words at that moment. Maybe it's "I love you" or just his name . . . they
are both the same to him. He calls back to her but something has caught her
eye out on the shore, and she's turned away from him, looking out over
the water.*

*Her hair's come loose and it streams behind her like the memory of a now
falling star.*

He goes to catch her, to hold her, before she reaches the ground.

This is a dream.

This is all it will ever be.

He's ready now.

He woke to a banging on his door, a pounding in his head, and the
bottle of Balcones, along with others he didn't remember finishing
off, scattered around the couch. There were chess pieces, too, flung
everywhere, as if he'd started a game and upended the board. "So
What" by Miles Davis was still playing, the last thing he'd heard before
everything had gone black. It was a nine-minute arrangement, but he'd
been out a lot longer than that. It had been dark before, and now it was
bright, early-morning sunlight burning through the thin curtains Modelle Greer had strung up in the place.

He had no idea how many replays of the song he'd gone through, had
no idea even what day it was. He felt as old as he ever had, feeble and lost.
He stumbled, searching for the Colt that had last been in his hand, only
to find it was still there. He'd passed out with the gun in his fingers and
grew cold even in the hot room at the thought of what that meant.

Far colder than the gun itself, which was still warm from his night-
long grip.

Maybe he'd dreamed of touching it against his temple or feeling its
metal against his teeth. That's all it had been, though, a dream.

He pushed the Colt beneath a couch pillow, unwilling to look at it again.

"Goddamn, I'm up, come in, it's unlocked."

The door opened, revealing Amé, her hands full. She looked the way he felt, only worse. Her eyes were hollowed, dark. At least he had drunk himself to sleep; it appeared she hadn't slept at all. He tried to stand and go to her, but his body wouldn't cooperate, not fully.

She took in the bottles around him but didn't say anything, just pushed a few aside with her boot to join him on the couch.

"We've both had better mornings, I see," he said, reaching for one of the coffee cups in her hand. "Are you okay, nothing happened, right? Nothing with the Earls . . ."

"No, not that. Not them." She had another bag, and pulled from it a bottle of Bayer and a couple of silver-wrapped packets of Certs. "You're going to need these, a lot of both. You have to pull yourself together. We have something we need to do today."

"That sounds serious. You know, Chris left for El Paso this morning." He blew on the coffee that was still too hot to drink.

"Sí. It might be better he's not here anyway, for now." She opened the aspirin bottle and dumped four into Harp's hand, followed by two Certs. "I talked to Azahel Avalos last night."

Harp struggled, reaching. "You mean that dumbass that hit Tommy, the guy still in lockup? The guy you punched?"

"Sí, that one."

He dry-chewed the mints and the aspirin before trying the coffee again. "Goddamn, why? He's got a lawyer. You can't talk to him."

"He wanted to talk to me."

"Was Paez there?"

"No."

Harp took one more aspirin. "Then it does us no good, it does him no good. It's like it never happened at all."

"Lo sé. I think that's the point." She sat back, felt something, and pulled out a chess piece and Harp's gun from beneath the pillow. She tossed the chess piece aside and didn't check to see if the gun was loaded, since they both knew well enough that it was. But she looked at it a long time before dropping the magazine and popping out the lone chambered round, catching it clean with her free hand. She put the gun and the magazine on the small coffee table, muzzle pointed away from them both, out of habit. It sat in the middle of his empty chessboard, but she held on to the single bullet.

"So that's where that went to." Harp tried to joke, giving up on the coffee and putting it on the table next to the gun, realizing that Jackie's Archangel Michael pendant was there on the little table as well, where it gathered up morning sunlight. He didn't remember bringing it in from the car.

"When I came in, you thought I was going to tell you something about the Earls?"

Harp shrugged, keeping his eyes clear of the pendant and the Colt; anywhere, really, but the gun. "I thought . . . I mean, yeah I did, something other than Avalos, anyway. I'd forgotten all about him."

"We all did," she said, but Harp could tell she was lying. She hadn't forgotten about him at all, not even close. "But this does have to do with the Earls. John Wesley Earl."

"I don't get it," Harp said.

She picked up the coffee he'd abandoned. "I didn't either, not at first. This is going to take a while." She tried to take a sip, found it too hot as well.

"It starts with my brother, Rodolfo . . ."

LATER, THEY WERE WAITING in the sun for Customs agent Elgin Bartlett.

Harp had called him over an hour ago, but Elgin was dealing with a tractor trailer full of onions crossing through Presidio—onions, and about two thousand pounds of weed. All the agents at the POE were tied up with that and would be a while longer, and it had been Bartlett's canine, Big Max, who'd found it. All those thousands of stinking onions from Ahumada in Chihuahua, and the shepherd-Labrador mix had smelled the weed hidden beneath them anyway.

Bartlett had texted Harp that he was on his way as soon as he could get free, but they were running some other trucks through secondary, and both he and Big Max were working their asses off. Sometimes the cartels tried to shotgun multiple loads through at a time, figuring if one got taken off, that upped the chances of success for the others. Sometimes, they *hoped* a load got ripped—it was easy enough to sacrifice a ton of weed if fifty or a hundred kilos of coke, meth, or even heroin got through behind it.

It was the cost of doing business.

The impound lot didn't offer much shade, and they could have waited together inside the department, but Harp wanted to be out here in the sun anyway, to give it a chance to burn away the last bit of his headache that the aspirin hadn't quite reached. Amé wasn't complaining, so they swapped turns sitting in his air-conditioned truck, taking small breaks, when they weren't walking around Azahel Avalos's— *Miguel Suarez's*—car examining it from every angle.

Searching it a third, fourth, fifth time; so many they lost count.

And each time, it stubbornly refused to give up its secrets.

BACK AT HIS APARTMENT, sitting with his gun in front of them on the table, Amé had finally told Harp about Rodolfo—how he'd worked as a BP agent in the Big Bend, but how his *real* job, the one that had mattered, had been moving drugs and money for a cartel called Nemesio back and forth over the river. Rodolfo had done it with the help of Big Bend's then sheriff, Stanford Ross, and his chief deputy, Duane Dupree. At some point, Rodolfo had learned that the sheriff and Dupree were double-crossing Nemesio, holding back money or just outright stealing it, and they'd killed him because of it. There was more than that— Dupree had also been fixated on Amé, stalking and threatening her, while he succumbed to a raging meth habit and rapidly fell apart, body and mind. But before her brother had died, he'd left her a gun and a phone that Nemesio had given him. Desperate and alone, she'd used that phone to make a call, and a boy named Máximo had arrived not long after, bringing with him revenge; fire and death.

Some of this Harp had suspected already, and other parts he'd picked up from Chris, who'd played his own role in it all. But Amé told him that Chris never knew about Máximo, and still didn't, or what had become of all that money Sheriff Ross had stolen.

No one had, except the sheriff's son, Caleb.

And her.

ELGIN BARTLETT WAS A BIG MAN, and his blue Customs uniform was soaked through. His hat was crooked on his large head, barely hiding thinning hair and a sunburned scalp.

He'd had a miserable morning, and looked every bit of it.

Big Max looked worn-out, too, sitting on his haunches in the thin shadows tossed by Bartlett's truck. The dog watched them with eyes that made it clear he knew who was going to do all the real work.

Bartlett wiped his head with his hat, but since it was drenched, too, it didn't help.

"Goddamn, Harp, you could have called Vazquez over at the BP checkpoint on I-67, or whoever's working Sierra Blanca or 118. You know they got dogs, too. We all get trained at the same damn place nowadays."

"Maybe, but they're not as good as you and Big Max. Not half as good. Blue shirts, green shirts, hell, I don't know the difference anymore with you guys and your uniforms, but I know a good dog."

Bartlett looked sideways over at Amé, who was checking her phone. "You just didn't want Vazquez 'cause he's Mexican."

Harp rolled his eyes. "My *partner* is Mexican, you racist dummy. And I don't even give a shit if Big Max *is* Mexican, will you just get to it?"

"Okay, okay." Bartlett patted his back pocket to make sure he had Big Max's rolled-up yellow towel, the dog's reward for doing a good job. The dog spied it and stood up, knowing it was time to get to work. As Bartlett walked past Harp toward the Nissan, Big Max loping behind him, Harp caught the sour smell of onions.

"Hey," Bartlett said, "did you call those breeders in Sanderson that we talked about? Did they get that dog for you?"

Harp watched Big Max start making his way around Avalos's car, nose down. "Yeah, thanks for that. I really appreciate it. I got him. But he wasn't for me."

HE'D BROKEN DOWN AND MIXED a lot of the too-hot coffee she'd brought with some ice and a little of the Red River bourbon he had above the fridge, just a fingerful, to help even him out. He'd made a point of holding up the bottle so that she saw him put it away; so she knew that was all he was having.

"No one cares about what happened to Dupree and Sheriff Ross, Amé. Sounds to me like they got what was coming, *what they deserved*, and it's what would have happened anyway, one way or another, no matter what you did or didn't do. As for the money? The sheriff isn't looking for it, and I sure in the hell don't care. If you need to unburden yourself about it, tell a priest. Otherwise, fuck it. I hope you bought yourself something nice. Nicer than that little house over in Beantown . . ." Harp had stopped, looked away. "Sorry about that, but you know what I mean. I hope you bought a lot of nice things."

"I don't know if I deserve nice things," she said. "Anyway, when I realized Avalos knew who I was, I got afraid he was here for that money. If he knew about it, then Nemesio knew as well. That's why I wanted to talk to him. I was worried for you and Sheriff Cherry."

"Fair enough, but we can take care of ourselves. But you said Avalos knows you?"

"He knows *about* me. He says that everyone knows about my brother and me, because of our uncle, a man they call Fox Uno. He's Nemesio, so was Rodolfo, and . . ."

"And so are you," he'd finished for her, sitting back next to her on the couch, shoulder to shoulder. "I get it, and that's complete bullshit. That man means nothing to you."

"*Él es la familia.*"

"You don't believe that. The sheriff is your family. Your Mel is your family. I and those other asshole deputies we work with are family, if you want us to be. We're the only family that matters, at least more than this bogeyman across the river. If people want to think differently, fuck 'em and prove 'em wrong."

"You make it sound so *fácil.* You didn't grow up here, you don't know."

"Maybe, maybe not. But I know it's going to be every bit as hard as you make it."

She'd nodded and took one of the aspirin she'd brought him for herself, chasing it with his coffee and Red River mixture.

"If Avalos wasn't here to scare you or take back that money, then what the fuck was he here for? And what does he have to do with the Earls?"

"It still has everything to do with money, just not the money I've been holding on to these last two years."

BIG MAX BARKED, once, twice, and then sat down by the left front fender of the Nissan.

"Looks like we got a winner, winner, chicken dinner," Bartlett said, mostly to himself, but loud enough that Harp could hear . . .

"AVALOS TOLD ME the car has a *clavo.* It means 'nail,' but what it really means is the car holds a big *trap*, a secret compartment for smuggling money or drugs or whatever. The people Avalos works for were working with Earl and the ABT. All the money Earl's been making all these years dealing drugs was being kept by those men. They provided him the drugs he sold, and held on to most of the money he made. Avalos was supposed to bring Earl that money, as well as a new license and passport. It's all in the car, and Earl is the only one who knows how to get it out."

Harp had laughed, bitter. "I can't believe Earl trusted those fuckers more than his own people, or his own family. The Mexicans have been the goddamn bank all along, and that car was the fucking vault, Earl's safety deposit box. I wasn't wrong about that, after all. I was just looking in the wrong damn place. He's cashing out."

"*Sí*. I didn't push, but that's what I understand. Last night Avalos was desperate and wanted my help getting the car and the money inside it to Earl. But today he will find out he's getting bonded out anyway."

"And yet, Santino Paez didn't tell him that right away, and instead got him to talk to you first? Why?"

"It has to do with his *familia*," she'd said, and left it at that.

"Whatever, the less I know, the better. But that lawyer's taking a risk, a big one. I'll give him credit for that." He'd started looking around for his badge and belt. "That fucker Earl never planned to help his son or Nichols or anyone. He's never going back and he's never going to testify. He's not going into witness protection to live out the rest of his days with Nichols or some other agent like him looking over his shoulder. He's going to run."

"So what do we do now?"

He'd put the mostly full glass aside, and reached over and picked up his gun and magazine from the table. Both had gone cold while sitting there, untouched.

He'd racked the magazine into place as Amé handed him the single bullet she'd been holding the whole time.

"First we make sure Avalos, or Miguel or whatever the fuck his name is, is telling the truth, and then we'll figure it out from there."

. . .

"Look, I can't tell you exactly how big it is, or what's in it, but it's there. Max alerted. It's dope, money, something."

Big Max was chewing through his towel, still standing guard on the Nissan.

"We looked all through it," Amé said. "All morning. We saw nothing."

Bartlett squinted at her. "They're pretty ingenious nowadays. They got these guys, right? That's all they do, build these sorts of traps. There may be a sequence of buttons in the car you have to hit, like first turning on the radio to a certain station and then the AC and then rolling down the left window. It may be magnetized, or the only way to get it open may be to cut it out. We can X-ray it at the POE and take a better look."

Harp kicked at the blown tires. "We'll have to tow it down there."

Bartlett nodded. "Yeah, it doesn't look like it's going anywhere fast and today's not good anyway. But if you bring it down tomorrow, or the day after, we can crack her open. Give my guys some time and we'll find whatever's in there."

"Okay," Harp said, reaching out a hand to Bartlett. "Thanks for coming up. I owe you a beer and burger."

"Make that two burgers, one for Big Max," Bartlett said, coaxing the dog from the Nissan and back to his own truck.

Harp stared at Avalos's car, furious. It sat on its ruptured tires, covered in dust, where it had been left and ignored since the day Tommy Milford had been run down.

Goddamn.

If he'd just done what Chris had told him days and days ago, when the sheriff had been on him about getting a dog on the car. But with Bravo's murder and then everything with the Earls, he'd let it slip. Like he'd let other things slip, far too many.

He'd talked a big game to Chris about action versus reaction, always faulting the young sheriff for being too patient, too deliberate and always waiting too long to act. But here he was with Avalos's car and he hadn't done anything at all.

It had been there all along, right in front of him, waiting for him.

Goddamn.

"Okay, now what?" Amé asked, moving next to him, staring at the car too.

"Well, it seems Avalos is telling the truth. Not much we can do with the car, but we can get Danny Ford the hell outta Killing. Now."

"*Sí*, I thought you might say that."

Harp shook his head. "There's no reason for him to stay down there even one more day. The whole situation is fucked. I'm going to go down there and get him myself, and put cuffs on that lying sack of shit Earl while I'm at it . . ."

It had been there all along, right in front of him, waiting for him.

"No, Ben, you don't need to do that—"

"I wasn't asking, *niña*. Every minute Danny's down there, *he's* in danger."

"*Verdad*, as he was yesterday, today, and tomorrow. And this"—she pointed at the car—"doesn't change that much. I feel the same way you do, but what we're going to do is tell the sheriff what we found so he can let Agent Nichols decide how to deal with Earl. *Ese es su problema.*"

Harp didn't believe what he was hearing from her, even though he could see her struggling with it: what she really wanted to do, versus what she thought they should do. What the sheriff would want. He'd watched Chris struggle the same way, and maybe the things Avalos had told her had affected her more than she realized. "Amé, Earl has to know by now this car is here. He's probably known it all along. His hands might as well have been on the wheel when it ran down Tommy. He can't let it go. He's coming to get it, one way or another. You see that, right? And that is *my* problem."

Amé shaded her eyes with her hand and took in the impound lot, the high fence, and the Nissan's wrecked tires. "It's our problem, and it won't be easy for him."

"You're right about that. It's not going to be easy at all, no matter what. But he won't stop now. And there's still Danny . . ."

Amé held up her phone again. "No, like I was trying to tell you, we don't need to go to Killing. Not for Danny, not for any reason. I've already heard from him, he texted me and he's on his way to meet us. He thinks Vianey Ruiz is in danger. So, while I'm checking in with her, you're going to call the sheriff and let him know what we found."

"Goddammit, Chris will go batshit. And after that, he'll order us to sit tight. He'll call that fucker Nichols, and Earl's going to catch wind of what we know and be gone."

"*Está bien.* Nichols *should* know, and if Earl runs, it's on him."

"You don't believe that, you want Earl as bad as I do. And we're not negotiating . . ."

"*Sí, sí, estamos*, Ben Harper. I want the man who killed Billy Bravo, but we both know that's Jesse Earl, not his papa. More than that, I want to make sure Vianey and Danny don't get hurt, so *that's* all we're agreeing to. If you insist we go down to Killing right now, we go down together, or we don't go at all. If you walk out of this lot on your own, I'll call Greer and Emmett and Holt to come grab you. I'll call the district attorney and tell him all about this. I'll have the *camisetas verdes* stop you before you get to Killing. And if I have to, I'll cuff you to that car there myself."

"You are one tough bitch, you know that?" But Harp couldn't help smiling when he said it. She'd outflanked him with the interviews, and she'd done it here again. She knew he would never let her go into Killing with him, not now.

She was a damn good chess player for someone who'd never played the game.

"I had a very good teacher."

"Well then, I hope you have a good place for Danny to meet us. Someplace safe. Once he's out of Killing, there's no need for him to ever go back. We won't let him."

Amé put her phone away. "*Sí*, I know just the place."

35

Earl had to hold the cell phone away from his ear while Nichols yelled at him during their daily check-in.

He thought at first that Nichols knew about Manny and his people, but it wasn't that.

Then he thought it had something to do with the little meet-and-greet he'd had with Sheriff Cherry earlier in the morning, but he'd believed the sheriff when he said that was for their ears and no one else's, and it was soon clear enough anyway, despite all of Nichols's barking, that the agent didn't know anything about that, either.

What he did know, and what he was righteously pissed about, was that Thurman Flowers was in Killing and Earl hadn't said a fuckin' thing to him about it.

The agent was going on about chat groups or the damn Internet, but it all came down to the fact that he'd been a busy little beaver all on his own, sniffing around and doing his best to keep an eye on Earl even from hundreds of miles away, and was furious to learn that Earl had been holdin' out on him.

Hell, he didn't know the half of it.

Earl had dealt with the agent agitated before, but not like this. Earl figured he was gettin' squeezed from somewhere above, or someone had burned up the phone lines one too many times to Washington, D.C., or wherever it was someone like Nichols had to answer to.

Earl told him to calm the fuck down, and that only made him madder.

Earl had always known *he* was runnin' on borrowed time, so it was no surprise to learn that the agent was, too.

He tried again to get Nichols to shut the fuck up, explaining that everything was still good and still on track. Flowers had arrived only a couple of days ago and Earl didn't expect any more run-ins with anyone in Murfee, so all he needed was another day or two, which they both knew was such complete and utter bullshit that Nichols laughed at him before he even finished. He told Earl that as bad as he wanted Flowers, and that was bad enough he could almost taste it, he wasn't going to jeopardize the cases they'd already made on the ABT trying to get him now. Jesse's little throw-down in Terlingua had fucked all that up, and everyone right along with it, and Earl had doubled down on it by not shooting straight about Flowers's arrival in Killing. So now he—Special Agent Austin Nichols—was on his way down to Murfee from Dallas to personally straighten this shit out, and Earl better be there waiting for him.

Earl had only as long as it was going to take Nichols to get a flight, and then, no matter what, Nichols was pulling the plug. Party over.

Really, Earl didn't give a flyin' fuck about that anyway, since he was gonna be long gone before Nichols had picked up his luggage, but he didn't like the man pissin' on him and told him so, suggesting Nichols go righteously fuck himself. He reminded the mouthy agent that he was nothing without Earl, that it was Earl who'd risked everything from the get-go, while Nichols hadn't risked shit, except his time.

That's when Nichols went silent for so long that Earl thought he'd hung up, or had thrown the phone across the room, until the agent quietly laughed and said, *I'm nothing? Risked nothing? There is no world for you without me. You only exist because I allow it, and I can unmake you with a wave of a hand. You're an inbred, ignorant cracker who'd still be rotting in jail if I hadn't stepped in. You're nothing but a signature on a piece of paper. Let me tell you a story . . .*

Then Nichols said a name.

Danny . . .

HE CAME BACK INTO THE HOUSE and walked into Jesse, Flowers, and Clutts, who were waiting for him.

He wasn't in the mood for this, not now, not after what he'd learned from Nichols, but it was clear they weren't gonna let him pass without having their say.

"Danny finally got the word from his friends up at Fort Bliss. He's gonna go meet them today," Jesse said. His face was blue turning to black where Danny had struck him, and one eye was red like a setting sun.

"Well, it seems to me that's what you all been waitin' for," Earl answered, waving at the three in front of him. And he almost laughed out loud. *And just a fucking coincidence, too,* this mysterious meeting coming on the heels of his talk with Nichols.

Let me tell you a story . . .

Flowers: "Do you still trust Danny after what he did to Jesse? Everything we're going to do here is based on trust. That's something I know you understand."

"Fuck, I don't trust *you*, Flowers. I try not to trust anyone." And yet he *had* trusted Danny, at least as much as he'd needed to, and look what that almost got him. "And I woulda whupped Jesse myself if I'd known first he was out pokin' around for this little wetback girl. But it don't matter, 'cause I made it clear to Danny he ain't gonna be hittin' Jesse like that ever again. I told him I'd near kill him myself if he did. The same way I'd do you, if you were to cross me or my boy."

Flowers raised his hands. "There's no worry about that. Jesse and I see eye to eye on a lot of things, including our concern about Danny. Jesse thinks he should be followed to see what he's really up to, and I agree."

Jesse added, "That old deputy in Murfee called him "Danny" when we were all in that bar, all familiar-like. Like they was old friends, JW, like they was *good* friends."

If Jesse had picked up on something subtle like that, Earl was impressed, not that it mattered now. It was too damn late. "Are you two here askin' my permission or my opinion?"

Flowers put a hand on Jesse's shoulder . . . *all familiar-like.* "Honestly, neither, John. We just thought you should know. That issue of trust, again. I wanted to see if it's going to be a problem."

Do you know who "Danny Ferro" really is . . . ?

Do you know why he's there?

You dumb cracker peckerwood piece of shit . . .

Think you can fuck with me?

No, Earl didn't think it was gonna be a problem at all.

"It mean's nothin' to me." He turned to Jesse. "You think you can handle it?"

"Yeah, he's goin' out on his bike. I can take care of it, no problem."

Earl figured letting Jesse follow Danny from Killing was no different from putting both of the boys' names in the hat, but he was okay with that. He was finally ready to put all the cards on the table anyway, push all his chips in, and for the second time that morning, he almost laughed out loud. The name Danny had given him, *Danny Ferro . . . faro . . .* just like that old card game.

A queen of clubs with a ragged black hole in the center, that his daddy said had come from an actual bullet, a faro game gone bad . . .

The boy did have balls.

Do you know who "Danny Ferro" really is . . . ?

You dumb cracker peckerwood piece of shit . . .

Do you know why he's there?

Think you can fuck with me? . . . I can unmake you with a wave of a hand.

Do you know why he's there?

Earl focused on Jesse. "Look, borrow a car from the Joyces, he won't recognize it as quick. Maybe even have Joker and Lee follow in the Marquis, too, way back, just to be sure. Keep an eye out for trouble."

He was specific about the cars, because it mattered for what he needed to do.

And he was gonna have to do it without Danny, because he was bettin' on this hand, one way or another, that Danny Ferro, *Danny Ford,* wasn't ever coming back to Killing.

"Do what you gotta do, and let's see if he's tellin' us the truth."

Although Earl already knew the answer.

HE COULD HAVE LEFT IT AT THAT, but didn't. He tracked down Danny, who was outside near his bike.

"They tell me your army boys are finally gonna meet you."

Danny looked up from where he was kneeling next to his Harley. It was a good-looking bike with a custom paint job, blue and chrome, and with Danny wipin' it down under the bright sun, it shined like quicksilver. "Yeah, they finally called. I figure I need to at least meet them since I was the one pushing so hard. They're coming down to Van Horn, so I won't be too long. Like you said, as long as I'm here, I need to come through with something for Jesse and Flowers. I'll be back tonight in plenty of time. If you need me to go through Murfee, I can do that, too, for one more look around."

"Is that right now?" Earl stood over him, casting his shadow. "I have a feelin' there ain't no army buddies meeting you in Van Horn, and maybe you're just gonna keep on ridin' instead. Is that what you're gonna do, *Danny?*"

Danny stood up, wiped his hands on his jeans. "You've shot straight with me since you saved my life back in Lubbock, and I owe you that much. I'm the one that asked for this damn meeting with these boys, so just let me take care of it, and I'll be back to do what you need me to."

Do you know who "Danny Ferro" really is . . . ?

"Okay, but before you head outta here, hand over that gun in your jeans. If you get stopped or somethin' bad happens, maybe it's not such a good idea to have you shootin' anyone with one of our pieces. Actually, that one was my daddy's. It's kinda special to me."

Danny hesitated, before finally slipping the revolver out of his jeans. He turned it around and handed it grip first to Earl, the muzzle pointed at his own stomach.

Do you know why he's there?

"You really worry about that now, JW? After all we've been through since we got here? I know Flowers is the one who's supposed to be a pastor, but sometimes I think I'm the only one that's been preaching any sense. How am I going to defend myself if I run into some trouble?"

Earl smiled and settled the gun into his own jeans.

"Oh, I wouldn't worry about that. These are your buddies, right? And besides, I've seen you twice now put up a damn good fight with just your hands. Like I said, you're a damn hard man to put down. Just like me. I think when this is all done, we're both gonna be just fine . . ."

36

The HIDTA meeting was held in an office building only a few blocks from the hospital where Chris had stayed after he was shot at the Far Six.

Mel had been at a hotel nearby, although he still couldn't remember exactly which one. She had visited him every day, sitting by his bedside and holding his hand, her blood mixing with his. One of the doctors told him he'd been dead for a minute, but Mel had helped bring him back to life. She'd given him all the blood she could to replace what he'd lost out in the desert.

He'd died and come back to her.

It was strange to think about that—how there was always a part of her with him. He carried her everywhere. She was his every breath, every heartbeat.

I love you more than life. Some people said those words.

He and Mel knew what they really meant.

THE MEETING ITSELF WAS MADE UP of federal, state, and local cops. The HIDTA—High Intensity Drug Trafficking Area—program was created by Congress to support drug-related operations and initiatives with federal money. For a small sheriff's department like Chris's, the West Texas HIDTA meant desperately needed funding, but it came with certain strings, one of which included this quarterly meeting. Although the money was good, Chris found it was the chance to meet other members of the law enforcement community—to share ideas and intelligence—that proved most useful. He was the youngest sheriff by far, and responsible for one of the largest regions in the state, one notorious for its outlaw history. All the reading and research in the world would never teach him what some of these men had learned in a lifetime of police work.

That's why he'd brought on Harp, and kept an eye out for others like him who might be willing to come down to the Big Bend. Yet he struggled, knowing that Harp's lifetime behind a badge and gun brought its own burned-in prejudices and attitudes.

Action versus reaction, the first always wins.

There are wolves in the world, Chris. Criminals . . . outlaws . . . bad men, whatever you want to call them . . . sometimes we gotta be wolves, too . . . we just do.

Maybe, maybe not. He often asked himself if that was how it had started with Sheriff Ross and Duane Dupree. Had they been wolves so often, for so long, that they couldn't turn back anymore, or had it been something else entirely? Sheriff Stanford Ross's shadow still hung over Murfee and the Big Bend like the Chisos Mountains, large, immovable, unknowable. The sheriff had never explained himself, even when Chris had begged him to know *why* at the point of a gun.

So Chris tried hard to be a different kind of lawman, nothing like Sheriff Ross. He wanted to bring his department into *this* century, leave its past behind, but was afraid he'd never quite get out from under that other man's shadow; damn worried each day, the longer it went on, that he might forget he was even walking in its darkness at all.

It didn't help that he had to see Sheriff Ross's face every time he came to these meetings. He'd won Texas Lawman of the Year five times, and all of his award pictures were still up on the wall. Each one *looked* exactly the same—the creased uniform shirt, the sheriff's tanned face smiling tight beneath a razored brush cut, the hair just slightly gunmetal gray.

And those eyes: piercing and somehow young and old at the same time, the color of moonlight reflected off the barrel of a gun.

Colleen Worrel, the HIDTA secretary, told Chris that each picture had been taken new when the sheriff had won the award. But they all sure looked similar, even though some of them were taken years apart.

He just never seemed to get old, never seemed to change much at all, she told him. *I wish we all were so lucky.*

UNLIKE THE PICTURES OF SHERIFF ROSS, Garrison had changed even over just the last two years. There was more salt-and-pepper in his goatee, and now some had found its way to his temples. He'd put on a little bit of weight as well, visible in his face and around his gut. His tie was a little too tight and he was quick to loosen it, leaving his neck red. Chris had seen him wear a wedding ring before, but not today, and he didn't know what that meant, if anything at all.

They weren't close in the way he felt comfortable asking, so he didn't.

They picked up a cup of coffee after the meeting at a little place downtown near the freeway, and then drove separately to the Concordia Cemetery, within sight of Ciudad Juárez and the border. The cemetery was fifty-two acres of stone and concrete markers and rotting wooden crosses, a bullet hole in the heart of El Paso. It looked like an abandoned movie set, the tilted headstones just props. Garrison told him that it had been in use since the 1800s, and more than sixty thousand people were buried somewhere under the scrub, although no one knew the exact number. The cemetery had its share of bald patches and worn areas, seemingly empty, but far from it, where the old cheap crosses had given way to time, dust, and storms. One epitaph Chris passed started with *The Good and the Bad . . .*

"They say the place is haunted, particularly in the children's section. No one knows how many kids are buried here. They run ghost tours all the time, and they do a big thing for Día de los Muertos," Garrison said, reading the sign along with Chris. "I live here in El Paso and I think I've only been out here twice, but there is a lot of history buried beneath our feet."

"Including the gunfighter John Wesley Hardin, right?"

"Yeah, he's some of that famous history."

"Okay," Chris said, walking through dust. "Let's find that headstone."

IT WAS MORE THAN THAT—a stone and barred iron enclosure that reminded Chris of a jail cell, protecting a stretch of empty dirt topped with the marble headstone and a raised marker sporting the seal of Texas. The peaked roof had a metal sign cut out with the initials JWH, over which hung two six-shooters. The guns looked like wings, flying those initials heavenward, and it was only when he got closer that Chris could tell how much they resembled the guns tattooed on Jesse Earl's forearms. He read the marker through the bars:

John Wesley Hardin (May 26, 1853–August 19, 1895). Born in Bonham, Texas, John Wesley Hardin was named for the founder of Methodism. "Wes" Hardin grew into a family man, cowboy, and outlaw who claimed to have killed more than 30 men. An unusual sort of gunslinger Hardin considered himself a pillar of society who killed to save his own life. Hardin served 15 years in state prison for murder, was pardoned, then opened a law office in El Paso in May 1895. He was killed 3 months later by John Selman, an El Paso City Constable.

"I read somewhere that the constable, Selman, shot Hardin in the back of the head. Hardin never saw it coming, never had a chance." Garrison shrugged. "Selman himself was no saint, spent equal time as both a lawman and an outlaw. He was later shot by a U.S marshal and is supposed to be buried out here, too, somewhere in the Catholic section. His grave was unmarked and it's never been found."

"You don't strike me as someone who'd read this much Texas history," Chris said.

"Yeah, and you don't strike me as someone who is comfortable wearing that gun. I think you're the one better suited for a book than a badge, Chris. No offense."

"None taken. God knows I feel that way some days. But you know that saying, you break it, you buy it? For me, that's Murfee and the Big Bend County Sheriff's Department."

"You didn't break anything, Sheriff Ross did. You're picking up the pieces, and if you ask me, you've done your part. You can walk away anytime. There is no glory in any of this, trust me." Garrison shook his head. "Anyway, you're not here for a lecture. You asked me to look into FBI Special Agent Austin Nichols, and I did."

"And?"

"And he's based out of their Dallas field office, an up-and-comer. He went to law school in Georgia before becoming an agent. Our guys in Dallas haven't worked with him because he's always been assigned to gang stuff and domestic terrorism, not really drug cases. But I have to ask, is this also related to that traffic stop that you e-mailed me about a couple of weeks back, your deputy getting run down?"

"No, not that," Chris said. "At least I don't think so." Chris had been reluctant to call Garrison after the Avalos incident, not wanting the inevitable discussion that he knew would follow, the familiar outlines of an old argument. Garrison saw everything through his own particularly dark lens, and couldn't get past the killing of one of his agents in Murfee and the near-fatal wounding of another. He took special issue with America Reynosa and he took it personally; he absolutely thought Chris had made a mistake bringing her on as a deputy. Amé's brother Rodolfo had been an informant and a drug smuggler and not particularly good at either, and either one more than enough to draw Garrison's antipathy. Rodolfo's activities had cost him and others their lives; he was tainted and everyone associated with him was as well. The DEA agent could go on endlessly about all of his intel about the extended Reynosa family across the river; about his informants and his finely honed agent instincts and experience, all of which, to him, made Amé an equally bad bet. But Chris knew it was more than Amé, it was Murfee itself, it was the *place* he couldn't trust, and never would.

So Chris had sent him a short e-mail instead, and the reply had been equally terse. The DEA had no information on Azahel Avalos.

Garrison continued. "Like I wrote you then, we ran the driver in our indices and didn't have anything on him, but that doesn't mean there *isn't* something. He's not speeding through your town and running from your deputies for no reason." And by *your town* and *no reason*, Chris knew that Garrison was referring to Murfee's drug-smuggling history.

"You don't trust anyone."

"And your problem, Chris, is you want to trust everyone. Life doesn't work that way, and this job sure in the hell doesn't."

"You sound suspiciously like one of my deputies."

Garrison watched dirty clouds move across the sky. "Speaking of deputies, how's Ms. Reynosa?"

Here it comes.

"She's doing very well." There was a long, uncomfortable silence that neither man seemed ready to fill.

Finally: "I'm glad to hear that," Garrison said.

"No, let's be honest, you're *surprised* to hear it. And we both know you don't believe it or mean it."

"It is what it is. I just want you to be careful, that's all."

"She was a young girl when all that went down with her brother. It's a non-issue for her, so it has to be for me."

"She's still a young girl *now* . . . a girl with an extremely complicated past."

"Given what happened with Sheriff Ross, the same could be said for me." Chris turned away from Hardin's grave, looked squarely at Garrison. "What remaining family she had in Murfee is gone. She never crosses into Ojinaga as far as I know. She lives by herself, works her ass off, and *wants* to be a good cop. I need her help with all the Hispanics in our community. They trust her in a way they don't trust me and the other deputies, and that means something. Whatever you and your people think you're hearing about her or her relatives, it's nothing."

"You should know better than anyone that it's never *nothing*."

"We're done talking about Ms. Reynosa. I mean it."

"Got it, we're done. And I just said I wasn't going to lecture you." Garrison went back to counting the low clouds in the sky. "So what is the deal with Nichols? Why does he matter?"

Chris turned back to Hardin's grave site. "It has to do with a man named John Wesley Earl."

CHRIS TOLD GARRISON EVERYTHING; he stood silent the whole time, listening. When Chris finished, the DEA agent checked his watch, pretending to care about the time, collecting his thoughts.

"I've had my guys work prison cases before, big-time crooks moving considerable weight both inside and outside. They get iPhones smuggled into them and make calls and arrange deals right in their cells. We had a Mexican snitch in Lynaugh who told his fellow inmates that he knew a guy on the outside who could drum up twenty, thirty kilos at a time. The snitch would pass a number we'd given him, and sure enough, his 'guy' on the outside, actually one of my agents acting undercover, would get a call out of the blue. Next thing you know, we'd have some Black Disciples from Chicago in a Motel 6 with two hundred fifty thousand dollars in the back of a rented Toyota Camry. It's a new world order, Chris. These gangs have all gotten so big, their criminal networks and activities extending so far beyond the prison walls, that they have to work together, inside *and* outside. Moving drugs, carrying out contract killings, whatever."

"Nichols said as much."

"Right, so this op he's running is dicey, edge-of-the-seat stuff. High risk, high reward."

"Would you do it?" Chris asked.

"He's looking to tear the heart out of the ABT leadership, and take a shot at a piece of work like Thurman Flowers? That's big game."

"Big enough? These people are in my backyard and Nichols let them in."

Garrison scanned the graveyard, remembering. "Well, speaking of backyards, about ten years ago, ICE, when there was such a thing before it was folded into Homeland Security, had an informant working right over there in Juárez." Garrison pointed across the freeway, where the nearby border ran past them. "He managed something they called the 'House of Death' where the Carrillo-Fuentes cartel carried out numerous killings, burying the bodies, naturally, in the backyard. This informant drove the victims there, handed weapons and tools to their killers, and even recorded one of the murders and played it over the telephone to his ICE handlers, who listened to the whole thing and *still* kept using him. He fucking held down a man's legs while they killed him, and they made a *conscious decision* that it was worth looking the other way while he did that. They 'handled' it by telling him never to do that again, but of course he did, over and over. He was credited with sixty arrests and was paid over a quarter of a million dollars for his efforts helping the government, but no one knows exactly how many people he also helped murder. Was it worth it? It was not one of federal law enforcement's finer moments."

Garrison turned to start walking back to their cars and Chris fell in step with him. "But this is what we do, Chris, these are the risks we take. I've flipped some very bad men and put them right back out on the street to work, and I was holding my breath the whole time. We have a lot of rules and protocols for handling them and they're there for a reason, both for our protection and the informant's. Still, you can't watch them every minute of the day. So, like I said, you end up holding your damn breath. No matter how much a piece of shit they might be, you don't want them to get hurt, and more importantly, you don't want them hurting anyone else. Not on your watch."

"Like Rodolfo Reynosa."

Garrison's jaw clenched. "Right, like Rodolfo Reynosa."

"But you still didn't answer my question."

Garrison stopped. "Yes, I did. I told you . . . *this is what we do.* Look, as far as Earl is concerned, I'm not saying I would, I'm not saying I wouldn't. But if I did, I would be very, very careful about it and I'd want to make sure this Thurman Flowers was damn well worth it. Given what you've told me and how it's playing out, that's a long damn time for anyone to hold their breath."

"And what about Danny Ford? What if he was one of your agents and was now in bed with the Earls because of some misplaced sense of duty?"

"Or vengeance? Because that's really what we're taking about, right? That's a tough one, too. But right or wrong, once they're mine, they're always mine. You never let the guys who work for you go, particularly if they get hurt, or worse, if they get killed. *Most importantly,* if it happens on your watch. You have to talk to the wife, have to talk to the kids. You have to help them make sense of it, try to explain to them why it happened, and why what their daddy did was important enough to die for."

"Is it? Is it that important?" Chris knew that Garrison was talking about Darin Braccio and Morgan Emerson, the agents Duane Dupree had attacked.

Garrison started walking again, turning his back to Chris. "Again, it's what we do. And that is a question I can't answer for you. Only you can. And you need to, every day you put on that badge."

GARRISON WAS NOW GONE, and Chris was left sitting in his truck, staring at the crosses and headstones. He'd tried counting the ones he could see but kept losing his place, starting over again.

Again and again.

The Good and the Bad . . .

He needed to start the long drive back to Murfee, but had one other thing he wanted to do, something for Mel. Something he'd been thinking about for weeks now. He called her first to check in and she was outside, letting the new dog run, and he could hear him in the background, barking at the wind.

She told him she'd repaired the bathroom doorknob he'd pulled off the other morning.

Then he called Harp, who answered on the seventh or eighth ring, and sounded preoccupied, tired. Chris asked him what was going on in town, worried that maybe his encounter with Earl had kicked up a hornet's nest, but Harp said all was quiet. *Boring* was the word he used. He said it slow, hesitant, and Chris thought for a moment he was going to add something else, but he didn't. Whatever was on his mind could obviously wait, so that decided it for Chris. He told Harp he was going to stick around El Paso then for a while longer to get some errands done. Harp told him to take all the time he needed, and if things stayed quiet, he and Amé might go out later and put holes in some paper out at Chapel Mesa.

Harp told him to take care before he hung up and Chris did the same.

Starting his truck, Chris checked the clouds—the sort that could threaten rain—wondering if they'd follow him all the way back to the Big Bend. But then the sun broke through, and he reached for his sunglasses.

He drove out past the crosses casting long shadows behind him.

37

I get there as the sun is hooked on the horizon; everything beneath it still bright, the sky above it slowly going dark. I've heard of this place that Deputy Reynosa texted to meet, the Murfee Ghost Lights, but there isn't much to it—a gravel drive and a small pavilion and some benches just off the freeway, all of it looking out over a whole bunch of nothing, just rolling caliche and creosote. When I get there, another car is just leaving—some parents and their two kids, a small blond boy and his sister. Their license plate says they're from Arizona and the whole family looks at me as I roll past them into the lot.

The little boy waves as if he thinks he knows me.

The deputies are there waiting in one of their Big Bend County trucks. Deputy Reynosa seems glad to see me, the other one, Chief Deputy Harper, surprised. We stand around by the hood of their truck and Deputy Reynosa tells me that Bravo's girlfriend is fine and somewhere safe, and then Deputy Harper explains all about someone named Azahel Avalos and a broken-down car full of money, but the only thing I hear is Earl's name. That was his damn *Christmas in July*. Since Avalos was arrested he's been doing nothing but planning on how to steal that car back out of the impound lot. That's what we were going to do tonight, or what he was going to convince me to do for him. He's been lying all along, lying to the FBI and to me and to Sunny and to Jesse and to everyone.

I tell them that Earl somehow met with Sheriff Cherry earlier in the morning, and they exchange a look I easily understand.

They care about him, they're trying to protect him. From the Earls, and me.

They ask me how Earl plans to get the car out of the lot and where he's going after that, and I tell them I don't know; I'm not sure and he's never shared that with me. They wonder out loud if he'll still make a try for it if I don't return, and that I can answer, that I am sure of. He absolutely will. He won't turn back now because there's nothing to turn back for.

When I left I think he knew who I was, and still he let me go.

Deputy Reynosa tells me there's no reason for me to go back then; that there's nothing there for me anymore, if there ever was. When Nichols finds out about Avalos, the FBI will descend on Killing and it will all be over.

It's just a matter of time.

THERE IS A MEMORY I have of my dad.

I'm maybe eight and he's standing tall above me, blocking out the sun, and I think we're fishing. I know it's hot and I can smell water and dirt; that heavy, oily stink of fish. He's trying to show me how to hook a worm, and I won't do it. I won't put my hands out and grab it and he's frustrated. Finally, he bends down to get on his knees next to me and he's been drinking beer so I can smell that, too, and he's breathing right in my face.

He takes my little hands in his, hands that are covered in dirt from the worm can, but mine aren't. Mine are clean and white because I've had them stuck in my pockets. But my hands disappear into his and I feel the coiling and turning of the fat worm and the prick of metal as he makes the movements for me, guiding me through the process of baiting the hook. He's talking the whole time and I want to cry because I don't want to kill the worm or ever hurt anything at all, and when we're done and he releases my hands they are now just as dirty as his, slicked with mud and water and blood.

I remember him later washing my hands. He has a bar of soap and he makes a long green hose appear as if by magic and he gets down on his knees next to me for the second time and he takes up my hands again and he hoses them off with the cold, clear water and scrubs them with the soap until they're pure again, until both of our hands are white and spotless, and then he uses the tail of his own shirt to dry them.

When he's done he stands up and runs his clean hand through my blond hair and tells me it was *a damn good day* . . .

Then I'm in the backseat of the car and he's driving with both of our windows down and singing to a song on the radio, and as many times as I've turned this memory over I don't know what the song is and I always wish I did . . .

Finally, I am home in my room in my bed and I can hear my dad and my mom talking and laughing down the hall in the kitchen and I can smell fish frying. There are a couple of posters on my walls, Spider-Man or Superman, and the sun through my window is lying flat on them and shadowing them, making them disappear beneath the last light of our damn good day. And as I lay there all I can do is look at my hands, turn them this way and that, smelling of soap and not of the blood or fish that had been there before, and it's not the struggling worm or the hook that I can still feel against my skin, but the calluses of my dad's hands holding mine tight.

IT'S OVER.

WHILE WE'RE TALKING, Deputy Reynosa stands there with her arms folded in front of her, like she's protecting herself from a chill that doesn't exist. There's a slight breeze, barely anything to it, and it messes with her hair, gets in her eyes. She's a beautiful woman, the kind to take your breath away, and when she asks me where I drifted off to, what I was just thinking about, I tell her fishing with my dad, and she smiles as if she understands exactly what I mean, and Deputy Harper looks back and forth between us and says that he loves fishing almost as much as a good whiskey and in the weeks to come we'll all have to go together up to Falcon Lake.

For a moment, we're laughing, and it's all good.

Deputy Reynosa watches me but is watching the road close as well, so she sees the two cars approach in the sunset even before Deputy Harper and me. She makes a small gesture for his benefit, not mine, and he glances around my shoulder and I turn to look along with him. I don't recognize the first car coming up the road, turning off into the gravel, but this is a tourist attraction so it's not unusual for cars to stop here all the time, mostly at night, with people searching for the ghost lights out on the flats. Just like the Arizona family I saw earlier. It's a public place on the main route to El Paso and Fort Bliss and Van Horn, where my phantom friends are never going to meet me, so it's a good spot, and if Deputy Reynosa grew up around here it was a natural choice for our meeting.

I want to ask her if she's ever seen the lights out here, if they really exist and what they look like.

But all of our attention now is on the approaching cars. The first rolls up beneath the pavilion and the other peels off a little to our right, their noses pointed at us like the hard tip of an arrow aimed at our hearts, their engines idling high and loud.

I think crazily for a moment that it is the Arizona family come back to take some more pictures, the blond boy still waving goodbye to me as if he'd never left, but even in the faded light I know these cars are far older, dirtier, as if they've been sitting outside a long time.

As if the dust has grown so thick that even blasting down the highway couldn't shake it loose.

They remind me of our cars and the RV parked in Killing; how their time in the sun ages them, and I'm just about to say something like that, when I recognize the second car.

T-Bob's old Marquis.

And then the door of the first car opens . . .

. . . and Deputy Reynosa's hand moves to her holstered gun.

38

Fuckin' Danny wasn't that hard to follow; out of Killing and away
from Alamito Creek, and then up to U.S. 67 that became U.S. 90,
before angling west toward Valentine and, eventually, Van Horn. They
stayed way back, losing him for stretches, only to catch sight of his
Harley throwing sunlight as it leaned into the curves. The bike was
a blur—eyeblink movement—as Danny cranked her up along the
straightaways.

Most of the time, it was the only thing in motion against the stale
desert and the mountains beyond.

But Jesse knew the area well enough; after all, he and Danny had
driven around it together on their trips to Murfee.

And after they cleared the town, Jesse thought maybe Danny really
was going all the way to Van Horn, so he settled in for the long ride. He
was a good distance ahead of them and they were playing catch-up, and
Jesse drank a warm beer and tried hard to ignore Clutts, who'd been
shitty company since they'd left Killing. Clutts had a story for each and
every goddamn thing, each one a taller tale, and if he'd done half the
shit he'd claimed, he was the most dangerous outlaw in four states, and
Jesse knew for a goddamn fact that wasn't true. Joker and Lee Malady
were a couple of car lengths back, and Jesse would have given anything

to have been trapped with one of those two instead of this idiot, and that was saying a lot.

He was about to turn to Clutts to finally tell him just to *shut the fuck up*, when he spied the Big Bend County Sheriff's truck pulled off to the side of the road in some sort of rest area or touristy spot. There was a wooden shed there and some chain fencing and benches. He recognized the truck from having seen it, or one just like it, outside the house in Killing, and, of course, during his two friendly visits to the department in Murfee. He finished off the beer and crushed the can quick and then slid it under his seat, making sure he was doing the speed limit, which still was seventy-five on this stretch, so he had room to spare. He was almost on top of the truck, passing it and wondering how Danny had blasted through and not gotten caught up in the speed trap, when he saw a last bit of sunlight flicker again off that chrome . . . *Danny's* Harley. It was pulled up next to the truck, and Jesse could just make out three people standing there: Danny, that older prick of a deputy who'd pulled a gun on him in that Murfee bar, and that little wetback girl with him. He hit the brakes hard enough to make Clutts go *What the fuck?* as he slid over the center line and the wheels crunched when the asphalt gave way to gravel.

Goddamn motherfucker.

He ordered Clutts to get on the phone and call back to Lee and tell him to get ready, and he pulled the car into the mess of shadows thrown by the wooden pavilion. He'd heard people talk about being so mad they couldn't see straight, and he'd experienced that before, plenty of times—the sort of pulsing anger that had caused him more trouble than it had ever gotten him out of—but this was something wholly different. He was so mad *all* he could see was Danny, everything else around him lost to a blazing white heat. The pavilion was suddenly gone and Marvin Clutts was no longer sitting next to him and the car had disappeared and even the mountains and sky no longer existed. All of it vacant, erased, burned away—revealing there had been nothing there to begin with. There was only Danny . . . that *lying piece of traitorous shit*, turning now to watch the two cars pull in, not yet under-standing who was behind the wheel.

Jesse couldn't even see the gun that had somehow gotten into his own hand, just inches from his face; could barely even feel the weight of the heavy pistol his daddy had taken off Danny and handed to him just before he headed out after him.

But by God he knew it was there.

39

Jesse Earl was out of the car, yelling, taking a step clear of his open door, but not by much.

One hand was still hidden by it, and Harp didn't need three guesses to know what he was hiding there. Amé knew it, too, but she was pivoting to keep the second car in front of her, so if she had to bring her gun up, it was already well in her sights. She ordered Danny to get back behind them, and Harp grabbed the kid's arm so he wouldn't walk toward Jesse, who was still yelling his head off.

"You piece of shit motherfucker! All me and Daddy done for you, and here you are? *Goddamn you.*"

Danny raised his hands. "Jesse, listen, hear me out. These folks have something you need to hear. It's all about your daddy. JW's been playing all of us. He doesn't care about you, me, or Thurman Flowers. He's using us and has been from the get-go. We're fucking *cover* . . . He's going—"

Even at a distance, Harp could see Jesse Earl trembling.

"You shut your lyin', fuckin' mouth. Don't talk about my daddy, don't tell me what he is or isn't going to do. You don't know him. You don't know jack shit, *Hero.* You hear me? You don't know a goddamn thing."

Jesse spit on the ground. "We ain't blood and he ain't your fuckin' daddy . . ."

Harp slid his eyes off Jesse, looking for more movement in the car, but in the setting sun and the gathering shadows, he couldn't make out a goddamn thing. He'd been slowly moving his hand toward his gun, Amé doing the same, but Jesse had the drop on them, as did whoever he'd brought with him in the other car. It was just like down at the house in Killing, guns could be pointed at them right now and they might never see the shot coming.

Amé was breathing, nervous but steady, almost as if she were counting to herself.

Danny held his hands up higher, desperate to show he wasn't armed. "The problem is I know too damn much, and I have from the beginning. I'm a cop and I have been from that first moment we met in Lubbock."

Jesse stopped yelling, trembling, and went still. There was nothing but sun and wind and the sound of the engines idling. Then, at last, he nodded his head and laughed to himself, as if he'd just heard a funny joke.

"Well then, motherfucker, I guess that's the first true thing you've said since I've known you."

Then his hand appeared from behind the door, aiming a gun at Danny's heart, and he started shooting.

40

Everything slowed down, even though it was all as fast as a heartbeat.

America *heard* the shots from Jesse Earl's gun but didn't see him shooting, still focused on the other car. She *felt*, but didn't see, Ben grab Danny and pull him out of the way. There was the metallic hum of at least one round spinning off the truck, another shattering the glass of a window, a third punching through the dirt right at her feet, and then, finally, one striking Ben. He made a noise, kind of a sighing, and nearly fell against her, while still firing his own gun from one knee. Something hot and fast brushed by her face and made her blink, but she refused to take her eyes off the other car . . . that old Marquis she knew from Killing. So when a back window rolled down and a face rose up, with the barrel of what appeared to be a rifle floating in the darkness next to it, she was ready to put her Tritium sights right on it and she pulled the trigger again and again and again, just like out on the desert range. Sparks flew high as her third shot caromed off the edge of the window, but she knew her first two had been true.

The face fell apart and disappeared and blood sprayed thick over the car door.

Backing up and dropping down to one knee against the truck, trying to make herself a smaller target, she swung quickly toward Jesse, who'd been hit by Ben at least once, maybe more, and was crouched down behind his own car door. He was using it as a shield as he tried to crawl back into the vehicle that was rolling backward on its own.

"*Driver,*" Ben barked at her, having flattened himself out on the ground. At first she thought it was because he could no longer stand; there was so much blood on him—so much more than she'd ever seen—but then realized he was just trying to find an angle to shoot out Jesse's legs, the only part of him not protected by the car door. He was sighting, taking his time . . . *too much time* . . . bleeding out all over the ground. But like he'd directed, she centered on the windshield of Jesse's car where someone working the steering wheel should be, and put two rounds tight in that spot, before emptying the rest of her magazine evenly across the front of the car, leaving flares burning in the air until it finally stopped moving. She dropped her dead mag, slipped in another and racked it into place off the edge of her boot, just in time to see the Marquis picking up speed, trying to ram them.

Danny was behind her, up in the cab of the truck struggling to get at Harp's AR-15, but he didn't have the time.

None of them had enough time now.

Ben was trying to stand again, calling her name, when the Marquis closed on them.

She rose up and put herself between the coming car and Ben and Danny, and started shooting at the tires and windshield.

Two each, over and over again, until her magazine went dry . . .

41

It had taken Chris a lot longer to get out of El Paso than he'd planned, not helped by the two-car accident on I-10 by Socorro that had slowed him getting out of the city proper. But he was finally clear of all that, driving back east toward Murfee and past the setting sun, into a distance that had already turned into twilight.

Stars were just showing in a long band of purple, so few he could still count each one. And below that was a thin squall of clouds, stretched horizon to horizon, so maybe, finally, they were going to get that rain out in the Big Bend after all.

He tried calling Harp and got no response, and then had the same luck with Amé. Harp had told him they might spend the end of the day out at the range, so he wasn't completely surprised. He imagined them grimly punching hole after hole in their targets beneath the shadows of Chapel Mesa, trying to outduel each other, not saying much beyond the occasional *Good shot*, while the sounds of their guns still carried out far and wide across the desert. They were probably going to have a lot of brass to pick up.

Instead, he dialed up Buck Emmett, who answered on the third ring. He was at the Hamilton grabbing a burger, and Chris could hear the background noise, the low, steady murmur of other conversations punctuated by the rattle of glasses and forks, and Buck told Chris not much was going on; everything was quiet. Just like Harp had said. Buck had been by the bank several times, and had seen Harp and Amé earlier in the day messing around with that Mexican kid's car in impound, but they'd been MIA since then. For some reason that bothered Chris, tugged at him, because Harp hadn't mentioned it when he'd spoken to him from the cemetery, but at least he'd finally gotten around to doing something with that car.

Chris told Buck to finish his burger and call it a day. He still had a couple of hours to go, and was going to head straight on to the house. If Buck saw Harp, he should tell him to give Chris a call, just so he could hear for himself what they'd found out about Avalos's car.

After he hung up he made one last call, this time to Mel, and told her he was on his way home. She was already at Earlys for the night shift. They talked for a few minutes about her day, about the new dog, and he asked her if it had looked like rain out on the Far Six. She said there were a lot of clouds and even some thunder during the day, but no rain. Not yet. It was coming, though, she felt it.

The Rio Grande was off to his right, marked by a green band of trees and grass that lined its course. There were farms tucked down in there, surviving only because of the river's water. He didn't get up to El Paso often, but thought that green looked a little paler this time around, worn-out; drained like everything else by the hot summer drought. Lights were coming on in the small river valley, ready to push back whatever darkness they could.

He rolled down the window, let some air into the car, and watched the sky slowly change colors with that coming night.

42

I drive into the desert, away from that little blond boy.

He's not actually there, but still I see him. I have to get this insanity away from the roadside pavilion and the main road, so stray rounds don't clip a passing car, or worse, another family just like his pulling off to search for Murfee's ghost lights.

I drive and T-Bob's old Marquis follows us, one headlight blown out but the other bleeding ugly light like a monstrous eye, still searching.

THE MARQUIS DIDN'T HIT US straight on. Deputy Reynosa drove it off target by emptying another magazine into it, punching out glass and puckering metal, but as it passed us it caught the back end of their truck, tearing away the rear bumper and knocking Deputy Harper off his feet and me nearly out of the cab. I heard the grinding of the metal as the Marquis tried to pull itself free, and still we were taking rounds, from either the Marquis's driver or Jesse and his driver, both of whom were hidden from us by the tangle of vehicles. I'd followed Deputy Reynosa's first volley into the Marquis and knew that was a kill, the blood still fan-tailed all over the window, but still it came on, refusing to give up, as if it was the car itself that was furious. I thought I caught a glimpse of Joker's bulk behind the wheel, and if it was him, he'd never let us go.

Deputy Reynosa pulled Harper up into the cab and pushed bloody keys into my hand and yelled at me to drive. She shoved the older man down in the backseat and pulled free the AR-15 he had back there, checking the load, and then shot out the back window, still trying to put down the Marquis's driver. The seat next to me exploded as a stray return round found its way into the truck and tunneled through leather and foam, before finishing its trajectory right into the dash radio. I got the truck started and crushed a small chain barricade, knocked over a picnic table, and then we were out and free across the open desert, bouncing up and down.

Deputy Harper was sprawled in the backseat, a bloody mess.

Deputy Reynosa had blood of her own all over her face, either from broken glass or a grazing bullet.

And then I realized that some of the blood all over the truck was mine.

I DRIVE INTO THE DESERT but the truck is giving out on us. I can feel it through the steering wheel shaking in my hands.

The radiator is spraying out fluid from beneath the hood and one or more of the tires are shot. The Marquis behind us isn't much better, but it's still coming, and this slow-motion chase might be funny if it wasn't so goddamn horrible. I don't know if Jesse is dead, since we left him and the other car back at the pavilion, but Joker in the Marquis is most definitely *not*. Not yet, despite Deputy Reynosa's best efforts. She can't get a clean shot off as we rumble and zigzag over the broken ground, but she keeps at it, her bloody face determined.

Both cars are leaving thick wakes of dust and smoke. We can barely see anything and we've lost our way in the world.

There is spent brass throughout the truck, still warm and bouncing in my lap and tap-dancing along the dashboard. I wipe my eyes with bloody hands and look for a service road or a mule track or anything to follow rather than this endless, empty stretch of twilight—something straight to give shape or direction or meaning to what we're doing and where we're going.

A rising moon appears for a second before slipping behind a cloud, leaving soft, pale light in its wake.

I aim toward that.

I CAN NO LONGER DRIVE. The truck is done, and Deputy Harper is as well.

I have no idea how bad I'm injured, it's hard to tell, there's so much blood everywhere. I'm cussing at the truck, banging at the useless steering wheel, and he's trying to sit upright, struggling, as he tells me to stop through clenched, bloody teeth. *Just stop.* Fifty yards behind us, half the length of a football field, the Marquis has gone still as well, with its one crazy headlight canted skyward, shining light back at the new stars. Deputy Reynosa is ready to slip out of the truck and approach it, finish what she started, but Harper holds her back, grabs the hot muzzle of her rifle with a bloody, shaking hand, and pulls her to him.

She resists, fights, tries to get out of the truck, but he won't let her. I know what he wants me to do, so I hold her back as well, as another bullet whines over the truck's roof. It's a gentle purr and then it's gone, like a big cat passing us in the dark.

She's whispering something in Spanish and I have no idea what it is, and I don't know that Deputy Harper does, either, but he understands it well enough. He grabs her face with both hands, holds it close to his, makes her look at him so she can see just how hurt he is, how bad it really is.

She won't do it, trying to look at anything and everything but him, but none of that stops the tears I finally see . . .

43

This is a dream . . .

He didn't know how much time he had left, but it wasn't much. He hoped it was enough.

"Listen, you two are not going to die out here, you hear me? *You are not.* You have to get back to town and tell the sheriff what happened. Tell him about the car, about Avalos, John Wesley . . ."

Amé grabbed his hand. "You *already* talked to the sheriff, you told him all this. You promised me earlier. *Te creí.*"

Harp shook his head, but stopped because it hurt too much. Everything below his neck was on fire and he refused to look down. He knew he'd been hit once in the gut and might have even caught another. "No, I didn't. I talked to him . . . but . . . fuck, I just wanted to make things right. I didn't want him calling Nichols yet . . . I . . ."

"You lied to me, Ben Harper." But she stopped crying, and Harp thanked God for that. He wanted her angry now, like he'd wanted Danny angry in Murfee. It was better for what was going to happen next.

"I did, I'm sorry. I'm a bad, bad man, and this is what I fucking get for it. I won't do it again, I promise." He spat blood, tried to wink, but the eye just stayed closed and refused to open again. He knew it never would.

"Fuck, I am getting too old for this . . ."

They are out on the lake and she's sitting in the front of the boat, her hair pulled up, laughing at something he just said. The water behind her is blue, capped white, catching the sunlight and sending it back skyward. Everything is bright and she has on her sunglasses so that he can't see her eyes and her head is thrown back and there is light playing on her throat and her skin shines like a new star . . .

He drifted for a second, slid back in the seat on his own blood, but then there were two sets of hands on him, pulling him back up.

There is wind between them . . .

"I'm not walking out of here, it's not happening. But you two can, and you goddamn *will*. I'm not running the risk of either of you getting hurt. Give me the rifle and get out of here. I'm going to take care of that son of a bitch back there. Then I'm gonna lie down for a bit. I'm goddamn tired."

"No, not happening. You're too weak already. We're not leaving you," Danny said.

"Trust me, I'm fucking strong enough for this. But you help get her out of here. You owe me that, 'cause I got all shot to hell trying to help you. And Deputy Reynosa, I'm giving you a direct order to leave with this man. I'm still the chief fucking deputy."

"*Vete a la mierda,*" she said.

"That's my girl." He laughed, coughed, spitting up blood more black than red. "I got a present for you . . ."

And he wishes he could see her eyes . . . goddamn wishes he knew what he just said to make her laugh like that, so he can say it again, forever and always. He can't take his eyes off her shining skin and wants to take her up

and hold her and feel that shine with his own hands . . . hold her tight . . .
so they can both glow together.

He pushed the small medallion and necklace into her hand. "It's Michael the Archangel, the cops' saint. Jackie used to have this and she'd pray all the time for me, for all the good that did, and neither of us need it anymore. Not now. Keep it. You've been a goddamn fine partner, America Reynosa." He closed her fingers around it. "One of the best cops I've ever met." He looked over her shoulder, to where the Marquis sat waiting. "Now help me out of the truck. It's time."

He didn't have to tell them time for what.

He is darkness and always has been and always will be and is ashamed that
he exists only when reflected by her, by stealing her light.

But it does not matter to her, it never did. She never thought he was
stealing what she was willing to give . . .

They got him out and he refused to kneel or take cover, knowing if he got down on his knees he'd never get up again.

As Amé handed him the rifle, she kissed his forehead; quick, fleeting, so that he barely felt her lips but knew they were there. And if she or Danny had any thought of stopping him, that ended when they all saw that Danny had been hit, too. One of Jesse's rounds had gouged him, a deep cut along his left side, even though Harp had pushed him out of the way. It may have been the same bullet that had gone all the way through Harp's stomach. It was that damn *outlaw luck*, the sort of luck that promised a fleeing felon would hit a cop with a blind shot over his shoulder—the wild round finding its way through a gap in the cop's vest and killing him midstride. The same sort of luck that guaranteed that cop would hit that runner four of five times and none of them would be enough to bring him down. That's why Harp wouldn't risk Danny and Amé forcing a confrontation with whoever was in the

Marquis. Because of that fucking outlaw luck, and all of it bad for the one with the badge. In the receding light he couldn't tell how bad Danny was really hurt, and the boy wasn't complaining, but there was a lot of blood, and he'd need it tended sooner or later.

There was a lot of blood everywhere.

"There's a med kit in the truck that will help with that." Harp motioned at Danny's wound. "It's not much, but it will get the bleeding stopped." He lurched forward, kept his balance, just barely. "The radio's shot up, so you two make for the main road and keep working your cells until you get reception. Don't head back straight toward the Lights, in case Jesse is still there, waiting. Get someone to pick you up. And then you go down there and drag that fucking John Wesley Earl out of Killing and put a bullet in him. Tell him it's from me."

Amé came to him one more time, put her hands on him, but he didn't feel anything, He was too cold and had stopped feeling anything at all.

"*Puedo hacerlo.* I'm in better shape than either of you. I'm a better shot now, too."

"I know, and that's why I won't let you." He breathed deep, but didn't taste air. "I gotta do this. I fucked up . . . with the car, with not being truthful to Chris, with a lot of things. Everything. I need to fix it."

"I didn't think you believed in any of that. You don't believe in second chances or making things right."

"Oh, I believe you owe it a try, at least for the ones you love." He hoisted the AR-15, aimed it downrange toward the Marquis. "I just don't have much faith in how it works out. But I'm ready for this. It's time, she's waiting for me. Be safe, Deputy Reynosa. Take care of our sheriff. He's a good man, and he's going to need you." He tried to push her away, but she hesitated, wouldn't move.

"Get going, *now*. It's time I finish what I started."

She says something to him but he can't hear it, the wind snatching it away at that moment. Maybe it's "I love you," or just his name . . . they are both the same to him. He calls back to her, but something has caught her eye out on the shore, and she's turned away from him, looking out over the water.

He moved out wide of the truck, keeping his head down but the AR-15 up, locked in a shooting position, as he circled back in on the Marquis, standing still every few steps and listening—but not too long, afraid standing still would lead to him falling over. The goddamn radio was playing, music drifting out above the ocotillos, and maybe he could make out the words, the song itself. He smiled. It was the Eagles, Jackie's favorite. They once had tickets to a concert in Dallas, but something had come up at work and he couldn't make the trip. He'd begged her to go on her own, or take a girlfriend, since the tickets were damn expensive, but she wouldn't do it. She wouldn't go without him, and she'd just put the unused tickets in her keepsake jar on the desk.

Her hair's come loose and it streams behind her, the trail of a now falling star.

He made out the outline of the Marquis, someone struggling to get out of the driver's seat, and he knew who it was: that big bastard Joker. *Death on dark wings.* And that one headlight also revealed swirling dust; so much falling upward where stars were coming on high above him like lights in distant rooms. He heard the radio again, her song . . .

And now, he thought, the night was nothing but stars.

They lit up everything.

But there wasn't a song. That was all in his head.

He goes to catch her, to hold her, before she reaches the ground.

He moved in as fast as his legs could carry him, as Joker tried to stand. He was hurt, too, and bad; Amé had done a number on him. Left alone he eventually would have bled out like Harp, but he was getting out of the big old car, propping himself up with a long gun of his own, with that music still playing behind him that really wasn't playing at all. Harp was singing along with it through ragged breaths. He wasn't done with the fight, either.

Joker heard Harp almost a second too late, but still swung his own rifle at Harp's face, ready to shoot blindly into the rising dark.

Goddamn outlaw luck.

This is a dream.

  This is all it will ever be.

He pulled the trigger and all the stars went white.

HARP HAD THE DROP ON HIM, *action versus reaction.*

Everything he'd ever told Chris, except the truth.

Sometimes it didn't matter.

44

It was dark by the time Jesse and Clutts came back, and Jesse was bleeding, bad.

His guts were a mess, blood everywhere, and he came in the house hollerin' and everything was in an uproar. Clutts was also yellin', about Danny meeting a cop or bein' a cop. It was clear that things had gone bad out on the road, very bad, and that Joker and Lee Malady weren't coming back. Earl told Sunny to help Jesse into one of the back bedrooms and get him some fuckin' bandages, and told Jenna to get him a beer.

No one noticed yet that T-Bob and Little B and Kasper weren't standing around.

But Earl saw Clutts talking low and fast to Flowers, and didn't like the look of that. He'd deal with that in a second, once he figured out just what the hell had happened, and once he knew whether Jesse was gonna die before daybreak.

"HE WAS MEETING those deputies from Murfee, the old one and that spic girl. He was *talking* with them," Jesse said. He was pale, shaking, his hair slicked back by sweat and blood, and some of that blood was fresh on the bedsheets, more of it dried and spotting his face. Sunny kept trying to wipe it away but Earl pushed her back.

"He said he was a cop. He's been spying on us."

"You killed him, right?"

Jesse nodded. "It all went to shit. I think I hit him, and that older deputy, too. The girl was shooting at Joker and Lee. Joker drove off after 'em into the desert."

Sunny was hovering at Earl's shoulder, Jenna appearing and disappearing as well. And Cole Malady was there, too, wanting to know what the fuck had happened to his cousin, and to make sure Flowers or Clutts didn't try to barge in.

Earl took his daddy's empty Ruger from Jesse's hand, where he was still holding it. "So you *didn't* kill them? They're still out there, somewhere, right now?"

"I don't know. Everyone was shooting . . . fuck . . . *Daddy.*" Jesse bit his pale lips. "Except for that shit stain Clutts. He was hidin' down in the car. I don't think he took a single shot. Not a one."

Earl sat back, tried to think, absentmindedly reloading the Ruger from the shell box by the bed. There were a couple of wounded *real* deputies being chased out in the desert, along with Danny. It was possible they'd all die out there, or it was possible they wouldn't, and in a matter of hours or even less this place would be lit up like fucking Christmas, which was kinda funny in its own way. Jesse should have followed Joker, he should have made goddamn *sure*, even bleeding like he was. Earl hadn't gotten any more calls from Nichols, so whatever had happened outside Murfee hadn't made it to his ears, not yet, but still . . .

Now Nichols might not ever call him again.

Sunny started in on him. "JW, what are you doing? We gotta get Jesse to the hospital."

"Goddammit, woman, if I wanted your opinion, I'd ask it. This ain't the fuckin' time." She stopped, took a step back.

Then Jesse grabbed at him, pulled him down close. "That wasn't all that Danny was sayin', Daddy. He was talkin' other shit, *about you.* Said we couldn't trust you, that you had plans of your own. He was all kinds of clear about that."

Earl glanced up to see if Sunny had heard Jesse, but he couldn't tell; her face was a mask. It was the same face she'd used to slip dope and other stuff into prison for him for all those years. He had no idea what she'd heard or what she was thinking now.

"And what do you think about that, boy?"

Jesse smiled, blood all over his front teeth. "He said all that shit and then I shot his traitor ass. But I did hear it . . . heard it loud and clear, and so did Clutts." Jesse turned away, his breathing thin, his eyes not so focused on the far wall. He was slipping away, somewhere. "I did all right, Daddy, didn't I?"

"Yeah, boy . . . son . . . you did. You did all right."

Earl stood up and pointed to Sunny. "You tend to him, see how bad it is. And I don't want anyone botherin' him or talkin' to him, not even that bitch of his."

Then he turned to Cole Malady. "You come with me."

It was time to deal with Flowers.

HE CAME OUT INTO THE LIVING ROOM, where his boy's blood was still smeared all over the damn place. Flowers and Clutts were there, and Jenna, who had retreated from the bedroom. He wasn't sure how much she'd heard, either.

"This is bad," Flowers said, "very bad. Marvin was telling me everything that happened. Jesse shot at cops, John."

"From what I hear, your boy Clutts didn't shoot at anyone."

"It doesn't matter. And if he hadn't driven Jesse back here, your son would still be back there, dying. I'd say that's a fair trade. We all need to be on the road now, we can't stay here."

Earl nodded, as if seriously considering the idea. "And where the fuck do you think you're gonna go? You wanted a goddamn war, I'd say you're about to get one."

"Not like this. This isn't what I wanted. We're not ready, not now." He stood up, straightened his glasses. "We're going, John."

Earl pulled the Blackhawk from the back of his jeans and aimed it at Flowers's heart. Like the room, it was sticky and hot with Jesse's blood. He was too fast for Clutts, who seemed to have half a mind to still go for his own gun, but thought better of it, when Cole Malady stepped out from the shadowed hallway behind Earl, a shotgun leveled at everyone in the living room.

Clutts took a half-step toward the door and then nothing else.

"No, no you're not. You're not going anywhere. No one is. We're gonna sit here and smoke some cigarettes and Jenna is going to get us some cold beers and maybe some whiskey. You and Clutts there can tell me all about this all-white kingdom you're gonna build, and I'm gonna pretend I give a grade-A shit about it. It's going to be real nice, like we're all fucking family. *That's* what we're gonna do."

"This is insane, John. You've lost your fucking mind."

Earl laughed, bobbed the gun up and down but didn't take it off Flowers.

"Well, I guess we're gonna see."

Surprisingly enough, it was Clutts who began to do the mental math, counting out who was standing in the room and who wasn't. It got damn easy, when you started by figuring out who might have a gun aimed at you and who didn't. He tossed one glance at Earl and *his* gun before flicking back the dirty curtain of the closest window. He looked back and forth through the darkened glass, whispering a *goddamn* that everyone in the room could hear.

Flowers shook his head and sighed. "What was that, Marvin?"

"Our van is gone, Thurman. *The van is fucking gone.* They tossed everything out of the back. It's all just lying there, blowing around."

Flowers locked glares with Earl. "There was no need for that. I would have let you use the van, if you needed it. All you had to do was ask."

"That's not all," Clutts said, turning away from the window and staring down Earl's barrel.

"They took the tires off of *my* car. They're fucking gone, too."

PART THREE

SUNDOWN TOWN

We started back for the boys when I saw a man coming towards the pen. We saw he was lost. He got within ten steps of me when I threw my shot gun down on him and told him his life depended on his actions. The moon was shining brightly and Jim Taylor had caught his bridle. He said: "John, for God's sake don't kill me."

I asked him who he was and he said: "I am your friend, but I am a ranger. We found your horses tonight and knew you were close by. They sent me to Comanche for reinforcements. By daylight you will have 300 men around you and escape will be impossible. If they catch you they are going to hang you."

I then said to Jim: "We had better kill him; dead men tell no tales."

He said: "Oh, for God's sake, don't kill me; I'll never tell on you and will do anything for you."

After satisfying myself that he would do to trust I gave him a $20 gold piece to give to my wife and told him to tell her to go to Gonzales, where I was going to start for next morning. I told her not to be uneasy about me; that I would never surrender alive and that Jim and I had agreed to die together. That if either of our horses were shot down we would take the other up, but that we expected to be run up on before we got out of the country.

—THE LIFE OF JOHN WESLEY HARDIN, FROM THE ORIGINAL
MANUSCRIPT AS WRITTEN BY HIMSELF (1896)

45

Kasper thought it was strange that he only got more and more scared with each mile he put Killing behind him.

He should have been happy, relieved, to be getting out of that place.

But that's not what he felt at all, trapped with T-Bob and Little B in Flowers's old van, ripe with the smell of air fresheners and fast food. T-Bob was driving, but before they left he'd swiped a bottle of Teacher's scotch he had hidden outside in the RV, and he'd been drinking it ever since with some serious determination. Little B was bouncing in the passenger seat, talking on and on to everyone and no one like he had the habit of doing, and both of them were ignoring Kasper in the back, where he was pushed aside by the tires they'd taken off Clutts's car, and the two big rusted cans of gasoline they'd gotten out of the RV along with the booze. At his feet there was also a Remington 870 12-gauge and a Browning rifle. He wished they'd just pull over and let him out, but that wasn't going to happen. Not until they got to Murfee and he hot-wired Mr. Earl's car for him. If he kept his mouth shut and did it fast, Mr. Earl had promised T-Bob would give him two hundred dollars and leave him in Murfee, if that's what he wanted. And right about now, that sounded like a good idea. Days ago Mr. Earl had tossed out the idea of stealing a car, making Kasper promise not to talk about it with Little B or even Danny, even though he'd said Danny would be in on it, too. But out behind the ranch house tonight, after Danny had ridden off on his Harley with Jesse and Joker following him, Mr. Earl had put a hand on his shoulder and leaned in close and said, *Well, I don't think Danny's going to be coming back, and you don't really wanna be here anyway, now do you?* And it was the sort of question that really wasn't much of a question at all, like his mom had been so fond of:

Now, Tyler, you don't want to go back to detention again, do you?

Dammit, Tyler, you're not huffing that fucking shit again, are you?

Are you a faggot, Ty, is that what you are?

How am I supposed to handle you, Ty? What the fuck am I going to do with you?

For years, his mom had done nothing but ask him questions they both already knew the answer to, or that just didn't have answers at all. He'd hoped things would be different with Little B and Jesse and Pastor Flowers and all the others—everything they were going to build down in Killing—but he had a feeling that in a matter of hours it was going to be broken to pieces before they ever even had the chance to put it together. Now he was trapped in a van that was starting to fill with the stink of cheap scotch and tire rubber and worse, leaking gas, and they were keeping their eyes outside the window for the red and blue lights of police cars. Both T-Bob and Little B had a couple of guns on them, and before they set out Earl had asked them all another of those questions that really wasn't one . . .

You boys don't want to get caught, do you? I explained it all and you know what you gotta do for me, right?

And they hadn't said anything, because there was nothing to say.

Kasper knew that none of this was quite right . . . that if Mr. Earl had had his way, it would have been Kasper and Danny making this run up to Murfee, and not T-Bob and Little B. But Danny was gone, and Little B would do anything for his father, and T-Bob would do whatever he was told.

That left only Kasper, forced to go along with them because he was too scared not to, and now more scared than he'd ever been in his life, even if he'd stayed in Killing.

He wished Danny *was* here with him. One of the worst parts of this whole thing was that Danny had ridden off without saying goodbye . . .

ALTHOUGH EARL HAD INSISTED they not waste much time, Kasper thought T-Bob was taking damn plenty of it, waiting so it got later and darker, but really just nursing that bottle.

They even had a map Danny had drawn of Murfee to help them find their way, but Little B crumpled it up and tossed it out the window.

So instead they drove around the back roads for a while, almost lost, before finally circling into the town, no one stopping or bothering them, until they were cruising down Main Street. It wasn't even all that late, but the place already looked turned down for the night. There was a Dollar General, a Pizza Hut, some restaurant called the Hamilton. They passed a few cars but no one paid them any attention at all; Earl had said no one would be on the lookout for a white van with Washington plates, anyway. Still, T-Bob steered clear of the Big Bend County Sheriff's Department before heading to the far end of Main Street and turning into a neighborhood of a few older houses, although it wasn't really what he was looking for. It was too close to the center of town for this *other thing* they were supposed to do even before he had to boost Mr. Earl's car. Mr. Earl had insisted on it, and it was this *other thing* that had Kasper scared most of all, biting at his nails. T-Bob and Little B started arguing about it, as Kasper stayed quiet in the back, fingers in his mouth. T-Bob was mumbling that *goddammit he'd only been to this shithole twice*, and both times had been in the daylight and *fuckin' Danny* had been driving, so he kept making random turns, circling back to where he started, until Little B took over, telling him how and where to go, and they left the town proper.

They passed a little bar with a neon sign spelling out Earlys, which drew T-Bob's eyes hard like a magnet, and then headed out to some railroad tracks, where beyond that, the lights of a lot of small houses tracked into the distance. They were squared together, none of them very big, and as they drove through the little neighborhood, there were dogs barking and music playing from some of them. They briefly pulled into the gravel lot of a small store where a handful of men soon walked out, shirts open; they stood around drinking beers, watching them and pointing at the van. With the window down, the Spanish they were talking to each other rose and fell, but he had no idea what they were saying. Little B grunted out *Goddamn beaners* under his breath and flipped them off, but smiled as he did it.

He turned to T-Bob and Kasper and pointed over to the little houses all lined up on the other side of the street, like they'd been put there just for him.

"And *that's* what we need, boys, right there."

46

Thurman Flowers knew that John Wesley Earl was shit-house crazy, no two ways about it.

Jesse Earl had his own moments; his anger like a second skin, always exposed and hot to the touch. But Jesse's anger made Thurman *relevant*, it was a pure energy all its own that Thurman and his coming kingdom needed. It was *fuel*, a purpose—an energy that through the years Thurman had figured out how to manage, direct, focus. He'd always need men like Clutts, who was a brutal and crude tool; forever a hammer as long as everything was a nail—and Thurman did see himself as a carpenter—but Jesse had always showed the potential to be so much more.

A knife, a well-aimed bullet.

He'd always been worth the risk.

Earl was a different matter altogether, and when Thurman had learned Jesse was coming to Killing with his daddy in tow he'd almost bailed on the whole thing. He and Jesse had circled Thurman's concerns through several tense conversations, but they were already too far down the rabbit hole and had too many plans in motion to seriously consider just letting it all go. The source and wellspring of so much of Jesse's anger was *his damn daddy*—a need for the long-absent man that over time had curled into hatred at the edges, a ragged scar that had been cut deep, and that Thurman had picked at over and over again and had always used to his advantage. He'd needed those scars, and made damn sure they never quite healed. Thurman understood far too clearly that men like Jesse mostly followed him *because* of those old wounds, suffered at the hands of friends and family they believed had abandoned them, and not because they actually believed in the visions he had to offer or in his ability to make them real. In truth, it was the most brittle kind of power, but that had been Thurman's life and he'd been smart enough to recognize his limitations early. He was well used to living on the thinnest of margins, and had known that having both him and Earl here in Killing at the same time would only cause conflict. It'd be like two devils playing tug-of-war over Jesse's soul, and that's more or less how it had played out.

Thurman had seen all this coming, like a biblical prophecy, and still he'd gone through with it, for the simplest of reasons.

He needed the damn money.

"So is there an endgame, John? Or are we just supposed to sit here at gunpoint and wait while a hundred other men with guns arrive outside."

Earl blew out smoke, almost a perfect ring, and took another drink of his Pearl. That girl Jenna had already asked a hundred times to go in the back to see Jesse, and Earl had told her each and every time with a smile to shut her fucking mouth. Clutts was still standing to Thurman's right, by the front door and the window, and kept looking out the window as if their missing van and his car tires would appear again.

Cole Malady leaned against a wall, swinging his scattergun back and forth, and just like Jenna, kept peppering Earl with questions: What had happened to his cousin? When was he coming back? When were they heading home to Arkansas? The simpleton, head as soft as a melon, didn't quite get it and never would.

These were the sort of men Thurman had always been forced to rely on.

And all the while Earl kept checking his watch as if he had somewhere to be. He also had two phones in his lap, like he expected them to ring any minute.

"Your son is likely dying back there, at least let's get him to a hospital. There's no reason not to do that. The women can drive him. We can get them clear of this place."

"You let me worry about my boy, Flowers."

"Well, that would be a first now, wouldn't it, you the doting father?"

"You have a smart mouth for a man with a gun pointed at his eyes."

Thurman took off his glasses, looked through them at arm's length, and put them back on again. "Maybe it has something do with what Danny was telling Jesse and Marvin about *you*. Is that what's going on here, some agenda of your own? Something worth sacrificing all of us for, even your family?"

Earl put the empty beer can down but didn't grab another from the six-pack at his feet, unwilling to shift his eyes off the others in the room, even with Malady beside him. "Let's not pretend you ain't got angles of your own, Preacher. My boy don't mean nothin' to you, never did."

"Why, that's where you're wrong, completely wrong. Jesse meant everything to me. I trusted and believed in him. He's the son I never had. I think in many ways I was the father he never—"

Something dark and dangerous moved behind Earl's eyes. "That's enough, *enough*. I will shoot you, Preacher. You ain't worth a damn nickel to me. *Not a fuckin' red cent.*"

Thurman smiled, glad for the small victory of getting under Earl's skin; hoping to keep him off balance while he thought through what to do next. The room was too hot and too close and his glasses kept fogging up with his own breath.

You ain't worth a damn nickel to me . . . Not a fuckin' red cent.

Then it all made sense to him.

"It's about *the money*, isn't it, John? From the beginning, that's all this was ever about. You're getting your money and running, aren't you?"

Earl snorted. "Like you're any different? Goddamn you and Jesse and that damn money. You think if I had any money I'd be trapped down here with the likes of you?"

"No, no, I don't. And that's the problem. You've been trying to get your hands on it. That's what we're doing right now, isn't it? You don't have it, not yet anyway.

"But you will."

AND IN THE END, that's how Jesse had got *him* to come around about sharing Killing with Earl, too: going on and on about all the money his daddy had tucked away somewhere, money Jesse thought they could get out of him or take from him if necessary. And Thurman had needed that money, not just to build his kingdom (Jesse had been the rock he was going to build that kingdom on), but for his own debts. He owed that fucking cunt of an ex-wife of his child support for the little boy she wouldn't let him see, and she'd been very loud about getting it, even threatening to have a warrant sworn out if he didn't come through with it, and he was months behind. There wouldn't be much kingdom building if the pastor of its first church was locked up on delinquent child support, and it didn't help that he was basically on the run, hiding from both her *and* the feds. In his darkest moments, he sometimes thought she was working *with* them, and fancied himself Lot, dreaming of his ex-wife looking back on the destruction of Sodom only to turn into a pillar of salt.

But it wasn't all about his ex-wife. It was also about the gambling debts he owed, roughly to the tune of seventy-five thousand. Killing had been an escape from turning into salt himself. Just before he'd left

Tacoma, two men had showed up at his apartment, ethnic Vietnamese who ran one of the gambling parlors he frequented. The slopes had been armed, one with a claw hammer with the price tag still on it and a cherry-red bucket and a thick roll of painter's plastic, and the other with a stun gun and packs of condoms and cigarettes, and if Clutts hadn't been there to put a gun in their faces, they'd have taken Thurman away.

Killing was going to be *his* safe place, his haven, and Earl's money was supposed to buy him the time and space to make it so. Now all that was shot to hell and back, leaving him trapped with a madman, waiting for the end. Earl was worse than his ex-wife and those fucking slopes with their stun gun and their hammer.

Earl was a problem that needed solving, and fast. He was a *fucking nail*, but at least Thurman still had a trusty hammer of his own.

That's what he was thinking as he glanced up at Clutts.

He could feel the other man desperate to reach for his own gun, just waiting for a signal from him . . .

47

Little B picked the house. It was dark, no lights. After they pulled up behind it and T-Bob shut off the van, they sat with the engine ticking, waiting fifteen, twenty minutes, but there was no movement. A few streets over a car passed, painting a long smear of light across a crooked fence, but that was it. Satisfied, Little B told Kasper to help him with the gas cans.

"We really got to do this?" Kasper asked, another not-question. Little B was his friend and in his dreams so much more than that, and they had talked for months about starting a band, with him on guitar and Little B on whatever instrument he finally decided on. He'd always gone on and on about singing, but as much as Kasper thought he loved him, he didn't think he had the voice for it. Not for the music they wanted to play, like the Bully Boys or RAHOWA. But since his dad had shown up, Little B had lost all interest in Kasper and the music and their band altogether.

It was Earl who had told Little B to do this thing with the fire, and Little B wanted more than anything to please his dad.

Still . . .

"I told your dad I can be quick with the car, lightning quick. It's not gonna take me any time at all. There's no need for this, B." He wanted to reach out and put a hand on the other boy's shoulder, but didn't dare.

Little B looked at him while T-Bob disappeared behind his upended bottle, the last of the Teacher's disappearing fast. "It ain't just about that, Kaz. And anyway, it's gonna take longer than just the hot-wire." He pointed at the tires bunched around Kasper as an explanation. "We're gonna be workin' fast anyway and it's still gonna be tight. Daddy said we could do that shitty bar, Early but this will be a lot better. We're gonna need every bit of this distraction, so let's just get 'er done."

They got out of the van, each holding a heavy can of gas. Free finally of that horrible space, Kasper stretched; his body sore and tight from the cramped and bumpy ride out of Killing. It felt good to stand in the dark, waiting for any kind of breeze, hoping to feel it on his face. He caught the sound of a television turned up loud, but far enough away, it came to him only as a whisper.

"I don't think I'm going back to Killing, B. You don't have to, either. We just keep going, you and me, please."

Little B appeared to be deciding about lighting a cigarette, but thought better of it with the gas can still in his hand. "You know I ain't gonna do that. That's my family back there. They're gonna need me. I ain't mad at you for goin', though." Kasper thought Little B was going to say he was sorry about the band, but he didn't, not directly. Instead: "One day you can write a song about all this. Some people are going to remember this here shit."

Kasper didn't say anything, finally remembering himself that he'd left his guitar down in Killing. His mother had bought it for him and it was the only thing he owned that was worth a damn, and like his friend, he was never going to see it again.

Angry at himself, he hoisted up the can. "Okay, let's get it over with, then."

THEY DREW LINES in the dry, brittle grass with the gas, connecting the house Little B had parked behind to the one next to it. Little B traced his initials in the backyard and sprayed a stunted mesquite tree like a dog pissing on his spot. Kasper emptied what was left of his can on a bed of withered flowers and then tossed the empty into the backyard.

He could smell their handiwork. Everything smelled like gas.

Little B wiped his hands on his jeans two or three times, and then got back to lighting that cigarette he'd passed on earlier. He offered a pull to Kasper, but he turned it down. He just wanted to get back in the van and get on their way. He wanted to disappear and never look back.

So he never saw Little B actually toss the burning cigarette end over end into the grass.

The ignition temperature of gasoline is only about 495 degrees, pretty low.

The business end of a cigarette, after a good draw, can hit 700 degrees. The gas itself, spread thin, was already hot, like everything else around Murfee because of the summer drought, and even more so after being trapped in those cans for days in the RV. The dry, dusty grass held the gas vapor tight; a layer as thin as smoke, and even more combustible than the liquid gas itself.

The fire started before the cigarette hit the ground.

There was a definite sound like a harsh intake of breath, and a white-orange flash that was visible for two blocks, if anyone had been looking. The flame took off and leapt skyward from the gas runways made for it, leaving behind a trail of hungry sparks that ate up grass, jumping from patch to patch, and before long, yard to yard.

The walls of the first house boiled, caught fire, and seconds later, so did the second house.

And by the time the white van with Washington plates turned out of the neighborhood and headed back toward the Big Bend County Sheriff's Department, some of the flames were ten feet tall.

48

I hear the first shot, then another. We both do.

There's no way not to, they're so goddamn loud. They echo back and forth and back again, like a dozen guns firing.

She's not going to leave him out here, and I wouldn't let her anyway. I learned that in Wanat—we don't ever leave our people behind.

So even before the shooting is done and the echoes have all faded away, she's turning back to the place we last saw Deputy Harper walk off, and then she's running.

I'm right behind her.

HE'S FACEUP, looking at the stars, and his eyes are open.

He's about ten yards from the Marquis, if that, the AR-15 still in his hand. He never let it go, even when he fell. I move up to check him, while Deputy Reynosa moves a little to my left, aiming in at the car, where there's no movement, only sound. The radio is on, but it's mostly static: maybe a bit of music, some Spanish really loud, then a hellfire preacher at a revival, before finally one long hum and a hiss. The radio clicks off and the lone headlight goes dark, an eye closing, plunging us both into a black so deep it's like falling down a hole.

We wait, let our eyes adjust to the stars, and I try to take the AR-15 from Harper's hand. I have to pull his cooling fingers from it and he's still reluctant to let it go. Once I have it, I get Deputy Reynosa's attention and let her know we can slide forward. If she nods, I don't see it, but when I move, she moves right along with me—my shadow.

We flank the Marquis, come up on it slow, and find the driver, Joker, sprawled in the sand. Unlike Harper, he's facedown, legs still back in the car, tangled up in it. Joker's rifle is an arm's length away, and his brains, most of them, are painted all along the car's roof and the doorframe. They're a weird color in the even weirder light of the night; they glow and steam like they're still hot. I taste the copper of Joker's blood and the acid of piss in the air; he also shit himself when Harper shot him through the face.

He was going to die anyway, sooner rather than later, because as I get up close, I find two other exit wounds. Even with all of that bouncing through the desert, all that firing wildly into the night, Deputy Reynosa got him. She is a damn good shot.

We find Lee Malady still in the backseat, everything above the eyes gone and violently sprayed around the inside of the car. I pull him clear of the Marquis and strip both of them of their guns and check the remaining ammo, while Deputy Reynosa drifts around Harper. She's pulled there, his body a magnet.

She kneels over it like she's praying and I give her a few minutes.

I fumble through the med kit I brought with me from the truck, which is better than I thought it would be. It's a combat tactical kit, containing a lot of things we used in Afghanistan. There's antiseptic and some emergency trauma dressings and several packs of QuikClot hemostatic bandages, more than enough to get my bleeding stopped and my wound bound up. It'll hold for a while. This stuff would have even kept Deputy Harper alive a while longer, although maybe not long enough to walk him out of here.

I try not to think about that; how he sacrificed himself for Deputy Reynosa.

For me.

When I'm done, I go back over to the Marquis and Deputy Reynosa is there. She left Harper with his arms folded over his chest, and she's trying to get the car started again, just like I did back at the truck.

"*Nada,*" she says. We have two vehicles and neither of them are a go. We spend a minute messing with all the cell phones we collected between us, standing in different spots, with neither of us getting a signal. For a moment she has one lone bar and tries to dial out quick, but loses it before the call goes through.

"There are dead spots all around this fucking place. If we get closer to the highway, we'll be okay," she says.

Dead spots.

We'll be okay.

In Afghanistan, after a firefight, there was always a moment like this; a moment when you realized that somehow, someway, you'd survived. A moment when you truly understood just how close death had slipped past you even as you were surrounded by all the dead; like catching a glimpse of a great shark sliding beneath you in dark water before disappearing into the depths. In that moment, everything was brighter, clearer. Everyone who talked to you sounded too loud. And everything that had happened so fast before suddenly slowed down again. Although you might be fighting back tears, and might still be shaking so hard you could barely hold your weapon, at least they were the shakes of the living.

You knew then you were okay, or as okay as you could ever be again.

I go and lift up Harper. With Deputy Reynosa's help, I get him hoisted over my shoulder in a fireman's carry without tearing wide my bandages. Unlike my dad's badge from the funeral or Jesse's bloody T-shirt, he's surprisingly light.

Like the real Ben Harper and everything that had been important about him has already flown away.

As we start walking, Deputy Reynosa flicks on the SureFire she took off Harper's body and looks past me, back into the desert, where there's a darker band along the horizon. It's eating up the stars, one by one.

"What's that?" I ask.

She turns, leading me back toward the highway. "Rain."

49

Buck Emmett wasn't much of a drinker, but he liked to hang out at the occasional bar.

Not as much as being out on the river or hiking along the Chisos Basin, or holing up along a trail for a whitetail buck, but you couldn't spend your whole life outdoors.

And, truth be told, he had a bit of a crush on Sheriff Cherry's girl, so whenever Mel was working a later shift at Earlys and it lined up right for him, he found a way to slip in. He'd get himself a Coors Light or a Bud, whatever was cheapest for the night, and park himself at the bar and let the beer go warm in the can. He'd talk to Javy Cruz or Terry Macrae or Ben Harper—who spent a lot of time in Earlys as well, doing some *real* drinking—and swap bullshit stories and tell the same old jokes and the whole time he'd slide his eyes over to Mel and smile at her whenever he got caught, and she'd never get mad, just always smile right back. She'd dump out the beer he wasn't drinking and get him set up with another and never say a word about it, and still take the time to lean over the bar close and ask him about his day or what was going on at work or how his brother Birch was doing. Birch had a girl in Nathan he kept time with, but everyone said she kept time with a lot of men, and Buck had seen her and she wasn't much to look at anyway. Not like

Mel, who Buck counted as one of the prettiest women in all of Big Bend County, although Amé Reynosa wasn't too hard on the eyes, either, even if he personally didn't much go for Mexicans. For a while Tommy Milford had been whispering around town that Amé was a *lesbo* (and that's exactly how he said it), until Buck had cornered him and told him to knock it off. Buck had decided long ago something like that wasn't his damn business and didn't matter to him one way or another anyway, and it sure in the hell wasn't Tommy Milford's business to talk about another fellow deputy. Plus, it just wasn't right to gossip about *any* woman. Buck thought Birch's girl in Nathan probably was a bit of a skank and ugly to boot, with her one cross-eye and those gaps in her teeth, but he'd kept that to himself, the way a gentleman should.

He'd brought his second burger and leftover fries from the Hamilton and was now finishing it all up at the bar. He knew he needed to lose some weight, could feel the way his uniform shirt was too damn tight in the shoulders and gut, and how the buckle of his river belt dug into him, but his daddy had always been big (until his heart gave out), and his brother was, too. It was the curse of the Emmett men, adding pounds every time they added years. Getting in and out of his truck, sitting at his tiny desk in the department, was starting to be a royal pain in the ass, but somehow he never felt any of that weight when he was out camping or hunting or fishing.

Somehow it all disappeared then, and he was seventeen years old again: tall and strong and sunburned, with his hair colored copper by the summer and his stomach smooth and flat.

He could've turned the head of a woman like Mel back then, but that was a long, long time ago. Talking with her did the trick, though, and she had a way of making him feel like that teenager again; like that's who she was seeing when she looked at him, instead of the heavyset, aging man he was. She made it all worth dragging his fat ass into the bar and perching on the uncomfortable bar stool to have those summers back, just for the price of a few beers.

She was leaning into him now, talking about her new dog. She'd toyed with the idea of bringing him with her into the bar, but had thought better of it, and was now feeling guilty. He was locked up in one room at the house, waiting for the sheriff to show up. They were going to have to make a dog door or something for him eventually, but she wasn't sure how big it would need to be.

Also, she laughed, she wasn't sure she wanted the sheriff taking tools to any part of her house.

Buck laughed right along with her. The stories about Sheriff Cherry's handiwork out at the Far Six were becoming legendary, and unlike Amé Reynosa or his brother's ugly girlfriend, those were fair game.

"Whatcha going to name him, your dog, I mean?"

Mel straightened some glasses behind the bar. "Don't know. I was trying on names all day." She laughed again, smiled. "He doesn't seem to like any of them."

Buck pretended to take a drink of his Coors. "I had me a pup once when I was kid. He was a mongrel, a little bit of this, a little bit of that. I called him Rocket, which was funny, 'cause he was kinda dumb and a whole lotta slow. I'd go to school and he would lie down at the kitchen door and still be lying right there when I got back. I don't know if he was missing me or just plain lazy, but boy, I loved that dog."

"*Rocket.* That's not bad. I'll think about it and see what Chris says. I'll see if the dog likes it, too." She winked at him.

"You call him whatever you want, Ms. Mel. Dogs and men ain't that different. We'll always come runnin' whenever a pretty woman hollers for us . . ."

LATER, HE STEPPED OUTSIDE THE BAR and stretched, popping his shirt free from his sweaty skin. Mel had a couple more hours of work, and on most nights he would have sat there the whole time and then walked her out to her car, even though it was only a few paces away in the lot, but he needed to swing by the bank again tonight, like he'd promised the sheriff, and Javy Cruz said he'd do the escorting for him. He was a bit surprised that Harp had never come in, and was thinking about giving him a call, too, when the van caught his eye.

He was standing in the gravel just outside the nearest circle of sodium light from the overheads in the parking lot when it cruised past, heading back into Murfee. It was coming from the direction of Beantown, and looked no different from any of those shitty vehicles some of the ranch hands and other Mexicans drove: more rust and primer than anything else, held together with duct tape and wire. At his angle he couldn't quite see the plate, but it wouldn't have surprised him if it was from Chihuahua. If he'd already been in his truck, he might have pulled it over just to have a little look and maybe luck out and grab a few illegals he could turn over to the green shirts, but it was going on down the road and would be gone before he even got his door open.

He was about to forget it until he got a quick glimpse of the driver.

Buck Emmett was too big and more than a little clumsy, but he had the eyes of an eagle, far better than his brother Birch or his daddy, who had loved to take him hunting for that very reason. Buck could pick out the breathing of an elk through a thick stand of oak or juniper, and could spot a fear-frozen rabbit in ground cover. Hunting wasn't just about *the shot*, it was about *seeing*, and Buck had a gift for it. He could block out all of the background noise and color and movement and just *focus*.

So even in that one fast look, he recognized the driver, and he wasn't just some beaner. It was that old man who'd come with Jesse Earl for the DNA test . . . *Bob* or something. And he was white-knuckling the steering wheel, his head on a swivel, peering into the dark.

He looked scared . . . scared shitless.

And then the van was gone—just a pair of taillights driving toward Murfee.

Toward the bank.

Buck fumbled for his keys and trotted out to his truck, breathing hard already, hoping he could catch up to the van. He hadn't liked the way Jesse Earl had mouthed off to the sheriff, or how he'd later walked into the bar and had words with Mel, too. The older man, Bob whatever, hadn't been as difficult, but Buck had no idea who or what else was in the van with him.

And as good as his eyes were, he couldn't see through the van's rusted flanks, no matter how hard he tried.

50

Chris was already on the long drive out to the Far Six, as lightning stuttered and shook and the long-awaited storm rolled down over the Chisos from Mexico, when his phone rang, once. He didn't even have a chance to pick it up before it went silent again, another victim of the dead areas that dotted the entire Big Bend. He didn't check to see if it had even captured the number, too busy marveling at how the world outside his windshield was slowly disappearing, going blacker than black and then falling off the ends of the earth. The storm wouldn't have to last long to swell the washes and gullies, and in the aftermath, everything that was copper and rust and bone would get new life again; turn green and breathe, at least for a little while.

He wondered how the dog was doing; if he was burrowed under the bed in fear or had already destroyed the bedroom while waiting for him to get home. They'd had the damn thing barely forty-eight hours and he was already worried about him. He was a puppy but would get big fast, and with a little training would be a serious handful for anyone or anything unwanted approaching the house. Chris was more relieved than he'd first realized that Mel wasn't going to be out here alone anymore.

He searched the distance for house lights, but the house itself was all gone, lost behind the approaching rain.

A hard wind hit the windshield, then a wave of raindrops, almost as if someone had tossed a huge bucket of cold water against the truck. He held on tight; felt the wheels rise as the storm wrapped itself around him and his truck. Everything rattled and he slowed down, finally coming to a stop, as his wipers became useless and his headlights washed away to nothing. He was caught inside the storm's furious heartbeat and counted out the passing thunder and the lightning, trying to figure out how fast it was moving and how long it would take to sweep all the way northward toward Murfee. The rain was desperately needed but it would tie things up for a while, since it wasn't unusual for a storm like this to flood the draws and pummel campers up in the national park, even sweep away the cars they'd parked too deep in a wash, despite the warning signs. He was about to call Mel and tell her to hang tight at Earlys until it blew past, when his phone rang again.

Then it rang a third time, fast, like the phone itself was desperately trying to hold on to the call.

It was a number he didn't immediately recognize, an unfamiliar area code, but the voice—distant, struggling; sawed in half by static—he knew right away.

Amé.

He was having a hard time hearing what she was saying . . . something about Harp . . . *something about trouble.* She said Danny Ford's name as well, or he thought she did, and one other thing, her last words before the call dropped, and they were the clearest of all.

The Lights.

He'd just been out that way an hour ago, a little more than that. He passed right by the roadside tourist attraction and hadn't given it a thought, before sliding onto one of the ranch roads to get out here without having to detour through Murfee. He didn't remember seeing anything out there, but hadn't been paying any goddamn attention, either, and it didn't matter. Amé *was* there, with Harp and Danny Ford as well. He didn't know what was going on, but it couldn't be good. He'd try to raise his other deputies on the phone on the way, or pick them up on the truck radio once he got closer to town, but it was clear where he needed to be. *Now.*

He flipped on his emergency lights, smearing the watery night red and blue. He still couldn't see much, but he couldn't sit and wait for the storm to pass. He had to try to get ahead of it and race it all the way back to Murfee.

With lightning on his heels, he pushed the truck as fast as it would go.

51

Fifteen minutes after Buck Emmett left Earlys, following the white van into Murfee, Mel was standing outside in almost the exact same spot he'd been in when it first caught his attention, taking a short break.

She liked to step out into the night air like this every now and then, rinsing off the smell of beer and breath and cigarettes and dust that defined the old bar. Sometimes she smoked out here, but tonight she'd left her Marlboros in her purse, and had her hands in her back pockets, trying to see if the moon was out or if the clouds she had spotted gathering at the Far Six had followed her to town. Chris would be getting home soon if he wasn't there already, and she was looking forward to seeing him. The last time the two of them had driven back from the city together, he'd been bleeding next to her in their car, still suffering badly from the wounds he'd received at the place that was now their home. She'd been driving so Chris could call Caleb Ross, desperately trying to track down Caleb before he confronted and possibly killed his father. Chris had then faced off with Sheriff Ross himself in the sheriff's old office, while Mel had sat in their bloody car with a gun of her own she'd stolen from the sheriff's collection. That's all that horrible night had been for her: one long, held breath—everything on pause—waiting to find out what would happen to Chris and Caleb and Sheriff Ross.

Waiting to find out what was going to happen to *her* future with Chris; their lives together suspended in midair, ready to fall.

She'd prayed since then to never go through another night like that, knowing all the while it was foolish and futile. That was the nature of being in love with a man who carried a badge and gun: forever and always *waiting*. Ben had talked enough about Jackie for Mel to understand all the sacrifices that poor woman had made—the worry and the sleepless nights and the fear that had followed every ringing phone. And she'd experienced that already here, too, at Earlys, whenever Buck or Ben or the other deputies stepped through the door with their hats off—a moment of pure, cold terror that they weren't there for just a beer or a cup of coffee, but for her. That they'd then have to walk her outside, gently, calmly—maybe even steadying her by the arm—to stand in the spot she was in now, so they could deliver through gritted teeth their bad news about Chris, away from the prying eyes of everyone else at the bar.

It was a hell of a way to live, always waiting to die, but it was the life Chris had chosen. More fairly, after that night she'd driven him back from El Paso, it was the life they had chosen *together*. She had to own that, but some days and nights were easier than others.

She wished she had brought out her cigarettes, but if she'd been drawing on one of the unfiltered Marlboros, she might not have caught the smoke that was already on the breeze. Maybe it was someone sitting in their car having a smoke . . . *waiting* . . . and for a second she thought about those men from Killing that had come into the bar, the men Chris had been so worried about. She looked around for a telltale cherry spot hovering behind a windshield, but there were so few cars in the lot she soon came up empty. Given how conscious everyone around Murfee was of the summer drought, she wouldn't expect many folks to be tossing their half-lits into the gravel or grass, but the smoke was now thicker than just one cigarette anyway. It had a deeper smell, almost metallic, like someone had flicked a butt into some grass along the ditch and started a small brushfire.

She walked off the porch out into the lot, looking up and down the street, when she found the glow.

It was back toward Beantown, that horrible name some of the folks in Murfee had given the Hispanic neighborhood clustered at the far end of town. There, against the darkness, was a ruddy smear, flickering wide, getting higher. It was more than a little grass fire, it was like a whole house was burning, maybe even more than one. She knew that Amé lived back over there somewhere, but was ashamed she had no idea where exactly the deputy's house was.

She walked a little farther, trying to get a better look and trying to gauge exactly how serious it was. She'd left her phone in the bar, but Buck Emmett hadn't driven off that long ago, and she could call him to go check it out, if not 911.

That's when she heard the sirens.

52

America didn't want to look into Ben Harper's face.

It was there, right beside her, eyes closed, like he was sleeping over Danny's shoulder, even though she knew he wasn't. He hadn't been a big man to begin with and seemed even smaller now; getting smaller the longer they walked. She was afraid he would disappear before they made the highway again.

She held on to the SureFire and the pendant he'd given her in one hand and her gun in the other.

She and Danny hadn't spoken in some minutes. There was so little to say, so there was only the sound of their joint breathing, their boots on the scrub. She kept the SureFire aimed low, sweeping the beam across the ground in front of Danny so he'd see where he was going without tripping. She'd been switching between her own phone and Danny's trying to get ahold of Sheriff Cherry, and she thought maybe, finally, the call had gone through. Despite what Ben had warned, they were angling their way back to the pavilion where the shootout began, and where the sheriff could find them, and she kept searching the night in that direction, looking for fresh headlights. But it remained stubbornly, agonizingly, dark.

Danny stopped, shifting down to one knee. "Please, give me just a sec, gotta catch my breath." Like her, he was looking ahead where the highway should be, searching, and she could see the strain in his face, from his own injuries and from carrying Ben. Still, he wouldn't put the other man down on the ground. He kept him held off the dirt and the cracked desert floor.

"I'm sorry," he said, still looking straight ahead.

"You're hurt, it's okay. We can take a break. It's still going to take a while for the sheriff to get to us, or whoever he sends." She knelt down next to him on the side opposite Ben's closed eyes.

"No, that's not what I mean. You all risked so much for me. I didn't know all this would happen. I just . . ."

She shook her head. "We can never know. That's what I tried to warn you. *Sangre exige sangre.* We never know the price of our revenge, and the cost is higher because we never have to pay it ourselves. That falls to everyone around us."

"Blood demands blood," he repeated. "You told me that in the car when we talked in town, with . . ." She knew he was going to say *Harper*, but stopped himself. He turned to look at her and saw the pendant still grasped in her hand. "Firsthand experience, right? That's really what you were trying to tell me in Murfee."

She hesitated. "*Mi hermano.* He was murdered by men like your Earls. They buried him in a place like this, forgotten, like a dog, until Sheriff Cherry came and . . ." She stopped, stood up. "And it doesn't matter anymore. He's gone."

Danny stood as well, slowly, making sure Ben didn't slip from his shoulders. "What did it cost you? What price did you have to pay?"

She turned the small flashlight ahead, pointing him the way to go. "Who said I'm not still paying it, Danny Ford?"

NOW HE TALKED AS THEY WALKED, about a place called Wanat and some sort of battle, and a man named Sergeant Wahl who died there. He told her how parts of the Big Bend reminded him of Afghanistan— the mountains and the harsh earth. He then talked about a girl who'd asked Danny to watch over her while she slept, to keep her safe, but something had happened and the girl was now gone. That story didn't make any sense to America, but she listened anyway, and let Danny keep talking as much to himself as to her. He needed to say all these things, maybe because he was trying to explain to himself how he'd ended up here, walking through the dark and sour creosote, carrying a dead man he barely knew across his back. He'd already said he was sorry and that was enough for her, since she didn't, wouldn't, blame him. How could she, given all she had unleashed trying to avenge Rodolfo's death?

Sangre exige sangre.

Unlike Danny, she *knew* the price. She'd learned it the hard way, so she clutched Ben's pendant tighter, unwilling to let it go. She'd told Danny the men who'd killed Rodolfo—like the men who had sent Azahel Avalos—were no different from the Earls, *hombres malos*. Ben had also called such men *lobos. Wolves.* They were dangerous, never to be trusted. They were always out there, circling, and there were always more of them. Look at what had happened to her brother, then Billy Bravo, and now Ben Harper.

When did it ever end? How could it end?

Sheriff Cherry wanted to believe in the law, in this *right thing.* His experiences with Sheriff Ross, a wolf all his own, made him hold tight to the idea that such a thing existed and the idea of anything else was unthinkable. Her experiences with Duane Dupree and the boy *sicario* Máximo, with Vianey Ruiz tossing the ashes of Billy Bravo into the river and with Azahel Avalos in his cell, and, now, with her dead friend draped over Danny Ford's back, made her afraid such a thing was impossible.

She'd tried, but there was no right thing; no *cosa correcta.*

There was only what had to be done—whatever it took to stand against the wolves.

That's what Ben had been trying to teach her all along—that once started, blood demanded blood, forever. That it never ended and you could never wash your hands of it, so you just accepted it. That was the real price of fighting the *hombres malos* and keeping *los lobos* from the door . . . that was the burden of wearing a badge and carrying a gun.

Like Vianey's prayer to Nuestra Señora de la Santa Muerte. She tried to remember the words, and with each step, a few more came to her. By the time the pavilion was in sight, she thought she had it all.

Santa Muerte, le convoco. Santa Muerte, te invoco. Give me justice, justice against my enemies . . .

DANNY'S BIKE WAS STILL THERE, crushed on its side, but Jesse Earl was gone. He'd put a couple of bullets through it, drained the tank, and then cut the tires.

In the SureFire's beam, all the spent shells glittered like gold coins, like fallen stars. They extended beyond the light, trailing off into the darkness. There were also darker stains that had to be blood. She and Danny walked up to the benches of the pavilion and Danny, at last, stretched out Ben's body on one of the tables, above the earth.

She started to reach for their phones, but Danny touched her shoulder, pointing down the highway, where emergency lights were speeding toward them.

They watched the lights for a long time before they heard the sirens.

53

Buck had heard the phrase *All hell was breaking loose.*

He thought it pretty much described Murfee at the moment. Beantown was burning.

TILL GREER WAS OVER THERE handling that with Murfee's Fire Department, and hollering over the radio that they were taking gunfire from one of the burning houses, which didn't make any sense at all, but Buck had heard it himself—all muddied up with the sirens and background squall and the sound of someone yelling over Till's open mic.

But even before that, Sheriff Cherry had reached out to him on the phone and then on the radio. The sheriff was hauling ass from the Far Six back toward town, where something bad had happened to Amé and Harp, maybe involving the Earls, which is why no one had been able to reach the two of them all night. One or both of them were injured out by the Lights and were waiting for help, and the sheriff had been heading that way, until Buck had told him right at that moment *he* was following a van driven by those damn Earls that had just come from the direction of burning Beantown. With the sheriff still on the radio and Buck giving him the play-by-play—almost whispering even though he was alone—the van had circled the department's impound lot a couple of times, lights off, while Buck had pulled in along the street, hunkering down in his seat. Not before seeing someone jump out with a set of bolt-cutters, headed for the lot's lone gate.

However, the sheriff had ordered him to sit fucking tight. To not approach any of the Earls or the impound lot at all, even if they drove off. The sheriff was going to radio Dale Holt and have him go out to the Lights instead, and then he was going to come directly to Buck. With Till over in Beantown and Amé and Harp lost somewhere out at the Lights, and Tommy Milford still laid up after getting hit by a car, they were all out of deputies.

But the sheriff had told him *again* to stay put and not move, no matter what, and then had signed off to find Dale.

THAT HAD BEEN TEN, fifteen minutes ago, and in all those passing minutes, Buck had sat quiet and still in his darkened truck just like the sheriff had ordered, even while listening to Till yelling about gunfire on the radio and Dale trying to raise Harp or Amé on the air as he raced toward the Lights. Everyone was doing *something*, while he was doing nothing, just hiding. *Goddamn hiding.* With the Earls, who he'd bet all of his paycheck had hurt his friends and then set fire to Beantown, only yards away. He didn't know *why* they were in the lot and was surprised when they hadn't gone on to the bank, but his best guess was that it had something to do with the car that had run Tommy down, the same car Harp and Amé had been messing with earlier, even if he couldn't draw a straight line between that Mexican kid and the Earls. It didn't matter, anyway—they were over there *right now*, but probably not for much longer. He had no idea how far off the sheriff still was, and was afraid it was going to prove to be too far no matter what.

So he'd end up just sitting here, watching the Earls drive away.

He imagined later holding down a stool in Earlys, being ashamed to tell *that* story; trying to explain to his brother Birch that he'd only been following orders. He remembered Chief Deputy Harper talking on and on about *action and reaction* and knew that sitting in his truck he was doing neither. He was worse: a bystander, a damn witness.

He might as well be a ghost or not even be here at all.

He unholstered his Colt and slid back upright in his truck, staring down the street at the last place he'd seen the van disappear into the lot.

He and Birch had hunted about every sort of animal you could in Texas. Exotics like Aoudad sheep in the Glass Mountains and Nilgai antelope on the H. Yturria ranches. Mule deer and whitetail over on the Sierra Escalera, even alligators at the Red Run ranch in Caney. Just last year, they'd taken a big mountain lion down in the Solitario, which wasn't quite legal, but it had cut down some sheep at Dave Wilcher's place and left the half-eaten carcasses to rot. Birch had found the tracks, but it was Buck who'd spotted it first, near invisible in a thick bunch of Hinckley oak, and it was Buck who'd taken the shot, clean as a whistle, at forty or fifty yards.

He was a lot less than that now from the impound lot, and would be even closer, if he just got out of his damn truck and did something.

Before he opened the door, he turned off his truck radio and made sure his cell phone was muted. He gave it an extra minute anyway, not because he was scared, but just in case the sheriff did come rolling up. But when the streets stayed dark, he took a deep breath and got out.

He told himself it was just like hunting.

54

Jimmying the lock and getting the Nissan Maxima started hadn't been a problem. Kasper had done that model car or one like it at least a dozen times before, so it had gone just as quick as he'd told Little B it would. What was slowing them down like fucking quicksand was swapping out the tires, using the ones from Clutts's car they'd hauled up from Killing to replace the ones shredded and blown out on the Maxima. The holdup was the lugs, which although more or less the same—5 lug, 4.5-inch offset—weren't factory-perfect matches. Mr. Earl had asked him about that when they'd stood together and shared a beer and he'd brought up needing Kasper's help, and Kasper had checked the Nissan's measurements (because for reasons of his own, Mr. Earl hadn't wanted to go to Murfee to buy four brand-new tires if he absolutely didn't have to) only to find there were close enough replacements sitting right outside the front door.

Mr. Earl had set his empty beer can on its hood.

Close, but not identical. So T-Bob, who was drunk and stinking to high heaven, was still fumbling around with the last tire. Little B was trying to help him, aiming a flashlight at the old man's shaking hands as he worked, but Kasper could feel the minutes ticking away with each slow-ass turn of T-Bob's wrench. Mr. Earl had bet the fire on the other side of town would buy them plenty of time, so even if they did set off an alarm cutting into the lot, no one would pay much attention to it with half the town burning, and so far that bet had paid off, as the streets around them stayed quiet. But Kasper had been stealing cars for years, and both speed and invisibility were critical. They were losing the first swapping out the tires like molasses, and they didn't even have the second: they were too exposed, too naked. Although there weren't many lights in the lot, just two big security lamps on opposite corner poles—wires exposed and metal hoods rusted—there weren't a lot of cars cluttering up the place, either. To anyone who bothered to look, they appeared to be exactly what they were—three men trying damn hard to steal a car.

And not doing it fast enough.

A successful boost also came down to good timing and a little luck, and the longer the whole fucking thing took, the less of those they had as well.

"Goddamn, let me do that," he finally said, grabbing the wrench away from T-Bob. "T-Bob, please take that light from Little B and hold it steady so I can see what the fuck I'm doing. Little B, maybe you could walk out to the gate, keep an eye out, just in case. Or even better, pull the van up a bit, it might hide us while I finish this up."

Little B mumbled something to his uncle, but gave the flashlight to him. Then he stood over Kasper, looking down. "You runnin' this thing now, Kaz? You got balls now? This your plan all of a sudden?"

And for all the world he sounded just like his daddy or his big brother.

Kasper spun a bolt, tried to spit on the metal to speed it up, but he was so scared it took him a few seconds just to work up anything in his dry mouth. "Goddamn, no, this isn't my plan or my idea or nothing. I'm just trying to get this done so we all don't go to jail. *Your* daddy is the one who wants this car, that's all."

"I know, I know," Little B said. "And I been wonderin' about that. Thought I might take a look-see, see what the five-alarm fire is all about." He laughed at his own joke. "I'm guessin' there's money enough in there somewhere for everyone."

For everyone.

But Kasper didn't believe that at all anymore. Whatever was in the car was for Mr. Earl and Mr. Earl alone. "It's not going to matter if we don't get this thing moving. Please, B, just help me out here." Little B was about to slip in behind the wheel of the Nissan, maybe even crawl into the backseat and look around, but changed his mind.

He rolled his eyes. "Fuck you, Kaz, you sound like a little bitch, like goddamn Jenna. But I'll move the van closer if that's gonna get this shit to go faster." Little B punched his uncle in the shoulder to make him stand straighter, because T-Bob was somehow slouching lower by the second, even while standing still—the flashlight beam sliding past Kasper's hands and getting lost underneath the car—and then he walked back toward the van and got in.

And you sound like someone trying to be something you're not.

Kasper said, "T-Bob, just keep her steady, *please* . . . I swear we're almost done . . . there's just not enough light . . ." But he never got to finish the sentence, because someone called out to them from the gate.

"Put your goddamn hands up where I can see 'em and walk back to me nice and slow . . ."

Good timing and a little luck.

Another couple of minutes more, that's all they'd needed.

KASPER STOOD AND T-BOB TURNED at the same time, both of them finding a big deputy standing by the front gate, his gun drawn, pointed at them. Kasper could make out the badge on his belt, a real gold star, even though there wasn't much light to reflect off it.

Kasper dropped the wrench into the dirt.

Thank God this is over. I'm gonna go home and I'm gonna call my mom and I'm gonna . . .

T-Bob raised his hands, showed they were empty, and the deputy took a step forward. "You two walk toward me, slow." The deputy kept looking toward the van, but didn't have an angle to see into the cab. He was cautious all the same.

"Anyone else in there?" he asked, trying to keep the two of them in front of him as he moved forward inch by inch, focusing on the front of the van; the passenger-side door and window. He'd already cleared the van's tailgate and was staying wide, listening hard for any movement from inside. Kasper was about to say *Hell yes*, when T-Bob spoke up for the first time in what seemed like hours.

"No siree, it's just the two of us, I think."

Kasper turned toward T-Bob, as the deputy repeated "You *think*" out loud, with an odd, not-understanding look on his face, when Little B popped out of the rear of the van with the Remington 12-gauge. He kicked open the swing-out doors—still unlocked from where they'd rolled out the tires—and was only ten feet from the deputy, who turned at the sound with his gun raised. Little B's first shot went wide, blasting apart the windshield of an old taxi, and the deputy dropped to a knee to return fire, several of his rounds striking true. But Little B's second shot found its mark, too, knocking the deputy's legs out from under him and throwing him facedown to the ground in a mess of his own blood. Little B was then falling, also, backward into the van, searching for his balance and shooting all the way down, while the deputy lying on the ground was trying to do the same.

Kasper knew he was watching two men die right in front of him and had never seen anything like it. The deputy and Little B were yelling at each other, and even with all the echoing gunshots and his hands over his ears, they were the loudest goddamn noises Kasper had ever heard.

Hell, maybe he was yelling, too, calling out for Little B or his mom's name like he was a little kid again, as the muzzle flashes and the heat from it all burned so bright around him.

Twice as hot and fast as the fires they'd started across town.

55

It was all over by the time Chris got there.

He knew that when he drove past Buck's empty truck.

Actually, he'd known it before that, when he hadn't been able to raise his deputy on the radio for the last twenty minutes. It was a long twenty minutes, calling out Buck's name again and again, getting nothing back but heavy silence. *The silence was deafening.* It was an old saying, a goddamn cliché, but he'd learned during those grave, quiet minutes that didn't make it any less true.

He couldn't even hear his heartbeat, his own breathing. He'd searched that emptiness for any hint of Buck answering him back, but there was nothing.

He'd already turned off his emergency lights and his headlights, pulling up to the open gate guided only by the impound lot's security lamps. Even in that weak light, he could tell the chain had been cut and, beyond that, could see a mess of stains going blacker by the second all over the ground. They'd been smeared and whorled around like finger paints, and it took Chris a second to figure out what he was looking at. But when he finally saw Buck spread-eagled in the middle of it, all that spray spiraling out in wider and wider circles from his dead deputy, he knew.

They'd driven fucking *through* Buck's blood to escape; *over him,* dragging him across the concrete. The van Buck had been following was still there, bullet holes stitched across the open rear cargo doors, so his attackers must have bolted in another car, and even though Chris knew he shouldn't assume they were really gone—he needed to clear that van—he couldn't take his eyes off Buck's ruined body. He tried to make sense of it and tried to put all of those odd, unrecognizable pieces back together and make Buck whole; make him stand again.

He prayed Buck was already dead when they drove over his head.

He got out of his truck with his A5 leading the way, keeping it aimed on the open van doors. He moved slowly, listening. A moment ago he couldn't stop looking at Buck, now getting closer; he wanted to look anywhere else. He was careful where he stepped, avoiding the other man's blood, and made out the tire tread stained in it. Checking the lot, counting the remaining cars, he guessed it was Azahel Avalos's Nissan they'd taken, and it wasn't lost on him that Buck was the second of his deputies who'd bled because of that particular vehicle.

When he found it, and he promised himself he would, he'd pull it apart to the fucking bolts. No one was ever going to drive it again.

There was a noise by the van and he nearly jumped out of his skin, before catching movement and a pair of raised hands rising from the dark. He had a moment when he could have pulled the Browning's trigger and no one would have said a damn thing; no one who later saw Buck's bloody body would have ever questioned him or thought twice about it, but he *willed* his finger off the trigger. It moved so slow, though, goddamn slow, like it had a mind of its own. He took a deep breath and settled himself, staring down at the man he'd almost shot.

The kid he'd almost shot, pale and shaking, walking slowly out of the van's shadows.

"Please don't shoot me . . . please."

"Get on the ground, now. Don't take another step." The kid did as he was told, grabbing as much ground as he could, trying to avoid Buck's blood as Chris had. His face was still down there, though, inches from it, and the boy squeezed his eyes shut.

"Anyone else here?"

The boy shook his head. "No, they're gone, drove off. Just the one, though, the other's dead."

Chris looked around for another body and didn't see it. Maybe it was in the van.

"Just the three of you?"

"Yes."

"Who were the others?"

The boy swallowed hard, trying not to cry. "T-Bob Earl, and his nephew, Little B . . . He's dead, shot down by the deputy. I heard him die, he was making noises and goddamn it was like nothing I ever heard and—"

"That's enough, son. Enough." Chris walked over to him, shouldered the A5, and cuffed him. He got him upright, leaned him against the van, and searched him but came up empty. Blue and red emergency lights were spinning a few streets away, coming toward him, and now, for the first time, he could smell smoke from the fires burning on the west side of town. He needed to check with Till and find out if they were getting that under control. As dry as it had been, that whole neighborhood could burn if they didn't get a handle on it. They might get some help, though, if they could hold on; if the storm coming up from the south didn't die out before it reached them.

The kid was saying something more, but Chris told him to stop, to just be quiet. This close to the van, Chris could almost taste spilled gas on the metal, and the sulfur in the night air from the shotgun blasts stung his eyes.

"The fires, you and the others started those, didn't you?"

"Yes, we did. That was Mr. Earl's idea. He told us to do that."

"John Wesley Earl?"

The kid nodded, went to wipe his face but his hands were still cuffed.

"All this tonight was because of John Wesley Earl?"

"Something else happened earlier, too. Jesse and Joker and Lee

Malady hightailed it after Danny . . . he was going somewhere. I don't know where."

Earlier. That must have been what Amé had been trying to tell him. She and Harp had somehow tangled with Jesse over something to do with Danny. And now, here, Buck had shot Earl's other son. Maybe both of Earl's boys were dead in one night, and although Chris knew the old outlaw didn't give a damn about them, it still gave him a *reason,* at least two of them, to hold Chris and his deputies accountable.

Whatever was going on was not going to stop with Earl burning Murfee.

He might just be getting started.

The kid was still talking, only to himself. "We were gonna start a band . . . a band . . . and I think I loved him . . ."

And for what? What the hell was Earl doing?

He was still wondering that when Dale Holt drove into the lot with his lights and sirens going.

AMÉ GOT OUT FIRST, and then Danny Ford. They were both covered in so much dust and blood it was hard for Chris to tell how much of it was their own or someone else's. Danny was definitely limping, almost doubled over, but that wasn't what caught and held Chris's attention.

It was the man still lying in the back of the truck, the man not moving.

The man as still and cold as Buck Emmett on the nearby pavement.

Goddamn, not Harp. Please not Ben.

But it was.

56

-Bob drove into the coming storm in the stolen car with his dead nephew in the back.

There was no doubt about that . . . about Little B being dead. His heart had stopped pumping his thick blood all over the backseat, but T-Bob could still smell how it filled the car, making everything coppery, like he had a roll of pennies in his mouth. He'd propped Little B upright at first, but he'd fallen over since then, slipping down in his own blood (and probably some shit and piss) and was now a jumble in the backseat, looking upward at the ceiling and the back of T-Bob's head. Yes, he was plum dead, but that didn't stop T-Bob from keeping his eyes locked forward, waiting for the rain to hit, refusing to glance back at his nephew. He was afraid those dead glass eyes might blink a bit, or Little B's tongue might dart out and wet his cold corpse lips, or worst of all, he might sit up and slide a bloody, gun-blasted arm around T-Bob and say something smart-ass . . . or something truly fucking horrible.

It was the booze talking, or the lack of it. The bottle of Teacher's had gone far, but not far enough. And with your dead nephew in the backseat, threatening to get up and say a few words, maybe no amount of liquor would. There could never be enough.

The first of the rain grazed the car, like spots of blood. He had the

AC blasting, hoping to blow away the stink around him. He was shaking, but it didn't have anything to do with the temperature.

He squinted through the windshield, trying to make sense of the road, trying to stay between the lines. It had been a drought for months and now the whole world was slowly being covered in water. The only thing still and forever parched was his throat, dry as a bone, desperate for a drink. That's what no one understood, not Little B or Jesse or even JW. That goddamn animal thirst—hot like rabies—that only plagued a real drinker. T-Bob, almost ten years older than JW, had been a teetotaler into his twenties since he'd been the one mostly responsible for his younger brother, what with their daddy's comings and goings and his own drunken demons. But once he had his taste, a little Jim Beam single barrel or some Maker's, he'd followed Daddy right down to the bottom of the bottle. It was the only thing they'd ever shared, their one family bond. JW had been Daddy's favorite from the get-go, and that had only been truer after T-Bob took up drinking—all of his mistakes magnified, all of his problems multiplied.

He'd ended up exactly like Daddy, and Mason William Earl had somehow hated him for it, blaming him for all of the Earl family ills.

When JW got sent up the first time, his daddy had sat in his trailer and listened to KTEX out of Beaumont, singing along with the Johnny Rodriguez songs he loved, drinking his tears away one glass after another. He wouldn't look at T-Bob, wouldn't hardly say his name, as if they both knew the wrong son had been locked up and Mason William was locked up right along with him, and as his brain went bad and he got more difficult to deal with, sometimes he'd call out for the son who wasn't there and lash out with his weakened fists at the one who was. Mason was dead and gone before JW was released, so it had been T-Bob who'd put him in the ground, and his brother had never once asked him about it or even where their daddy was buried.

That was all JW, though, single-minded. Like with this damn car. He'd moved heaven and earth to get it, and it was going to cost him at least one son, maybe the other. Not that JW would see it that way or even care. A part of T-Bob knew that none of this was about him or those boys and never had been. There was nothing in this damn car for any of them, not even Sunny. Little B was dead for a handful of that nothing, but it didn't change the fact that it was T-Bob's fault; that it would be laid at his feet.

He could almost feel Daddy's eyes pressing on him from the back-seat, judging him; his corpse or ghost or whatever it was sitting back there in Little B's blood and holding the boy's dead hand, nodding in agreement.

Damn right it's your fault . . . always is . . . always was . . .

That was almost enough to make T-Bob turn the car around and drive right out of Texas altogether, maybe on to California or Nevada. First there was that fuckup at the Wikiup with Jesse, and then the run-ins with the law in Murfee, and now this thing with Little B. He'd been there for all of it, so that every bad thing that had happened since they'd come to Killing was marked up with his fingerprints. He needed a drink something fierce to make his dead daddy in the backseat stop looking at him that way, and to make his dead nephew stop whispering shit he didn't want to hear. Soon enough, he was also going to have to face a brother who'd probably just as well kill him as look at him, and who, in the right moment, T-Bob could admit to himself that he pretty well fucking hated, too.

He *did* hate JW, but could no more abandon him than he could their daddy, who'd called him all those names and one time, in a real mad fit—his brain burning out its last fuse—had pointed that old Ruger at his face and asked him where his real boy was.

His real boy.

But no matter what, he couldn't leave Sunny behind, either; and really, how far could he get with that body in the backseat and carrying all those other dead around with him?

JW had been very clear about where he'd wanted T-Bob to stash the car. He'd drawn it on a little scrap of paper and made him memorize it and then tore it up. He wasn't supposed to drive it right up to the ranch house, because Earl didn't want Flowers or Clutts seeing it. With the fresh rain and mud, T-Bob wasn't sure that was a good idea—it's not like this little Jap car was good for off-roading—but he wasn't going to fuck up again.

JW always told him not to think, just do what he was told, so come hell or high water, that was exactly what he was going to do—he'd get this goddamn car to his brother.

He laughed at that . . . *hell or high water* . . . as the rain started even harder and washed the night clean away in front of the car and his dead nephew watched him.

He pressed some buttons, trying to get the windshield wipers working and the radio going, maybe even a little Johnny Rodriguez singing "Ridin' My Thumb to Mexico" or "Pass Me By"—anything to stop the murmurings from the backseat—when the AC cut out, followed by a weird grating noise. He yelled, thinking at first it was Little B crawling over the backseat to sit up front with him, but realized it was just something shifting beneath the dashboard, a little panel popping open. He'd never have found it even if he had been looking for it, and couldn't imagine what he'd done to get it going. The wipers were now locked in place, though, useless and not moving, and though the AC stuttered and kicked back on, it was only blowing hot air this time.

When it did, a piece of paper also spun out from under the dash into T-Bob's lap.

He grabbed it, nearly sliding off the road, and when he crumpled it up, realized it wasn't quite paper at all. He held it up close, held it up high, so his nephew and Daddy in the back could get a good long look, too.

It was a hundred-dollar bill.

57

Murfee burned.

And the first house Kasper and Little B burned belonged to Amé Reynosa.

THE MURFEE FIRE DEPARTMENT had recently purchased a used Ferrara Intruder 2 custom pumper. It was their Engine 1, their primary fire truck, with a seven-hundred-fifty-gallon main water tank. Counting the fire chief, Ross Everly, and the first and second captains—his brothers, Ron and Rick—and every current, reserve, and probationary firefighter (including Ross's twenty-year-old daughter, Becky, who was sometimes dating Tommy Milford), the entire department counted eight people, many of whom were Everlys or closely related, and all of whom handled double duties as paramedics, EMTs, and even the department's treasurer. Their last callout had been two weeks earlier to a one-vehicle rollover, and the week before that, they'd dealt with brushfire ignited by a blown-out truck tire on Highway 90. That had stretched for about seventy-five to a hundred yards along the road, setting three fence posts ablaze as well, and took them close to two hours and over seventeen hundred gallons of water to contain.

The fires in Beantown were going to be a hell of a lot worse.

.   .   .

IT WOULD LATER BE DEBATED just how bad the final damage would have been if it hadn't been for the storm. When it hit, those eight firefighters had been battling for at least thirty minutes across an area of roughly three acres, encompassing about two blocks of small, close-set houses. Everything was dry and brittle from the drought and many of the houses weren't up to any sort of code and they were all filled with stuff that was ready and eager to burn.

The flames had free range to bounce from yard to yard, roof to roof, and they did.

Still, those eight fought them every step of the way, with Second Captain Rick Everly sustaining second-degree burns on both arms when a porch roof partially collapsed, as the vinyl siding of the home he'd been searching melted around him.

The fires were so hot that even the homes not burning suffered radiant heat exposure: baby pools boiled, plastic yard statues ran like wax candles, and the rubber tires of old bicycles and baby strollers blistered and popped.

A family chicken ran around in circles in the street, flaming, leaving ashy feathers and embers in its wake.

The Everlys drained Engine 1 almost immediately, went to the backup tanks, depleted every bit of Class A foam, and brought out their reserve pumper. They tried to use the one hydrant in the area, but hydrants had been an issue around Murfee for a while and a constant source of complaint for Chief Everly. They were painted in random colors, from traditional red to yellow to green, making color-coding them nearly impossible. Some didn't work at all, others didn't have enough water pressure, and a few weren't even hooked to a water line. This was true for the nearest hydrant to the Beantown fire, and when the chief realized they were going to run out of water, and fast, he said a small prayer, and started calling his counterparts in Artesia and

Nathan, even though he knew the fire would be well out of control before they could arrive.

But then the rain came.

The storm that had swept up from the Chisos and followed Sheriff Cherry into Murfee slammed into town.

It was the first rain in over sixteen weeks—a brutal, heavy downpour—and in less than an hour, it dropped nearly twenty-nine thousand gallons of water on those three burning acres.

58

He was aware they were all watching him.

Watching and waiting to see what he would do next, as if he hadn't done anything at all.

But he'd already called Nichols, staying calm at first with his hand choking the phone, then gripping tighter with each measured word as he recounted the chaos John Wesley Earl had brought down on his town, *his home*, before finally demanding Nichols get his ass down to Murfee and help him unfuck this situation. Nichols had told him he was already on the way, and ordered Chris and his people to stand down; that Nichols and the FBI would handle the situation from here on out.

Chris had told him he already had a front-row seat to how Nichols handled things, and ended the call by throwing the phone across the room.

And there were also the other calls he'd made, but from a different phone. He'd alerted Bethel Turner and the Rangers and all the green and blue shirts in the area, making sure a Nissan Maxima or any of the other cars or motorcycles the Earls might have couldn't pass through any of the checkpoints or points of entry, and he'd reached out to the sheriffs in Midland and Pecos and Terrell, and had Till Greer fax out the names and photos of everyone from Killing whom Danny had been able to identify for them. With each phone call, each fax, each e-mail, a noose was being drawn tighter around the Big Bend, fitted for Earl like the one tattooed around his neck, and anyone with him.

But still, Danny Ford and Amé remained watching him through the open door of his office, not quite accusing, but expecting something . . . *more*. They'd been waiting there since they all came in from the impound lot, after they told him everything that had transpired at the Lights. Dale Holt was dealing with their prisoner and Till was dealing with the bodies.

The bodies.

He sat back, closed his eyes, but still he could see them—Harp and Buck. Not just as they were now, those broken things they'd pulled from the Lights and the lot, but as they had been before.

Harp listening to his jazz and telling his stories on a bar stool at Earlys. Laughing at something Chris had said and complaining about something Chris had done.

Buck talking about hunting with his brother and his big hands trying to relay the size of an even bigger antler rack they'd taken. The way Buck was always the first one in the department, sitting at his desk and typing his reports one finger at a time, and reading the words out loud.

Chris knew he'd be seeing both men like this—before and after—for a long time, long past the moment when they were put into the ground. Like Major Dyer and even Garrison had said, they were his men, and always would be.

They'd passed on his watch.

WHEN HE OPENED HIS EYES AGAIN, Amé and Danny were sitting in his office. Danny's wound had been tended by Becky Everly, but he needed to be over at Hancock Hill, getting real attention. This was the first time Chris had put real eyes on Danny, and he was taller than he'd appeared in his pictures, his head shaved close but just starting to grow out. He was wearing a spare deputy's shirt over the bandages, since his original T-shirt had been scissored off by Becky, but it didn't hide the swirl of tattoos on his chest and up his arms. Eagles, guns, skulls, super-heroes . . . comic book stuff. Becky had bagged up the cut strips of the T-shirt, the blood turning the clear plastic red, while Danny had talked about how Ben Harper had jumped in front of the bullet Jesse Earl meant for him.

"Where do you need me?" Amé asked.

Chris wasn't sure. "Here, I guess, for now. We're going to have folks showing up later tonight, more in the morning, so we're not going to run around chasing the Earls in the dark. With the storm and the BOLOs, they don't have a lot of options, at least for a while. They're trapped down there." He couldn't even tell her to go home, because her house was gone, one of eight that had burned down. The gunshots Till Greer had dodged while responding with the fire department had been all of her spare ammunition and guns popping off in the heat. When Ross Everly told her that the house and everything in it had burned to the ground, she'd started laughing. It was something he'd ask her about later, but not now.

"I'm not sure about that," Danny suggested, from where he was sit-ting behind Amé. He was trying hard to look at the old map hanging on the wall behind Chris's desk.

"Not sure about what?"

"That they're trapped in Killing, at least not Earl. I think I know what he's going to do. He's been planning this awhile, and if we wait, he'll be gone."

Chris pointed at him. "There is no *we*, got that? You're a civilian, nothing more, and you need to be in a hospital."

"I understand the way you feel, Sheriff, I do. But—"

"*But what?*" Chris cut him off, reaching for anger he didn't really feel. He'd lost his anger after he'd thrown his desk phone across the room, with Nichols still talking. Now he was only numb, empty. "Look around you, look at what's happened here tonight. This has gone so far beyond you and your father and whatever the hell it was you thought you were doing."

Danny said, "I know, I know. But I watched a good man take a bullet for me tonight. He barely knew me and he died trying to help me, and the one who set that in motion is still out there hurting people. People *you* know, people you care about, your town. We can sit here or I can help you do something about that. I need to."

Chris yelled past Amé, who stayed silent. *"You need to?* Now? You're a goddamn visitor here, and an unwelcome one at that. *My people, my town?* You had your chance to play judge, jury, and executioner, and right now I'm not sure if Earl set all this in motion or you did. You're not a cop anymore, Danny, no matter what Harp and Dyer wanted me to believe. Right here, right now, this is a police matter."

Danny looked out past the door, to where the bodies of Chris's friends had been wheeled away. "So what are you going to do, arrest me?"

Chris stood, some of that anger he thought he'd lost coming back. "Yes, that's exactly what I'm going to do. I'm going to have Deputy Holt come in here and escort you under guard to the medical center at Hancock Hill, where you're going to stay until the FBI shows up. Then they can deal with you. Don't you dare tell me my duty—"

"Sheriff, please," Amé said, but Chris turned on her, too.

"No, not you, either. You and Harp were hiding information from me. You knew about the car and Avalos and then you went to meet Danny without telling me. I half expected that sort of bullshit from Harp, I should have predicted it. But not from you, Amé."

"I thought Ben *had* called you. And the rest of it—"

"Is this where you say you couldn't trust me, after everything we've been through?"

"No." Amé shook her head. "Not that, I thought I was protecting you."

"From what, my job?"

"From *me*, from the things I've done and what Avalos knew about me and *mi familia*. But it doesn't matter, not now. Ben and Buck are dead and I can't let the men who did that get away, and I don't think you can, either."

"*Can't?* You are both out of your minds." But Chris wouldn't look at her.

Amé stood, stepped closer. "No, Sheriff, but if Danny's right about the things he's been telling us, we're almost out of time. Just listen to him."

Just then, Dale stuck his head in the door. "Sheriff, it's Mel. She came over from Earlys."

Chris nodded. "Send her in. I need to talk to her. And Dale?"

"Yes, sir?"

Chris gestured at Amé and Danny. "Take these two out there and watch them. They're not to leave or make a call or do anything, is that clear?"

Dale swallowed hard and wouldn't meet Amé's glare. "Even America, sir?"

"Yes, especially her."

Mel already knew about Ben and Buck, so when she came in she grabbed Chris right off, held him tight, as much for her sake as his. She also didn't want him to see how much she'd been crying.

"Dammit, Mel . . ."

"I know, Chris. I know." And she also knew this was the point where he'd start blaming himself, chasing shadows at all the things he could or should have done. "Whatever happened out there at the Lights is what Ben wanted. You know him, and you know that."

He pushed away from her, gentle. "It doesn't make it any easier. It was about money, Mel. That's all. The car that ran down Tommy Milford was full of drug money owed to John Wesley Earl. Murfee was just the drop-off point. Earl was traveling with his son Jesse, and since Jesse and Thurman Flowers had decided to set up in Killing, they all ended up here. If they'd chosen anywhere else, none of this would have happened."

"True, but you can't think that way. It's useless."

"Two of my men are dead, babe."

"Okay, so what do you do about it? What happens now?"

Chris leaned against his desk. He was exhausted, and she wanted to hold him again, just to help him stand. "I've talked to the FBI and they're taking the lead on dealing with the Earls and Thurman Flowers in Killing. No one needs another Waco or Ruby Ridge, so they don't want me and the few deputies I have left rolling up on it. But I've got everyone I know with a badge and gun across four counties on the lookout for anyone and anything connected with the Earls. So we wait."

"You're not happy about that?"

He looked out the door to where Amé and Danny stood close, talking, with Dale awkwardly standing nearby. "Honestly, no, and they're not happy about it, either. Danny thinks he knows Earl's next move and he wants us to get to him before he makes it."

"And Amé?"

"Same. If I'm not careful, they're going to both slip out of here and try to deal with the Earls on their own."

After a long moment, Mel asked, "Is that such a bad thing?"

Chris looked at her twice as if trying to remember who she was. "Yes, yes it is. We're not bounty hunters, and we're not in the revenge business. They'll get themselves hurt, probably killed, and there's been more than enough of that tonight."

Mel nodded. "Okay, and I guess they've accepted that, or they wouldn't be in here trying to convince you otherwise." She grabbed Chris's hand back. "What would Ben say?"

He pulled away a second time and shook his head. "Don't ask me that, not ever again. It's not fair. Ben's approach is exactly what got him killed, action versus reaction and all that crap. He saw wolves every-where." Chris's eyes were as dark and wet as the earlier rain. "And maybe, you know, he wasn't even wrong, babe. That's the part I can't let go, that I struggle with. He warned me again and again, and still, here we are."

"Waiting," she said.

"Yeah, waiting." He rubbed his face, wiped at his eyes. "I want to think all of this is just bad luck, like the Earls showing up in Killing. But what if it isn't? What if it's *me*? Would any of this have happened if Sheriff Ross had been here? Could he have stopped all this?"

She moved in close and took his hand a final time, held it tighter. "And you think Ross was such a mean bastard Earl wouldn't have crossed him?"

Chris didn't answer, but she knew that's exactly what he thought—that he wasn't tough enough, strong enough, to protect his own.

"It doesn't matter what Ross would have done, and you're right, it doesn't matter what Ben would've said or done, either. You're the sheriff now. I trust you, love you, and I'll support whatever you decide. I knew that the minute you chose to stay in Murfee. I'd be lying if I said I didn't worry all the damn time, but that's what comes with the territory and I accept it, just like you have to."

"That's a helluva non-answer."

"It's the only one I have, and it's the truth." She fought to stay steady for him, to stay strong, even as she knew where this conversation was carrying them. "A while back you were on our porch talking about helping Danny, and we both knew you were going to do it. You talked around it, tried to talk yourself out of it, but we both knew. Like you said: *As far as the eye can see, that's my responsibility.* And that, Chris, *is* the territory." She made him look at her. "So, what if you wait for the FBI because they gave you an order, and then Earl goes on the run and hurts someone else before he gets caught? Someone without a badge and gun . . . someone who doesn't get a choice on how and when to deal with him. What if it was me, Chris? How would you deal with that?"

"That's another unfair question."

"No, but it matters. You don't get two choices, Chris, one for yourself and one for everyone else. I understand all the good you're trying to do here and the sort of man you are. I know what you believe and I also know, no matter what, right or wrong, you're never going to be him."

"Him?"

"You're not Sheriff Ross. I know that's what you're afraid of, what drives you to do the job the way you do it. Whatever you decide here tonight, you'll *never* be like him. I know that and you need to know it, too."

Chris stood silent. "Did you come over here to tell me all that?"

"No, I came over to tell you I'm going home. Our new dog is still there all by himself, the poor thing has been cooped up all night."

"You can't go by yourself. The storm . . . the Earls . . ."

"And you can't spare the men. You're running out of them . . ."

He smiled, faint, grim. "I'll have Tommy ride out with you. He can't walk, but he can shoot, if necessary. He'll stay out there with you until I'm done here."

She squeezed his hand and let him go, not bothering to ask him when that would be. She was going home, where she'd try and fail not to cry about Ben Harper.

Where she'd wait for Chris until it was over.

Goddamn waiting.

But like she'd told him, it's what came with the territory.

He left Mel in his office, and went out to where Amé and Danny were standing. He told Dale to reach out for Tommy and let him know that Mel was driving over to his house, and that he was going to ride with her out to the Far Six, where he was going to stay until he heard otherwise. He'd need his badge and his gun, both his duty pistol and his rifle. Then he told Dale to come back and help Till, who was going to be in charge of handling things in town.

He'd made all the calls, done everything he was supposed to do, and it wasn't going to be enough. Not for him. Not with his men, his friends, dead. It wasn't even close. He wasn't going to sit here and wait for Nichols and the FBI to handle things their way.

His men, his choice.

And the Big Bend, all of it, *was his*, as far as he could see.

Chris turned to Danny and Amé. "Okay, tell me . . ."

59

Earl was eating an apple, contemplating *again* just being done with it and shooting Flowers and Clutts, when T-Bob appeared in the living room.

Alone.

He'd come in through the back, quiet—the same way he'd left what now felt like days ago with Little B and Kasper—but had gone to the kitchen first, and walked in holding a six-pack of Pearl. He had something else held tight in his other hand and all of him was soaking wet, his jeans and the front of his shirt muddy, even his face. It was dark clay, almost red, and it looked like he'd been crawling around on the ground on his belly like a damn snake.

He'd got caught by the rain that had just started lashing the house.

"The Devil . . . ?" Earl said, standing back to get a better look at his brother. Cole Malady stood aside to make room for him, and everyone now was taking in the muddy, horrible apparition. He'd left footprints all the way down the hall behind him. "Where's them other two, T-Bob?" Earl said it through clenched teeth, knowing he wasn't gonna like the answer at all.

His brother had fucked up again, just like he always did.

T-Bob made a face and a noise halfway between a laugh and

something else, not quite human, that made Earl's skin crawl, as he tossed the object in his other hand at Earl.

It was a soaked-through hundred-dollar bill, crumpled up.

"Little B's dead, JW. You'd be proud of him, though. That other one done run off or whatever . . . I left him behind. But I done what you told me and I brought it, it's right where you told me you wanted it. Still runnin', lights on, easy to find. I said I'd do it, I swear I did, come hell or high water." T-Bob then made that weird noise again and pulled a Pearl free and cracked it open.

Goddamn T-Bob makin' a sight and mess like this, a spectacle. And Earl knew that his older brother was finally, after all these years, makin' a statement of his own.

Flowers watched Earl closely, and the wadded money in his hand.

"Well, by God, I was right, John. *The goddamn money,*" he said. "The money you swore you didn't have and that you didn't see fit to share with Jesse. I hope it was worth your sons. It's all in Corinthians . . . *nor thieves, nor the greedy, nor drunkards, nor revilers, nor swindlers will inherit the kingdom of God.*"

Earl took the bill and slipped it into his pocket. He turned his back on his brother and steadied his daddy's ole Blackhawk that he'd never stopped aiming at Flowers's skull.

"Go on, preach some more to me about swindlers. Seems like I'm looking at the biggest fuckin' one of all, right here in front of me . . ."

IT HAD BEEN A LONG WAIT for T-Bob and the others to come back, trapped in the living room with the retard Cole and Flowers and his fool. They'd drunk a few beers and smoked, and he'd gone back and forth a bit to check on Jesse, who'd looked worse by the minute—pale and fading, turning into a ghost right in front of his eyes. Every time he went in that reeking bedroom to see him, he'd half expected him to have disappeared altogether, leavin' only blood in the bed where he'd lain. It hadn't helped that Sunny had been after him to know what Little B was doing, and that back in the living room, Jenna had been cryin' a goddamn flood, beggin' to see Jesse. Her caterwauling had gotten on his nerves enough that he'd finally let her back there, where seeing all the blood had only made her wail more. She'd held Jesse, kissed him, but Earl wouldn't let her stay, 'cause he'd wanted her where he could see her, just like the rest, so he brought her back into the living room, where she'd sat with his son's blood on her hands; at last, finally fuckin' quiet.

She'd kept looking at her hands, though, turning them over and over as if she couldn't quite see the blood on them that she knew was there; couldn't make sense of whatever it was she *was* seein'.

It had been a long fuckin' wait.

If all that shit hadn't been bad enough, there was also that thunderstorm that had rolled down on top of them, a real fuckin' boomer, making the lights in the old ranch house flicker long before the rain itself hit. Every time they went out, he'd clenched up, ready for Clutts to make his move and imagining the darkened room filling up fast with fire and heat. He'd been about ready to pull the trigger first himself one or two times, but the lights had always come back up too quick, leaving him and Clutts still staring at each other and reading each other's thoughts.

And he really hadn't wanted to shoot Clutts or Flowers, not too soon anyway, thinking they might still be useful. They'd all sat there, trapped with one another, the lights flickering on and off like a weird heartbeat, listening to one another breathe and the storm murmur as it slowly worked its way over them, until T-Bob had walked in like the Devil himself . . .

"So this is what's going to happen, Preacher. Cole is gonna give you boys the keys to the RV and then you can get on your merry way. You're gonna go yours, and me and mine are gonna go ours."

Flowers shook his head. "So you can send us away in the one vehicle that's the easiest to find? *That everyone will be looking for?* While you slip out in *our* van or whatever other car it is your brother brought to you, the one with all the money? That hardly seems fair, John." Flowers forked his fingers at T-Bob and Cole. "You two understand what's going on here, right? He's using us as bait, *a distraction.*" He focused on T-Bob. "Just the way he sent you and Little B to do his dirty work. He didn't want to get caught himself doing that, but had no problem risking you. All his big talk about Jesse being a coward, and now we learn he's the biggest one of all."

Flowers laughed, kept going. "So when we drive away and leave you here with him, what do you think he's going to do? *He's letting his own son die back there.* Do you honestly think any of his plans involve you walking out of here with him? How long have you been planning this, John, weeks, months? You've been breaking bread with these folks, most of them your family, knowing they were all going to die. You've been living with dead people all along. How do you live with yourself?"

Earl checked his brother, tried to read what was going on behind his eyes, but T-Bob wouldn't even look at him. Cole, *the fuckin' retard*, on the other hand, was blinking slow, eyes going up and down like the lights had been. Was it possible he'd lowered the scattergun he had on Clutts and Flowers, just a little?

"That's a nice speech, but lots of words that don't mean shit. I'm giving you the keys and a way out. You don't want to take it? Fine, don't make no difference to me. We'll leave you here and . . ."

And then Sunny was in the room, standing at T-Bob's shoulder, pulling at his muddy shirt. She was looking around, searching all their faces for her boy, until she started screaming at Earl.

"Where's Little B, John Wesley? *Where's our son?* You said he'd be right back. That's what you said, that he was coming right back."

"There was a problem, Sunny. I don't know all about it, so we gotta talk to T-Bob, figure it out. Now ain't the time. There is no more time. I need you to go back there with Jesse and I'll be there in a minute. This is almost over."

Flowers spoke, barely a whisper, but it carried all the way across the room. "Sunny, Little B is dead. You see, John sacrificed him. It was no different than if he had put the boy up on the altar and wielded the knife himself. He killed your son, and before he's done, he's going to kill you."

Sunny's eyes were wide, big enough to reflect the whole room and everyone in it.

"Goddamn you, Flowers," Earl said. "Goddamn you . . ." He raised the Blackhawk for what seemed like the hundredth time, but Sunny was on his arm, holding him, her hands like claws and all muddied from T-Bob's shirt.

"Tell me that ain't so, JW. *Tell me* . . ."

"Dammit, bitch . . ." He tried to push her back, and . . .

. . . everything started to tip over, like the room itself was tilting. Sunny was latched on his arm, holding fast like a gator, holding his gun hand. And she was standing in front of Malady, blocking his scattergun, which he had, in fact, lowered, far too much. Then fuckin' T-Bob was in the way, too, tryin' to pull Sunny off of him, and he'd dropped the rest of the beers in his hand and they were rolling around between their feet and his brother was crying big tears that left tracks in the mud on his face.

The *blood* on his face . . . from Little B.

They were all jumbled up together in each other's way, and Earl felt the room turnin', threatening to toss them all on the floor.

That's when Flowers said, *Now, Marvin*, and Clutts went for his gun.

60

I'm in the backseat, giving directions. Sheriff Cherry and Deputy Reynosa are up front. We're somewhere outside Killing, off road, driving through the rain-soaked desert and following the swollen lines of the creek called the Alamito that I picked out on the sheriff's old map, searching for the unmarked dirt road the map didn't show that I knew stretched behind the house. The same road that Earl used to go and stare at . . . that I once saw him riding along on his Harley and that gets lost in the mountains and the rolling hills.

That I bet if you follow long enough, takes you right into Mexico.

How he's going to get across the border, much less the river, I don't know, but I know that's his plan. It's been his plan all along.

It makes sense. It's what old outlaws used to do—run south for the border when the heat got too heavy. Dirty Dave Rudabaugh did it. The infamous Ike Clanton from the O.K. Corral did, too, though he later came back north to Tombstone and was shot by lawmen for cattle rustling.

But Earl is never coming back. If he gets past those mountains and over that river, he's gone for good.

I DON'T HAVE A GUN.

That was the deal. I promised to help, as long as he promised to bring me along, but he flat-out refused to arm me, and when we find what we're looking for, I'm not even supposed to get out of the truck. He seriously thought about handcuffing me back in Murfee, and he might yet do it.

I still wear that deputy shirt but he's made it clear I'm not one.

Small lights flicker and fail way off to our left. That should be the ranch house and out behind that the bluff, and hidden somewhere nearby will be the Mexican's car Earl had T-Bob, Kasper, and Little B steal. The car he wanted me to steal for him. I talked to Kasper about everything that happened just before we left, the boy still crying over Little B while sitting in a Big Bend County jail cell, the same cell the Mexican had been in earlier in the day, at least that's what Deputy Reynosa told me.

It's hard to imagine that Little B is dead. He wasn't enough like Jesse or Earl, although he so, so badly wanted to be.

Deputy Buck Emmett shot Little B, but it was Earl that fucking killed him.

SHERIFF CHERRY PULLS OVER and cuts the lights. The truck is getting bogged down in the loam and clay. The long tail of the storm has all but passed here, but it's left its mark, and it's still north of us somewhere, dropping a lot of water. The creek roils and turns, in some places you might even promote it to a river, and in other places it's already broken free from its banks to search out the low places in the washes and draws. It's almost biblical, a desert flash flood coming to life in front of us.

The sheriff pulls out his SureFire and then a set of handcuffs.

He turns to me and tells me to get up front.

He cuffs me to the steering wheel. Both he and Deputy Reynosa have portables, and he'll be able to raise me on the truck's dash set if something happens. He tells me that no matter what, if they're not back in an hour, I'm to turn the truck around and get back to Murfee and

418 | J. TODD SCOTT

meet with his other deputies and the FBI agent Nichols and his men. Otherwise, I'm to keep the channel clear and stay quiet.

"You don't have to do this," I tell him, raising my handcuffed arm.

"I'm sorry, Danny, but I do. If you go down there and shoot Earl or anyone else, it's nothing but revenge, and everyone will know it. A district attorney might just call it murder, and I won't let you walk into that."

"And because you happen to be wearing a badge right now, it's not?"

He checks the cuffs to make sure they're secure, but not too tight.

"No, I guess not. No matter what happens, I can still call it my job."

Deputy Reynosa shoulders her AR-15. She doesn't say anything, doesn't try to argue with her sheriff. She's been quiet most of the drive out here. She does that, lapses into silence, just watching. For a few minutes out near the Lights, when we were walking in the desert, I thought I got a real glimpse of her, or at least understood her a little. But you could spend an entire lifetime with her and never unravel everything behind her eyes. She's younger than me, not by much, I guess, but getting out of the truck, getting ready to walk into the dark and face a man who will absolutely kill her if she gets in his way, she shows no sign of nervousness or fear.

If anything, she's impatient, ready to go, welcoming whatever comes next.

Earl has no fucking idea who's coming for him.

I watch them walk off and disappear.

I want to chew my arm free from the cuffs, tear the steering wheel clean off and follow them. I think about the guns I spent days hiding out in the desert behind the house and whether they're still there, or if Earl found them or if they were washed away by the storm. There are occasional stray raindrops on the roof, like fingers tapping, marking time, and that's all I'm doing, handcuffed in this goddamn truck.

Then I look over to where Deputy Reynosa was sitting just a few moments before and catch sight of it, tucked down in the edge of the seat, near the seat belt. If Sheriff Cherry had glanced over at any point, he might have seen it. But he didn't.

It's a stretch, but I get my fingers on it. Deputy Reynosa was counting on that the whole time.

It's a handcuff key.

61

Sunny thought at first she was dead.

Released.

But . . . her ears were ringing, so that probably meant she was still alive, more or less. She fell over Jesse's body, protecting him, as bullets and buckshot continued boring holes through the cheap plaster. A lamp next to the bed rocketed toward the ceiling and the back window gave way, showering her with glass, letting in cooler air and some of that thunderstorm that had been rolling through. She opened her mouth, screaming, and tasted rain, felt glass on her skin and damp on her face. She wouldn't have even gotten this far . . . she wouldn't be alive . . . if it hadn't been for T-Bob, who'd pushed her down the hall from the hell in the living room back toward the bedroom, helping her retreat.

His face was the last thing she saw before she closed her eyes and ran. T-Bob. Not JW.

Jesse was trying to sit up beneath her, awakened by the noise, but she held him down. It sounded like someone had driven two cars through the front door and they'd crashed into each other right in the living room. More bullets left bite marks in the wall, trailing corkscrews of plaster that spun around like mouthfuls of blown smoke.

"What, what the hell . . ." Jesse said, and she held him tighter, waiting for the car crash to end.

. . .

SILENCE CAME, EVENTUALLY, and at first she thought it was because her hearing finally had gone south. Then there was a lone gunshot, still so loud it made her jump. More silence, followed by another. She could pick out the click of boots walking across the old wood, then one last blast, not as loud as the first, and she *knew* what was going on in there and didn't have to see it at all. Not like that night in 1979 when she'd watched her daddy get shot in the head, kneeling outside their apartment.

He'd taken her to see the elephants Bertha and Tina and used to sing to her you are my sunshine, my only sunshine . . .

JW appeared at the door. He had two pistols stuck in his belt, his daddy's revolver in his hand, and there was blood speckling his shirt and his face. He leaned against the frame, resting, like he was thinking.

"JW, what . . . ?" Now she could barely hear her own voice.

"It's bad, Sunny, real bad. You don't want to go back in there."

"T-Bob and Cole . . . ?"

He shook his head and looked down at the gun in his hand.

Jesse struggled, pushing on her to get a look at his daddy. His eyes were glassy, not focused—they rolled sideways in his head, back and forth, like coins disappearing down a jukebox—and his lips were thin and almost invisible. "It's okay, Daddy, we good now, right? We gettin' going?"

JW continued to stare at the revolver in his hand, turning it over once or twice, weighing it, and Sunny went cold. She held on to Jesse, who had no idea his brother was dead and that the living room was full of more bodies. He didn't understand at all what was about to happen.

"John . . . please . . . no . . ."

Earl stepped in and raised the gun; it seemed to hang in front of Sunny's face forever before he turned it around and handed it to her. "Look, that fucker Flowers got out, used Jenna as a shield, pulled her right in front of him. He's runnin' around outside somewhere. I don't know if he's armed or not. Clutts had *two* pieces on him, one in a goddamn ankle holster, and got T-Bob and they're both dead. Cole took most of his fuckin' head off with the scattergun. There ain't nobody else." He straightened up, getting ready to walk out. "Like I said, it's bad."

"What are you doing? Where are you going?"

"Jesse can't walk, Sunny. That car T-Bob went and got me is our ticket outta here, our only ticket. I'm gonna go down the way and get it and drive back here and then we're goin', just like Jesse said. You stay here. Keep that gun on you in case Flowers comes back round. Pack up whatever you and Jesse need, we ain't never comin' back."

"The RV, we can just—"

"No, not the RV. That's registered to T-Bob. We can't run in that thing. Flowers was right about that. Everybody will be lookin' for it. Leave it be."

"How long you gonna be gone?" Sunny asked, sitting up now with the gun in her lap.

He winked at her. "Hell, you waited for me for years when I was inside. This ain't gonna be no time at all." He took one last look at Jesse, and disappeared.

She sat there for a while, thinking about Nevada; about her daddy bleeding to death below her bedroom window.

And the Bee Gees singing how sometimes you loved with your heart hanging out . . . how sometimes there was just no other way . . .

She popped the cylinder on the old revolver, and when she saw it wasn't loaded, that's when she knew for sure JW was never coming back . . .

Earl moved through the house, searching for T-Bob's big old JCPenney duffel bags—the ones he dragged all of his clothes around in—and when he found them, he emptied them out on the floor, kicking the clothes and books and photos and a couple of empty bottles and whatever other trash his brother had held on to out of his way.

He folded two of them inside the third and then slung that one over his shoulder.

He finally stopped to check the Nichols phone and there were about twenty phone calls and a dozen missed messages in the last hour or so alone. *The cat was finally out of the bag*, which was a good joke, what with T-Bob's duffel bag over his shoulder, and then he put the phone on the ground and stepped on it hard with his boot.

He wasn't taking any phones with him. He knew they could track them.

There was a moment when he thought about going back into the bedroom and finishing that business. But he didn't want to look either of them in the eye again. It already reminded him too much of Phyllis in Corpus, how her eyes had flickered in and out before she'd flatlined, and the way she'd gone limp in his arms but he'd still felt her there for a long time afterward. She'd stayed with him for far too many years, fuckin' with his dreams, and he didn't need that ever again.

Like all the phones and his own bag of clothes and his daddy's gun he'd dropped in Sunny's lap and everything else he'd brought with him to Killing—a lifetime's worth of shit, in so many ways—he was leavin' it all behind.

In fact, other than the empty duffel bags and the guns he'd pulled off of Clutts, he wasn't takin' a goddamn thing with him at all.

62

They moved through the desert, not needing their SureFires. The world had been washed clean by rain and the sky scrubbed free of clouds, although a silver moon had slowly started filling it in again, turning everything around them neither light nor dark, but a gunmetal gray. It was a weird light, but more than enough to see by, and they cut along the rocky ground, getting lower by the moment, moving past mesquite and ocotillo and cat's-claw and rainbow cactus, listening to the water breathe in and out in the creek bed around them. The new clay sucked at America's boots, tried to pull her down, but she got ahead of Sheriff Cherry, almost running in places, and even though he whispered after her to *slow down*, she couldn't. She didn't want to. She wanted to find John Wesley or Jesse Earl first and end it with them once and for all. Ben had asked her to look after the sheriff because he was a good man, but also because Ben had seen through her and had accepted exactly who she was and what she was capable of and what she was willing to do.

And she did, too.

Ella era un lobo, ahora.

Everything she'd worried about—all of her guilt—had burned up with the last of the money hidden at her house. It was a weight she hadn't even known she was carrying, the last tie to her old life and the person she'd been before—to Rodolfo and Caleb Ross and Duane Dupree and Máximo. The money was gone, nothing but smoke and ash now, and they were all gone, too, but she was still here, running.

Libre.

She was far ahead and had left the sheriff behind, when the low ground crumbled away and she was left standing on the rough edges of a deeper arroyo, a finger of the Alamito now filled with water from the storm that was keeping the creek swollen and angry and alive. In that gray, unsteady light, she realized just how much of the flatlands around Killing had flooded, and how many of the mesquites were waist deep in water. The road Danny had talked about was somewhere beneath it all. No one was driving out of here anytime soon.

Then, before the sheriff made it down to her, she picked it out of the wet haze. She had seen it only hours ago in the impound lot in Murfee, but now it looked strange and unfamiliar, out of place.

It glowed with its *own* light.

Azahel Avalos's car.

There was something else inside it, something she had to look at twice as she made her way to it, just to be sure.

She was almost there, wondering what to do next, when she heard laughter.

63

Jesse was dyin'.

He'd heard somewhere, maybe on one of Jenna's reality shows, that you got to see your whole life in flashes, all the good stuff anyway, but he wasn't seeing jack shit. Just black holes he kept falling into, over and over again. He was waking up in bits and pieces, once to thunder, or maybe gunshots.

The whole of his world was torn paper he couldn't hold on to.

Next it was Sunny breathing over him, talking about RVs and keys, and his daddy standing in the doorway, winking.

Then the sound of the back door slamming.

In fact, the only thing one hundred percent clear for him was the face of that lying cocksucker Danny—his ass driving out in the desert with that crazy fucker Joker giving chase, while Jesse's own fuckin' guts were looped up in his arms. He'd ridden all the way back to Killing holding them, pushing 'em back in, and it had hurt like almighty hell. You could live a damn long time gut shot, but it was a painful way to go, and he was most certainly *going*. He could smell his own blood, his own *real* shit, and knew he was dyin' right there stained and wet in his own mess and still not gettin' a glimpse of anything good.

Which meant his whole life hadn't amounted to shit, either, and he was gonna leave this world never knowing his mama and with the last thing he really remembered being Danny . . .

Somehow that just didn't seem goddamn fair.

Someone was banging around deeper in the house, maybe Sunny looking for the keys she may or may not have talked about, but other than that, he was alone. His daddy *had* been there a few minutes ago, he was pretty sure of that, but he was gone, too . . . the sound of that door slamming. When Jesse struggled to sit up, his guts moving sideways and sending pain like lightning all through his body right up to his eyes, he realized there was a gun in his lap—his daddy's and his granddaddy's before that, the trusty ole Blackhawk. He'd shot Danny and that old deputy with it, and he'd always wanted this gun. He'd had it before he collapsed into bed and he picked it up now; glad to feel its weight again. It anchored him, kept him out of the holes and firmly in *this* world, and when the pain like lightning came again, and it did, he just willed it all the way down his arm and into the gun.

He thought the gun itself glowed. *It flashed*, far brighter than those glimpses of his shitty life.

Bright enough for Jesse to see by, as he got up out of bed, to figure out where his daddy had gone . . .

64

Earl was laughin', 'cause there wasn't much else to do.

Hell or high water. That's what T-Bob had said, and now it made perfect sense—why he was all muddy and why his brother had that weird look on his face as he threw the money at him.

It *had* been his statement after all; a goddamn inside joke that only T-Bob knew the punch line to.

Hell or high water.

Goddamn right.

T-BOB HAD PARKED THE CAR that Manny Suarez's son had brought him close up beneath a stand of mesquites, just where Earl had told him. But water had since rolled up around the Nissan, as high as the wheel wells and still rising, and T-Bob had left the hot-wired car running, lights on, and even left the goddamn front door open; on purpose or not, Earl couldn't say. So creek water, dark as a snake, was now moving around in there, twistin' in and out, and carrying some more of his money with it. The stray bills were floating on south down the creek, the direction he'd wanted to go all along. And propped up in the backseat was Little B, his head against the window, like he was staring up at Earl, waitin' for him to get in and drive.

A little father-and-son road trip, like the boy had always wanted.

The little beaner deputy was there down below him, looking at the car, too, and when she heard him she turned fast, but he already had one of Clutts's guns leveled at her.

"Goddamn, girl, you've been some trouble for days. Now what I need you to do is put down that rifle." He slipped the duffel bag off his shoulder and tossed it at her feet. "And then you're gonna crawl up in the car and save us as many of those pesos as you can. Good thing I brought these here bags, although they're gonna be a bit lighter now. My money was supposed to have been packed in there all nice and tight, like good pussy, which is why I needed to get the whole damn car outta your town in the first place, but my brother went and fucked all that up. Hell, I was gonna use it to get *me* outta this dump, too . . ." He shook his head, watching his money disappear into the dark water. "But I gotta get something for all my troubles, right? I can't have it all wash away." He motioned at the car with the gun. "There's also a passport and some other stuff in that hole under the dash, so whatever you get, you slip nice and easy into that bag. And don't mind Little B sittin' there in the back, he's harmless. Looks like *you're* gonna be my way out now."

She lowered her rifle but didn't drop it all the way, and she ignored the duffel bag, where it had gotten lost on the darkness on the ground.

He drew out the second gun from his jeans and pointed that one, too, at her heart. "You hear me, you beaner bitch? I said—"

There was now a bright light switched on his face, a flashlight, and someone calling out to him.

"It's over, Earl. It's done."

Earl searched past the light, where he finally found the other man, Sheriff Cherry. He had some sort of sawed-down long gun aimed at him, along with a small flashlight that seemed way too bright for its size. He was looking at Earl and the waterlogged car between them.

"I knew we needed this damn rain . . ."

65

Chris made sure he was loud enough to be heard over the rushing water.

"You're going to drop both pieces at your feet and then come on down to my deputy nice and slow. She's going to cuff you and then we're going to talk about who might still be in that house back behind you. Are we clear?"

Earl laughed again, the same sound Chris had followed when he was trailing behind Amé. "Fuck me, if it ain't one goddamn thing after another with you folks. Can you not leave me be?"

"We never invited you here."

Earl nodded. "Fuck, I know, trust me, I didn't wanna come here, either. But here we both are, and it was gonna be so simple, my little Christmas in July. I was gonna get my payday and be over there"—Earl waved the muzzle of one of his guns toward the mountains neither of them could see—"drinkin' tequila on a beach. Beaches full of beaners, like your pretty deputy here, but I was done with all that anyway. And you people woulda been done with me."

"You couldn't have hidden in Mexico, Earl. Not you, not with all those tattoos. You could have cut your hair, changed your name, but you couldn't have changed your skin, *who and what you really are.* Like I said, it's over. Put the guns down, or I put you down."

Earl still had one gun on Amé, but the other—the one he'd used to point toward the mountains—had come to rest between Chris's eyes. Chris wanted to get Earl dealt with, fast, because he had no idea who was still out there roaming in the darkness—Jesse or any of the others. His gut told him Earl was alone but he couldn't be sure.

Wolves.

He almost could hear Harp at his ear, whispering to him.

And as if on cue, there was another voice: "He's not ever going back, Sheriff. If he said it once, I guess he said it a thousand times. So we're probably going to have to shoot him."

Chris searched out Danny Ford, where he was stepping into the light just past Earl, holding a badge and some sort of muddy gun Chris didn't recognize, like he'd dug it up. *Holding it* and aiming it at Earl, because he wasn't cuffed to the steering wheel of the truck anymore.

"Danny, step back," Chris warned.

Earl swept up Danny with one hard look, at the deputy's shirt he was wearing and the gun in one hand and a badge in the other. "Ain't this a fuckin' reunion? A goddamn cop the whole time. You're damn good, I'll credit you that. Nichols said he didn't put you up to this, but I ain't so sure. Did he send you out to spy on me?"

"Danny," Chris ordered, "do not talk to that man." Everyone's nerves were rising, like the water around them, and everyone had a goddamn gun pointed at each other.

Danny raised the badge up, even higher than the gun. "No, this was all about me, you fucking bastard. You killed my father, Texas Ranger Robert Ford."

EARL DOESN'T DENY IT, but doesn't admit to it, either. He looks at me and the only thing he says is, "Never even knew he had a boy, didn't know that at all."

It's not enough.

This is how you stop a man's heart.

Breathe . . .

"I want to hear you say it. I want to hear you tell me how you shot my father down in the road. I want to hear you say that and then I'm going to fucking kill you."

Relax . . .

Sheriff Cherry yells something, but I don't hear it. I can't hear it. The last thing I'm ever going to hear is whatever comes out of John Wesley Earl's mouth next.

Aim . . .

Earl says, "Fuckin' pussy, is that all you been waitin' for all this time?"

Then the lights on the drowning car below us wink out.

And right after that he's falling backward and the night is full of gunfire . . .

EARL'S HANDS WERE MOVING. The guns *were* moving . . .

Or were they?

Goddamn action versus reaction.

Chris knew if he didn't do something, Danny was finally going to kill Earl right there in front of him.

He's never going back.

He would swear the guns were moving. The barrel of the one pointed at Amé getting bigger by the heartbeat, threatening to swallow her whole, and the one that had been pointed at him, now turning toward Danny, just a little bit.

But just enough.

The guns were moving.

So when the Nissan's lights went out and then Jesse Earl appeared out of nowhere behind both his father and Danny—silhouetted in the lone remaining halo of Chris's SureFire beam—Harp was suddenly there, too, right at Chris's shoulder, telling him he really had no choice but to pull the goddamn trigger.

A lifetime's worth of decisions in a second.

In a heartbeat.

It's your goddamn job, Sheriff . . .

Do your job.

And Chris did.

EARL FALLS, REPLACED BY JESSE, who I didn't know was there and who comes out of the blackness behind me roaring, striking me across the face with his daddy's gun, breaking all the bones around my left eye.

He hits me there again and now his arms are around me and the gun is against my temple.

It burns a hole there and I lose my grip on both my father's badge and my gun.

I struggle not to black out and Jesse's shouting at Sheriff Cherry and Deputy Reynosa and telling Earl to get up, to *get the fuck back up, Daddy*, and I fight him with everything I have left until his gun slips off my temple to rest beneath my already damaged eye like a heavy finger, and I feel and hear the hammer of the big old revolver drop into place.

It's the loudest sound I will ever hear.

I am dead.

EVERYTHING HAPPENED FAST.

The sheriff shot the older Earl, just as Jesse Earl appeared out of the night, striking Danny and grabbing him, using him as a shield, a hostage. It was hard to tell who was who in the shadowed, stray light where they grappled—life and death—with Jesse's gun at Danny's head and Jesse yelling at his papa to stand up, which America wasn't sure he would ever be able to do again. She brought her rifle up but there wasn't a clean shot.

That didn't mean there wasn't a shot.

America Reynosa would never know it, but as she looked down the barrel, relying on the AR-15's iron sights, she used the same marksmanship techniques Danny had learned in the military.

All she knew was that she was just doing what Harp had always taught her.

Endless hours.

All those paper targets, moving in the wind.

Breathe.

Relax.

Aim.

Slack.

Jesse Earl's face was so close to Danny's, like lovers, the barrel of his gun beneath Danny's eye . . .

Squeeze. Tight.

And that was how you stopped a man's heart . . .

PART FOUR

BLOOD OUT

Ridin' my thumb to Mexico
It don't matter when or how I go
 —Johnny Rodriguez, "Ridin' My Thumb to Mexico"

Goodbye stranger it's been nice
   —Supertramp, "Goodbye Stranger"

66

TWO DAYS LATER

I'm not dead, but not quite alive, either.

I wake up, fall back into darkness, and do it all again. It's like climbing out of a deep well full of cold water. I come to the surface for a mouthful of air before sinking beneath my own weight.

I see only half the room and the rest is shadowed.

There are people I don't recognize, a few I do, and some that aren't really there at all. Major Dyer is one of them, looking serious. There's Deputy Reynosa leaning over me and we're back in the desert again, stars all above us. The girl from Ballinger is across the room, sleeping. She rolls over and asks me if I'm still watching her—if I'll always watch her—and she's crying and her face is blue and black . . .

Once, even John Wesley Earl is sitting next to me, smoking a cigarette.

He says, *Howdy, Danny*, and puts a gun to my head.

My dad is there and then he's gone.

"LAST TIME I WAS IN A HOSPITAL, I was laid up pretty much the way you are now," Sheriff Cherry says. "A bunch of men ambushed me on a ranch outside of Murfee. It's where my house sits now, and I was so damn scared, I just started shooting back, shooting wildly. I didn't think about it and didn't have time to, and somehow I killed three men. Not like Killing, where I had the time to think, *to decide*, and couldn't even kill just one."

"What do you mean?"

Sheriff Cherry leans back in the hospital chair. "I shot John Wesley Earl but he didn't die. He was still breathing when it was all over, and was in this same hospital with you up until yesterday, but he's since been moved. He's in a bad way, bad enough he might never walk again, but he'll likely live. Ben Harper once called it *outlaw luck* . . . or something like that."

"You should have let me shoot him. I was right there next to him."

Sheriff Cherry nods. He's exhausted, haggard. He still seems waterlogged, muddy, like we never left the desert, even though his uniform shirt is clean. "You were standing next to him for a long, long time, Danny. You had your chances, but I don't think you're a murderer, no matter how hard you wanted to be."

"Did he . . . did he ever say anything about my dad?"

"Only what we both heard. Other than that, he never said a word."

SHERIFF CHERRY TELLS ME how Deputy Reynosa shot Jesse Earl in the head and killed him, and how fortunate I was that Jesse's gun was empty all the time. I know he put it to my face and pulled the trigger, so he must have never realized it. He showed up to a gunfight without any damn bullets, so I guess I got a little outlaw luck of my own. The sheriff says Jesse still worked me over pretty good and the damage to my eye is serious, but the doctors will tell me all about that. It will be a while before they get the bandages off and can determine if I'll ever see out of it again.

Sheriff Cherry looks at his hands when he says that and won't meet the gaze of my one good eye.

Then he tells me the rest of it . . .

. . .

ALL ABOUT THE CAR with Little B's body and the money.

A handful of bills washed away, but when the waters rose up around it, the whole car was submerged; buried in a grave of mud and water. Somehow they got Little B out just in time, but not fast enough to save the car itself, or the rest of Earl's money hidden in it. They'll recover it someday just so they can crush what's left and leave it in Murfee's junkyard.

ALL ABOUT THE RANCH HOUSE.

An FBI Special Response Team surrounded it for three hours without any movement inside, before sending in a robot. Cole Malady, T-Bob, and Clutts were all dead from what appeared to be a massive shootout in the living room, and no one can figure out how Earl ever made it out of there; that damn outlaw luck, again. It will take a while to reconstruct exactly *how* things ended inside the house, but early postmortems revealed the three were shot execution style in the head as they already lay either dead or dying.

Just to be sure.

ALL ABOUT THURMAN FLOWERS AND JENNA.

Both were bloody but very much alive when they walked up to a Border Patrol mobile checkpoint that had been hastily thrown up on 169. If Flowers's side of the story checks out, no one is quite sure what, if anything, they'll be able to charge him with.

It looks like he's going to keep on walking right out of Murfee.

AND ALL ABOUT SUNNY . . .

She was pulled over in that old Fleetwood Southwind RV on 67, trying to make the I-10, headed west to Arizona and then on to California. Deputy Till Greer stopped her and she brandished a gun at him, refusing to come out of the RV for two hours, but Sheriff Cherry wouldn't let Till or anyone else go in after her. He didn't want to face one more dead body, so with the FBI tied up in Killing, he took control of the scene and he talked and talked and talked some more, until he was able to convince her to come out without another shot being fired.

She walked into his waiting arms, shaking and crying, and he took her to see the body of her dead son before he took her to jail.

"AMERICA, DEPUTY REYNOSA, stopped by a couple of times to check on you."

"I thought I saw her . . . I don't quite remember." But maybe I do. Sitting quietly by the bed, giving me a gentle smile when she thought I was awake. That mysterious smile, and all it might mean . . . *that's how you truly stop a man's heart.* I wait for him to ask me about the handcuff key or the gun that I dug out from beneath the Bonneville hood behind the Killing house, but he doesn't. Maybe he's already had that talk with her.

"It was an unbelievable shot she made. One in a million, and you're probably alive because of it. Jesse might have beaten you to death with that Ruger, empty or not. You two were all tangled up, and with the dark and everything else, I could barely tell one from the other, and I was still trying to make sure Earl didn't stand up again and shoot us all. There's only one other person I know who would've pulled the trigger on that shot, and I'm not ashamed to say, it wouldn't have been me."

I don't have to ask him who that was.

"I BROUGHT YOU THIS," he says, and reaches over and hands me my father's badge, the one I held up to Earl's face. The one I've been carrying forever. He's shined it all up and it glows in the white hospital light. "I found it out there where you dropped it. It was your father's, right?"

"Yes, they gave it to me at his funeral. I was nine years old. I've carried it with me since then, pretty much every day."

"You gave up your own badge but kept his? That's a long time to hold on to it, a damn long time."

Then he stands, slowly, to go.

"Thank you," I say.

"Don't thank me, Danny." He hesitates, motions toward the badge. "I didn't shoot Earl for you. I wasn't trying to kill him for what he did to your father, or even what happened to Harp or Buck. It wasn't revenge. At that moment, he was pointing a gun at one of my deputies. He refused to comply with my lawful commands. He was a life-threatening risk to her and to others. *I stopped that risk.* That's my job, nothing more or less. If he'd surrendered . . ."

"He was never going to surrender, Sheriff. I know that and you do, too. He was never willingly going back to jail. It ended the only way it could, the way it had to."

He stands silent over me for a while longer, like there's more to say, but when he reaches for his hat, I know he's finished. "Good luck to you, Danny Ford, I wish you the best. I really do."

"What happens now?" I ask.

"You heal. You answer a lot of questions, for both Nichols and Major Dyer." He settles his hat on his head. "And I go to some funerals . . . and then we both move on . . ."

AFTER HE'S GONE, I walk myself to the bathroom, still holding my dad's badge in my hand, where I look at myself in the mirror. My head is wrapped in bandages, a thick band of gauze covering my left eye, and there's bruising extending out from beneath it all the way down to my jaw. It's the color of blood, spreading over my skin, and that's what it reminds me of—a bloodstain on pavement. My other eye, the good one, is also bull's-eyed by a bruise, and the veins are blown out, turning it red. My hair had been starting to grow out, but some of it was shaved back down again to the raw skin for the bandages, and the damage they're hiding. I'm unrecognizable to most people, and after the surgeries to repair my damaged face, who knows exactly what I'll look like. Not the same, not anymore.

This is not my face.

But then again, it is.

And for the first time in a long time, I see myself clearly.

When I go to lie back down I realize that I left my dad's badge in the sink, but I'm okay with that. I don't go back to get it.

It'll always be there later, if I want it.

67

ONE WEEK LATER

America stood outside the charred remains of her house, ready to be bulldozed, still wearing her uniform and the black armband from Ben Harper's funeral. It had been held in Midland that morning—even that early, the hot sky had been the color of sand and windless as well, so all the flags had hung limp—and over three hundred current and retired officers had showed up from all over the area, as well as dozens of people from Murfee who'd driven up in a long convoy.

He was buried in a tree-lined cemetery next to Jackie, the two graves close, almost inseparable.

She and the sheriff had come back together. Melissa had been there, but Dale Holt brought her back to Murfee, giving her and Sheriff Cherry over two hours alone to talk. He drove and drank a Coke while she stared out the window and told him about taking one of Billy Bravo's old guns for Vianey Ruiz, about leaving the handcuff key for Danny, and then all about Santino Paez and Azahel Avalos and what he'd said to her that day out on the highway. She told him the things he had claimed about her family—about her uncle, Fox Uno—and how two years ago she'd used her brother's phone to call a ranch across the river, summoning a boy named Máximo to kill Duane Dupree. She told him it was Máximo who'd cut off Dupree's head and burned down his house with his body inside it, and that he'd come to her later with ashes in his hair and blood still beneath his fingernails. Finally, she told him that Caleb Ross had left her a large suitcase full of his father's drug money—everything that Sheriff Ross had stolen from the cartel Nemesio—and how she and Máximo had fled Murfee with that for a while, until she left him in Houston with a thick stack of bills and her brother's gun. The gun had been an ugly silver thing etched with images of the narco saint Jesús Malverde and grinning *calaveras* that she guessed had been a gift from her uncle.

She said all the remaining money had been hidden in her house and now it was all gone.

The sheriff had listened and didn't ask any questions, and when she was done, he'd filled in the rest—his side of it—the *real story* and not what was printed in the papers. How Caleb had come to the hospital in El Paso and told him about the money, but never said where it was or what he'd done with it, and how he'd returned to Murfee with every intention of killing his father. How the sheriff, with help from Mel and the English teacher, Anne Hart, had rescued Caleb from himself and then confronted Sheriff Ross in his old office with a gun in his hand—a confrontation that Ross had walked away from, right into an ambush by Dupree.

And how it must have been sometime after that when Máximo caught up with Dupree and finished it for all of them, for good.

By the time they'd both told their sides of it, they were just pulling up in front of what remained of her house, and they'd gotten out together, to stand there silent, staring.

She thought if she looked close enough, she could see a blackened piece of a dollar bill, still trapped in the charred wood.

"You remember the first time we stood together in front of another burned-out house?" the sheriff asked.

"*Sí*, Dupree's house. That's when I came back to Murfee and you asked me if I wanted to be a deputy."

"And you had all that money then?"

"In my truck, I used some of it to buy this place . . ."

"And a lot of guns, right?"

He was talking about all the ammunition that had cooked off in her house; that had slowed efforts to save it. "*Sí, muchas armas.* I was always afraid someone would come looking for that money, or for me. After what happened to Rodolfo and Máximo, I never wanted to need anyone's help ever again."

"I know that, I understand that."

"*Lo siento.*"

The sheriff looked at her, his eyes hidden behind sunglasses, before turning back to the ruined house. "I've been hearing that a lot lately."

She pushed ahead. "I'm sorry about not telling you everything sooner, and not being honest about Avalos . . . Suarez. But I'm not sorry about Duane Dupree. These past two years I've struggled with guilt over these horrible things I thought I'd done, but it really wasn't guilt, not the way you think. I hated myself for not feeling *bad enough* about any of it, not at all." She shrugged. "I'm glad Duane Dupree is dead. I'm glad Máximo did what I couldn't. Like Danny with John Wesley Earl, I had chances to kill Dupree myself and I was too scared and waited too long, and I probably shouldn't have. And I'm not sorry about the Earls. *Eran hombres malos.* Buck and Ben are dead because of them."

"It's not about revenge, Amé, it's supposed to be about justice." He shrugged, too, defeated. "You know who you sound like, right?"

"*Sí*, and maybe Ben Harper was right and you're too good to see that."

"And you're not?"

She put a hand on his arm. "I don't know. But I didn't need Ben Harper to show me there are *hombres malos* in this world. I learned that from Duane Dupree. *He* showed me what a really bad man will do."

The sheriff didn't have anything to say, and she let her hand drop. She went to grab her badge, to give it back to him.

"What the hell are you doing?"

"I said I'm not sorry, and I'm not. I helped Danny get free and I lied to you, and if Azahel Avalos was right, most people in Murfee and all along the river think I'm a drug smuggler working for my uncle anyway, just like my brother. That's more trouble for you than it's worth."

The sheriff held her hand, stopped her. "Let me be the judge of that. I've lost two deputies and I have a third on the mend. I can't afford to be down another. And if you hadn't slipped that cuff key to Danny, maybe we're all dead. I don't know which one of us was right or wrong, and maybe I never will. Maybe it doesn't matter. You still want to quit again in a few months? Fine, we'll talk then, just not now. I won't let you. Besides, with Ben gone, you're the best damn shot I have." He released her, pointed instead at her badge. "You've earned the right to carry that as much as anyone, but no more secrets, though, for either of us." He looked down at his own hands. "And since we're being so honest, maybe Ben wasn't right about me being a good man."

"¿Por qué es eso?" she asked, holding on tighter to the badge she'd almost unpinned from her shirt.

"When I shot Earl, he had a gun aimed at you, at both of us . . . but for a moment, and just a moment . . . I could've sworn he was about to drop them and give up. Another second . . . maybe . . ."

She shrugged. "Another second? Maybe he kills me. *Está hecho.* And anyway, you didn't kill him."

The sheriff's jaw was set, hard, like he was biting down on a bullet. "Not for lack of trying. I *wanted* to put that sonofabitch in the ground."

"Well," she said, "next time, aim higher . . ."

He turned away from her and got lost staring at the house. Maybe he was embarrassed, or saw those scorched bills as well. "Are you still checking in on Danny?"

"A couple of times," she admitted. He glanced at her from beneath his sunglasses, and she raised her hands. "Okay, more than a couple of times. He's alone and the doctors are still not sure if he's going to keep his eye. We just talk. Or he talks, and I listen. Not about his time with the Earls, that's all been with Agent Nichols and Texas DPS, but before that, when he was in Afghanistan and the undercover work he was doing. I don't think he's ever really had anyone to talk to about it all."

"I've checked with Major Dyer. None of his resignation paperwork was formally put through. He was supposed to be seeing a police psychiatrist before he bolted to track down Earl, and probably should be now. They'll take care of him, if he'll let them."

"I don't know that he's ever going back. I think he's going to be around here awhile."

The sheriff sighed and got ready to get back in the truck. "That's what I was afraid of." Then, "He's staying because of you, you know that, right? There are a thousand worse reasons, but that's the one."

"I don't . . ."

"Hey, it's not entirely my business. I'm just your boss. I think I told you Danny Ford wasn't your brother, and he isn't Caleb Ross, either."

"Lo sé." And she did know that, better than anyone.

"So, now that you've been doing all this listening, what do you think about him?"

She hesitated, remembering sitting next to him in the hospital. The way the uncomfortable chair felt; the way his hand felt, when the room was dark and he reached out to hold hers to remind him that someone was there. He asked her once or twice to watch him while he slept and to be there when he woke up, but he never said why.

"I think it's like he just woke up from a very bad dream. He's not sure where he is or how long he's been asleep, and the whole world's changed. He doesn't know where he fits into it anymore or what happens next."

"He's not the only one, Amé, not by a long shot." The sheriff opened the door for her. "Let's get out of here. After Buck's funeral tomorrow, his brother is throwing a barbecue at that place they have in Pecos. Mel and I are going to stick around for that, and most of Murfee will be there. I know that's not typically your thing, but this is your town, and these are your people, just as much as they are mine. All these whispers you worry about will stop when they see you the way I do. Stay with us, and we'll bring you home."

"Okay," she said.

"Oh, and one other thing, please get that gun back from Vianey Ruiz."

"I already have," she said, not mentioning that it was Santino Paez who'd returned it. She owed him that, and more. But it made her think about Billy Bravo. "Did you ever get the results on the DNA?"

He looked at her. "Not yet. Soon, though. Given what happened, and how it all turned out, does it matter anymore if we prove that Jesse Earl killed Billy?"

Again she hesitated. Her hand went briefly to the Saint Michael's pendant around her neck, turning it in the sun; the one she never took off. "*¿Honestamente?* No, not to me it doesn't. But does it matter to you?"

He started the truck, and if he had an answer, he didn't share it.

68

ONE MONTH LATER

He'd thought he was going back to Walls Unit at Huntsville, but he needed more care than that, a lot more, so they transferred him instead to the Texas Department of Criminal Justice Hospital in Galveston, where he shit and pissed in plastic bags under the watchful eyes of armed guards. Not that he could do a damn thing about it, because his body refused to move below the waist, no matter how much he willed it. So he had to lay there and listen to 'em make jokes about him, laugh about the way the nurses had to come in and clean up after him like a goddamn baby, and how there was still a stink on him that they could never scrub off.

It wasn't just the prison walls that trapped him now, but also his own fuckin' flesh.

Earl wouldn't look at his reflection in the chrome and glass of the machines that helped keep him alive; always making sure he looked the other way instead. He didn't want to see himself like this, so he just spent a lot of time with his eyes closed, in darkness.

He tried to ride his motorcycle in his mind, the way he used to, but even that didn't work anymore.

HE WOKE FROM A DREAM OF WIND—hot wind moving over dry grass, the touch of it against his skin and the weight of a scattergun in his hand—to the face of Agent Nichols. Nichols was reading something on his phone, and when he realized Earl was awake, he lowered it and didn't smile.

The guards were all gone.

"My star witness, how are we feeling today?"

"Fuck you, I ain't got nothin' to say to you." His voice was strange to him since he hadn't used it in a while.

Nichols looked down at his phone again and then slipped it into his pocket. "You had a lot to say months ago, a whole lot, John Wesley."

Earl remained silent and looked at the far wall, where he wouldn't catch a glimpse of himself.

"You're alive, you're getting better. Not good enough to walk, you're never going to do that again, and certainly not run. That's really what you've been doing all along, right? *Running.*"

Nichols looked at the ends of his fingers. "When you're done here, I'm having you transferred to the U.S. penitentiary in Beaumont. That's a fed facility, no more state prison time for you. I'm actually probably doing you a favor, and trust me, I'm not in the mood to do you any favors. You really wouldn't want to be back in any of your old haunts anymore. My sources tell me word's gotten out about you."

Earl didn't want to ask, but he did anyway. "What the fuck you talkin' about?"

Nichols stopped looking at his hands and stared right at Earl. His eyes were as dusky as his skin. Earl thought he should be at a country club, playing tennis or something, and realized just how young he really was, a kid, not any older than Jesse.

Nichols leaned in close and Earl caught a whiff of his heavy and expensive aftershave and saw a spot of blood on his chin, where he'd nicked himself shaving in the hotel bathroom mirror in the morning. The blood had dried as dark as his eyes. "The Wheel's figured out the *real* reason you did George Chives. They know *he* wasn't the federal snitch. Word gets around, even behind bars. You were just cashing out

George's chips, too, right? So when you made your run for the border, you had all the money?" Nichols reached into his suit coat pocket and pulled out a brand-new deck of Kem Arrow playing cards. He opened them and began a slow overhand shuffle, practiced and easy. "It doesn't matter. I've run down the Manny Suarez connection."

"Don't mean shit," Earl said. "Like Manny would say, fuckin' *nada*."

Nichols laughed, still shuffling. "You are one fucking tough nut, Earl. And you almost made it. By the way, when we kicked in the front door of Manny's nice house in Arizona, he didn't say *nada*. As a matter of fact, when I threatened to really hammer down on *his* son, Miguel Suarez, aka Azahel Avalos, he fucking *sang*."

Earl opened then shut his mouth, and searched the far wall again.

"It seems your federal cooperation leaked. It's rare, actually I've never heard of it happening, but the ABT is now well aware it was *you* that tried to sell them out. And because of what transpired down in Killing, now I can't, and won't, put you on the stand. Your grand jury testimony is so much worthless paper. Plus, Sheriff Cherry has been very vocal about your little bloodbath in the Big Bend. So there is no deal anymore, that's gone up in flames like that fire you had that fucking worthless son of yours start in Murfee. There's no WITSEC, nothing, *nada*. All I can do is fucking bury you. You will never be a free man as long as you live."

"If the word is out and there ain't no protective custody, they're gonna kill me, even in a federal pen," Earl said. "I'm a dead man already."

Nichols shrugged. He looked down at a card and slipped it into the middle of the deck. "Yes, most likely. I figure *your* name finally went 'in the hat.' Isn't that what you and your inbred friends call making a hit?" Nichols stood up, cards in hand. He slipped into a picture-perfect Hindu shuffle.

"I talked once to Deputy Harper, and he said for a good cop, sometimes the work *should* be personal. I told him I thought that was bullshit, but just like *you*, this whole time, I wasn't being completely honest. You see, hanging Flowers *was* personal for me. I was very close with my grandfather, a good, decent man, and then there was this church shooting in Georgia . . ." And then Nichols leaned down and whispered some more in Earl's ear, and when he was done, he stood up and patted Earl on the cheek.

But not before dealing out a final hand of Texas hold 'em, two hole cards facedown for each of them, and tossing the rest of the deck into the trash.

"You aren't the only cardplayer, Earl."

"It was you, you fuckin' prick. You let 'em know I cooperated."

Nichols stopped, thought about it, and pulled out his phone to make a call as he walked out the door.

"I have no idea what you're talking about."

AFTER NICHOLS LEFT, he dozed again, fitfully. He expected to dream of Jesse or Jesse's mom or Little B or T-Bob, even Sunny, but that wasn't who haunted him. It was only Phyllis, and she came for him with fire in her hair from the muzzle blast of a shotgun, the one that had killed Robert Ford in Sweetwater. Her hair was burning and there was sea salt on her skin and her eyes were rolled up in her head and she told him over and over again that *she and their baby had been waiting, just waiting, for so long . . .*

When he woke, the four cards Nichols had dealt were still there, untouched, and he realized that if he made it as far as USP Beaumont, he'd be home.

He also realized that the guards that had been around his room and sometimes his bed were gone.

HE RECOGNIZED THE ORDERLY, even though he'd never seen him before. He knew *the eyes.* They were his own, staring back at him from over twenty years ago. The boy was nervous, but determined.

A prospect . . . *Blood in.*

He had on a long-sleeve T-shirt underneath his uniform, probably to hide the tattoos; the ones they'd given him with pen ink and needles and sharpened guitar strings, attached to the small motors of electric toothbrushes. The boy's first stint inside wouldn't have been for very long, maybe just a few months for robbery or assault or something, but the next one would be for longer, a whole lot longer, if he got caught for what he was about to do. And Earl wanted to tell him it really didn't matter anyway, that he was already going to spend the rest of his life in some kind of prison whether he was ever put back behind bars are not. A prison of his own making; 'cause you made your choices, placed your bets, and you lived and died with them.

You made your deals with the Devil only to realize it was just you all along.

The kid slipped the cards away that Nichols had left behind without looking at them, leaving Earl still wondering what they were . . . but jokers or aces, it was all the same now.

"Come on, then, peckerwood. Let's do this thing . . ." Earl closed his eyes, searching for his boys or Sunny or his brother or his daddy or Phyllis, but there was no one there.

"It's okay, son . . ."

No one at all and he was alone.

The boy moved in close to him, leaned in the way Nichols had. The boy breathed on his closed eyes and Earl thought he might be crying, or maybe not.

"*Blood out, motherfucker . . .*"

69

SIX WEEKS LATER

Chris was having trouble with the words, getting them right, or maybe it was the whole damn story itself. He didn't know how it ended or even where it began.

It didn't help that Rocky kept staring at him, as if the dog was trying to read his thoughts.

He put the pad down and watched the sun drop in the sky, leaving long, burnished shadows across the Far Six. After the big thunderstorm the night of the fire, everything had gone dry again. There was dust on the pages that he hadn't been able to fill, and on his fingertips. He'd brought a bowl of water out for Rocky and the dog had already finished it.

Giving the dog a good name had been tough. They'd considered "Harp" for a bit, but that just never quite worked. It was too easy, and also, it hurt far too much. Mel remembered that Buck used to have a dog he called "Rocket"—the last conversation she had with the deputy, just before he walked out of the bar and into the path of the Earls—but that didn't quite fit, either. But it did give her the idea for "Rocky," and they both liked that, so it stuck, even if they weren't sure if the dog did. Sometimes he came to it, sometimes he didn't (and that would have reminded Chris of Harp if everything else already didn't), but his ears always went up when they called him. He knew his name and recognized it. He just chose to ignore it every now and then.

Maybe it was the name that was giving Chris such a hard time with his story, or rather the loose jumble of ideas he hoped to hammer into a story. The name for his main character was important; he and the reader and the character all had to live with it, page after page. He could easily picture everything about his character, except for the name. Nothing worked.

Hell with this.

He tossed the pad down, knowing that he'd come back to it anyway, sooner or later. He always did. He'd wake up in the middle of the night with the ideas still turning over and over, just like he'd secretly practice the words and dialogue on Mel to see if it all sounded right. He guessed she really knew when he was doing it, but she never said anything about it, or asked him what he was trying so hard to get down on his endless sheets of paper.

Just a story.

THE GUNS MOVED.

That was another thing that woke him up at night, those dreams of John Wesley Earl, and that moment just before he had pulled the trigger on his A5. Sheriff Ross had once told him that killing a man was different when you knew you were doing it, when you were looking him right in the face and had to see the life and light leave the other man's eyes. Chris had thought Ross had just been shining him on, saying something—anything—to keep Chris from pulling the trigger of the gun he had aimed at him. And on that night, Chris hadn't. He'd let Sheriff Ross walk out of the Big Bend Sheriff's Department and it had ended up not mattering anyway, because Dupree had been waiting for him and gunned him down in his own living room. Chris hadn't killed

Sheriff Ross by his own hand, but he'd ended up dead all the same, just as if Chris had.

The same was true for Earl. Two weeks ago, Earl had been stabbed to death in a state prison hospital, still recovering from the wounds Chris had given him.

The guns moved.

For the first few days after that night in Killing he'd written letters and made phone calls about Nichols. He'd figured out that Nichols was already on his way to Murfee after Ben and Buck's shooting because he'd either guessed himself what Earl was up to, or because he'd told him about Danny Ford. Earl had even admitted as much: *Nichols said he didn't put you up to this, but I ain't so sure . . .*

The last Chris had heard there was going to be some sort of inquiry or investigation about Nichols's handling of it all, but Chris had since let it go.

Nichols had to live with it, and it wasn't like Chris's own conscience was all that clear.

Except in his dreams, where *it was so clear,* so obvious. Everything that had happened was lit bright by its own high sun, and Earl was at the very center of it, aiming a gun right at Amé's head. But then when he woke up, when he tried to think about what exactly had happened that night and make some sense of it, it got all dark and unseeable again.

I wanted to put him in the ground.

And I did.

The guns moved.

And maybe that was just the story he wanted to tell himself.

MEL CAME OUT, hiding something behind her back. Rocky stood up, yawned big, and walked over and then sat on his haunches next to her. The dog tolerated Chris, maybe even liked him on good days, but he adored Mel. Sometimes, though, they both caught him sitting at the end of their long drive, looking back down it into the heat and haze, like he was waiting for someone to appear. No amount of calling would make him come, and he'd stay there until he was done searching for whatever it was he was looking for.

"How's it going?" she asked, nodding toward his empty pad. It was all she ever asked about it.

"Ahh, not so good."

"It'll come," she said.

"Yes, I figure so."

"Vianey Ruiz starts tonight at Earlys. We'll see how she works out."

"I appreciate you putting in a word for her, getting her hired."

"Well, your deputy can be pretty insistent. America wasn't going to take no for an answer. I think it'll be good. It'll cut into my hours, but I'm fine with that. It's probably necessary."

Chris nodded, but his own thoughts were elsewhere. He'd had the DNA results for Billy Bravo's murder sitting on his desk at work for a week before bringing them home, and he still hadn't looked at them. He'd asked Amé outside her burned house if it mattered whether Jesse's blood was there or not, and she'd said it didn't, and then she'd turned the same question on him, and he hadn't answered. But he had to think it did matter. It was the difference, after all, between revenge and justice. That's what he desperately wanted and needed to believe.

The guns moved.

He sat up, focused now on something Mel had just said. "Why is it necessary you get your hours cut?"

She grinned, embarrassed. Her hair was down and it was longer than it had been in some time. It was in her face, covering her eyes, but they were still so damn bright. "You've been a bad, bad man . . ." She reached around from behind her back and held up something for him to see.

It was a small purple box with the letters EPT in white. It took him a moment to even understand what he was looking at.

"Is that . . . ?" He stopped, remembering the night he'd come back from Lubbock after meeting Nichols and Dyer. She'd sat up talking with him and then a whole lot more than that.

. . . taking him back inside, sliding her robe off with nothing underneath, and letting him have a good long look, before pulling off his T-shirt and peeling down his shorts . . .

"Yes, it is. And very keen investigative skills you have there, since it says it, you know, right on the box. But I haven't taken it yet. I mean, it's still so early . . . I'm pretty sure, but . . ." She held up the purple box. "Well, I was going to do it now. Not very romantic, I know."

He took the box from her and slipped it under his chair. "No, babe, don't. It's like reading the last page of a story first, just to know the end. Let's be surprised . . . just see how things turn out." He stood up. "And speaking of not very romantic, stay here just a second, I'll be right back."

He went in and fished around under the bed, where he'd been hiding what he'd bought in El Paso that day after talking with Garrison. It was the errand that had kept him there later that night when Ben and Buck were killed, and although he would never tell Mel that, she'd probably figure it out anyway.

He came out with his own box in his hand, smaller than hers. "You know, after the last few weeks, there just wasn't a good time to do this. Harp kept telling me I needed to make an honest woman out of you and all that, and if we're going to be parents, well, then there's no better time than now."

He started to open it, but she put her hand over his to keep him from revealing the ring inside. She put her other hand over her stomach, protective, like she was searching for the life she already knew was there. "No, not yet. Like you said, let's just see how things turn out."

"You know, babe, one doesn't have anything to do with the other. I don't want you to think that, ever."

"I know, Chris. It's not that. It's just . . . are we ready for this, for any of this?" Now, with both hands wrapped around her stomach, she looked into his face, his eyes, for a long time, and the moment was broken only when Rocky suddenly barked, tearing off the porch into the flowering scrub, chasing a rabbit or shadows or whatever bad men or wolves he was afraid were out there.

Chris pulled Mel close, holding her and the baby inside her tight against him as he watched their dog run free.

"Hell no, babe, but we will be. We're going to finish this story together . . ."

LATER, AFTER SHE WAS LONG ASLEEP, he went back into the room they'd turned into his study, which might have to be a nursery before too long. He sat down at his makeshift desk and turned over the envelope holding the DNA results, weighing it. Everyone they suspected of Billy Bravo's murder was already dead, and maybe the DNA results would prove nothing at all, but it was still an unsolved crime that had occurred on *his* watch. Harp had always stressed that Chris was responsible for his deputies and that he always had to be ready to deal with the bad men of the world, but he was responsible to all of their victims as well. *That was his job, too.* Maybe it was the most important part of it. He'd felt that way when he first found the skeletal remains of Amé's brother in the desert, and his need to solve that murder and bring the killer to justice was what drove him to face Sheriff Ross. He'd felt it just as strong for Evelyn Ross, even as the empty months slipped by with no answers. He couldn't lose sight of that, not ever again.

That's why he carried a badge and a gun.

And Danny had said that Jesse Earl had made him burn a bloody T-shirt . . .

He tore the envelope open and read the single paper inside by his small lamp. When he was done, he smiled, satisfied, and then folded it in half and put it away.

. . .

HE FOUND HIS YELLOW PAD and tapped his pen against it, as moonlight moved outside the window.

The night glowed, just for him, showing him the way.

He just needed a good name, and then he could finally get on with his damn story.

He'd never finish it, if he never got started.

Ben.

La Chica con la Pistola

She was coming out of the apartment that used to be Ben's and that was now hers until she figured out where she wanted to live, when she found the box. It wasn't very big; sitting on the top step, unaddressed, and wrapped in paper.

Her first fear was that it was some sort of explosive, so she backed away from it, fast, but the longer she looked at it, the less likely that seemed. It was more of an intuition, a guess, than anything else, but she bent down and carefully picked it up and brought it inside.

It was heavier than she thought it would be.

She contemplated calling Danny before she opened it, since she was already running late to meet him at Earlys, but decided against it. She wasn't being secretive, necessarily, but she wanted the moment to herself when she finally pulled open the paper to see what was underneath.

There was no writing, nothing to even indicate it was for her, but she knew it was.

Slowly, she pulled back the butcher paper and found an ordinary cardboard box folded shut. She turned it around a couple of times, and when she couldn't find anything else, she opened it. The overhead light scattered off something bright inside, something silver and pearl.

A gun.

At first she was afraid it was her brother's gun, the one she would recognize anywhere and had left with Máximo in a hotel outside of Houston, but looking closer, she realized it wasn't. It was very similar, but the etchings were different; some of the same *calaveras*, but no Jesús Malverde or Pancho Villa or the Virgin of Guadalupe. Instead, there was only one figure, obviously a woman, but skeletal and horrible— wrapped in a massive cloak, its own tiny skull-face smiling up at her, its hands holding a scythe and a globe.

Nuestra Señora de la Santa Muerte.

It was just a skinless skull with no face, but she could swear it had been carved to look just like her.

La chica con la pistola.

America pulled the gun out of the box, and just like Ben Harper had trained her, she checked to see if it was loaded . . .

ACKNOWLEDGMENTS

I faced a very different writing experience with this novel from what I faced with my first.

The Far Empty had a life all its own; it carried no expectations, no deadlines, no competition or comparison. *High White Sun*, however, was born in the shadow of that first book (interesting, given its title), when I hadn't originally committed to a sequel, and wasn't even sure there'd be a second novel (the fear of probably every debut author, I guess). I did have some earlier notes about a young cop going undercover in an Aryan gang, but I just never found a way into that story I liked . . . until I wrote the opening Sweetwater sequence for what became this book, and the very first Danny Ford chapter: *This is how you stop a man's heart . . .*

From there, it was an easy decision to set Danny's confrontation with the Earls against the backdrop of my fictional Big Bend County, along with a little help from Sheriff Cherry and America Reynosa.

Although writing this second book was a helluva lot different from writing the first one, what did stay the same was the amazing team of people who brought it to life. So, here we go again . . .

Thanks to my agent, Carlie Webber, who continues to insist that I know what I'm doing, and Sara Minnich, Ashley Hewlett, Allison Hargraves, Anna Jardine, and everyone else at Putnam who has helped prove her right. Neither of these books would exist without their tireless efforts. Next up: Delcia Scott (each and every word is yours), the Scott girls, the Scott and Martin families, and all my friends—both personal and professional—who've supported me over the course of two books and nearly a thousand manuscript pages. When I'm working through a long novel like this, some days are definitely harder than others, but there are always a few people who drop in to see how I'm doing. This time around, that included Julianne C, Angie D, Vianey M (the "real Vianey"), Brian P, and my former boss, Will R. Glaspy, who's the most authentic Texan I've ever known. I'd also like to thank/recommend a few other writers I've met along the way: Jeff Abbott, Ace Atkins, Jay Busbee, Reed Farrell Coleman, David Joy, Robert Knott, and Brian Panowich. These gentlemen are amazing storytellers, and more than a hundred years ago they would have made a damn fine posse, too.

I also need to recognize District Attorney Rod Ponton, who was kind enough to answer some very specific questions. All factual errors are mine.

And finally, thanks to you . . . to all of you who've saddled up for what I hope will continue to be a very long ride.

I don't know when or where we'll meet again, but the Balcones and beers are on me . . .